JANE HARRIS

SUGAR MONEY

A Novel

FABER & FABER

First published in 2017
by Faber & Faber Limited
Bloomsbury House
74–77 Great Russell Street
London WC1B 3DA
This export paperback edition first published in 2017

Typeset by Faber & Faber Limited
Printed and bound by CPI Group (UK) Ltd, Croydon, CR0 4YY

A CIP record for this book
is available from the British Library

ISBN 978–0–571–33693–7

2 4 6 8 10 9 7 5 3 1

For George Young Mulvagh

I. de l'Anguille

les Chiens

P.te de Sable   I. S. Martin

I. S. Barthelemi

de Saba   P.te Ragged

de S.t Eustache   St. Christophe

V. et F.t Charles Town   C. Nord

la Basse Terre   I. de Nieves

P.te S.te Croix

Charles Town

P.te Reyerson   Rade de Parham

la Redonde   S.t Jean   P.te Indienne

Basse Terre   Falmouth   I. d'Antigoa

P.te de Carlisle   P.te Anglois

I. Montferrat   P.te d'Unique

Port Louis   Terre   P.te du Nord

I. de la Desirade

le gros Morne   P.te du Sud Est

I. DE LA GUADELOUPE   Fort Louis   P.te des Chateaux

Fort F.te Anne   la Petite Terre

Cabesterre   Bourg du Vieux Fort

Bourg du Bailly   S.t Sauveur   I. de Marie Galante

la Basse Terre   Bourg de Terre   Bourg de la

Basse terre   Cabesterre

P.te du Capucin

Rade du Prince Rupert   Anse du May

I. de la DOMINIQUE   C. François Monteur

Bourg des Roseaux   Charlotteville

P.te de Cachacrou   P.te à Crabes

I. DE LA MARTINIQUE

la Perle   Macouba

la Trinité   Cul de Sac de la Trinité

F. S.t Pierre   Cul de Sac Robert

Cul de Sac François

Fort Royal   Cul de Sac Vauclin

Cul de Sac S.t Martin   C. Ferré

I. des Salines

le gros Islet   Cul de Sac de l'Esperance

Anse du Choc

le Carenage   Anse Mabouya

Cul de Sac

des Roseaux

P.te Chimachiti   Ste. LUCIE

le gros Piton   Cul de Sac des Savennes

Vieux Fort   P.te Moulachique

P.tes Iles

P.te Tarratou   P.te Espagnole   Petit Bristol   André

Chateau Belair   Holetown   Joseph

Kingstown   I. S.t Vincent   Bridgetown   S.t Jean

I. de la Barbade

Becouya   Port de Cariacou

Balesso

Consouan   les Moustiques

l'Union

Cariacou   P.te Martinique

Islet Rond   Islot de Levera

C. David   Morne des Sauteurs

Anse Goyave   I. de la Grenade

Fort Royal   P.te du Requin

Banc de la Grenade   P.te des Salines

ISLES ANTILLES DU VENT

28

17

16

15

14

13

12

Based on a True Story

PART ONE

St Pierre, Martinique, Western Antilles

DECEMBER 1765

Chapter One

I was tethering the cows out by the pond when a boy came into our pasture saying that Father Cléophas himself want to see me tout suite in the morgue. Never having set eyes upon this child before I simply looked at him askance. He must have been somewheres about my own age; a mulatto, like myself, perhaps a shade darker than me, a hair smaller. His jaw hung loose and he had froth at the corners of his mouth from which signs I deem him to be of no startling intelligence. I spat on the muddy ground that lay between us to show my scant regard for him. Then I told him something he could do if he had a mind to.

The boy he scowled and thrust out his hand. There upon his palm lay a silver-mounted rabbit foot. This grisly talisman belong to Cléophas who found it on the Sugar Landing in St Pierre and kept it to remind himself of home, though it were a superstitious charm and most likely inapt to his faith. I had seen that pitiful scrap of fur and claw manys a time hence knew the Father must indeed have sent this chuckle-head, now telling me he would tend to my beasts once I had gone. And since I knew no different then, I thought he meant whiles I went to the morgue.

'*Hé! Poté mannèv!*' said the boy, in our kréyòl tongue. '*Ou kouyon, wi!*'

Though it would be unwise to make Cléophas wait, I refuse to be hurried by this poor fool, and I daresay I took my time strolling over to Victorine to gather in her rope. My chief employment was to tend livestock for the friars and since I would rather do that than toil on their plantation, you can bet I slung to my chores like a Hercules. Those animals so spoil they fancy themselve kings and queen. Victorine she leaned against me, entirely companiable, whiles I moored her up to the stake. She had the fluffiest most velvety ears of any cow you ever did see and her milk always came plentiful and sweet. I had no fancy to abandon her and her sisters to the care of this stranger; some might say a half-wit at that.

Meanwhile, the boy puffed up his cheeks and paced about, inspecting the little herd. The way he strutted and squinted and stroke his chin you would have took him for some Béké colonial cattle-merchant.

'What's your name?' I asked him.

'Descartes,' says he.

Now, I might have been a young tom-fool back in those days but whenever the friars discuss the world beyond the islands I kept my ears open and I had heard tell of many great men, René Descartes among them. Seem to me some former master must have name this boy in cruel jest, for I have known game-fowl with more savvy.

I watched him strut about a-whiles then asked him:

'They name you after the philosopher?'

'Filo-*kwa*?' says the boy.

'The scholar: Descartes. They gave you his name?'

Boy shook his head, emphatic, then dealt an imaginary hand of Piquet.

'*Mé non*,' says he. '*Dé KARTES, tu vwa?* You damn silly. Playing cards.'

Poor boy had more teeth than brains. I could only hope none of my cattle would suffer whiles in his care.

'Well, Descartes, you best not harm these ladies,' I told him.

'Or else.' And I showed him my fist, mostly in jest. Then I snatch the rabbit foot from him and took off running like a redshank to the hospital.

Chapter Two

The Fathers had constructed the morgue a short distance from the main building in the shade of abundant trees; a stone house in miniature, small enough for to make you laugh had you not known its gruesome purpose. High jalousie windows and walls three feet thick kept the temperature inside cool. I hesitated at the doorway, turning my straw hat in my hands. Not that I felt afraid; I had been in that morgue before. Just the dim light of the interior did blind me awhile. When my eyes adjusted, there stood Father Cléophas and, on the table before him, a naked field hand, dead as a dead herring. Since August they had been perishing at the rate of about one a week, struck down by a raging distemper no amount of prophylactic or purges would cure. For now, the poor dead fellow lay there all of a piece but only a matter of time before Cléophas finish washing him and then he would slice the belly open and haul out the inners. It was a known fact that our surgeon Fathers like to hack up a cadaver, poke around inside. They put our livers and lights in pickle jars and called it Learning. The very thought of it – and the ripe smell of the morgue – would have made a person of delicate disposition queasy. The field hand lips had all shrunk back; his teeth expose; eyes open. There be a fly stood on one of his eyeball but the poor dumb clod would never blink again; he had gone *kickeraboo*, most certainly.

That corpse had me so hypnotise, it took me a moment to notice my brother Emile stood nearby in the shadows. Blow me tight. The sight of him there made me jump in my linen. I took him for dead too, just propped against the wall – until he opened his eyes. Mary and Joseph! I laughed out loud and was the gladdest kind of boy alive until, slapdash, it occur to me to wonder exactly *why* he might be return to the hospital. Emile gave me a dismal look as much to say: 'Well, here we are,' just as Cléophas beckon me in with a '*Bonjour*' and bid me put his rabbit foot on the bench. I set the hairy toes beside some medicine jars. Meanwhile, the old man turn to drop his cloth into a bowl and whiles his gaze averted I whisper to my brother:

'*Sa ou fé?*'

But before Emile could tell me how he was or explain his presence, Cléophas had stepped around the table toward us, one finger raised as though to reprimand me. He had been with us several month by that time and the sun had tawned his skin such that it now shone like beeswax in the gloom.

'Prattle all you like in that gibberish,' says he, in his same-old fussy-fussy French. 'But I'm reliably informed, Lucien, that you speak another language.'

At first I thought he must mean his own tongue. Our friars hailed from Paris, *Fwance* and wanted us slave to speak as they did but we converse mostly like our mothers, in a hodge-podge of their own languages and French and – though we knew more of *la langue française* than our elders – we were prone to vex the friars with bombast kréyòl.

'English,' says Cléophas. 'I'm told you speak it like a native.'

Perhaps this knack of mine might be a misdeed for which he would scold me inasmuch as, though the war had ended, we still considered England to be the enemy. I cut a glance at my brother. He seem calm enough but I could spot that his breath came fast and shallow. For what purpose he had been summon now I knew no more than a moth. But life had taught us to expect the worst; we were both full of dread and would have twittered in our shoes, had we worn any.

'No need to look worried, my son,' the old man said. 'I speak a little English myself. I gather you learned it in Grenada from that man-nurse, Calder.'

I nodded.

'Pray let me hear you,' said Cléophas. He picked up the rabbit foot and slipped it into the folds of his cassock. 'Say something in English.'

I thought for a moment and presently did as bid, allowing old phrases to come to my lips just as I remembered them; though I took care to leave out the abundant foul curses I knew and use to spout with relish.

'Good day, Father. How do you do? My name is Lucien. I am thirteen or fourteen years old or thereabouts. Monday, Tuesday, Wednesday, Thursday, Friday, Saturday, Sunday. Where is the ipecac? Good boy. Give this man a medal. Bring me a jug. The fault, dear Brutus, is not in our stars, but in ourselves, that we are underlings. The fever has broken. The fever has return. They all have a fever. Fetch bandages and hot water. This leg must come off. She is dead. He is dead. They are all—'

Cléophas raise his hand.

'Enough,' said he. 'I believe you.'

For true, I had not sought his belief but it would have been rash to point this out; and since I had deference ingrained in my very bones, I bessy-down and made him an obeisance.

'Now then,' says he. 'There's something I want you boys to do for me.'

And in this manner here the whole entire enterprise did commence, exactly so.

Chapter Three

Some masters are swift to get to the point when they give instructions; you might say they go directly through the main door, cross the threshold, no hesitation. Father Cléophas was not one of these. He would walk around the property first, try the windows, then wander off into the garden to gaze at the roof before eventually he retrace his step to the front of the dwelling and give a tentative knock and – whiles he went on this bumbling circumbendibus – you oblige to go with him, wondering what abominable toil or trouble might be in store for you whenever he finally came around and stated his requirement. With this rigmarole and in other ways, Cléophas like to cultivate the impression of being an absent-minded, kindly fellow and he would beguile you with that bilge awhile until you became better acquainted and began to cognise just how sly he could be, for true. My brother and I had encountered all manner of individual among the friars: a spectrum of humanity, from gentle coves who scarce could bear to swat a musquito to the most heartless bully. Whiles Cléophas might not be the worst kind of tyrant, for true, he was surely as slippery as a worm in a hogshead of eel.

As for my brother, they said he had enough brains for to run a parliament. He was more than twice my age but I considered myself to be just as much a man, though in those days I lacked his talent with the pigeon peas and mummy apple. Beforetimes, he had slave for our friars, planted their growing grounds, first in Grenada then Martinique, until they sold him to some Dominican monks on the far side of the island, a long-day hike away. He had lost weight since last I saw him, about a year previous, when his masters had sent him back to the hospital with a gift of wine for the Fathers. Beneath his clothes, his body look to be naught but pure muscle and bone; a sculptor could have used him as a model for a fine-figured deity. His skin *peau-chapotille*, like mine – the pale bronze of ripe sapotillier fruit – but on that day his face had a chalky tinge and I fell to wonder about his health. Whiles listening to the Father, he appear to be the embodiment of patient attention but he had a gleam behind his gaze – a gleam such as only I, his brother, could detect – and it struck me that he must be taking the measure of this friar and would soon reach a verdict akin my own.

Meanwhile, Cléophas had finally crept up behind his point. Well, he required us to deliver some few medicinal plant to a colleague on Grenada. My brother and I were no strangers to that island, a former French territory now in English hands. We both had served *les Frères* at the hospital in the main town of Fort Royal and I was born there by all account. What Cléophas describe was a task of some magnitude, a voyage by sea to the place we had once called home. Listening to the old bolus drivel on, I grew thrill to the very marrow. An expedition with Emile to *La Grenade* struck me as naught but an adventure. Thus, when I turn to my brother, I felt all a-mort to see his shoulders droop. He look twice as miserable as before.

Cléophas must have observe this too, for he said:

'You surprise me, Emile. I was led to believe you might like to see Grenada again.' He awaited a reply but my brother simply composed his features, drew himself upright, so. 'There was a girl, I'm told,' Cléophas continued. 'Her name – perhaps you can remind me . . . Estelle?'

My brother pursed his lips so tight you would have thought he wish them seal for the course of ages but the Father continue to stare at him such that Emile had no choice but to respond.

'Céleste,' said he, his voice hoarse.

'Well,' says Cléophas. 'I expect you'll be glad to fetch her back with you when you return to Martinique.'

Perhaps the old buffer had took leave of his senses for this could scarce be a serious proposition. Céleste – along with our former confreres at the Fort Royal hospital – was now in the hands of the English. What the friar said next did little to dispel our bewilderment.

'You can bring her as well as the others.'

A moment pass, then my brother said:

'Beg pardon, Father – what others?'

Cléophas spread his hands as much to say the matter self-explained.

'Our other Negroes in Grenada. You may as well bring them too.'

'. . . The hospital slaves?' says Emile.

'Indeed, those at the hospital.' The Father gave a careless pout in the French manner. 'And also the field hands from the plantation.'

Emile threw me a startle glance.

'But that would be – please you, Father – many slave.'

'Forty-two, at the last count,' says Cléophas. 'A number of them have perished recently. And some might be too old or sick but the fact is, the healthy ones should be here with us. No need to tell you what brutes those English are; they treat their Negroes so badly. We must get our own slaves back into our possession. We've lost so many this year to fever; we must replenish. There's the rest of our land to clear and plant, not to mention our plans for the new distillery. With so few of us Fathers left, it's too much. Also, we could use those hospital Negroes, the trained nurses, particularly Céleste; I understand she is very skilled. There is free passage to Grenada now and the treaty with England seems to have endured – the time is right to bring these Negroes here to us, to where they rightfully belong. It is the will of God.'

For true, I knew that Cléophas had been buttering the authority in Grenada and had even sail to Fort Royal for parleys with the English, angling to recover those slave. Emile may have heard the same rumour but he still look puzzled entirely.

'Forgive me, Father,' he said. 'Perhaps I misunderstand. You want us to round up the hospital slaves and all the plantation hand and bring them back here with us?'

'Certainly, those that are capable of labour, those that can make the journey. And, of course . . .' Cléophas waved his hand vaguely in the direction of the medicine jars, '. . . deliver these dried roots and leaves to Monsieur Maillard, the physician.'

But I saw now that those herb were naught but a cloud of mundungus sent up as distraction before the old sawbones reveal his true purpose.

'If you please, Father, you will not come with us?' enquired Emile. 'Or any of the other friar? We would need your authority, surely?'

Cléophas gave him a smile.

'There's a skipper has agreed to take you, a Spaniard. I'll join you in a few days, of course, but for now you boys must go ahead.' He indicated the body cooling on the table. 'As you can see, I'm too busy here.'

Emile frowned.

'Please you, Father, but do we have permission – from the English, from their Governor? I expect we would need that – to take the slaves.'

'Indeed.' Cléophas reached into the folds of his cassock and extracted a document. 'This is a Power of Attorney from our Order, drawn up by the notary, Monsieur Emerigon, in the presence of our Governor, the Comte d'Ennery, and signed both by him and by our very own Reverend Superior, Père Lefébure, and this permission includes, of course, the approval of the English Governor of Grenada.'

He handed the parchment to Emile, who held it up to the light. A pang seize my heart as I watched him squint at that page. My brother was no kind of fool – no indeed, not one pound of him. But that paper might as well have been bum-fodder for all the sense he would make of it since he was unable to sign his own name. Emile would have cut off his own thumb for a chance to learn his ABC, whereas I could spell out a few simple word, though – for all practical purpose – I was illiterate and only educated myself, little by little, in later years.

The manuscript looked hard to read, close-writ in a backward-sloping scrawl, and before I could cipher a single word Cléophas had retrieve the thing.

'I'll return this to you when you leave,' said he, as the document vanish within the folds of his linen. That was some magical robe he had on him: a Power of Attorney in there now and a rabbit foot – and what else besides his jiggumbobs – a bag of many eggs? A silken handkerchief? A turtle dove?

'You should be aware,' he continued. 'The new physician at the hospital in Grenada – Mr Bryant, an Englishman – contests our ownership of the Negroes and hopes to retain them for himself. Both he and the new overseer at the plantation are of the same mind. They would keep the Negroes if they could – *our* Negroes, Negroes that were either bought or raised by us, *les Frères de la Charité*. It matters not to them what may be right, or what the English Governor may think, or the Comte d'Ennery. This is the one slight impediment we face in this matter.'

Emile turn his head a fraction. His gaze met mine then he resume looking at the floor. The room lay mortal still, so quiet I could hear a flame gutter in one of the lamp. Cléophas scrutinised us with his little grey eyes, first me, then my brother. He appear to weigh something in his mind before he continue.

'Nevertheless, there is nothing that cannot be overcome now that we have this Power of Attorney. Be very careful with it.'

My brother breathed out hard through his nose: not quite a sigh, but similar. Cléophas studied him and presently spoke again, his voice stern.

'We chose you, Emile, because you and Lucien are best suited to succeed in an enterprise of this sort. You're familiar with Grenada and the town and since you know the hospital Negroes they ought to trust you. You've been hired back from the Dominican Fathers until such time as you return with the slaves.' Here, he fixed his eye on me. 'I imagine a trip to Fort Royal will please you, my son.'

No doubt in my mind that our old confreres would be glad to quit Grenada. Our French masters treated us bad enough but we all had heard stories about the English and what fiends they could be: they would hang you out to dry soon as look at you or squeeze you, bones and all, through a cane press. Most certainly, the hospital slaves would greet us as saviours and I had a mighty fancy to the notion of myself in such a role. Last time our Fort Royal compeers had seen me I was but a sprat of six or seven. Whereas now – in my triumphant return – I considered myself well nigh a man and though I might not part the waves and lead them toward the land of Canaan, I could see myself chaperone them to *La Matinik*, safe and easy, like eating pastry. In sum, I was noways cast down about the prospect of our allotted task, and would have said as much except the 'Talking Machine' had already turn back to my brother, palavering on again.

'Who knows? It is not impossible, Emile, that Père Lefébure might see fit to grant you your freedom, if you succeed. At the very least – with the increase in sugar money once these Negroes are brought to us – we may, in time, be able to buy you back from the Dominicans. You could set up quarters with Céleste here and resume tending our vegetables – as I'm told you did before you became so morose and impudent. Your talent in the garden is missed, you know. None of your successors has shown much aptitude. Father Damascene still goes into raptures over your avocato pears. I daresay you and Céleste might even grow old here together. To my mind, this venture will be a blessing for all of us. So, there you have it.'

All through this soft sawder my brother stood with head bent, his lips down-turned. It would have been unwise to pay much heed to these allusions to freedom. Howsomever, Emile did not even seem cheered at the prospect of a reunion with Céleste. Once upon a time, back in Grenada, he had been a hearty soul with a smile for everyone and such a natural ability for growing plants he could coax cassava from a rock. Originally, we thought he had been sent to Martinique for just a few week but when those week turn to month I'm told he began to lose interest in the earth and all that grew there. By the time I arrived in St Pierre a year later he was a change character, stubborn and sulky. The Martiniquan friars suffered him somewhat longer until they tired of his insolence and sold him on to the Dominican monks, just prior to the English invasion. I half surmise that parting from Céleste was what had caused him to languish in the first place.

Cléophas folded his arms. Oh, he was a weary-o!

'Now then, Emile,' said he. 'You cannot refuse to carry out your duty.'

My brother said nothing. His fists clench, unclench and clench again. In silence, I willed him to use them on the friar – for that would be a sight to see – then told myself not to be a fool, and prayed he would do no such thing.

'Well, my son,' the old man persisted. 'What do you have to tell me, hmm?'

Poor Emile look sick as a poison dog. When he spoke, his voice sounded tight and dull.

'Father, I must do what you ask.'

'Excellent,' said Cléophas. 'The matter is settled.'

My brother looked up and stare the old man in the eye.

'Except one thing,' said he. 'Please you, Father, I'll go alone. No use for this boy here. He will only dilly and dally and cause trouble.'

His choice of words – 'this boy' – stung me to the core but I should have expected as much. Trying to get me left behind, no doubt; always treating me like a baby. For fear that I would miss my chance to act the big don for our Fort Royal compeers, I open my mouth to object but Cléophas had already clicked his tongue in disapproval.

'Stuff and nonsense. You'll need him.'

'Beg your pardon, Father,' Emile said. 'But this is a child. What is he – ten years old? He'll ruin everything. He is too young and silly.'

My cheeks grew so hot they burned.

'*Cho!* Father, I'm not ten years old, I'm—'

Cléophas lifted one hand to silence me.

'Be sensible,' he told Emile. 'We thought you would welcome this opportunity to spend time with your brother.'

Emile scowled at me. We sucked our teeth, same-time, me thinking: 'Ten years old. I'll give you ten years old.'

Meanwhile, Cléophas regarded us with a kind of detach amusement like he might survey the twitching of two sand-flea on the shore. I had no desire to give him the pleasure of observing us quarrel and Emile must have thought the same for he fell silent, though his eyes were all a-blaze. He look taut as a yellow viper all set to strike; you would not wish to encounter him in the forest.

Cléophas drew him aside for a quiet word.

'Listen, my son. Whatever language you boys jabber on in is incomprehensible, even to most Frenchmen. What would happen if you were stopped by an Englishman or one of their redcoats, and questioned? You would have difficulty being understood. But Lucien here can talk to them. None of them has any command of French, believe you me, and an interpreter is never to hand, as I learned when I was there, in August.'

Here, he step back and raised his voice to include me.

'By the by, if such an eventuality did occur – say, if, upon arrival, you're stopped by soldiers and questioned – perhaps it would be better to avoid mention of your purpose in Grenada, if possible. The less said, the better. Christmas is almost upon us. I shall give you each a ticket, stating in writing that you are in Grenada to run various errands for me. If I were you – just in case they question you more closely – I might dream up some other story to explain your presence on the island. For instance, Lucien can tell them that you're delivering medicinal plants to Monsieur Maillard and that you must prolong your stay on the island for a few days in order to . . . to . . .'

Since an idea had already formed in my mind, I spoke up:

'Please you, sir, I'll say that, since it's Christmas, our masters let us return to the island to visit the grave of our own dead papa.'

'You see?' said Cléophas to Emile. 'Not silly.'

My brother simply gave me a look of disgust.

Cléophas turn back to me.

'Your father was some . . . settler, no doubt – now deceased.'

'He is gone *kickeraboo*,' said I. 'Quite so, he is, *mon père*, most certainly.'

Cléophas nodded.

'At any rate, it will probably take more than one of you to manage all that must be done over there. You will have to speak to the field hands and to the hospital Negroes, first of all, and one or two of the nurses have been hired out – at least they were a few months ago – so you'll have to track them down and instruct them on how to get from wherever they are to the point of embarkation. Believe me, I have been thinking long and hard about this venture, and how it might be achieved.'

Then he proceeded to jaw on so long I reckoned we might be there until the crack of doom. Most of his remarks he address to my brother, who kept feeding him judicious questions. A fine pair they made, old Socrates and Plato; paid me as much heed as they might a lizard, and I leave you to fancy if I soon grew tired of that or not. The old man droned on and on. I won't record his orations here; besides, I was only half listening, caught up in imagining my triumphant return to Grenada. The long and short of it, a skipper and vessel had already been hired and my brother and I were to set sail on the morrow.

Chapter Four

By the time we quitted the morgue, dusk had crept up the foot-hills of Mont Pelée, though her summit glowed bright jade in the sun. I had presume that Emile might walk with me back to the pasture to talk but he began to head toward the main gate so fast I was oblige to call out to him before he vanished.

'Emile!'

He turn to look at me, all the while backing off beneath the trees.

'What is it, little britches?'

A few question came to mind but none seemed worth asking in that instant. Besides, it pained me, the sight of him all hotfoot in retreat, as if I were some kind of leper. Scarce the blink of an eye together and already our great reunion gone sour.

Perhaps Emile read my mind for he came to a stop, saying:

'What's the matter?'

'Nothing. Just – a person might – well, it might be good to talk with you is all.'

Somesuch nonsense came out of my mouth and I could have kick myself all around the hospital for sounding like a fliperous coquette.

'Child, I would like nothing more,' said he. 'But we have no time for chit-chat.'

Contrary as a hog. Of course, from birth, we had been at the beck and call of others – my brother slaving first for *les Frères* and then, after they sold him, for those Dominicans; but also, for that matter, any Béké white colonial in the islands. Back in those days, since Emile could not be master of his destiny I suppute he like to hold sway over the few paltry element that lay within his control. Thus, he tended to avoid any other slave dictating his affairs, even in a matter so slight as when he might be engage in conversation. If ever you ask to speak to him he would imply – though he would gladly talk with you – he had far too many demands on his time; he a busy-busy man, a regular Bashaw: such would be the implication. Well, I could have cuffed him right where he stood for he was nothing but a stubborn, miserable slave, same as me. However, I knew better than to provoke him and so came at it sideway like a crab.

'Will you sleep here tonight in the cells?'

'Mm-hmm,' he said, clearly thinking about something else. Then he asked: 'Tell me, do you remember your birdcall signal?'

'Of course.'

'Let me hear them. You might be out of practice. Not too loud now.'

I cup my hands to my mouth, then press my fingers to my nose and gave three short descending hoots, one upon the other. The untrained ear might mistake those sounds for a dove but we knew otherwise. Compare to a real bird, the calls were a fraction short and came too express, one upon the other. This was one of the signal we used on the hospital estates to attract attention in secret, though some slave were disincline to whistle or hoot after dark for fear of rousing spirits. Emile himself had taught me the calls when I was but a sprout.

'Not bad,' he said. 'Now the pigeon.'

Whereas a dove hoot meant simply 'Here I am' or 'All clear' or 'I'm coming', the pigeon call constituted a warning, especially at night when most of those bird would be tucked up in their nest. A pigeon was more difficult to mimic than a dove.

I put my tongue to the roof of my mouth and gave a few tentative coo. My brother frowned.

'Again,' he said. 'Not so loud.'

I tried once more. He shook his head.

'You need practice. Go on now, back to pasture. Try and get it better out there where there's nobody around.'

'Perhaps we can talk later then,' I said, as he turn to leave. 'See you at the cells?'

He spread his hands, full of regret, as though even this would be impossible; I may as well have ask for an audience with the Pope in Rome.

'I have some errand to run in town,' he said. 'I may be late. But we have abundant time for talking tomorrow, on board.'

'Oh,' says I, and gave a sniff. 'You need a ship to get to Grenada, do you?'

He frowned.

'Of course.'

Quick-sharp, I toss back at him: 'And here am I, expecting you to walk there upon the water.'

My intention, to take him down a peg, but he only gave me a familiar look of fond despair.

'Listen, Lucien. This is no adventure, nor a child game. Sometimes, I wonder if you still have the sense you came born with.'

And so saying he sped off toward the gates. Just as well for him, since I was blazing with such a wrath I could have punch the head off a hammer.

Chapter Five

On the following day, the tiny whistling-frog (or *'ti gounouys*) cease their overnight song and the sudden silence woke me as usual, just before first bell. Emile had return so late the previous night I had not seen him, hide nor whisker. I doubt he had a girl in town; no woman interested him save Céleste. First, I check the row of cells in search of him then ran to the main building. Young Father Boniface was in one of the empty sick room, sitting up and darning bandages, despite his belly complaint. Once, he had been a swarthy fellow but for weeks now his skin had taken a greyish pallor. When he saw me at the threshold, he pointed to a bowl of vomit at his bedside and said:

'No blood this time, Lucien. We shall gain the whip-hand yet.'

But he shook his head when I asked if he had seen my brother.

I found our superior, Père Lefébure, in the refectory, his cheeks already florid and sweating, his gooseberry-coloured eyes somewise bloodshot. He glanced up from his plans of the new distillery to inform me that my brother and Cléophas had already left for town. No doubt they had some business of Olympian importance to attend to down there. As a mere mortal, I was under instruction to join them at the Sugar Landing once I had shown the new boy, Descartes, how to keep the livestock from perishing in my absence.

Lefébure peered into his ink well.

'Before you go, take a breakfast to Damascene,' he said. 'There's a good boy.'

Old Father Damascene lay in bed, awake, his face fish-white. The room smell like a new-fill chamber pot. As I cross the threshold to prop open the jalousie, he fail to recognise me and call me '*Maman*'. Then he look shame-faced and murmured:

'*Bonjour, mon fils.*'

'*Bonjour, mon père. Il fait beau aujourd'hui, non?*'

I found it no hardship to speak a little of *la langue française* with the Good Father, just the two of us. He had shown me naught but kindness and had save my skin by bringing me to Martinique. I helped him to his chair, checking his nightshirt en route but – thanks be to great Jehosaphat – he had not soiled himself.

The only food left to eat that morning was some *corossol* fruit. I passed him a slice and set his coffee in front of him.

'Pah!' he said, with one glance at the pale liquid in the bowl.

But before he could make a whole simmy-dimmy about water-down coffee, I distracted him.

'Now then, Father. Me and Emile are to – you remember Emile, Father?'

'Ah, what a gardener. He was a good boy – before.'

'Father, he still is, mostly. Do you know where we are to go, me and him?'

His eyes grew wide.

'Where?'

'Please you, Father, back to Grenada. Remember: where I first saw you, when you came there to the hospital – when Father Prudence decease this world?'

Damascene looked appalled.

'Prudence is *dead*?'

'*Oui, mon père.* Remember? He died years agone.'

'Ah yes,' says he, but he looked wily and I doubt he did recall, for true.

'We sail this very morning, Father, because we have to—'

'Who is sending you? Cléophas?'

'*Oui, mon père.*'

'That speck of shit.' He bang his fist on the table. 'I told him not to pursue this reckless venture. Confound him.' He grab my hand. 'Don't go, my son. Stay here!'

'Now Father, you mustn't upset yourself. What is reckless?'

'Oh my child. Those Goddams!'

Back then, Goddams was what we sometimes call the English. They had invaded our French Antilles some years prior, causing turmoil, and for small return since a mere nine month later they handed back most of their Caribee spoils, except some few, including Grenada and her sister isles. Now, King George reigned over those territories and the slaves in Grenada toiled for Goddam masters.

'Father – the war is over, remember? They sign the treaty, three years since.'

'All the same, those English, one cannot trust them. Why does Cléophas not send someone else?'

Then he said something all gibberish, just a jumble of words, but I was accustom to his ramblings, more frequent these days now he had become diswitted.

'Father – I'll be back in one week.'

'A week!' Poor old soul; his eyes fill with tears. 'But if you go, Lucien, who shall bring me my *corossol*? My *cocoyage*? What if you never return?'

'I will, *mon père*. And the other Fathers will take care of you until then.'

At least, I hoped they would. Now that most of the friar had died or gone back to Paris or St Domingue, only four remained. *Les Frères de la Charité* in France were suppose to provide replacements, but months had gone by since the arrival of Cléophas with no sign of anyone else, not even a new nurse-man. Young Father Boniface had been ailing for weeks, and Lefébure had no time for quotidian cares, always up to his neck in alchemy, trying to make his special silver rum and planning his distillery. I had my doubts about whether he would remember to take much care of the Good Father.

Damascene sipped his coffee then scowled into the bowl.

'My piss is darker than this,' said he. 'How many times did you use the grounds?'

'Now then, Father. Soon there will be strong coffee every morning. With those extra field hand from Grenada, we can grow more cane, sell more sugar and make rum to sell. Besides, I shall bring back some old faces you might remember, Father – Céleste and the others . . .'

'Ah, Céleste.'

He smiled and, for a flash, seem so much like his old self it occur to me he might be on the mend. Lately, he scarce knew where he was, often wandering from one place to another and talking stupidness. To have such lucid conversation with him was a wide stride, for true. Howsomever, by the time he had drunk his coffee and I bid him farewell, he had already forgot about my voyage, for he told me he would see me that night, and I had not the heart to contradict him.

The boy Descartes I found by the chicken pen, laughing at the hens, mocking them with a 'buck-buck-buck-A!' Then he bob his head up-down like a pullet pecking seed and by mistake banged his skull off the hen-house. Well, bless my stars. He yell fit to raise the Devil and jumped about the place, cursing all kind of curse.

'*Tambou! Puten bordow do mèd!! Fé shié!*'

It pained me to leave my poor Victorine and the rest at his mercy.

Chapter Six

The St Pierre Hospital sits behind town at the foot of a vast cliff so abundantly overgrown that the forest seem to surge down the rock face like a green waterfall. Just a few years theretofore, I had witness with my own eyes the blockade of St Pierre, prior the English invasion, when those Goddams had dropped anchor offshore and done their utmost to knock the place to fritters with bombardment, firing great guns without cease, their bursting bombs raining down upon us for days until our batteries were silence. It was a miracle that any structure along the waterfront had been left standing. Parts of town were still under repair since the war and through certain gap between buildings you could glimpse the bay. As I walk down the straight road toward the ocean, I saw nine, ten large vessel moored up – drogher, sloops and merchantmen – all floating there, majestic, as though suspended in blue light.

St Pierre has no true harbour and no pier of any account, just the Mooring, an open roadstead. All the big ship coming in, they toss anchor seaward and fasten to a chain brought from shore and any cargo is ferry to land in smaller craft. Here and there among the larger vessel, a few piddling yawl like little children clinging to the skirts of their mother. No sign of any slaver: that was a mercy at least, and no warship either, save one frigate the French kept there now on watch, lest those English Goddams attempt another invasion. My gaze picked out this or that rig and my veins began to tingle as I wondered which ship might be ours and what would be her name. Something impressive and manly, I hoped, perhaps a

Triomphant or *Persévérante.* In those days my head always and ever full of stories about ships such as the *Royal Fortune* and the deeds of buccaneer pirate like Blackbeard and Bartholomew Roberts.

Down at the quayside, people crowded around the market stalls. One bacchanal in the place: invalid soldiers and sailors begging, some blind, some with blacken stumps where once grew an arm or leg; whole dugouts full of fishes for sale, longside fruit of every hue and form piled up in basket; the whisper of naked feet on the stones mostly drowned out by high-pitch cries of vendors calling their wares in a mish-mash of French and kréyòl, their words alone enough to make your mouth fill with water.

'*Çe moune-là, ça qui lè di pain aubè?*' '*Ca qui lè bel avocato?*' '*Mwen ni bel poissons!*' Who wants my little loaves this morning? My avocato? My beautiful fish? '*Oh, qu'ils sont bons, mes patisseries! Oh, qu'ils sont doux!*' Oh, my pastries are good! Oh, they are sweet!

I spotted Father Cléophas and Emile at the end of the quay among the barrel at the Sugar Landing so I headed toward them through the crowd with a 'Good day' and a tip of my hat to those of my acquaintance. '*Bonjou – Bonjou ché – Bonjou Manzell – Bonjou Missié.*' The friars sent me somewhiles to market and often as not, I had to persuade sellers that they should hand over fish or other goods with promise of payment in sugar 'tomorrow self' or 'next week'. More than anything, I hated to beg, ashame that my masters so poor. Thus, by way of compensation, I always tried to be extra genial, quick with pleasantry and laughter, offering compliments fore and aft and up and down so no one heart would groan if ever they beheld me coming.

My brother now wore a battered straw hat. The face on him hard-hard like stone; his shoulders up; his arms folded. Father Cléophas carried his old burlap bag on one shoulder and, on the other, a satchel made of leather. He was clearly holding forth to

Emile in earnest and though I felt disoblige that they had left me behind, I took some comfort at having escaped an ear-load of friarly chatter.

Out in the shallows, I could see the usual flotilla: a few large canoe or *pirogues*, but mostly about a dozen flat-bottom *'ti canot* or tub made of tea-chest and the like. In these preposterous craft, little boys sat entirely naked, paddling about the bay hoping to be hire to take passengers, messages or small cargo to and from the ships at anchor. From my previous trips to town, I knew some of these wharf boy – the *'ti canotié*. They were younger than me, by and large, so I mostly ignored them but I had an inkling they would be impress by the great adventure I was set to embark upon. The Father had warned us to be discreet once we reach *La Grenade* but he had said nothing about here in *La Matinik*. I thought it could do no harm to drop some hint to those boys, just enough so they might wonder about the important mysterious business I had been chosen to conduct. With this in mind, I waved and call to them as I approach the water.

'*Hé! Zenfants-la. Kouté.*'

But right then old Cléophas descended on me with a cry.

'There you are.'

And before I could say a word to the boys, he sent me off on some blasted errand, to get a scoop of fried Jackfish and some Kill-Devil, alias RUM.

'Tell the vendors I'll pay them next week, in sugar,' says he. 'And be sure to get the cheapest tafia, just a small jug – a sealed one. Then come and find us. We'll be down there on the sand.'

Seem to me the old man just wanted rid of me. I curse my lot, having to beg yet again – and on this of all days. Old Blackbeard, before he set sail for some ruffian escapade, you can bet nobody sent him to market upon the spunge for Jackfish.

My brother let himself be led away, walking stiff and stilted as a heron. By the time I persuaded two vendor to give me rum and fish for a promise of sugar, he and Cléophas had reach the sand. Emile watch me approach, the look in his eye telling me something – but what I did not know.

'*Viens*, Lucien. *Vite*,' says Cléophas when he notice me. 'Ah! My Jacks.'

He grab the parcel from me since those fishes a delicacy and his favourite. The rum he refuse to take.

'No, no,' says he. 'That's for Captain Bianco. Give it to him when you go aboard. Just be aware, my son, as I've been telling Emile, your skipper is a Spaniard but he's also a deaf mute. He cannot hear what you say but makes himself understood with signs and he's an experienced sailor. You're in safe hands with Bianco, yes, quite so, *pas de problème*.'

Behind his back, I could see my brother. He raised an eyebrow, poked his tongue in his cheek: his sceptic face. No doubt, so far as he saw it, the friars being poor and scrimp of means, Cléophas would have found the most cheap and nasty vessel that could be hired in the whole Caribbees.

Meanwhile, a canoe had come skimming to shore and out jump Descartes. That boy was everywhere. Only a short while before, I had left him back at the hospital. My brother must have recognise the boy, for he knew his name.

'*Bonjou*, Descartes,' he said. 'Peace be with you. How is your mother? And how's my friend your brother? And your cousin, Baptiste – is he well?'

Here I saw a vestige of the old Emile. Our mother was of the Mandingo people and she had taught him to greet acquaintances in ritual manner by enquiring about the health of every family member, every sister, brother, father, mother, every cousin, uncle, aunt. Emile like to observe the custom and would have continue to question Descartes about more distant relatives had Cléophas not grown impatient.

'Enough,' he said and then he made us all kneel down on the sand whiles he offered up devotions. I must confess, a few line into the prayer, I open my eyes and took a peek at my brother. Back in Grenada when I was small, he use to carry on all kind of macaque during prayer. He might pretend to smoke an imaginary pipe or knock back invisible drams of rum, then yawn and stroke his chin as though bristles had sprouted there, or find supposititious insects in his hair, or a lizard or a crab – all to try and make me laugh. But those days were gone. Now, he contemplated me with an expression most grave before bestowing upon me the strangest smile, full of melancholy. Then with a sigh, he closed his eyes.

Descartes had hunched over, his face hid from view. Cléophas, meanwhile, was lost in hocus-pocus, head tilted back, smiling up at his compeer, the Divine Being. No other friar did pray quite like Cléophas. He always talk directly to God, smiling or chuckling now and again over some badinage that only he and the Supreme Being could hear. The way he spoke with the Lord you might suppose they were the best of friends; that Cléophas knew more about his Creator than anyone; perhaps he knew better about the Almighty than even God knew himself. Sometimes the old goat palavered on so long his orisons were like a monologue in six act but mercifully, on that day, he made short work of it. In his final remarks, he knew the Lord would watch over our journey; he knew the Lord would assure our safe return to Martinique; he knew the Lord would want to provide us with fair winds and untrouble seas; old Cléophas he knew the Lord back and front and upside down – yes he did, for true.

After we said our Amen, the Father bestowed his blessing upon us and handed over our tickets – written passes to show to anyone who might accost us, each in a small burlap bag with string to hang around our neck. He gave Emile the leather satchel then thrust us toward the 'ti canot.

'Go now, my sons, *vite, vite*.'

Descartes held the canoe steady whiles my brother and I climbed aboard, fore and aft; Emile so careful with the satchel you might suppute it full of holy relic.

'What's in there?' I asked. 'A pique-nique?'

Naught but a slice of *corossol* had pass my lips that morning and my belly was biting me. My brother open the bag. Inside, muslin-wrapped, the jars of herb from the morgue; also the Power of Attorney and a flask of water. Nothing else. Emile gave me a consoling wink.

'Never fret, little one. I'll make sure you eat.'

'You're the one fretting,' said I. 'Nothing amiss with me.'

Descartes shove the boat out and sprang inside, between us, perfectly balanced and fit as a flea in a hound-dog ear. The canoe sat low in the water but it did not seem to bother the boy. As we pulled away from shore, Cléophas called out:

'Emile, I have every faith in you.' And then: 'Be sure to tell Lucien your slight change of approach.'

I looked at my brother.

'What change of approach?' I asked.

But he just shook his head, with a glance at the boy. Then he lean forward and spoke to him.

'Give me that paddle.'

'*Non mèsi*,' Descartes said. 'We change places now, we tip over. Besides, I'm use to paddling.'

'Who is your master now?'

'Monsieur Siboulet. He's half kill me six times. But I'm hired out for a few week to the Father. If I can show them I work hard then they might buy me.'

'Oh well,' said Emile. 'In that case, keep paddling.'

Instead of heading for any of the big ship out at anchor it seem to me that we were bound only a spit and stride offshore toward a dilapidated craft no bigger than the smallest kind of fishing yawl. She had a tattered mainsail fit for a twopenny pirate, a dirty, flapping mizen and her hull needed a coat of pitch. A leanish colonial type stood amidships, arms a-kimbo, observing our approach. Emile grinned at me as much to say 'I told you so', his pessimistic prediction come true.

'Gloat all you like,' says I. 'But we won't fit forty-some slave in *that* calabash.'

'Ksst! Do you never listen? This is just to get us there, you and me.'

Back onshore, the Father all smile-smile and waving. He called out a few word but the breeze snatch them away.

'What's he say?' I asked.

My brother stitched up his lip like he might spit but made no reply.

'*I di, bon chans, mes fils,*' said Descartes.

Since Cléophas had wished us luck, I yell back thanks to him across the water.

'*Mèsi, mon pè a mwen. Ô rèvoi. Mèsi.*'

And then Emile did spit: noisily, over the side, into the blue-green ocean. All at once I consider myself insulted for it seem to me this constituted some kind of a slight against me for calling out pleasantry and thanks to the Father. I glared at my brother, all fired up.

'What do you mean by that? You want to say something then say it.'

Emile gazed at me, perfectly serene.

'Easy now,' said he. 'We should try and keep our temper.'

Well, of all his habit this infuriated me the most: when he took on superior airs of condescension. I might have jumped on him there and then, at least for a tussle – except I feared that the *'ti canot* might flip and neither of us could swim a stroke even though we had resided by the ocean all our days. And so, instead, I spat over the side myself; a great big *crache* that landed near his. We watch the pair of foamy oysters float off on the unruffle surface of the sea. I hoped my sputation would overtake his or that the two would drift apart; whereas, in fact, the water stirred up by the paddle carried mine forward, such that the two spit join together and became a single entity.

Thus far the day had presented me with but one vexation after the other.

I turn to take a closer look at the yawl. Some letters had been etched on her hull in paint now flaked and barely legible. Two short word and I could spell them both: *THE DAISY*. An English-sounding appellation, for true, but – at the time – that did not strike me as strange. All I could think was that we would make our voyage in a vessel named after a pretty little flower and how that fairly put the cherry on the cake.

Chapter Seven

Captain Bianco was a pale-eye Béké: small and wiry; russet-skinned; his beard trim neat with a scissor. He wore tight britches and, in his belt, a keen-blade cutlass that glinted in the sun. As we came alongside, Descartes grab the yawl to steady the canoe whiles Bianco lean down and helped us climb aboard. Then he indicated where he would have us sit: me amidships and Emile in the prow.

I gave Bianco the Kill-Devil and – not forgetting his affliction – made a big pantaloonery of obeisance, pointing toward the shore where Cléophas still stood. The skipper eyed the jug with some amusement as though he had surmise it contain the worst kind of gut-rot. By the look on his face, this hombre knew the Father of old. In jest, he pretended to jettison the rum but he only made-believe to pitch it overboard: fact of the matter is, I saw him stash it in a coil of rope. Then he face the island and – putting thumb and finger to his lips – let forth a piercing blast of a whistle, his other arm raised. In response, Cléophas gave a last wave then picked up his bag and began to walk back toward Place Bertin. I watched him go: a lonely figure now, diminish by distance.

Meanwhile, Emile had stowed his precious leather satchel and slump down glumly in the prow. Something had vex him, no question. I would have given my left liver to know what Cléophas meant by a 'change of approach' but if Emile thought I would sweat him for answers he was sore mistaken; I cared the devil of a Hindu dam for his condescending ways. When I turn back, the captain pro-

duced a silver denier from thin air and flipped it so it fell, twirl-
ing and glittering, toward the *'ti canot*. Quick as a skink, Descartes
caught the coin and stowed it in his mouth for safekeeping. Then
with a muffle squeak: '*Ô rèvoi*,' and a wave, he took up his paddle
and set off for the shore.

After that we had a lot of dumb show as Bianco pointed to his
ears and shook his head; and pointed to his lips and shook his head;
then pointed to his brain-pan and NODDED wide-eyed just to let
us know he was nobody fool. Then more pantomime as he warned
us not to bang our skulls on the boom or fall overboard or get underfoot whiles he went about his boat business. Next, he chopped
open a few green coconut and gave us the sweet water to drink and,
presently, when he lean down to rummage in a basket, I heard my
brother, behind me, speak in an undertone:

'Take this knife and kill him.'

Convince I had misheard, I turn my head. Emile sat there, arms
folded.

'What?' said I, bewildered.

He said it again, louder this time:

'Take this knife and kill him.' Then, keeping his eyes fix on Bianco, he yelled it: 'Kill him with this knife quick!'

All throughout, Bianco continue to rummage in his basket,
oblivious.

My brother thrust out his bottom lip, then flex his knuckles,
evidently satisfied.

'*I bon*,' said he. 'Looks like he's deaf, for true.' Then he murmured: '*Hé*, Lucien – watch out for him with that cutlass.'

'Why bother to whisper?' said I. 'You just proved he cannot hear
you.'

'Just watch the cutlass, is all.'

'Cutlass,' I scoffed. 'He had six cutlass I could still put him over the side with one hand.' Then I call Bianco a name, not a pretty one, I will admit the fact.

'*Cho!*' said Emile. 'No need for that. Poor man's only a dummie.'

Just then, the skipper span around with a madcap grin, holding up a handful of small cod-cake, like they were a trophy. He tossed us two a-piece.

'Thank you, master, sir,' I heard my brother say. 'Thank you very much.'

Well, of all the hypocrisies. First he disapproves of me for thanking Cléophas, next he bessys-down to this Spaniard. There and then, I vow to cease all dialogue with Emile and – since I was ignoring him – my next remark I address to my cod-cake.

'Can this old lobster hear you thank him?' I asked it. 'No, he is deaf as a bat.'

Emile just shook his head.

Whiles we ate, Bianco began some intricate business with ropes, hauling on them and tying them off. *The Daisy* was bleach with age and her sails much mended but on closer inspection she seem sound enough. Despite my phantasies regarding pirates and the like I knew precious little about the sea in those days and thus watch the skipper in fascination. At one point I stood up to offer a hand but he shove me back down, fair and square; and quite right too for a novice can wreck a vessel quick as hell can scorch a feather. With nothing else to do, I sat back and listen to the creak and tick of the hull, the air currents out there in the bay like cool caresses on my skin.

From this place, out on the ocean, the whole Martinique was a mass of verdant green. A wreath of cloud sat about the crown of Mont Pelée with St Pierre like a pile of red rubble that had slided down the mountainside and come to rest by the shore. Despite the English bombardment, she was still a fine, handsome settlement. Just behind town, the hospital estate stretched out below the cliffs.

I strain to see my cows but the trees grew too high all around and I could only glimpse the roof of the hospital building among the lush vegetation.

Meanwhile, Bianco continued his preparations. I could scarce help but cast curious glances at him, not least at the almighty bulge that strain the front of his britches. Deaf mute he might be, but he seem well equip in other respects. Either that or he stowed all his worldly goods in his pockets. It did cross my mind that his pink segar might be upstanding for some reason. I wondered if Emile had notice the same thing but he was staring at the horizon in silence. A dummie Spaniard and a brother in the doleful dumps, such would be my company on our great voyage. I gave thanks that I had not brag to the wharf boys about my illustrious venture, only to be witness sailing off in such a miserable tub.

Just then, Emile gave a sigh, no doubt lost in memory of Céleste – or perhaps just gazing across the ocean, yearning for the land of our Mandingo ancestors. I took up my second cod-cake and spoke to it in scolding fashion:

'Some people might believe Africa is over in that direction,' I told it. 'But they be silly. They are looking west not east. Only land over there is St Domingue.'

Well, I thought that might get a rise out of my brother, but he just yawned. Then the light in his eyes darken as they fixed on something behind me.

'Company coming,' he said.

I followed his gaze. Heading straight for us and within pistol-shot, here came a pinnace with about a dozen French military aboard, four soldiers of the marine rowing, the rest of them Royal Grenadier, staring at us in hostile fashion. Despite their faded and tattered uniforms, they look to be a stalworth crew, all a-bristle with weaponry. I counted six musket with fix bayonets, eight pistol, four cutlass and two boarding axe. A well-knit officer with the build of a swordsman sat in the prow and as they came up to our stern he called out:

'Ho, lads!'

The marines lifted their oars such that the vessel slowed to a near standstill close aboard of us. Bianco notice me craning my neck for a better view and turn to see what had caught my attention. He and the officer came so close they could have reached out for an embrace but naught so tender came to pass. Bianco simply glared at the man who, in return, made no gesture save to lean forward and inspect our yawl, glancing along her deck then taking a good study at each of us, and all the bluejackets in the pinnace also stared at us with menaces. I held my breath, wondering what might happen.

Then the officer smiled at Emile.

'Is that you, Mandingo?'

My brother snatched off his hat and stood up.

'Yes, sir, Lieutenant Fournier, sir. Good day to you.'

The officer glanced at Bianco then back at Emile.

'Is this man treating you well?'

'Oh quite so, sir,' said my brother. 'He can't hear you though, sir, he's a dummie.'

'A dummie, is it?'

The lieutenant look Bianco up and down with frank curiosity.

'Well, we shall detain you no longer,' he said, loud and slow, to the Spaniard. 'Strange boat, you see. Need to check you aren't up to no good.'

Then – blow me sideways – he gave my brother a wink. Thereafter, he turn to our skipper and spoke in his face, slowly, whiles pointing at Emile.

'You must be careful with this man here. He saved my life at Morne Grenier.'

'Sir,' said Emile. 'If you please, sir, you exaggerate.'

All this, I found most intriguing. For true, the French had con-scripted some slave to help fight off the Goddam invaders and my brother had been among their number but he had told me that since the east of the island was mostly unaffected by the conflict, he had seen no combat; the English had more interest in the towns on the west coast. Morne Grenier, a lofty well-defended hill with many guns and batteries, was in the south-west. So far as I knew, Emile had never been there.

A few of the Grenadier stared oddly at Emile, their eyes shining. Meanwhile, he appear to be avoiding my gaze. Lieutenant Fournier grinned at him again.

'What are you now, Mandingo, a fisherman?'

'No, sir,' said Emile, with a glance at the Spaniard – who had loop his arm through a hanging rope and was swinging from it by his elbow, quite composed, as he watch the proceedings, following the conversation by studying their lips. 'This is not my master, sir. I'm hired out, sir. We're – we're bound for Grenada, sir, on behalf of *les Frères de la Charité*. Delivering medicinal plant to a physician there.'

The officer looked surprise.

'*La Grenade*, eh? Well, be careful. We cannot have those God-dams steal you away from us. Can't have you spying for the enemy.'

My brother gave a short laugh, somewhat hollow.

'No, sir.' He frowned. 'But – please you, sir, if you would be so kind.' Here, he gestured toward me. 'Take this boy ashore with you. Turns out we have no need of him.'

I stared at Emile, aghast, as Fournier pointed at me and asked Bianco:

'You need this boy?'

Much gesticulation ensued, the gist of which being that the skip-per required both me and Emile, most definitely. The lieutenant gave my brother a quizzical look.

'Well, Mandingo. I know not what tricks you're up to but it looks as though the boy goes with you.'

'Please, sir,' said Emile. 'This is my brother. He'll be safer here in Martinique.'

But the officer was already calling out over his shoulder, keen to be off.

'Nothing to concern us here, men. *Allons-y. À la frégate.*' He turn back to Emile. 'He'll be fine, Mandingo. We're not at war any more, you know. You can sail right into the harbour at Fort Royal, nobody will bother you.'

The marines dip their oars and began to row. In parting, the lieutenant bid our skipper farewell and, for reply, Bianco gave a kind of salute. Slow-slow, the pinnace got underway and Fournier called out to Emile:

'Good to see you again, Mandingo. You have my thanks, as ever – *et bon voyage.*'

He raised his hand in farewell but my brother did not respond in kind. The pinnace ploughed a wide arc in the water then surged away toward the frigate, north of the bay. A few Grenadier wave their hats and grinned, calling out as they went:

'Goodbye, Mandingo. Farewell.'

I was not altogether convince they knew Emile in person but they were evidently well dispose to the notion of him. Meanwhile, their commander seem lost in thought, gazing back at my brother as though reliving some memory. Emile resumed his seat. Forgetting my vow to disregard him, I asked:

'Who was that?'

'Nobody you should worry about.'

'When were you at Morne Grenier?'

But he just clicked his tongue and gave me a brief smile, which I returned, only mine were entirely sardonic, a grin so forced and wide that it hurt my face. Confound him and his mysteries. He replaced his hat on his head, then spent a moment adjusting his sleeves: His Excellency, Prince Mandingo.

By this time, the pinnace was just a shimmering spot of colour in the distance. Bianco gave an exaggerated shiver and, with that, began to hoist his sails. The breeze must have been favourable because no sooner did he haul up his mud-hook than the yawl began to move, feeling herself free. Along the hull, came a crisp sound of water hissing and then with a snap the mainsail caught the wind and we were away, slapping through the waves.

Since I had already broken my vow to ignore Emile – and we could scarce spend the entire journey in silence – I decided to strike up an innocent conversation with him from which origin I might coax some revelation. For true, I was intrigue to hear the story of the lieutenant and how Emile had saved his life but I also wanted to know what Cléophas meant by a 'change of approach'.

Howsomever, when I glanced around, I saw that Emile had curled up beside the little skiff in the prow, his hat over his face and his head in the shade of a thwart, by all appearance, already asleep. I turn back to shore for a last glimpse of our plantation but we had almost rounded the point at Morne aux Boeufs; the red roof of the hospital no longer visible and even the town of St Pierre herself had faded from view.

All at once, I became aware that – from his place at the tiller – Bianco was watching me close-close. A kind of uneasiness settled across my heart, for I dislike the way his pale eyes seem to stare into my soul. Jésis-Maïa! In haste, I turn to face the prow. That way I could keep lookout for sharks and make sure that Emile slept safe. I had no fear of the Béké, not one iota, but if he could not get sight of my countenance then that was an added bait and bonus.

PART TWO

At Sea, Western Antilles

Chapter Eight

To begin with our course took us down the west coast of Martinique. We were scarce underway when the skipper reached into some cache neath his seat and produced a wicker-cover flask – perchance a better class of taffey than the one I brought aboard – and on this liquor he commence to swig. Devil the bite to eat had passed his lips, yet a pottle of rum on empty guts in noways impaired his faculties; I could only suppute that he was well accustom to strong drink.

We sail beyond that mossy great rock in the sea that resembled an old back tooth and yet – for reason unknown – is dub the Diamond; then we tack south of the island past the Islets des Salines. Bit by bit, *La Matinik* began to recede, the hill shapes fading from green, to bluish-grey, then to a vapory smoke. So far as I could see, we would progress down the windward side of the Antilles, retracing the route I had travel some years previous, only this time in the opposite direction. The breeze blew strong and warm and soon we were in the open sea, the two piton of St Lucia visible on the horizon. No sign of any shark as yet but – from time to time – flying fishes came to visit with us. They skimmed along the waves as they overtook the yawl, twitching their tails and shining like polished metal birds.

All this while, my brother lay in a dead sleep but toward the mid of the afternoon he sat up and made some sign to Bianco, seeking permission to move closer to me. The hombre beckoned him forth, warning him with gestures to keep low in case of accidents. Emile bessy-down along the deck until he sat alongside me.

'Speak up if you need to puke,' he said.

'*Cho!* Puke yourself. I am not sick at all.'

Admittedly, on my previous voyage between the islands I had been somethingish queasy, but I was only little then, six or seven years old. Besides, that had been a particular rough passage; Damascene and everyone else aboard said so at the time.

Emile glance toward the aft. There, Bianco sat, sharpening his cutlass, lost in his own thoughts, whatever they might be: the reveries of a Spaniard, a sailing man. For aught I knew, he was dreaming of hard cheese or doubloons of gold.

My brother lean closer to me.

'That bug's been watching you since we left St Pierre.'

'Says the man who was napping the whole time,' I replied.

'You silly. I was awake, watching through the holes in my hat. Turns out he did nothing save keep his eye on you lest you tried any mischief. He likes that old cutlass of his. I would wager he might like to use it in earnest.'

'Who was that soldier back there, that lieutenant?'

'Never mind him. We need to talk about this change of plan. You see, all that macaque yesterday, Cléophas talking, was only palaver. He was just buttering us, nice and sweet.'

'Is that so?' said I. 'What other shocking fact am I to learn from you this day, I wonder? Will you tell me next that the sky is blue, perhaps? Or that the sea is made of salt water?'

He gave me his sour face.

'You want to hear what that old jackal said this morning or not?'

I raise my hands.

'All ears,' I told him.

'*I bon.* Well, he said this idea came to him overnight – this so-call different approach – after hearing my concerns about what we have to do. The way he framed it, you might think I gave him the idea.

But my guess is, this was his intention all along. He fail to tell us yesterday because – well – I half suspect he would not have us think about it overnight.'

'Think about what?'

Bianco was squinting up at the heavens, making some calculation about the hour or wind. Emile cast an eye at him, then his gaze wandered upward to the tip of the mast. There, his thoughts seem to drift. When I flicked his arm with my finger, he took a breath and held it awhile before he spoke again:

'What he says is, overnight he got to worrying about this English doctor, Bryant, and the overseer – that they might try to stop us taking the slaves. So this morning, he told me that instead of approaching them with the Power of Attorney, we're to go straight and talk to the slaves at the hospital and plantation – without those English finding out. Keep ourselves hid so far as possible. He says those poor wretches at the plantation won't need persuading; he's convince they want to leave. But fact of the matter is he wants us to do it all in secret and get them away without being seen.'

'How are we suppose to do that?'

'By night, foremost. Cannot be done by day. And we can't take them to the harbour at Fort Royal; you know what a bacchanal it is there, and right next to the barrack. Cléophas says a boat will be waiting for us up the coast at Petit Havre on Christmas Eve. We have to take them there *dousman-dousman* – gently-gently – whiles all the Béké are groggy with rum. There's the truth of it, so far as I can tell. He wants us to steal the slaves without asking, right from under the nose of those English.'

'*Tambou!*'

I slap my own legs, partly in disbelief and partly through a kind of half-craze nerves or shock. Emile looked at me askance.

'Think on it, before you start puffing yourself up like a bombast mome.'

A concentrated silence ensued as we stared first at each other and then out across the waves. My heart opened and close like a fist in my chest, a rising panic at the back of my throat as I considered our predicament.

'At any rate,' Emile said, 'I told Cléophas we should wait a few week. That's what I tried to persuade him this morning but he refuse to listen.'

'What difference does it make?'

'By Christmas, the moon will be almost full. If there's no cloud, we'll be lit up like a boiling house. I told him we should wait until the wane. For true, I was hoping to delay, such that we might find some means to wriggle out of it. But Cléophas insists it must be Christmas Eve. He says the moon will be full but so will the English – full of rum – and moonlight will help us on our way.'

'So – what do you think we should do?'

My brother rubbed his eyes.

'I've been debating that back and forth since this morning and I am still at a loss. What do *you* think?'

It was a surprise and some gratification that he did me the honour of consulting my opinion. Alas, I had no answer for him and could only shake my head.

Chapter Nine

By the end of the day, we had borne down upon the isle of St Lucia, a monstrous black shape against the flambant glow of the sunset. I wondered if we might berth there overnight but with vigorous gesticulation Bianco made us to understand that since the weather condition were most favourable he intended to sail on through the night, guided by the stars, and take dog-sleeps every otherwhile at the tiller. For nourishment, he gave us coconuts along with a bunch of plantain and when darkness fell with a heavy dew he threw us some old sack to use in case the wind grew chill.

Slumber did not come easy to me that night. I was wary of sharks and ill accustom to sleeping under sail. At first, I tried my sack as a pillow but its coarse fibres did itch my skin, ergo I tossed it aside. The constant motion of the yawl – along with a certain lingering mistrust of our hombre – kept me alert as a four-eye fish. Bianco sat in silence at the stern, just a shadow against the starlit sky. Up in the prow, my brother had stretched out longside the skiff. For all I know, he slept; leastwise, he hardly stirred whiles I laid there awake for what seem like forever.

Only yesternight, our venture had promise to be an escapade, a chance to rejoin our old confreres at the Fort Royal hospital, to spend time with my brother and escape the friars, if only for a week. But here we were now, bidden to steal forty-odd slave from what amounted to enemy territory and smuggle them away across the sea. If that were not an act of piracy equal to any by Blackbeard or Bart Roberts then I was the Duchesse de Bouillon. Now that I knew the true nature of our allotted task, trembling had seize my body. My skin grew clammy; my hands clench so tight in two fist that my fingers began to ache.

In an effort to overcome my fears, the mirror of my mind conjured scenes in which we two brothers – somehow armed with cutlass and musket – fought skirmishes with redcoat soldiers along the carenage at Fort Royal. Having vanquish our foes, we freed all the slaves in town then led them aboard a galleon, firing cannon at the fort as we sail to safety. In the grand finale of my imagination, Céleste threw herself at my feet, weeping tears of gratitude and hailing me a hero.

My waking dreams full of such nonsense, I gazed up at the heavens until a flare of light caught my eye and I beheld a shooting star fall across the Milky Way. Magical sight. Perhaps it were a good omen. For a brief instant, I allowed myself to feel encouraged. But as the star died, trailing silver embers, old Bianco let flee a fart, startling as a blast of musketry, and the precious moment was ruined. All at once, my childish fancies of courage and audacity vanished and my mind became uneasy once again. Emile and I had no weapons and – in the immediate – not even a boat sizeable enough to carry off our bounty. What had old man Damascene called our mission: a reckless venture? Well, it was certainly noways as simple as I had first thought. It seem to me, now, that there might be good reason for his anxiety.

My inners filled with dread and my visions became too dark and terrible to dwell upon. Some comfort then it was to see the recumbent shape of my brother stretched out within a few feet of where I myself lay. Though we had never lived life in clover – and he would insist, at times, on treating me like an infant – I felt sure that no real harm could come to us whiles we were together.

Chapter Ten

The weather held fair enough overnight, with a fine breeze to carry us, the only sound the slap of waves against the prow. In the small hours, came a drenching downpour as though God in Heaven had emptied all his buckets, but it passed almost as soon as it had commence. At some point, I must have fallen asleep and – since there is no whistling-frog at sea whose silence would rouse me, nor no morning bell – I slumbered on beyond break of day. When I finally came to my senses the sun had ascended on another clear morning. Bianco stood at the stern, one hand on the tiller as he attended to a call of nature over the transom. Emile sat against the starboard side, already awake.

'*Bonjou, ché,*' says he.

'*Bonjou.*'

I rouse myself and saw, close at hand, a low-lying land of forested hills. A few vessel had moored up just offshore near a tiny settlement, the wide bay so turquoise-blue it hurt your heart to look at the water. My brother nodded at the island.

'Carriacou,' he said. 'Little sister of Grenada.'

I gave a yawn.

'Everybody knows that,' I said – though, for true, I had fail to recognise the place.

Bianco resumed his position at the tiller. Like as not, he had scarce slept overnight yet he did not stagger or sway. The sole hint of his condition was a smouldering behind his eyes, something red and fiery. In dead of night, he must have steered us windward of

St Vincent and then south-west through an archipelago of islets and cays taking us to the leeward side of the Antilles. By my recollection, our destination lay at least a half-day sail further south but we were heading for the mid-point of the blue-green bay.

'We're making stop here,' said Emile.

'*Pou ki sa?*'

'For food. Though I expect there might be some other reason.'

His gaze strayed to the deck and a coil of rope, inside which lay the Kill-Devil jugs – both of them uncorked and empty.

Just then, our hombre leapt up to drop sail and throw his mud-hook over the stern. A boy in an old candle-box raft sculled over to us, wight as a water beetle. The Spaniard gave him a dumb show and paid him to fetch what vittles could be found in haste. Once the boy had paddle for shore, Bianco sat down by the tiller and soon began to nod off.

My brother was staring across the bay. I interrupted his thoughts with a question that bothered me.

'Those slave in Grenada – who do you reckon they belong to?'

Emile blew air through his lips.

'Impossible to say. It's complicated.'

'But *les Frères* bought all our elders, did they not? Our mother – may God rest her soul in peace – and Chevallier, and Angélique, all of them, yes?'

'Correct.'

'And when those slave had their babies – like you and me, through the years – those infant belong to the same friars, did they not?'

'Yes,' said Emile. 'But it's more complicated – because of the loans.'

I looked at him.

'What loans?'

'All those slave, the friars bought with borrowed money.'

'Who told you that?'

'Father Prudence, years agone. They took a loan from the French government and another from some merchant in London. Being the case, the French authority might say those Fort Royal slaves and their descendant belong to them. The London merchant might say the same. Of course, the friars would argue otherwise but some would say they lost the right to the slave because of the debt and their misdoings.'

'They might have repaid those loan since.'

'No,' Emile replied. 'I asked around St Pierre the other night. They never repaid one sou, to this day. Everybody knows they are in debt from Salines to St Domingue. That's why they want those slave back, to grow more cane. Cane is sugar, sugar is money. That's all we are to them. But loan or no loan, the English will care not one farthing. Now they rule the land of Grenada, they must surely lay claim to the slaves at the hospital. And if we take Céleste and the rest without permission, those Goddams will say we stole them.'

'But what about that Power of Attorney? That gives us permission to take them. Sign by the English Governor in Grenada himself.'

'You believe so?'

'That's what the friar said.'

'Well, a person might think that – if he weren't listening. Your old Cléophas has a way of making words sound like he want them to. I *did* listen and – from what he told us, that parchment might well be sign by the two French, Ennery and Père Lefébure, but never once did the old man say that the English Governor made his mark on the page. If you ask me, I would be surprised if he's even seen it.'

I glance toward the prow. There lay the satchel with the Power of Attorney inside. Father Damascene had taught me all the letters of the alphabet so that I could recite him his Scripture, but before I learn to spell many words he got too giddy in his mind and our lessons ended. Nevertheless, it seem to me, any confirmed idiot could count signatures.

'Let's take a look,' I said.

Yet, when I made a move to fetch the bag, Emile grab my wrist.

'*Atjelman, non.*' He jerked his head toward the dozing skipper. '*Capitaine Couilles* there is deaf but he's no numps. We should wait until we're ashore, alone.'

'But if it's not sign by the Governor in Grenada then what earthly use is it?'

Emile scratched his head.

'Perhaps he has signed it or approved it in some way. Perhaps he told them what to write in it. At any rate, Cléophas says it may help us – depending on the circumstance.'

'Circumstance . . . what does that mean?'

For true, I knew that the Fort Royal hospital and all its slave had once upon a time been under the care of *les Frères de la Charité*. The Fathers had establish their Martinique hospital in the days of old langsyne. Then, some nine years before I was born, the French Government handed them control of the Grenada hospital. Two of the friar – Fathers Damien Pillon and Yves Prudence – did sail from St Pierre to Fort Royal. They took with them a nurse-man and some half-dozen slave, including our mother and Emile who was but five years old at the time. Pillon and Prudence bought additional slaves in Grenada and started up a plantation to fund their good works. However, as the years went by, the Fathers began to lose their reputation due to certain scandals and malpractices. The main culprit in all of this was Damien Pillon, though we seldom spoke his name – and even now I find it hard to write down on paper.

Nobody liked Father Damien; not even the other *Frères*. He was the most notorious of all the friar, known for his tendency to lash out. In secret, the plantation hands called him '*le Pilon*' or 'the Pestle', a name to reflect his crushing cruelty. The Pestle liked sugar money better than treating the sick and he was known to dole out more beatings than charity. Despite this, he acted as superior of the hospital in Grenada for years. Every otherwhile, a new Father would be sent from Paris to take control but somehow the Pestle always manage to oust them: they would conveniently die of fever, or he would send them packing to St Domingue or Martinique, or they would lose heart and return to France and then it might be months or even years before a replacement could make the journey from Paris.

In this manner, the Pestle continue to reign supreme. When, at last, he decease this world – about a year after I had gone to Martinique – another friar took his place but within a month he also died, leaving just young Father Boniface and he had no experience to run a hospital and plantation. The French authority were only too delighted to resume control of the estate, having long since lost patience with the friars. They sent Boniface packing to Martinique, and the French Governor of Grenada appointed M. Maillard, a local physician, as head surgeon. There was an understanding that our Fathers could return to the hospital at Fort Royal as and when more experience friars arrive from Paris, proviso *les Frères de la Charité* submit in future to closer supervision by the authority. However, before that could happen, the English invaded the islands and what had once belong to the French passed into the hands of the Goddams.

My brother took a sip from the water flask.

'I've been thinking,' he said. 'Way I see it, if we fail to do what Cléophas wants, we have a few option.'

'*Di mwen.*'

'First option, when we reach Grenada, we take foot and hide out.'

I looked at him.

'Take foot where?'

'We could try the mountains. Live off our wits in the forest. But we risk being hunted down forevermore by every Béké white colonial on *La Grenade*. And we might get caught. In which case . . . well . . .'

'Second option gets my vote,' I said.

'You don't know what it is yet,' Emile replied.

'I still prefer it.'

He gave me a doleful smile.

'*I bon*,' he said. '*Vwala*. We hand ourselves over to the English when we reach Fort Royal; tell them Cléophas sent us to steal all the hospital slave.'

I could only laugh.

'You had a stroke of the sun? They will kill us dead on the spot.'

'They might. Or they might put us to labour on one of their estates; murder us just the same, but slow-slow, with slaving.' He rubbed his finger across his lips. 'Or they might send us back to Martinique under escort . . .'

His expression betrayed how little he relish that prospect. The friars would be unhappy if we failed in our task but Lord only knew how they might punish us if they heard we had thrown ourselves on the mercy of the Goddams.

I grab the brim of my hat and began turning it around on my head. Emile threw me an enquiring look.

'What are you doing?' he asked.

'Trying to think of a third option.'

'Well, there is one.'

'What?'

'We do exactly what Cléophas ordered. We steal the slaves. I've been thinking until my brain-pan hurts but seems to me that's our only alternative – provided we are not caught, in which case . . . that would be . . . well . . . tiresome . . .'

'One way to describe it.'

I couldn't help but remember the previous night: my racing pulse, and the sudden enchantment of a shooting star spoil by the crack of a white man squib. For a moment, I did consider telling my brother what had happen, then thought better of it. No doubt, he would deem talk of bad omens infantile.

'Well, what's your suggestion?' Emile asked. 'You don't like any of my ideas.'

Just then, Bianco woke up and began to scratch himself all over, twitchy as a mud crab, due – most likely – to rum, or lack of it.

'We could wait until we're out at sea again,' I said. 'Sling this one overboard and sail to Africa, live like two king.'

My brother threw back his head and laughed, guffawing from the back of his heels to the tip of his nose. I had not heard him roar so much in a long time but it seemed a ferocious kind of merriment.

'Sail to Africa,' he said. 'In this tub. Now that I would like to see.'

And he laughed again.

'What's so funny?'

'Damned if I know. I might be crazy from lack of sleep. But just one thing – neither you nor I can sail a boat. We would have this calabash capsize in less than five heartbeat and drown ourselves in six.'

'Speak for yourself. I've been watching this old mackerel here with his ropes. It's not difficile. I could manage.'

'Oh yes?' says he. 'Silly! Besides, you tell me you disapprove of stealing slaves but you would *murder* a man – because that's what it would amount to – murder; no matter he's an old rum-hound or a dummie, he's still a man and if you threw him overboard out there in the ocean you be killing him. You prepared to do that, on your own? Because I wouldn't help you – hell-fire, I'd have to *stop* you, even if it meant hold you down and sit on your head, that's what I'd do.'

We both looked at Bianco. He had hunched over now and was scraping out the dirt from neath his toenails with the tip of his knife. Never did I see a more worthless-looking creature. And yet, once I gave the matter consideration, I knew I had no real desire to end his miserable life.

'He fed you,' Emile was saying. 'There's many would let you starve on this trip.'

I kicked at the side of the hull.

'You can bet what he gave us came from his self pocket,' said Emile.

'I heard you first time.'

'And you would repay him by slinging him overboard?'

'I am not going to sling him overboard. *Tambou!*'

We glared at each other for a stretch. I was first to look away, somewhat ashame by my own suggestion – which was only a passing fancy, after all, though I would never admit as much to Emile.

Meanwhile, the skipper had finish grooming his feet and progress to matters of a dental nature, prodding his back teeth with his finger then smelling it. In any other mood, such antics might have amuse me but my head ached and I was thrumming like a fiddle. Indeed, so embroil had we been in discussion that I had fail to notice the boy in the candle-box raft paddling back toward the yawl. Bianco quit prodding his ivories and leapt up to receive the delivery which turned out to be more Kill-Devil and some over-ripe paw-paw.

Our hombre cheered up no end with a full jug in his hands. As we watch the raft scud back to the shallows Bianco gave us a wink and made a start upon his new taffey. Though my belly was growling, I let Emile take his pick of the fruit for I had no desire to share repast with him. Even after he finish his paw-paw, I left a decent interval before even considering mine, but once started on them I fairly slonk them down. We had reach no decision about what to do and the dilemma hung over us. However, it seem to me that we had to eat, no matter what.

Having despatch a good slug of tawny liquor, Bianco cork the jug and began to rummage in his lower garments, presently pulling out a long knob, both fleshy and scaly, deformed by protuberances. The sight of this thing emerging from his britches pocket unsettle me greatly until I realise with relief that it was not attach to his person. Thuswise was solve the mystery of what had cause the bulge in his inexpressibles: only a large hand of root ginger.

He put one knuckle of it in his yam-trap, snapped off a good inch, then – chewing mightily – offered me a bite. Bearing in mind how long this rhizome had spent in the clammy depth of his most intimate pocket, I declined. My refusal sent him into a frenzy of gesture; he pointed at the ocean then smashed his hands together and waggle them: some tale about two current of water meeting and rough waves – from which I gather that ginger was a cure against sea distempers. Since the weather looked set absolutely fair and I had felt fine since we quitted St Pierre, I shook my head. Forthwith, the skipper played out the same mime for my brother and to my surprise Emile took the root and availed himself of a big old bite. Like as not, he did it to spite me and be different. Well, he could choke on ginger, for all I cared.

Bianco wave the root in my face one last time but – when I forbore to accept it – he thrust it back in his pocket with a shrug of his shoulders and set about hauling ropes.

Provided we encounter no problem, the next place we dropped anchor would be Grenada. I wondered how much longer Emile might wait before deciding what we should do. In a matter of hours, we would be at our destination.

Chapter Eleven

We sail down the coast of Carriacou and out again into the open sea. On a sudden, my breath stopped at the sight of a shark-fin breaking the surface of the water. Then, all at once, the ocean grew lumpy. Though the sky remain clear, waves began to buffet our vessel, splashing over the sides and banging the hull so hard she shuddered each time. The sound only intensified my dread and the paw-paw I had so recently devoured did slosh around sour inside my belly. In due course, *The Daisy* was rolling to her scuppers and Bianco tossed us two coconut shell and set us to bail. Now more than somethingish qualmy, and still on the lookout for that shark, I crouched amidship and threw bilge water over the side for all I was worth. Whenever the yawl did pitch or reel the content of my stomach threaten to gush up into my throat but I was determine not to submit to *mal de mer* lest my shipmates tease me. Meanwhile, neither Emile nor the skipper seemed in any ways consternated by the sudden swell.

Came a time my inners twisted in agony and my mouth fill with saliva. I clap my hand over my face and moaned. Bianco saw me – curse him – and with a grin he whistle to Emile, drawing attention to my plight. One glance at me and my brother sprang to his feet. He pick me up, threw off my hat and lean my head over the side. For a flash the ocean surge toward my face like a green wall then my throat erupted and I spewed, again and again, in gushes. The force of heaving cause me to strain over the rail and I would have tumbled into the depths, down amongst the cold tangle-weed and shark, had Emile not kept grip on my shoulders and waist, despite the drenching waves.

'*Vwala, 'ti pantalons*,' he said, as I puked again. '*Kam-twa, kam-twa, respire.*'

He stroke my back and held me until my purging diminish to a dry retch. Then he drag me back in, sodden, and laid me beside him on the deck whiles he bailed alone.

'You rest, little brother,' he said, in my ear. 'You lie there and get some rest.'

Before my eyelids closed over, I caught a glimpse of Bianco. He could grin all he liked. Much as I might appear maladif and miserable, he would never know how glad I felt inside – for Emile had showed me kindness and call me 'little brother', and I saw this as proof that he held me in his heart, no question.

Of course, sometimes, the difference in our ages did seem like a prodigious chasm between us. Emile was twice my age, at least. After our mother, Aphrodite, gave birth to him, several other infant were born to her but every one of them died and by the time I came along, my brother was almost a man, slaving for the friars, tending their growing ground under supervision of Father Prudence. Alas, less than two years after I arrived, our mother perished in the throes of yet another still-birth.

After her death, Emile could scarce care for me since he was oblige to toil the earth from dawn to dusk. Normally, I might have been given to one of the field women but a Scottish nurse-man, John Calder, took pity on me, perhaps because his own mama had perish when he was an infant. He brought me to live in the hospital where he and Céleste (then in training) looked after me. Calder allowed me to sleep in his chamber – firstly in a drawer and then, when I grew older, on a mat – and it was he who taught me to speak English. I loved nothing better than to hear his stories of old

Caledonia. He had read many a book and when he was in his cups he would recite what he could recall of the plays he had seen at the theatre.

Some said Calder had been a pirate; others that he was a convict on the run. But the true story told to me by the man himself is that he had been training as a surgeon when he got all fired up to the Jacobin cause and abandon his medical studies. He had gone on to fight at the mighty battle of Culloden, whereafter – force to flee his own land – he became a nurse-man for the friars at their hospital in Paris. Some time later, when a party of Fathers set out for the Antilles, they took Calder with them and that was how he ended up at Fort Royal, arriving there a few years before my birth.

If only John Calder, this man-nurse, had been our parent, life might have been easier for my brother and me. Unfortunately, it was a known fact that the man who sired us was one of the friar, none other than Damien Pillon, the Pestle. Over the years, he had pestered our mother with his lascivious attention and my brother and I were the sole surviving children of that union. Each-every day, it was a horror to know that the blood of such a vile devil ran in our veins and perhaps, every otherwhile, this came between us. No doubt, Emile would rather that one of the other friar had fathered him, such as the gentle Prudence who taught him to grow provision. However, Father Prudence never tampered with the female slave like Pillon did – though, for his part, Prudence never acknowledge that such abominations took place.

It was hard to forget our parentage. On occasion, when Emile looked at me, I knew from something dark in his eye that he was thinking of the Pestle. My very presence in the world reminded him of where he came from; my image made him think of our father – his father – and perhaps made him want to turn away from the sight of me. I cannot say that I felt the same, partly because

I found myself too much in simple-hearted awe and adoration of my brother. Perhaps, a few times, I caught a fleeting glimpse of the Pestle in his features, but nothing more. On one occasion, long ago, after a disagreement about something, a squabble which ended in a scuffle, Emile grab me by the shoulders and said, through his teeth: 'Remember our mother. Her blood flows in our veins too, just as much as his. We never have to be like him, not ever.'

We had our disagreements, for true, and could put each other in a rage with naught more than a single word or glance. Yet, despite all, despite that sometimes Emile seem distant or remote, despite his evasions, his mysteries, his temper and his pride, even back then I knew that nobody could break the bond of blood – good and bad – between us.

Chapter Twelve

Presently, I became aware that the sea had return to calm. A shadow fell across my face and I open my eyes. Bianco stood over me. I sat up with a groan, thinking he wanted me to bail, but instead he pressed his jug into my hands and encourage me to take a drink. This was not the first time I had tasted liquor. Now and then, Père Lefébure gave us small batches of his new-made silver rum to test and on one of those occasions I had even got myself a trifle rocky. Bianco tip the jug to my lips. The Kill-Devil burn my mouth but warm my inners on the way down. Slapdash, my legs grew heavy but after a few more swallow I could scarce feel them at all. My sea distempers faded; my spirits began to lighten. Indeed, after several further swig, I came over all misty inside and considered myself to be quite invincible. The skipper pass the taffey to Emile but my brother cared little for rum and only took a sip for politesse before handing back the jug. With a wink at me, Bianco resumed his place at the tiller where he continue to quaff.

Up ahead, I could see Grenada, at first pearl-grey in outline then violet like the distant ocean. As the island grew closer, my notion of myself as unconquerable began to wane. I found myself wishing that we might never reach her shores. Over the years, I had often imagine returning to the island of my birth but never under such dire circumstance.

'There she is,' said Emile.

He shook his head and gave a hollow laugh.

'What?' I asked.

'Just thinking about Cléophas.'

'What about him?'

'I've met some artificious friars in my time – but that quack-salver. Dangling Céleste in front of me like a ladle of molasses.'

Well, stone me down. He had spoke her name. I could have seize this chance to discuss her but I knew he would become evasive should I dare to question him. Thus, forbearing to take the bait, I simply said:

'Correct. The man is an old sly-boots. But it strikes me, if those English lobster are half as bad as everyone says then we should get her and the rest of them out of Grenada. The more I think on it, the more I reckon it might be our best chance of – well, our best chance.'

Emile nodded.

'For true,' he said.

He glanced off to starboard. Hard to tell what went through his mind in that moment because his face was averted.

'Will Cléophas really come and help us?' I asked.

'He's bringing a bigger boat to Petit Havre on Christmas Eve. So he claims.'

I raised my eyebrows.

'Mm-hmm,' said Emile. 'Well, we'll see. Do your growl.'

'What?'

'Your growl. Do one for me.'

When I was only small fry, Emile had taught me to bare my teeth and growl like a wild animal or rabid dog. We use to amuse ourselves with such nonsense. Over time, I practise so much that my growl got better than his. It use to make him laugh.

'Go on,' said he.

And so I bared my tooths and made the scariest growl noise I could muster. I growl so hard the hairs rose up on the back of my neck. My throat did rasp until I near choked, after which I make-believe to die of an apoplexy and was rewarded by a weak smile from Emile, though he soon grew serious once more.

'So, are we agreed?' he asked. 'We do it?'

'*Wi.*'

'Have you still got your ticket? You might need it if we're stopped.'

I showed him the pouch around my neck.

'*Tjenbé rèd, 'ti pantalons. Pa moli,*' he said.

Be strong, little britches. Don't give up.

Chapter Thirteen

As we drew closer to Grenada, her forest summits became more sharply defined and green patches began a glimmeration among the inky blues. The distant mountains of the interior were veiled in grey mist, whiles to the west – as the afternoon gathered in – the sun melted the sky into the sea, turning them both pale-pale lemon. We began to coast down her western flank and, once we were leeward of the island, the wind dropped and Bianco worked hard, resetting the sails and chasing every little gust and breeze.

I watched Emile, staring up at the towering wall of green mountains. Eventually, without taking his eyes off the heights, he asked me:

'How many runaway stories you heard about in Grenada?'

'Some few.'

'Any of them get away? Aside from those that die trying?'

'Hard to tell. I did hear about one man, he stole a canoe and paddled out to sea. They never saw him again.'

'Probably drowned,' said Emile. 'Or sharks got him. There's no point taking a canoe. Nowhere safe to paddle that's close enough. All these islands own by the Béké and no matter be they French or English, Spanish or Dutch, they all have us under the yoke. But some people have escape, for true. Those Maroon. Living their days out in groups now, up in that high forest.'

'*Cho!*' I said. 'You trust them? I heard they turn other runaways in for reward.'

'Some of them aren't so bad,' said Emile. 'The ones that hide out near the big lake. They might help us.'

'Nn-nn,' I said. 'They'd tie you up, drag you like a hog to the English.'

Although I had never told my brother, I once found a Maroon in the shed where Father Prudence kept his pots and tools. This was back when I was only a spratling, not yet task with work about the hospital. One day, I crept into the shed to hide from one of the Fathers and just about leapt six foot in the air at the sight of a poor wretch standing there, eating seed; a full-grown man, rake-lean and fidgety as a cornered rat. The smell of him was worse than any wild animal. He grab me and made me promise not to tell anyone he was there. Then, under pain of death, he told me to fetch whatever food and drink I could scavenge. All a-tremble, I stole two corncake from the hospital kitchen and found some rainwater in a bucket. The Maroon swallowed the two cake whole and wash them down with water. Then he told me he hardly slept because he always had to keep on the move. That morning, he had only come down from the heights because he was gut-foundered. He warned me he'd be watching to make sure I never betrayed him. At last, to my relief, he went scurrying off up into the trees on Hospital Hill. Although I never saw him again, the memory still made my blood run hot and ever since I had been terrified of those Maroon and the mountains.

'Well,' said Emile. 'Just in case it looks too dangerous at any point, I vote we take foot, head for the lake. You know how to find it?'

'Of course.'

In fact, this was far from the truth, but since I had no mind to throw myself on the mercy of any Maroon it hardly seem to matter.

Just then, we were sailing past a black stretch of sand. A movement up on a rocky outcrop at the end of the beach caught my eye and, presently, I was able to discern some few English troop loitering in the shade of the trees on the point, their scarlet coats visible at a distance. Emile gazed up at the cape, his eyes narrow and watchful. I plucked at his sleeve.

'Already seen them,' he said.

Having assume that Bianco would carry us all the way to town, it came as a surprise when we sheer toward this lofty bluff. Close and close we sailed until we pass beneath the point and could most probably have held a shouted conversation with the soldiers. Bianco snatched off his hat and waved it at them as we skimmed around the headland but nary a one of those men return his greeting; they simply stare down upon us, a few of them cradling muskets. I kept my gaze fixed on their ruddy faces until they seem to lose interest in us and strolled away, slipping out of sight as we rounded the point and entered a cove. There, the wind dropped further still. I looked around. No settlement in this lonely place. To the left, a narrow shore gave way to trees and behind them up-sprung a coffee plantation, the estate house on a distant hill. Over on the right, the forest came down to meet the water. Two small vessel had moored up there in the bay: a pair of drogher, no doubt waiting for coffee. Bianco peered past them at a dark stretch of sand ahead. Evidently, this was where he intended to seek harbour.

I look to Emile, wondering what he would make of this development. He had his arms folded across his chest, his leg jiggling.

'What is this place?' I asked.

'Petit Havre, unless I'm mistaken. That old sawbones Cléophas must have given this bug instruction to bring us here. He wants us to step ashore somewhere quiet. Which means coming here in secret was his plan all along – like I told you.'

'How do you know that?'

'Back in St Pierre, yestermorning, what instruction did he give this dummie about where to take us?'

I thought awhile then replied:

'None.'

'*Vwala*,' said Emile.

'They might have met after he spoke to us in the morgue.'

He shook his head.

'Somehow I doubt it.'

Our skipper darted glances right and left, busy-busy at the tiller as he guided the yawl between the two drogher. I peered at them in passing but they had the air of abandon vessel; no doubt their crews on land somewheres, enjoying themselve, or below deck, avoiding the afternoon sun.

We had scarce enough breeze to carry us along in the shelter of this small harbour and the water lay so tranquil that Bianco could run *The Daisy* slow and easy, right up to the shallows where he drop sail and anchor. No need for the skiff to take us ashore. He stuck his cutlass through his belt and shove the rum jug down the back of his britches. Then he clenched a strand of coir-cable tween his teeth and sprang off the side and landed in the sea, chest-deep. He staggered up onto the sand and tied the rope to a big almond tree at the edge of the forest. Thereafter, he beckoned us to join him. We clenched our burlap bags and tickets in our teeth then Emile swung over the side into the shallow water. I handed the satchel to him and he put it on his head to keep it dry. Then I lowered myself in after him and together we floundered up onto the shore.

There, on the sand, I hesitated, the earth heaving under me like a ship deck. The baylet lay deserted, the only sounds watery ones: the sluggish surf caressing the shore and the gurgle of a muddy creek that oozed out of the forest, spilling across the sand into the sea. I could see little sign of activity among the coffee trees but a thin column of rising smoke told of a cooking fire nearby. Along with the scent of burning charcoal, a faint smell of rotting vegetation hung in the air.

'You know how to get to Fort Royal from here?' I asked Emile.

He gazed over to the headlands and then up at the forest.

'This the west side of the island,' he said. 'If we follow the coast south, that way, once we hit the St Jean river we're at the hospital plantation. About a half-day walk.'

Meanwhile, some ways off, our skipper had found a spot to rest in the shade. Alas, he had chosen to sit beneath a Manchineel, most poisonous of all trees in the island. Eating the fruit could be fatal and any contact with the leaves or branches or sap, or even to shelter beneath such a tree during rain, might cause the skin to blister and send a soul into agonies. Bianco had taken off his hat and press his jug into the sand beside him. He appear quite content there, all set for a proper nap at last.

My brother had also notice the Manchineel.

'Look there,' he said. 'Poor fool. We should tell him.'

'You tell him if you want,' I replied. 'But he might take against you for being procacious. What will he do after we're gone, do you reckon?'

'My guess is he'll finish that jug,' Emile said. 'Then find another one.'

Bianco gave a spluttering cough. Then – blow me tight – if he did not open his yam-trap and speak.

'*Au contra*, boys,' says he. 'I intend to careen this boat here on this beach, if I can find enough locals to help me drag her out of the water.'

And then he grinned and raise his jug to toast us. His words were a mingle-mangle of English and bad French mixed up with some of our tongue. My brother and I stared at him – and then at each other – so thunderstruck you could have knocked us down with a hummingbird wing. The man was no more deaf nor mute than we were.

Furthermore – as it swiftly began to dawn upon me – he had been present for our every conversation since the previous day. He must have eavesdrop on our petty disputes; would have noted the names we called him; had surely listen to our discussion about runaway slaves and would most certainly have heard my hot-headed proposal to sling him overboard.

'Well may you look surprised,' said he. 'Father Cléophas cooked up this jape of me being a dummie so that I might fish out if you half-breeds have the good sense and obedience to carry out your orders. Seems you made the right decision. Very wise – though you can forget about running for the mountains if you take fright. They have dogs and men here would find you quick enough and – fear not – I'll tell them where to look.'

I hardly dare to glance at Emile. The Béké kept talking without pause:

'And if I were you, I wouldn't be handing myself over to the authority here. What are you – a couple of chickens? Would you pluck yourselves and lie down in the oven? I'm an Englishman myself and take my word – you boys are better off with your monks back in Martinique than you would be here under English rule. *Voo comprendee?*'

Well, I was speechless as a statue, but my brother did manage a nod in response.

'Boys, I might try to find a bed up at that estate on the hill but I'll be hereabouts, somewheres, if you need me. My name is White – Mr Theobald White. Now, *alley veet*, before those redcoats wander down here to poke their nose into my business – which they will do, shortly, I assure you. I'll tell them some balderdash and send them packing.' He glanced at the sky. 'You have about three hours until sunset. Should give you enough time to find your way to town before dark.'

His entire demeanour had utterly transform. Gone was the toe-nail-rooting, tooth-prodding dummie, replace by a man with a deal better polish and infinite more wiles. No wonder I had often felt uneasy beneath his gaze.

'Incidentally, boy,' he continued, to my brother, 'that was a rather cunning ruse, when you called out, pretending to have a knife – to test if I was deaf or not. Very clever.'

Emile gazed at him, unsmiling.

'Please you, master,' he said. 'Not clever enough, for true.'

'Ah well, I have an instinct for such matters,' said White. 'A man with murder on his mind does not usually announce his intentions. In most cases, the first thing you know about a knife is the pressure of the blade as it slices through your windpipe.'

The look in his eye made me suppute that he had done some windpipe-slicing his own self. Emile regarded him, now something-ish wary.

The Béké wagged his cutlass, shooing us toward the trees beyond the creek.

'*Alley-alley*,' said he. 'If you go now you can be there by tonight. Cléophas wants you to stay out of sight if you can, so avoid the road and any plantations you pass en route.' He pointed at the hill that sloped up from the bay. 'Cross the road up there when it's quiet and cut across the headland. Keep the coast in view and you won't get lost.'

'Thank you, master, sir,' my brother said.

'One other thing: watch out for that Scotch overseer at the plantation – Addison Bell. You might be accustom to a different cut of fellow, with those French fribblers of yours. Now, Addison Bell – you would be disappointed to fall into his hands, believe me, especially when he has drink taken. I have heard that he is a notorious drunkard.'

He closed one bloodshot eye and leered at us out of the other.

'Thank you for the advice, master,' Emile replied, without a flicker. 'Please you, sir – will you be here when Father Cléophas brings the other boat?'

'All being well, my boy,' said White, with a grin. 'I'll be lending a hand.'

Just then, a drop of water splash my face. I glanced up. Unnotice by us, a cloud had come creeping over. Raindrops began to spatter the sand. My brother gave a sigh as he contemplated the Englishman. I knew what was going through his mind.

'Beg pardon, sir,' said Emile. 'But – *lapli* – it's raining.'

'Hah!' scoffed White. 'Scared of a little shower?' He laughed. 'What are you, a muff? You and your parly-voo. Cléophas told me you were fearless.'

'Oh no, sir,' said Emile. '*Pa ni pwoblèm.* Only – if it please you, master – it might be for the best, pray, sir, if you found shelter elsewhere.'

'I'm quite happy here, thank you.'

'Quite so, master. It is a good spot. But, beg pardon, you may notice that this tree right behind you is a Manchineel . . .'

With a great oath, White sprang to his feet and – snatching up his hat and rum – took several leaping steps across the sand, shuddering head to toe and uttering cries of revulsion much as though he had fallen into a stinky nest of cockroach. It was all I could do to keep a straight face. Emile pressed his lips together and raised his brow, such that he might not lose countenance. From a safe distance, the Englishman hurled a piece of driftwood at the Manchineel. Then, he glowered at the trees until he found a plain old seagrape and settle himself down in its shade.

'Alley-alley, veet,' he urged us, in his clumsy lingo. '*Lez sodias arreevee.*'

Indeed, he was right. As Emile and I set off, southward bound, I glanced over my shoulder and made out on the far side of the cove three bright crimson shapes flickering in and out of view behind the trees: a trio of English soldiers in red jackets, descending from the point. They were heading for the narrow stretch of sand where Bianco – or White, as we must now call him – sat quaffing rum, awaiting their arrival. I scuddled after my brother, across the muddy creek and up out of the bay. We climb toward the road in silence, both of us perturb by how gullible we had been, after all, and by the revelation that the Englishman had eavesdrop on our discussions, such that we were reluctant to talk long after he was out of sight, lest he might somehow overhear.

PART THREE

Grenada

(FIRST DAY)

Chapter Fourteen

This was a rough part of the island, inhospitable for cultivation: all steep foothills, their spines descending to the sea, and scraggy woodland of black sage, dogwood and blackthorn. We soon found the coastal highway – the *Chemin de Gouyave* or Gouyave Road – and were about to cross inland to deeper forest when Emile drag me back into the undergrowth. Moments later, a *porteuse* came around the bend, northward bound, swaying along with a springy step; black as a black-bone hen; her feet bare and on her head a trait of produce well wrap against the rain. I was simple-hearted enough then to believe we would be acquainted with all those we might encounter in Grenada and it came as a blow to realise I did not know her face. She move so fast, she pass before our eyes like a leaf on the breeze. Splish-splash, she went, through the shallow muddy river where it bisect the road. Then she turn the corner and was gone.

Nobody else in sight, we scuddle like a pair of *zaggada* across the highway and into the forest. There, somewise inland, we found an overgrown goat track, little used, but it seem to lead south, across several steep ridges that rose toward the mountains of the interior. A forest trail can be treacherous in the wet but the rain that day was no more than a shower and the foliage above us made a fair umbrella. Emile went first, keeping an eye out for prickly plant and other hazard. The ground lay thick with debris – dead leaves and vine, shards of bark and rotting orchid – and the underbrush kept catching at our legs. Everywhere rose the scent of decay like earth newly upturned or mould; and always, in the near distance, to the west, the boom of the breakers. Soon I could see nothing overhead but gigantic trees and the lurid greenish light of the forest.

All this while, devil the word we spoke but presently, my brother came to a halt in the shelter of a large, leafy tree, where the ground mostly dry. He prop himself up among the roots, glancing around to check we were alone, and when I caught up with him he open the satchel and took out the Power of Attorney. The seal had been broken already; Cléophas had simply folded the document and bound it with an old leather cord. Emile loose the knot and unfurl the parchment before handing it to me. Straightways, my eyes were drawn to the foot of the page. I could make out five different signature, one below the other. With so many, perchance this might mean that the English Governor could be among them.

'Five name,' I told Emile.

'Who are they?'

The first signature comprised a lengthy appellation in a round and sweeping hand, simple enough to read. I began to spell it out:

'V – I – C – T – O . . . Victor—'

My brother interrupted before I could cipher the whole name:

'Victor-Thérèse Charpentier, Comte d'Ennery – ?'

'. . . That's right.'

'Like Cléophas said: Governor of Martinique. Who's there next?'

'P – É – R – E . . . Père—'

'That will be Lefébure. Go on.'

Though I squinted at the writing on the page, the next hand was only a scrawl and I could make neither head nor tail of it. I shook my head.

'It's too ill-written.'

'Never mind,' said Emile. 'What about the next one?'

But again, the scribble-scrabble on the page made no sense.

'I can't read it,' I said.

'What about the last?'

The final signature had been inked in a backward-sloping scrawl. It took me a short while to make out the name.

'P – I – E – R – Pierre. E – M – E – R – I – G . . . Pierre Emerigon.'

'That's the lawyer,' said Emile. 'Cléophas mentioned him – the notary that drew up the document. Those ones you can't read – could either of them be Robert Melville? He is the English Governor here.'

'Hard to say.'

'Check again.'

I peered at the names once more then shook my head.

'The writing is too bad.'

My brother just stood there, staring at the ground between us. At our feet lay a fallen branch, swarming with ant, a thousand tiny dark speck, busy-busy.

All at once, I heard a quick, stealthy scurry, close at hand among the fern. I wheeled around and peered at the bushes.

'Just a bird,' said Emile. 'No need to worry – that old English mackerel won't follow us. He's back there laughing into his jug. Reckons we're a couple of bufflehead. He might well be right.' With a sigh, he folded the parchment and returned it to the satchel. 'Well, at least it's sign by the Governor of Martinique. That ought to be worth something, if we wind up in the suds. We'll just have to get someone to read it properly and tell us what it says.'

I had hoped he might be impress by my ability to spell – since he had nary knowledge of letters himself – but no praise was forthcoming. He simply patted me on the shoulder, saying: 'You just need more practice.' Then: '*Annou alé* – let's go, bug. We would do better not to be stumbling around here in the dark.'

With that, he clambered out of the tree root and we set off again toward Fort Royal. Every so often, as we laboured along, Emile would pause and listen to the forest. I listen too but the only sounds I could hear were the distant waves, water drip-dripping from the leaves and, once in a while, birdsong: the long, sad note of a dove, forever asking: 'Who? – Who? – Who?'

Chapter Fifteen

The overgrown path coiled on and on through the forest – an everlasting green tunnel. In places, the ground slope steep as a ladder and every otherwhile we had to haul ourselves up the track with the assistance of roots and branches. Like rigging strung from mast to mast, giant creepers bound each-every tree trunk to its neighbour. As we crested the spine of another ridge and began to descend the other side, the rain eased off, then stop altogether. Bright light burst through the foliage overhead and presently steam began to rise up all around us. From certain vantage point we could glimpse the ocean – blue-black in this light, the sun a silver disc in slow descent toward the horizon – and, between the trees, the *Chemin de Gouyave*, somewhiles visible. Not much of a thoroughfare, for true; at times no more than a wide beaten path along the cliff-edge, and the cause of much complaint among settlers since whole sections of this coastal highway were forever crumbling into the sea.

Presently, we found ourselves at the skirt of the wood, overlooking a river valley. Here, the land had been clear to some extent to make way for cultivation. The river flowed wide and deep on its approach to the coast hence the Gouyave Road veered about half a mile inland where the water ran shallow enough for to cross. On the other side of the ford, a lane quitted the highway and snaked up a hill toward a large plantation house. Two Béké settler on horseback had stop near the ford to converse whiles half a dozen *porteuses* strode along the highway in both directions and far off, in a bend of the river, a team of slave were clearing a patch of land. In order to avoid the house and the open ground we would have to stay in the forest and make our way inland for quite a stretch, then cross the river far behind the estate, in the hills, keeping under cover of the trees all the while.

Emile hesitated, staring at the plantation house.

'Beausejour,' said he.

Never once had I been in that part of the island but I had heard of the Beausejour Estate. When I was four years old or thereabouts, Céleste had been hired out to look after newborn twins at the Beausejour house until a proper nursemaid could be sent from *La Fwance*. Back then, I felt closer to Céleste in some ways than I did to Emile. He spent his days toiling over at the surgeon growing ground whereas Céleste stayed around the hospital and quarters, ergo I pass more time in her company. I thought of her as my wise older sister, perhaps even a mother. Sometimes, the sight of her gave me a strange sensation inside, as though I was made of wax that grew so hot it had begun to melt. She had eyes as jet-black as her curls and her flesh shone dark and glossy like a melongene. For true, her large features and dusky skin meant she was never seen by most as the prettiest girl on the hospital estate. Nevertheless, she had the most wit and kindness which is why she made such a good nurse. Her voice would make you think of honey, the way it flowed and rose and fell, a little catch in it sometimes as though she was about to laugh or cry. And when she did laugh, you could see her tongue, pale pink, and her teeth, so white, against her skin.

Of course, I was inconsolable when they sent her to Beausejour. Emile was allowed visit her there on Saturday night, if he could persuade Father Prudence to give him a ticket, but being only small, I was not permitted to go with him. One Saturday, I did follow him down to the river after he finish work and caught up with him at the ferry but as soon as he saw me trundling along behind him, he pick me up and carried me back to the quarters. There, he gave me to Angélique Le Vieux, the laundrywoman, and she put me in her cabin then sat against the doorflaps and though I kicked at them and howled and pounded, she held me prisoner inside and only release me after dark, when Emile had long gone.

Once the new nursemaid arrive from France, Céleste return to us at the hospital. She had only been gone a few month, but to me it felt like the course of ages. When she got back, she told me that she had lived inside the plantation house itself, next to the nursery. Her room had a huge window that looked out toward the ocean and she slept in a real bed with a mattress and sheets.

Curious now to see Beausejour at last, I took a good look at all the windows.

'Which room did Céleste sleep in?' I asked Emile, but got no reply.

To my surprise, he had wandered off and begun to make a pile of short fallen branches. He pointed to some twig on the forest floor.

'Gather up those stick there.'

'For why?'

'Firewood.'

'It's too wet to burn,' I told him. 'Besides, we have to hurry. What do you want to build a fire for?'

'No fire,' said he. 'We carry it.'

'What?'

'Just grab all the short branch you can, put them in a pile.'

I shook my head in disbelief but it were pointless to resist my brother once he got an idea fix in his mind, thus I simply did as bid. Emile bound his bundle of branches and twig with a length of creeper and did the same with what I collected.

'*I bon*,' said I. 'What shall we do now, I wonder? Let's pick some flowers and press them, then smoke a pipe.'

'You silly.' Emile indicated the bundles. 'Now we can go down there, walk on the highway and nobody notice us. We're just two half-breed, hauling wood to our master for charcoal. Works every time.'

A sudden pang of alarm ran through me.

'But old Bianco – whatshisname White – he said—'

'I know what he said but go too deep into those mountain and it will take all hell eternity to find a way back out. We have to get to the hospital quick, start spreading word among the slave. Let me hear you cough.'

'What?'

'Go ahead and cough.'

I cleared my throat: a polite tussication. My brother rolled his eyes heavenward.

'Not like that. Think how the Fathers sound when they have a fever – like they might yelk up their lung. Do that, like you're about to drop down *kickeraboo*.'

I tried again, hacking harder, until my throat did burn.

Emile nodded.

'You see a person on the road, you cough like that. Nobody will come near us.'

He crouch down to adjust his bundle. Something about the set and angle of his shoulders made him appear obstinate in the extreme.

'When did you do this before?' I asked him.

'What?'

'Bundles of wood. You said they always work. Was it something to do with that lieutenant? The invasion?'

Emile adjusted his hat and hoist his burden of wood onto his shoulder. Evidently, his mind was busy-busy: he chose to disregard me. When he began to walk again I notice he had change his gait somewise, so he look like an older man.

I called after him.

'But how do we know if the road is safe?'

'What's the matter with you? They won't arrest us just for being here. We've done nothing wrong. Leastwise, not yet.'

'Well – if that's the case, why do we have to carry stupid branches?'

'Just a precaution. To avoid questions. Believe me, this wood on our backs is like a cap of invisibility.'

He took a few step and then, because he knew I was watching, stuck out his foot and waggled it in jest, personating some kind of Frenchified *gigue* dancer. I had to crack a laugh. Emile carried on walking but when I hesitated, he turned and looked at me.

'There's no time to waste. You go up behind that house if you want, but you're liable to get lost in those mountain, and then I'll only have to come and find you, unless those Maroon get to you first.'

I turned and stared up at the great forest. Whiles the low slopes look shadowy and mysterial, the lonely summits and jagged heights were veiled in mist and an air of menace. How many Maroon were hiding up there in those high peaks, skulking about and watching from the forest? I shuddered. All around me, the hillside swarmed with insect; the air filled with the high, throbbing rattle of their song. Enough to drive a person crazy. I hefted up my bundle and trailed after my brother, feeling sick to my stomach and wary as a beaten dog.

Chapter Sixteen

Down in the valley, on the muddy earth of the highway, Emile and I fell into step together. My heart beat like a *tambou* drum. Here in this place, unconstrain by cliff or ridge, the road grew wide, though it were still churned up and barely cartable. I fix my gaze on the ground ahead, glancing up time to time to check who might be approaching. On the far side of the river, the team of slave bent to their task, hauling and hacking at a tree stump. An overseer stood behind them, his whip trailing on the ground. Every otherwhile, he jerked his arm to make the lash twitch like a crosspatch cat tail. Up ahead on the road, four *porteuses* were striding out in pairs toward Fort Royal but those girls walk so fast we would never overtake them. The two Béké horsemen had cease their conversation and gone separate ways. One set off up the lane toward the Beausejour big house at a canter – and fine riddance to him. The other had cross the ford and was now trotting toward us.

'*Dousman, dousman,*' said Emile, to me, under his breath.

We kept to the edge of the highway and I swap the firewood bundle to my left shoulder, better to conceal my face. When the rider drew near I began to cough just as my brother had instructed but I need hardly have bothered: the Béké paid us less heed than had we been two butterfly flopping along the wayside. He was possessed of a broad, ruddy countenance; I would have guess more English in appearance than French. In passing, he gave us nary a glance, only applied his spurs such that his pony broke into a gallop and away he went.

'Well done, bug,' said Emile. 'Now watch this pair coming.'

I had already seen them: two more carriers, young women, slender as beanpod, with *peau-chapotille* like us. Despite the great load upon their head they kept step and step with each other on their way across the ford, swaying their hip, their damp robes clinging to their legs. As they drew near, they glanced at us, my brother in particular, appraising him tip to toe as though to reckon his worth by the drachm. Those girls were strangers to me but they look so pretty – and tired, poor souls – it was only courteous to raise my hat to them:

'*Bonjou, Manzells. Bonjou. Sa ou fé?*'

Slapdash, before they could reply, my brother began to cough like a sorry plague-struck ass: a honk so vile that the girls took fright and sped on down the road. Only when we had cross the ford did Emile cease his racket and hiss at me:

'Are you brainsick? You suppose to cough, not stand there with your tongue hanging out.'

By this time, the *porteuses* had receded into the distance, just two lithe shapes, shimmering in the heat-haze between us and the sea. I paused in order to stare after them. I would sore have like to sit on the sand with them and hear their stories.

'Keep walking,' said Emile. '*Tambou!*'

I fell into step with him.

'They're only girls,' I said. 'Gentle dove.'

My brother gave me one sour look and muttered:

'*Chyen pa ka fè chat.*' Dogs don't make cats – a remark that stop me in my tracks for I believe he meant to draw some insulting comparison between me and the Pestle, our vile parent.

'What's that suppose to mean?' I said.

'No fuss now,' said Emile. 'Keep moving.'

I put a lid on my rage and carried on. Before we had gone ten step we came to a signpost painted with the word *Beausejour* and an arrow that pointed up the lane. A stand of trees now hid the mansion from sight but I knew it was up there. Ordinarily, I would never mention Céleste as I knew the sound of her name pained Emile but that gibe about dogs and cats had provoke me and so now I asked, all innocence:

'*Di mwen*, when you use to come here, those nights – where did you meet with Céleste? Was it down here – or up in her quarters – or where?'

My brother gave me an astonish look as though he could scarce believe my impudence. I went on:

'Remember how you use to be so tired all day when you'd been to see her?'

Again, apart from some rapid, affronted blinking, no response. I was quite enjoying myself.

'You know, the other night, I dreamed they sent Céleste to Martinique. I was bent down, cleaning out the chickens, and when I stood up – there she was, right beside me. She took me in her arms and stroke my head. Then I woke up crying, I was so happy.'

I turn to look at Emile – only to find him no longer beside me. He had stepped off the road onto a track that led toward another forested prominence. I threw my bundle of wood to the ground.

'Stone me down. Where to now?'

'Let's get off this highway,' he said. 'Unless you want to strike up more conversation.'

'I won't talk to anyone else. I promise.'

He gazed off into the distance, along the road.

'You want to talk to those soldiers?'

Through the heat haze, I could just make out a few bright red spot moving toward us. Say what you like about my brother but his eyes so sharp he could see two flea fornicating on a rat in the dark.

'Bring that wood,' he said. 'You never know who we might meet in the forest. These bundles are a good disguisement, wherever we go.'

He set off again toward the trees. I stared at his back for a while. Then, with no little reluctation of spirit, I heave my burden up onto my shoulder and traipsed after him. Both of us carried a similar load but all the same I felt like his packhorse.

I called after him:

'What do you reckon to my dream about Céleste?'

'Enough of your dreams,' he said. 'Stop talking about her.'

Well, it was a mystery and no mistake. Something must have happen to make him so averse to the mention of her name, but whatever it was, I had not one iota of an inkling. Of course, once upon a time, my brother and Céleste had been inseparable. They were born in the same year and grew up together. By the time I was old enough to notice, Emile had taken to following her around like a whelp whenever he could, kissing her after dark if he thought nobody would notice. I suppute they did more besides because once or twice I saw them sneak off into the forest.

Back when I was peeny-weeny, neither one of them would ever shoo me away but everything change soon after they began their smouching. If I followed them, they would tell me to run along or shut themselves away in one of the hut. In the end, came a time if I saw them together, I knew to leave them alone. Every otherwhile, I would catch sight of them, walking hand in hand, or standing still with their arms wrapped around each other, her head on his shoulder, neither one of them aware of my existence. Then my heart would throb with loneliness and I came to dread Sunday afternoon, for that was when they were mostly able to spend time together.

During the week, when Emile was over at the surgeon growing ground, I would follow Céleste around the hospital. She use to let me ride on her back and sometimes, if the sick room were quiet, she would try to improve her nurse skills by wrapping my arms or legs in splints, the way John Calder had taught her to bind broken bones; supporting my limbs so tenderly that I almost believe myself to be an invalid. (Other times, she was oblige to tend my real wounds, mostly the torn flesh of my back, and of this I was naturally less enamoured.)

One morning, she was about to fit my arm in a sling for practice when we heard a bird-call outside the sick room – three plaintive hoots. We both knew who it was, at once, and ran to the window and looked out. My brother stood in the courtyard, hat in hand, a burlap bag at his feet. Céleste started to laugh when she saw him there but we knew almost at once from his face something wrong.

'*Pou ki sa t'e là?*' she call to him. 'You should be working.'

Emile notice me peering over the sill and frowned.

'Lucien, *pa rété la*,' said he. 'You run off now.' But when I show no inclination to budge he fail to scold me for he had something more pressing on his mind. 'I only have a moment. The Pestle is sending me to Martinique. I have to go now.'

Céleste breathed in sharply. The bandage in her hand fell to the ground.

'But – why?' she asked.

'The old gardener at St Pierre died,' Emile replied. 'They want me to tend the surgeon growing ground over there, just for a few week, until they find someone new. Augustin is to take over from me here.'

'*Attention*,' said Céleste, softly. 'Look out.'

She jerked her head, indicating something on the far side of the courtyard. Emile glanced over his shoulder. I saw Father Damien emerge from the stable, leading a mule. My brother turn back to us, quick-sharp.

'Take care of Lucien,' he told Céleste. 'And tell Calder what's happened – I can't find him anywhere.' Then he spoke to me. 'Listen, little brother, I have to go somewhere but I'll be back soon, so you must not worry. *Tjenbé rèd.* You hear me?'

'Yes,' I replied.

'Then say it.'

'*Tjenbé rèd. Pa moli.*'

He nodded.

'Don't you forget it.'

Then Céleste spoke his name, just that:

'Emile.'

Father Damien had seen us. By this time, he had mounted his mule and was staring over in our direction. I shrank back from the window and heard the Pestle shout at my brother.

'What are you doing there? Get over here, boy! Hurry up!'

By the time I dare to peep outside again, Damien was urging the mule across the yard, digging his heels into the sides of the poor beast. I leaned out further and saw Emile trotting longside him, turning back every so often to look at us. They pass through the open gate onto the High Road, heading down toward Fort Royal and the carenage. As they descended, Emile twisted around one last time to look at us and raised his hand as he disappeared out of sight. Céleste reach down and put her arm around me. We watched a while longer, though we could see him no more. Then she turned away from the window, her eyes full of tears, her face contorting as though it had begun to melt. My skin tingled with fright to see her on the point of collapse. I picked up the fallen bandage and held it out to her, but she turned away.

'Not now, Lucien,' she said. 'You run along. I have to work.'

That would have been the last time she and Emile saw each other.

After that day, with my brother gone to Martinique, I was more at the mercy of Father Damien. Céleste and Calder did what they could to protect me but Pillon was sly and would wait until they were out of the way before he took out his wrath on me. Even now, all these decade later, my back is ridged with an island of scars, a map of tyranny, and a permanent reminder of our father. If no whip were available, he would simply use his fist. On one occasion, he knocked me cold as a wedge with a punch to my jaw and everyone thought I was dead until my eyes opened. Another time, he broke up a chair and beat me with one of the leg, such that I could scarce sit down for a week.

To make matters worse, soon after Emile had gone, first Prudence then Calder died of some burning fever. The Scotsman tried but fail to save Prudence and then he himself fell sick, whereafter I help Céleste tend him until his final breath. Father Damascene arrive shortly after to replace Prudence but, alas, he also succumb to bad fever almost as soon as he got to the hospital and was laid up for weeks. Left to his own devices, Pillon became yet more unpredictable. One morning, when I had spill some water on the floor by accident, he tied my hands and fasten me with a cord around my neck to a tree in the courtyard and then he took a whip and proceeded to beat the flesh on my back to a jelly. He might have kill me too had Céleste not intervened. She grab the lash but he turned on her and tried to strangle her with it. Fortunately for us both, Léontine had already run to fetch Father Damascene. He came hobbling out and attempted to restrain his fellow friar but Pillon was strong and the Good Father much weaken by fever. In the end, the Pestle threw him to the ground and stormed off to the mill where, I'm told, he took out his rage on some of the women.

Next day, Father Damascene packed his bag and return to Martinique, taking me with him. He would have brought Céleste too but

Pillon refuse to give her up, saying he needed her in the hospital. Lucky for Céleste, she was so dark: Father Damien only pestered women with lighter skin. As for me, the Pestle said he was sick of the sight of me and good riddance. No doubt, he viewed me as the walking emblem of his sin. Céleste change my dressings before we left and came with us across the courtyard to the gate. That was as far as she dare to venture. My back was too cut up for her to embrace me properly and so she held my hands and kiss my fingers until the little bell rang inside the hospital summoning her to the sick room and she hurried away. Damascene led me downhill but I look back in the same moment as Céleste and she reached out one hand to me and then turned and was gone.

All through the voyage to Martinique, Father Damascene sweated with a violent calenture and once or twice he fancied the sea to be green fields. Although he was taking me to relative safety, to join Emile, I spent much of the journey with my head in my hands, weeping bitters tears for the loss of Céleste. And, no matter how I missed her, my brother must have felt worse, having been separated from her for so long. I doubt the Pestle could have got him on board a boat had Emile known it would be seven whole year before his return to Grenada. All that time wondering when he might see Céleste again, the weeks and month passing – then turning to years – until he could scarce bear to hear her name. That was why his mood now seem so strange, as though the prospect of seeing his true-love again had fill him with dread. Why was he so down-at-mouth and chagrin?

Chapter Seventeen

I followed Emile along the track, into the trees, then up a steep scarpment and over a wooded hill. From the edge of a felling on the far side we gaze down upon another bay. Fields of cane and coffee had been laid out along the valley. Here the road divided, one branch veered off into the mountain, the other continued alongst the coast. The four *porteuses* now specks in the distance whiles various white settlers made their way in both direction, some on foot, some with handcarts, others on horseback or mule. A group of slave in shackles had been set to fill the holes in the highway with gravel, watched over by another Béké with a whip. To the south I could see two plantation house. In the hills behind them, a dark-skin boy drove a herd of sheep up the slope.

My brother blew air between his lips, exasperated.

'This use to be an empty valley.'

Near the shore stood a small sugar mill, the kind drove by cattle. A few slave hurried in and out of a store, carrying logs, and there was a gang in one of the field, stripping trash – or *bagasse* – off some lush old cane. A well-fed Béké with tawny skin stood on a tree stump, leaning on a stick and smoking his pipe as he watched over his scrawny charges. The slaves look starved and ragged. An air of gloom and desolation hung over the landscape.

'Look at that Goddam with the whip,' I said.

'He could be French,' Emile replied. 'A lot of those French stayed behind. Not all of them sold up to the English.'

I sighed.

'Sometimes I wonder what it must be like.'

My brother looked at me.

'What?'

'To speak,' I said. 'And not be contradicted.'

He jab his elbow at me but I dodged out of the way, just in time.

'Do you know any words in their language?' I asked him, thinking he did not, but was surprised when he replied, in English:

'Yes, master sir.'

'Anything else?'

'No, master sir.'

'What else?'

He looked around then pointed to the boy and his beasts on the hillside.

'Muttons,' he said.

I had to smile.

'No, those are sheep.'

'Sheeps.'

'You are quite the linguist,' I told him, feeling pleased with myself.

But he paid no heed to my satirical remarks. He had turn to stare down at the travellers on the Gouyave Road, weighing some thought in his mind. At one point, he cast a doubtful look at me. Then, eventually, he scratched his head.

'I would have propose going down to the road there and around the point but it's too busy.'

Hard to tell whether this was true or if he simply no longer trusted me to keep my yam-trap shut. He began to head along the ridge. I trailed after him, saying:

'This way must be longer.'

'A little,' he replied. 'But in any case, the St Jean is too deep and wide to cross at the coast. We would only have to walk upstream if we went by that road.'

'What about the ferry?' I said. 'The ferryman might still take you for free.'

'You think that same fellow is still here? There might not even be a ferry.'

I was considering this possibility when Emile stop short and set down his bundle. He reached into his pocket and pulled out a twist of thin linen. This he unravel to reveal a few coin: one half-joe, clipped light, two sous and three deniers – about as much money as I had ever seen.

'Where did you get those?' I asked, in wonder.

'Cléophas.'

'*Tambou!*'

'You should have seen his face as he put them in my hand. You might have thought he was giving me his fortune.'

Emile stare down at the coins, an absent look in his eyes, behind them his splendidious brain no doubt whirring. Like as not, he was supputing whether we could afford to take a ferry. Then he began to bind the cloth tight around the coin such that they would jangle less in his pocket.

'Sorry, bug,' he said. 'I can't waste this on a ferry when we can walk there almost as quick. And that road is busy as a half-day market. *Tout bagay chanje, 'ti pantalons* – nothing stays the same for long in these Antilles.'

He stuff the twist of linen in his pocket and lifted his bundle onto his shoulder. Then he strode off amongst the trees. I caught up with him in a twinkle.

'Emile? *Souplé?* Can I carry those coin? I'll take extra special good care of them, *mwen sèmante* – you have my word.'

I leave you to imagine his reply for it is hardly printable here.

Chapter Eighteen

We pressed inland, keeping out of sight among the woods. At one point, we came to a highway that headed up into the hills. As we crossed over, Emile scraped a line in the muddy road with his toe.

'This is the *Chemin des Hauteurs*,' he said. On the far side, he patted the trunk of a tree. 'Now we're in the hospital estate.'

All this country was new to me. By my reckoning, we had reached a spot only a few mile from the very place where my life began. And yet, there I was, just as lost as had I been set down a naked babe in the wilderness of Beersheba, entirely at the mercy of my brother and his superior knowledge of the island. Perhaps that is why a thrill ran through me as we came around the side of a hill and I heard the sound of rushing water.

'The river St Jean,' I cried. 'Over there – listen.'

Emile shook his head.

'That's the Mahots. We must cross that first. Then there's another river just beyond it and when that joins up with the Mahots, both together, they form a bigger river and that's the St Jean you remember – but what you hear now is the Mahots.'

'They should make you a geographer,' I said. 'If ever we get to be freed – that would be my strong recommendation.'

'You – meanwhile – will be on the stage,' said Emile. 'The hired buffoon.'

He was a dry dog; you had to give him that.

'Why not just cross the St Jean?' I asked. 'Why make us cross two rivers?'

'Like I said, the St Jean is too wide and deep where they join. We should go upstream, ford them one at a time. Mahots is bad enough this season, after rain.'

But despite all his fuss and bother we forded the Mahots easy as scratch. On the far side, we had scarce gone forty paces when we came to another river, this one narrower but fast-flowing. So far as I could tell we were somewheres in the V of land between where the two watercourses met. No path here to speak of, just mud up to the ankle.

Emile led me into the thickest part of the woods. Then he sat me down on a fallen tree and spoke in a low voice.

'You wait here with the bag, out of sight. I'll take a look at the mill.'

'What mill?'

'The hospital mill.'

'Will anyone we know be there?'

He raised his eyebrows.

'Might be nobody there at all.'

'But – if you find someone – will you speak to them?'

'Don't talk stupidness. Nobody will see me, come or go. I only want to take a look.'

'But aren't we suppose to talk to the field hands?'

He sighed.

'We can't go crashing in at the mill like a couple of whip-cat niggers, talking to this one and that one – you think any overseer would tolerate that? No, we need to get to the old quarters, speak to the hospital slave first – whoever is remaining. I'm only going to check if the mill is quiet, see if we can use the ford there – otherwise we'll have to cross further up. *Kompwan?*'

'Mm-hmm.'

'Well, stay here until I get back.'

He listen for a short interval then disappeared through the under-growth, headed upstream. As you might imagine, I took a stitch at having to wait there like a pricket whiles he went ahead to scout. Why he wanted me to stay behind I knew not: any fool could sneak around just as well as him. So far as I was concern, I could con-duct myself in an entirely sensible manner. He had made overmuch simmy-dimmy about those two *porteuses*. After all, I had only said '*Bonjou*'. Some people might argue it would look more suspicious NOT to greet two young ladies if they pass you on the road. Giving them 'Good day' was only polite, or so I persuaded myself as I sat there alone.

In plus, I would have like to see the mill, for as a child I had strayed no further from the hospital than the ferry road and the plantation village. I tried to cheer myself with the thought of an imminent reunion with our old compeers, the hospital slaves: most of all, Céleste, of course, but also my childhood playferes from the hospital quarters, Vincent and his cousin Léontine. Both their mothers had died long since, and they grew up in the care of their grandmother, laundrywoman Angélique Le Vieux. Beforetimes, I used to trail around after them, trying to keep up when they ran down to the river and the plantation. Léontine was a bold child, always leading us into scrapes. She could outrun and out-climb her cousin and her sharp wits meant that she often acted as lookout for the adults from a young age. As for Vincent, some older boys might have scorned me as a whipper-snapping baby, but he always stood up for me and one time, when I fell and got coated in stinking scumber from knee to neck, he took the trouble to wash me down himself.

Vincent and Léontine had been the best compeers of my child-hood and the thought of seeing them again improved my humour somewise for, all afternoon, it had been naught but encounters with strangers and one unfamiliar place after another. I had a yearning just to see someone or someplace I recognised: the ferryman, the mouth of the St Jean, or even old Angélique, who was mainly known for chopping the heads off hens and trapping spirits in jars. In fact, I knew her *soi-disant* spirit were nothing but smoke from her tobacco pipe, since I had spied the old sly-boots puff and blow into her silly jars when she thought nobody could see. Back in the old days, she used to scare the britches off me, but now I would have traded every coin we had just to see her spit in a fire.

By then, it were that tranquil hour of day in those Antilles that comes creeping before the last of the light. The forest smelt of tree sap and smoke and blossom. In less than an hour it would be dark and the tiny frog would start to pipe their night-time song. I sat so still and quiet waiting for Emile that I might have been invisible. If only he could have seen me. Why, an old iguana fail to notice me altogether and climbed a tree right before my eyes. Next came a manicou limping along just a few feet away. I lean down to whisper to him: 'How do you do, sir?' but he keeled right over on the spot and even when I stroked him with a long leaf he pretended to be stone *kickeraboo*. Well, that provided middling entertainment for a snipper-snapper such as me in those days. But as time went along and Emile fail to return, my impatience grew. I began to think it would do no harm to get the lay of the land on my own account, perhaps take a look downstream and see what could be seen before nightfall.

Leaving the bag, I crept along through the underwood to the tongue of land at the conflux of the two waterways. Here, at last, the St Jean. I could see for myself that the river flowed wide and high, a mite too frisky to cross. Above the leafy canopy, to the south, a long stretch of high ground rose up against the sky. For true, something about those heights reminded me of Hospital Hill – though I had never viewed it from so far inland. Besides, in my memory, trees shrouded the slopes, whereas this ridge had been half-cleared.

I was puzzling my noddle about that when a movement downstream caught my eye. There, on the opposite bank of the river, stood a bacon-face Béké of middle years, peering down into the water as if in search of fish. He wore a broad-brim cloth hat, loose shirt, faded nankeen drawers and dingy stockings. I had just noticed him when he glanced up and saw me. Slapdash, the breath quitted my body. My impulse was to scuttle for cover like a scalded cockroach except it struck me that – if I fled – his suspicion would only be arouse. Ergo, I raise my hat instead to greet him.

'Good day to you, sir,' says I, in English, in case he might be a Goddam: 'How do you do? Lovely weather today, master, sir.'

The Béké just narrowed his eyes at me. It struck me that he might be the overseer – Addison Bell – the one White had warned us about. If it were him, I was surely done for. But the man just frowned at me then turned and ambled away downstream. I watched him until he disappeared from view. He did not give the appearance of one intent on raising the alarm. Perhaps he had mistook me for a freed man since Grenada then had a few hundred such fortunate souls. Nonetheless, the incident gave me quite a jolt. My heart beat fierce and fast as a beggar with a clap-dish. So much for seeing the lay of the land: the devil to that. In haste I sped back to the thicket, arriving just as my brother reappeared.

'Where have you been?' he said.

Well, he would go up in smoke if I told him what had happen, hence I led him to believe that I had merely step behind a tree to 'pump ship'. After all, the Béké stranger had strolled off without a word. I told myself not to fret or foam.

'There's a dog at the mill,' Emile said. 'But he's tied up asleep. No sign of anybody else. They're stocking wood but they haven't begun the harvest yet. We'll have to take care – they've chop down half the trees up there so there's less cover. Now – follow me and be quiet – specially near the mill. Let's not wake the dog. I can see no sign of a watchman but someone might be lurking. *Dépéché kò'w.* Hurry up. Bring your wood.'

He put his finger to his lips. His eyes were blazing, alert. I should have guess he would be twined up tight as a tourniquet now we were closing in on our destination, on Céleste. Of course, I know that now. But back then, I just felt too vex to care, all up in the snuff with him for flinging orders at me what seem like a thousand times per second.

Chapter Nineteen

Soon enough, we arrived at the ford, where a highway approach the river from the east. All seem tranquil until we heard the thud of hooves on the road. Emile pull me down into the rushes at the water edge and held me tight-tight. The hooves turned out to belong to a couple of Capuchin friar, one young, one old – or rather to the mangy mules upon which they sat. The elder friar was clacking away like an old babelard on the subject of nothing, whiles his youthful companion look fit to die of *ennui* and for that he had my fellow-feeling. The pair took their time negotiating the river but at last they trotted off on their way. When we judge them out of earshot, we left our hiding place and cross the ford. On the far side, the rutted highway followed the course of the St Jean to the sea.

'Is that the River Road?' I asked Emile. 'The one I know?'

'Correct,' said he.

I had never been on this exact stretch of highway, yet it was some comfort to reach a familiar landmark at last. Nonetheless, by then, Emile had grown exceeding cautious and even though the road would take us in the right direction we ran across it and onto the back of the ridge. Getting up there was a scramble but we stole along quiet as two slipper-shod snake and had soon gone high enough to look down upon the former property of our friars, *les Frères de la Charité*.

The mill turned out to be not much more than a few ramshackle building: a boiling house made of rough stone with a squat chimney, the mill itself and the curing house. A massive hound lay asleep in his kennel next the woodshed. Otherwise, the courtyard seem deserted; all the machinery lay still. So often beforetime I had heard talk of this place, I must have built it up somewise in my mind. Well, it was less grand than I had imagine; in fact, the boiling house was smaller than the one we had in Martinique and from what I could see there was no distillery, just the curing house.

Emile pointed across the yard to a low structure of iron bars and hinge planks. He put his mouth to my ear and whispered.

'That's new. Bilboes.'

I whispered back.

'I can see what they are.'

But he persisted in explaining:

'You put your feet in the holes, they keep you locked up long as they want.'

'Instruments of torture,' I replied. 'A Caribee tour, conducted by his excellency the Prince Mandingo.'

Emile twitched his shoulders.

'You and your mouth,' he said. '*Annou alé*. Let's go.'

We hurried on, keeping to higher ground where the woods gave us some small amount of cover. Further along, we could survey the wide valley all the way to the coast. Some still call the plantation land the *Indigoterre des Pères* though the Fathers had long gone and only cane had grown there for years, first planted by the friar themselve when sugar became a more valuable crop than indigo. Now, the cane looked lush, bright green, tall enough to be cut. I peered ahead to a bend in the river where the field hand quarters use to be, right in the midst of the cane-pieces. The dwellings seemed much as I remembered: a huddle of thatch roofs, seven timber cabins of different sizes, set together in haphazard fashion on the north side of the St Jean.

Eventually, we came to a halt in a dense thicket of campèche.

There, in the shadows beneath their branches, we were invisible. The sharp scent of the trees hung in the air. I could hear the thwack of axes chopping wood somewhere along the ridge. Voices floated across the hillside. Down near the coast, a dog was barking. Below us, the river St Jean snaked along the valley. The field hand quarters lay on the far side. Someone had built a narrow bridge across the water, a rough structure of planks just wide enough to allow one person to cross on foot. Most likely, this was so the hands could move from one part of the plantation to the other without heading up to the ford which had always been a time-waster. A few infant amused themselve on the riverbank. Behind the cabins, lay the provision ground and beyond that, prospecting the village on the low slopes opposite us, sat the cabin that housed the overseer. As we watched, an aged field hand hobble behind the huts toward the growing ground, a hoe upon his shoulder. Almost in the same moment, the chock-chock of axe blade ceased and soon a group of figures emerge from the trees and began to assemble on the road below. Evidently, the field hand had just finish work for the day. We were too far distant to recognise anyone for certain but close enough to make out that two of the women wore spike collars.

I glanced at my brother. He studied the quarters, then looked up and down the valley, a keen expression on his face as though he were calculating something or measuring a distance – but what exact form his thoughts took I could not hazard a guess.

'How are we suppose to get them all the way up-island to Petit Havre in collars?' I asked. 'Up and down ridges, on goat tracks, in the dark. What about the old sick ones, and the children? They'll be too slow. We have to leave them behind. Cléophas said take the fast ones, those fit for work.'

'We're not leaving any that want to go,' Emile said.

He took a few step then stopped again, staring down at the village.

I followed his gaze and saw a single field hand standing alone against one of the hut. For a sudden, I thought that the light was playing tricks on me. The man was bone-lean and entirely naked. He had his head press to the cabin wall, as though to eavesdrop on some conversation inside. His skin gleamed strangely. He had an iron weight attach to his ankle by a chain: not enough to stop him working, but it would slow him down.

Something about the position of his body seemed wrong, as though he stood there against his will. His head met the boards of the hut at an awkward angle, his back twisted. If he was eavesdropping, he did so in plain view, because the other field hand had begun to stream across the bridge and the man did not try to hide what he was doing, as though unable to move from that spot. In fact, he raised his hand to greet them, though it cost him some effort. It was only then that the truth of the situation dawned on me. His ear had been nail to the hut.

My brother gave me a look, as much to say: 'You see what they do?'

'Why is his skin shining so much?' I asked.

'Molasses. I expect the overseer tarred him with it, to attract flies to bite him. Flies in the daytime; musquito by night. Send him out of his mind. Wonder how long he's been there?'

Indeed, the poor wretch did seem weary. His knees kept giving way as though he had nodded off but then he would jerk himself upright again.

'That ear is lost, no matter what,' said Emile. 'Likely they will slice it off to set him free. Or pull him away from the wall, leave his flesh in shred.'

I squeeze my own ear, glad to find it intact.

'Enough,' whispered Emile. '*Annou alé*. Follow me.'

Toward the western end of the hill, he paused and pointed at the heights. Since I now had my bearings entirely, I knew at once what he meant: we should avoid the redoubt at the summit in case the English kept soldiers up there on guard. In peace time, the fortified position were mostly unmanned; no doubt, the redcoats would all be in town or down at the fort but, cautious as ever, my brother headed down the slope.

Without a word, we made for a line of woods beyond which the hill had been cleared entirely. Above us, a winding path descended from the redoubt. New trenchments had been dug across the hillside all the way to the cliffs and palisades erected. A tunnel led through the battery. On the other side lay the hospital – but the last thing we wanted was to show ourselves there in the courtyard. Our true destination was the huts, uphill and downwind of the main hospital buildings.

Beyond the cliffs, the sea had begun to glow in shades of pink and orange, reflecting the sunset and a long scatteration of violet clouds at the horizon. Dusk was creeping up on the land. The first little frog began to whistle his song – and then another joined in, and another, until the whole entire landscape came alive with the piping chorus of those invisible creatures.

Emile beckoned and I followed him up into the trees, past the end of the battery. Although it was unguarded, we moved along in pure silence. We crested the ridge just as the last golden sliver of sun slip down behind the ocean. And there – at last, laid out below us, in its healthy position – *L'Hôpital des Frères de la Charité*, a few white building arranged around a courtyard, beyond which forested cliffs dropped away to the sea. In the deepening shadows between us and the hospital lay the familiar slave quarters, in two rows divided by a narrow yard. Six small cabin made of board, with thatch roofs, and at the bottom end, an open kitchen, all clinging precarious to the hillside like a cluster of shaggy burrs. The sight of them in the last glim of day made me tenderhearted and sad.

I took a step toward the huts but Emile grab my arm.

'Wait,' he whispered.

'What for? We're here.'

'Just wait and listen.'

He crept further along amid the tall grass and after a moment I followed him to a spot that overlook the town. Well, I never thought to have seen that place again – but there she was, Fort Royal: bright flambeaux already burning here and there; a forest of mast in the carenage; and, out on the bluff, the dark shape of the fort.

Emile crouch down among the grass and after a moment I sank to the ground beside him. The sea was just a surge and a hush below us in the dark. Every so often, I could hear a goat bleat in the distance. We waited – and waited. Soon, the stars came out and bathed everything in silvery light. Some nights in those Antilles are so clear that – even with no moon – the heavens shine bright enough that you can see your own shadow. All around us, the sound of a million million insect and creatures assaulted my ears. I thought about the poor field hand down on the plantation with his head nail to the cabin wall. Would he remain there, awake all night, taunted by the peep of those frog?

Down below in town, I could see the church spire, glowing in the starlight. Most likely, our father – which art not in heaven – had been buried somewheres in the cemetery yard. Several month after I had left Grenada, word of his death reached us in Martinique. The story we heard was that when one of the field women resisted him, he beat her about the head until she bit him in retaliation. Soon thereafter, he fell sick with blood poisoning and decease this world just a few days later. For true, there could scarce have been a more apt demise for Father Damien Pillon.

Had he been alive, I would have dreaded even more this return to Grenada. Howsomever, it was some comfort to know that he no longer walk the earth. I was wondering whether I might have time to see his grave with my own eyes when my brother began to speak, his voice so soft I had to strain to hear him.

'Now then, Lucien – listen to me . . . I've been thinking . . . I want you to go down into town and find a boat bound for Martinique.'

'What? Why?'

'Because you're going back to St Pierre.'

'But we just got here.'

'I know,' said he. 'But your part in this matter is finish. You came in case we needed to speak with any Englishman. Well, here we are, safe. We did not have to talk to anyone. I'll just keep to the huts out of sight while I'm here. So – you see – I have no further need of you. Makes sense you should go back now.'

'What about taking everyone to the boats? Is that not what we're suppose to do? In small groups? Cléophas said it would take two of us, at least. What about going to find all the hired-out slaves and fetch them?'

He tried to press the twist of cloth with the coins into my hand.

'Take these,' he said. 'You'll need to pay your fare.'

I pushed him away and sprang to my feet.

'You just want to do it all by yourself – play the big Don Diego.'

With that, I began to walk toward the quarters.

'Come back here,' I heard Emile say. 'Come back, you—'

He fell to cursing me. But I paid him no heed and carried on, straight for the huts. I would not have him lord it over me any more. Besides, I was gut-foundered. I could smell no fire yet, but surely our old compeers would return from their labours soon and start to cook.

Next thing I knew, I was on the ground with Emile on top of me. He grab my arms and lay his full weight on my body. Although I struggle with all my might, he held me fast, his face in my face.

'Go back,' he said. 'Go back, Lucien. This will not end well.'

I wrestled him again, trying to free my arms, grunting and gasping with the effort. Then, without warning, there was a clatter and a change in the light. A bright flash shone in my eyes and a deep voice said:

'What the tumpty-tum are you boys doing there?'

PART FOUR

Grenada

(FIRST NIGHT)

Chapter Twenty

Although we had not seen him for years, we would have known those grumbling tones anywhere: it was Chevallier, one of the hospital slave; and if we had fail to recognise his voice, we could have distinguish him by his 'tumpty-tum' profanities for old Chevallier swore harder than any fellow you ever met. I caught a glimpse of his sconce (mostly bald now) and on his chin some patchy grey whiskers, before he thrust a lantern in our faces. His mouth dropped open as the light fell upon my brother.

'Jésis-Maïa! What the tumpty-tum? Is that you, Emile?'

'*Wi*,' said my brother, somewhat sheepish, perhaps because we had been skirmishing around, undignified, like two frigatebird squabbling over stick. '*Bonswa, tonton. Mwen kontan wè zot.* Good evening, Uncle. Good to see you again. How is—?'

'*Mèd*,' the old man interrupted. 'Thought we saw the last of you. Who's this here?'

He held up the smut-lamp to my face.

'It's me,' I said and, when he look none the wiser, was oblige to add: 'Lucien.'

'*TAM-bou.* Little Lucien. I would hardly know you. Well, boys, stop standing there like a pair of stones.'

He span around and began to head for the huts, muttering to himself:

'Well, I'll be tumpty-tummed . . .'

Emile called after him, in an undertone: 'One moment – we must fetch our bag.' Then he drag me back, all the while speaking in my ear. 'First sign of trouble, you run. Don't wait for me. Head for the mountain, north of the big lake – I'll find you. You understand me?'

I tried to wriggle out of his grasp but knew he would only let go if I replied.

'*Wi*,' I said.

'And keep your mouth shut at the quarters. I'll do the talking. *I bon. Annou alé.*'

He grab the satchel and followed the old man. I trailed along in his wake. Emile stepped into the yard as wary as a dove but the place seemed empty save for Chevallier who was now crouch down in the open kitchen in front of the fire pit.

'Just let me light this,' he said. 'Else she'll tan my tumpty-tum hide.'

By that, I suppute he meant his woman, Angélique. He lit a piece of dry *bagasse* from the lamp then held the flame to some kindling. I stood behind him to watch. When I was a child, Chevallier use to go out in the boat every day to catch fish for the Fathers, cursing all the way down to the shore and cursing all the way back. He had been a sturdy fellow back then but now he look much scrawnier than I remembered and the shirt he wore hung on him like a sack.

Meanwhile, Emile was stalking around the huts. He peered circumspect inside any open doors and cast uneasy glances downhill through the trees, toward the hospital. Inside those buildings – no doubt – were a Béké doctor or two, perhaps some nurse-men and patients: settlers of the less wealthy kind and even sick soldiers from the fort.

My brother paused in front of the smallest cabin at the end, where he had lived alone after our mother died. That hut was also where he and Céleste had shut themselves away all those time. Now, the door lay ajar.

Chevallier fed the flames with charcoal and the twigs began to crackle.

'You boys on the run?' said he.

I cast a glance toward my brother but he was peering inside the little cabin.

'No, *tonton*,' said I. 'Not at all.'

'Your brother seems agitable.'

'He's just wondering if you can still have visitors here.'

Chevallier gazed up at me, his dark, rheumy eyes glistening in the firelight.

'Depends on the visitor. We can't take no runaway.'

'We're not runaway,' said Emile, returning abruptly. 'That redoubt up on the hill there – do they keep it manned?'

'Not lately. They send someone to clean the cannon on the battery every otherwhile but mostly the redcoats stay down at the fort. Greys, they call them – Glasgow Greys. That's the regiment.'

'What about this English doctor? How often does he check on you here?'

'Most Sunday he looks us over. He was here this morning. Not every Sunday, though, depending how drunk he was the night before. So long as we keep toiling obedient they hardly bother us much here. But that's about the only thing has stayed the same. Everything else topsy-turvy, Emile – you would scarce believe.'

'*Di mwen*. Tell me.'

'Oh! *Tout bagay chanje. Mèd.* Everything changed. They don't let me fish any more because Bryant don't like fish. They got me working the surgeon provision ground, since they demoted Augustin to field hand. All he said was "*Bonjou*" and then they – but of course, you ought to know we're not permitted to speak French any more. *La la la! Pa de Fwancé. Puten!* Anything from the old days is bad: French language is bad; French food bad; French dancing bad. Anything French, they forbid it, these Goddams.'

He made a vulgar gesture with his arms.

'They think the French too soft on us. Bring a new regime all over the island, harsh-harsh. This overseer now, Addison Bell, that man would string you up soon as look at you. Him and Bryant together – *puten!* They make us bessy-down and speak English: "Yes, master sir; no, master sir." Well, nobody likes it, of course. *Pèsonn! Pèsonn vlé pale Anglé.* Now French – that's a language. *La langue Fwancé. Bel; dou; ravissonne.* A man can say what he wants in French. But this English – *mèd!'*

By no stretch of imagination was he speaking French, but we were too polite to point it out to him.

'Well, you know our friend Augustin. He's stubborn. Every time they want him to say "Yes, if it please you, sir," he pretend to forget, talking French: "*Wi, messié, souplé.*" And that, they do not like. They shout at him: "Speak English, dog!" But he kept forgetting – on purpose. So first, they punish him, stop him taking any rest. Made him work all day, *sans pause*, no time to piss, nothing. Then, five, six markets agone – *plam!'*

Chevallier banged his hands together.

'He gave the doctor "*Bonjou*" instead of "Good morning" – and right there and then Bryant told the overseer to put him in the field. They got shackles on him, set him to work felling tree. He's been there ever since. And now – we heard just last night – Addison Bell nailed his ear to a wall. For no reason.'

So – the poor wretch down at the village was Augustin. To my recollection, he had been a mighty man, somethingish wild and reckless, with broad shoulders and powerful hands. It was hard to reconcile this memory of him with the haggard fellow hammered to the cabin.

Emile caught my eye across the flames. I wondered if he would mention what we had seen at the quarters but a scarce-perceptible shake of his head told me to keep my yam-trap shut. Chevallier had bent down to set a pot of water on the fire, perhaps to hide the anguish on his face. He dropped in some salt-fish and vegetable. When he stood up again, Emile put a hand on his shoulder.

'That must be hard to bear, *tonton*,' he said. 'But Augustin is strong.'

Just then, I heard a sound on the path from the hospital, someone coming up the slope. Emile seem to panic. He span around, scanning the dark beneath the trees.

'Here she comes,' said the old man. In the same instant, Angélique Le Vieux hobbled out of the gloom. When she caught sight of Emile by the fire she stop dead.

'There you are,' she said, then turn to Chevallier. 'Is it him?'

'It's him all right.'

'Well,' said Angélique. 'I can't believe it. How long you been gone now, boy?'

'Seven Christmas,' replied Emile. 'I hope you are well, *tati* Angélique.' She was not our aunt, no more than Chevallier was our uncle, but we call them such to be polite.

'Seven Christmas,' said she. 'And I haven't thought of you once.' She held up her finger. 'Until today.'

I looked at my brother. He raise both eyebrows.

'Correct,' said Angélique. 'Not one time have you cross my mind and then, this afternoon, you came into my head and I spoke your name out loud. Is that not so, *ché*?'

She look to Chevallier who gave her an apologetic smile.

'Well, *ché*,' said he. 'I haven't seen you since this morning. But I'm sure you're right. You spoke his name out loud.'

'I spoke his name out loud. "Emile Mandingo." Someone was there – I said it to somebody. Léontine. We were folding sheets in the laundry. She heard me. "Emile Mandingo," I said. And then I said: "What has become of him?" And now – before the day is out

– there you are, right in front of me. I conjured you up. Yes, I did. Exactly so.'

'Quite so, *ché*,' said her man. 'You still got your powers. Strong as ever they were.'

'Conjured you up out of nothing,' she told Emile. 'And it was no more trouble to me than eating pastry.'

Of course, my brother might have pointed out that when she had thought of him that afternoon he was already in Grenada, at Petit Havre. But perhaps out of respect for her age, or for the bad news about their friend Augustin, he only bowed his head. Angélique hobbled over to Chevallier.

'Any news of Augustin, *ché*? How is he? Have they set him free?'

'Not yet,' the old man said. 'I went down just before sunset, took a look from the hill. He was still there. But he will be fine. He's strong.'

Angélique had already turn back to Emile.

'Did you hear? They made him work with those dirty dogs down there. And now they nail him to a wall. I get sick to think of it.'

She clutched her stomach. Chevallier slipped his arm around her shoulder.

'I told them all about it,' Chevallier said. 'Come, *ché*.'

Meanwhile, Emile fiddle with his hat and clung to that satchel as if he might depart in a twinkling. Then Angélique notice me at last.

'But who is this with you, Emile?'

Chevallier forced a laugh.

'You must recognise him?'

The old woman cast her eye over me, her mouth downturn. Then she took a step back.

'Ha! Just like his mother – big ugly lips and skinny face.'

Well, that was nonsense for my mother was known for her

beauty and I would have said as much except Emile shot me a warning glance.

Angélique sat down and took up her pipe. The firelight threw flickering shadows across her face. Sharp creases ran from the corners of her nose to the ends of her lips. The skin below her eyes look puffy. She was old and lame. Nevertheless, she was still tough as old turtle, for true.

'Well, Mandingo, what the dickens you doing here, hmm? You back for good? You know they got us working the surgeon provision ground now, so they'll have to find other work for you to do. Watch out – they could put you down in the field, get you cutting cane. You might have to break a sweat. *Tant pis pou ou.*'

She laughed and then fell to coughing.

'He could cut cane if he wanted,' I told her. 'He's plenty strong enough.'

'Lucien,' said Emile, sharply. '*Souplé – tati Angélique*, I need to ask – is there somewhere we can rest our head for a few night?'

'Well, so many of us gone these days, we all spread out – but the two hut at the end are empty.'

Perhaps she had fail to remember that one of these was where our mother and Emile had slept in bygone days. My brother glanced over his shoulder and his face grew mournful again as he looked at the smallest hut, visible now only in outline. Across the yard stood a slightly taller construction, more ramshackle, with a broken shutter. Emile pointed to it.

'What about that one? Is that empty?'

'Mm-hmm,' the old woman said. 'You can use that. So long as the Goddams never find you. But you still haven't told us why you're here.'

My brother cleared his throat.

'Well, we – we've been sent by *les Frères*.'

He tried to sound light-hearted but Angélique must have heard the grave tone in his voice, for she paused in the act of relighting her pipe.

'What for?'

Emile glance down toward the hospital buildings.

'I'll tell you but – when will the others get here? I should tell everyone.'

She waved her hand, dismissive.

'Tell us now, instead of making us peck at dust.'

My brother place the satchel on the ground then sat by the fire. When he spoke his voice was no more than a whisper, such that Chevallier had to crouch down with us.

'Well – you might not believe this but *les Frères* want you all to come to Martinique. We're to take you back with us, everybody from the hospital here and anyone that's hired out and all the field hand too.'

'*Puten!*' exclaim Chevallier.

Angélique just blew smoke into the fire, trying to take it in her stride.

'They're sending a big boat in a day or two,' Emile continued. 'We have to get everybody up-island somehow. And they want us to do the whole thing in secret, at night, on Christmas Eve. We have to get away without the English finding out.'

'*Puten!*' said Chevallier again.

'Who sent you here?' demanded Angélique. 'Damascene?'

'No,' said Emile. 'There's a new superior now at St Pierre. Père Lefébure.'

'What's happen to the Good Father? Is he sick?'

'Just old, his mind wandering,' said Emile. 'Lefébure is in charge now. We're acting on his instruction. Him and another Father from Paris – man they call Cléophas.'

The old woman gave a hollow laugh.

'Well, that makes sense. He came sniffing around here himself a while back, that Cléophas, in the hurricane time. Came and spoke to us about Martinique, the land of milk and honey. Hah! I told him that hellhole is nothing but a bad memory. Oh yes. That's where they took us first, you know. I will never forget it. But he tried to tell us everybody in *La Matinik* speaking French and if we go there we would be just like in Paradise. Fool of a man.'

Chevallier said: 'Most of the time, he was down at the plantation there, persuading them they belong to *les Frères* and then—'

'For true,' his woman interrupted. 'Until the overseer saw what he was up to – tampering with the slave. Then Bell told the surgeon doctor and he scared that silly Father off the plantation. Threaten him with the Glasgow Greys.'

'Told him to go and tumpty-tum his-self.'

'That's right,' said Angélique. 'But that Cléophas swore he'd come back to fetch us. Told us he'd bring a document that prove the friars own us – and all the plantation slave – and the whole jiggumbob would be settle in his favour.'

My brother narrowed his eyes at me, across the fire.

'There is a document,' he said. 'But I'm not sure it's proof of anything. And with or without it, we have orders to take everybody in secret. Besides, I expect this Bryant and the overseer might try to stop us if they find out.'

The old woman snorted.

'You expect? No question. These Goddams aren't about to let the slave all go skitter-scatter across the water, nevermore to be seen. How would they run this hospital? How would they bring in the cane? They need the sugar money. If we all scamper off like fools, they're going to come after us and then—'

She shook her head, grimly.

My brother said: 'Well, let's see – there might be a way.'

Angélique looked at him, sceptical, whiles Chevallier scratched his head.

'I would like to see my sister again,' he said, suddenly wistful. 'Does she still work for *les Frères* over there? Tattio? They call her Thisbee. Last I heard she was on the friar plantation, looking after children whiles everybody else in the field. Have you seen her?'

Emile glanced at me for the answer.

'Mm-hmm,' I said. 'She's still there.'

Chevallier turn to his woman.

'I haven't seen her in twenty Christmas or more.'

Angélique gave her teeth a loud suck.

Emile lean forward.

'So – would you come with us?'

The old couple stared at each other across the fire. Nobody spoke until eventually Emile said:

'Well, no need to make up your mind tonight. We need to get word to everybody on the plantation and everybody hired out, and find out what they want to do. Now, tell me, who exactly is left here beside you two?'

The old man reached up and pulled at the chicken-skin on his own scrawny neck.

'Not many,' he said. 'Our grandchildren – Léontine is down there at the refectory, serving Bryant his dinner. Vincent is over there somewhere.' He jerked his thumb at the hillside. 'Picking grass or catching rat. They got him tending stock mostly. Thérèse, our oldest grandchild – you remember Thérèse?'

'Of course,' said Emile. 'When I left, she was hired out in town to the jeweller.'

'That's right,' Angélique replied. 'She spent nine year wiping his mother filthy old Béké bung-hole – but at least his wife taught her to read, that's something. Then a few month back she got hired on again. Now, she works for Governor Melville himself.'

Emile tilted his head. I could tell that this interested him.

'The English Governor?'

'*Wi*,' said Angélique. 'In his kitchen and sometimes at his own self table.'

Emile frowned.

'I see. What about the nurses? Marie-Rose? And Joseph? And LeJeune?'

'Well – LeJeune is hired out too,' said Chevallier. 'Three hurricane season agone. She works now for a French family over in Megrintown. Serving table and dusting their silver and tumpty-tum whatnots.'

'And Céleste?' I asked. 'Where is she?'

Emile glared at me, whiles the old couple exchanged a look I couldn't fathom.

'Oh,' said Chevallier. 'She's still here at the hospital. She's – eh—'

My brother interrupted.

'But what about Marie-Rose and Joseph?'

Chevallier sat back and a shadow passed across his face.

'Well, that's not so good.'

He went on to explain that Joseph – father to my playfere Vincent – had been demoted to field hand soon after the invasion. But at the turn of that year, just before the last harvest, he had been found in a tree, down at the plantation. He had hung himself. And Marie-Rose had been pulled out of the river a few month afterward. They reckon she had drowned her own self and the baby in her belly.

'You see, Bryant and Bell hardly flog much,' said Chevallier. 'The whip stops people working. So they use – other punishment.'

'Like what?' Emile asked. 'Collars? Those bilboes?'

Chevallier looked uncomfortable. He glanced at me and shook his head.

'Well, sometimes – but – worse than that.'

'*Di mwen*,' said Emile.

The old man stared at the ground.

'Hard to say. Bad things.'

Clearly, he was not about to divulge more in my presence. A mood of gloom descended. We sat there awhile, nobody speaking, until Angélique got to her feet.

'Well – you boys want fed, I suppose?'

Chevallier grab her hand to detain her.

'Listen, *ché*. If we all creep off on Christmas Eve, after dark, we'd be gone long before those Goddams even wake up and notice.'

The old woman sucked her teeth again as she pulled away from him and shuffled off behind the kitchen. We watched her go, then Chevallier spoke to Emile in an undertone:

'Bryant and Bell tipple most nights. The doctor is invited to dine with this one and that about the island. Meanwhile old lonesome Bell staggers off into town for the billiards. Most Saturday, both of them so full of Kill-Devil and wine, you could drive five hundred hungry goat through the valley, they be none the wiser.'

A disembody voice came from behind the kitchen:

'Do not talk STUPIDNESS.'

Chevallier cracked his knuckles.

'Christmas Eve, they'll both be over at the Anglade place in the hills. Old Monsieur Anglade stayed on after the invasion, kept his estate, and he still has his Christmas soirée every year. Bryant and Bell will be there. Last Christmas, they got drunk as fiddlers. Of course, we are not invited to the dance. Be lucky if we get a day of rest.'

'Talking of that,' said Emile. 'Why are the hand working today? It's Sunday.'

Chevallier blew air through his lips.

'These days, if they fail to finish a task, they have to make up for it by going out again on Sunday. So, on top of everything, they have no time to tend their provision ground. They have to do it whenever they can, mostly at night. These tum-tum English been working us to death.'

Angélique return to the fire and dropped a few handfuls of leaves in the pot.

'Listen, *ché*,' said Chevallier. 'Just think how it might be if we went with these boy here. No more speaking English, *tou ça bordel*. I could see my sister. And Augustin – the Fathers would make him a nurse again.'

Angélique cast him a filthy look.

'Not to mention you go back to fishing,' said she. 'All day lie slugging in a boat.'

'Oh, now, *ché* . . .'

'Who's head driver down there now?' my brother asked.

'Saturnin,' said Chevallier. 'Nobody likes him but the field hand do what he says.'

'Well,' said Emile. 'If he decides to go with us, the rest might follow. I need to talk to him, sooner the better. Is there a watchman down there after dark?'

'Just Old Raymond. Keeps an eye on their produce ground. No Béké watchmen except Bell himself. He likes to sneak around the tumpty-tum plantation, trying to catch people doing what they ought not, spies on them making *chouc-chouc* in the bushes.'

There was silence for a moment. My brother stared into the flames.

'What do you think? Would the field hand want to leave here?'

'Some of them are old,' said Angélique. 'Some dragging weights and collars. Where is the boat?'

'Petit Havre,' said Emile.

'All the way up there? With children and babies? No matter how bad it is here, I doubt most of them would take the risk. I could hardly walk there myself with my knees.'

'We could go in the old row-boat, *ché*,' said Chevallier. 'I can fit four, maybe five, in there. Won't take long to row to Petit Havre. You won't have to walk.'

'Talking stupidness again, old man. That boat is locked up. No man can get in the boat-house without the key.'

Chevallier gave Emile a wink.

'For true,' said he. 'Without the key no man can get in. But what about the man who knows where the key might be? What about him?'

Just then, we heard the sound of someone else approaching from the hospital, someone singing soft-soft. Emile jumped up, grabbing the satchel.

'Who's that?' he whispered.

Angélique was watching him, a gleam in her eye.

'Your old sweetheart,' said she, then called out: 'Is that you, Céleste?' She turn back to my brother. 'You must be all exagitated to see her, Mandingo.'

Emile strode away from the fire just as a figure emerge from the trees, carrying a lantern. It was indeed Céleste, in a pale head-wrap with dark stripes, a light shawl draped about her shoulders. She glanced at me – apparently without recognition – then she notice Emile and came to a dead stop. He stare back at her and I saw the two of them exchange a look of pure anguish. Céleste reached out to him with one hand, her mouth half-open as though to speak but no sound came from her lips. Emile appear to waver for an instant but then I saw his gaze drop to her waist. Something passed across his face – as though whatever he dreaded was now confirm – then he span around and off he went down the goat track, striding away until he was swallow by the night.

By this time I was on my feet, yet rooted to the spot, my heart beating so hard it hurt my chest. It was so long since I had seen Céleste. And there she was, just as I remembered. She step further into the yard, her head held in the air like a couresse-serpent might swim a river. Yet, her eyes were brim-full of tears; I could see them glisten in the lamplight. I felt that old sensation again, like a hot candle melting inside me.

Angélique called out to her.

'*Bonswa, ché. Vien manjé.* Come and eat.'

Céleste shook her head.

'*No mèsi,*' said she, softly, in her own dear voice. 'I'm not hungry. *Mwen pa fin.*'

She made her way toward the nearest hut, a sound construction with a well-trim *bagasse* roof. As she reached up to unhook a hanging lamp, the shawl slipped off her shoulders and I caught a glimpse of her belly: big and round and tight as a fat melon, pushing out the front of her skirts. That was all I was able to see before Céleste stepped into her cabin and close the leaves of the door.

Chapter Twenty-One

The old couple began to exchange all manner of significant look: Angélique pursed her lips and shook her head whiles Chevallier made one-handed chop-chop motions at his throat. There followed a sort of consultation, of eyes only. Hard to tell what they were communicating.

Angélique called out to me, her voice too bright and cheerful.

'*Vien ché*. Sit down now and eat.'

They began to serve themselve from the cooking pot but I just stood there, obstupified. A moment previous, I could have dog down a leper lung but my hunger had vanish. For true, the old couple might answer any question I had on the subject of Céleste and her belly. Yet I was disincline to enquire. My brother and Céleste and our two dead mothers had been like family to each other – moreso than we ever were with this Arada pair and their offspring. To consult them for tittle-tattle seem like a failure of sorts: as though we had been fighting a battle and now my side had lost.

Céleste remain shut away in her cabin. I could see light behind the little jalousie and wondered what she might be doing in there. It occur to me that she knew my brother at once but – apparently – had fail to recollect me. No doubt, I had done some growing and changing since I quitted Fort Royal six years agone. Céleste could hardly be blame for not recognising my face but it stung that she might have forgotten me. And yet, there she was herself, transformed, getting baby, perhaps seven or eight month into her term. Her obvious condition made me feel betrayed in a way that, back then, I could not understand. Worst of all, the sight of her had sent my brother into a state of turmoil. Without him, I grew ill at ease, sensing myself to be expose. At any rate, I could bear to stay there no longer, thus I set out across the yard to follow him.

Angélique glanced up from her calabash.

'Mm-hmm, go fetch him,' she said. 'But careful now. Watch out for Addison Bell. You can tell him by his hat, cocked hat, made of straw. He'll eat you for supper then shit you out into a pot.'

I fled the yard, her words ringing in my ears as I set out along the goat track. My guess was that Emile would head for the plantation quarters and cross the river at the new bridge. Thus, I more or less retraced our steps from before, except this time, alone. The moon had yet to rise entirely. Sometimes the stars were enough to light my way but every otherwhile it fell so dark beneath the trees that I stumbled. My ears strain to discern any sound beyond the massed flutes and recorders of a million frogs and insect. Now and then, fireflies sparkle past my face like fragments of charcoal carried on the breeze. They say even a cripple likes to walk *au clair de la lune* but on that night every shadow held a threat. I kept spinning around to check the path behind me. Of course, it was not *La Diablesse* I feared, none such superstitiosity – the Fathers had taught me better than to pay heed to old-wife tales. Neither was I scared of serpents for Grenada has no venomous snake, just cribo and the like. No tiger, lion or wild beast. Only dogs and men, and a peck of English Béké ones at that.

At a fork in the path I paused, trying to pluck up courage to head down to the plantation. Huge branches loomed over me, black against the stars. Whiles I stood there, deliberating, three plaintive hoots floated down from the slope above: 'Who? Who? Who?' Some might mistake those calls for a mountain dove but I knew otherwise. No doubt in my mind, this bird was my brother. I whooed back and headed uphill toward the source of the signal. Soon enough, I found him seated beneath an old campèche tree, jabbing a stick in the dirt. He greeted me with a furious whisper:

'Where do you think you're going?'

'To find you. I thought you went to see Saturnin.'

'Just wanted to sit here awhile and think.'

'What's the matter with you?'

He gave no answer to that, only an angry sniff. I threw myself down beside him.

'How did you see me in the dark?' I asked.

He gave a laugh in the back of his throat.

'No need to see. You make more racket than a goat dancing on a tin trunk.'

Despite my youth, I knew it was just his wounded pride that made him chastise me: something to do with Céleste and her belly, matters I did not yet fully comprehend. In my bountiful mercy, I decided to refrain from vexing him with further reference to Céleste – at least, that was before he carried on:

'You walk around like an old woman gone to market, panting and puffing. You might as well jangle your bracelets and sing to the trees and sky.'

I shot back at him.

'Well, if I'm an old woman, you're a mouse. Why run off like that? Did you know she is getting baby?'

He held his hand up to my face, turned away.

'No more of that word.'

'What? Baby?'

'There you go again. That's enough now, Lucien. Go back to quarters.'

I kicked out my leg, disconsolate, begging him:

'Don't make me stay with those old Arada. Let me go with you.'

Emile set the satchel of herbs in my lap.

'I'm sick and tired carrying these. Take them back to the huts.' He fumbled in the bag then withdrew the Power of Attorney and tucked it into the pouch around his neck. 'Tell them I'll be back soon.'

'Do I have to?'

'And be polite. They're old people. They carry on sometimes but that's just how they are, those old Arada. They had a hard life.'

'Eating dogs,' I said.

'They don't eat dogs. You ever see them eat a dog?'

I thought about it and made no reply.

'Well then,' said Emile.

'Everybody knows they eat dogs,' I muttered.

'Talking stupidness. Now, will you be careful?'

'*Wi.*'

Yet still he hesitated, hacking at the dirt with his stick. I could smell the stale salt of him, feel the heat rising from his skin. Eventually, he spoke again:

'Did you – did you talk to Céleste?'

'No. She went in her hut.' After a while, I found the courage to ask: 'So you knew about this – the – baby?'

'Only rumours. I had to see for myself. And stop saying that word.'

'Who is the father? Do you know?'

The stick he was holding snapped in two with a loud crack. He tossed aside the broken pieces and stood up.

'No. Go and eat something. I'll see you back at the huts.'

He started downhill, toward the river. I listen carefully as he went, hoping to hear some trace of him above the racket of the night – one breath or a footstep – but he made no more sound than a shadow. Within a twinkling, he was gone.

Never once had I seen him so discomposed. My brother was known for his steady head. Now, he seemed off the hooks and high-strung. It made me sick with nerves.

Something scuttled in the dirt behind me and I jumped up, sweating, armpits prickling, but I could see nothing beneath the trees. With Emile gone, I bethought myself very small there, alone on the hillside, beneath the vast Milky Way. The ground tilted neath my feet. I felt panicked and winded, as though someone had close their fist around my heart. Quick-sharp, I slung the satchel of herbs over my shoulder and headed back to the cabins on the side of the hill.

The yard look deserted; the remnants of the meal cleared away. I walked up to the ramshackle hut at the end and set the satchel inside. No sign of the old couple or Céleste though a light still burned behind the jalousie of her cabin. Hearing soft voices inside, I crept closer and was about to listen at the wall when the door flaps flew open and Angélique almost fell over me.

'Where's your brother?' she said, crossly.

'Gone to talk to Saturnin.'

Behind her, inside the hut, I could see an old smut-lamp on the table and Céleste, slumped in a chair. She gazed out at me, her face a mask of sadness.

'Shoo away from this hut now,' said Angélique, to me. 'I left some food for you in the kitchen, wrapped up.'

At that, Céleste hauled herself to her feet with the help of the rickety table. Her belly so big it made everything a simmy-dimmy.

'No,' she said. 'Let me talk to him. Come inside, Lucien.'

Chapter Twenty-Two

I step past Angélique and close the door flaps on her scowling face, leaving her outside. Céleste came toward me as I turned, opening her arms to embrace me. I was surprise when my cheek touched her throat. Beforetimes, I had stood no higher than her waist. Her swollen belly – solid and wide as a boulder – pressed against me. She smelled like vanilla. Then she step back, holding me by the shoulders to take a better look at my face. I could see the beat of the pulse in her throat; beads of perspiration on her upper lip.

'Forgive me for ignoring you, child. I was confuse, seeing your brother here after all this time, then him running off like that.'

Could this be true? Had she recognise me, after all? I wanted to speak up, to say something, but my mind had gone blanker than Canada snow. Rather than stare at her, I glanced about at the few stick of furniture: two touchwood chair, the lamp on the table, a thin mat on the floor; other than that the hut contained only a few female garment hanging from nails on the wall.

'I want to hear your news, of course,' Céleste said. 'But later. Just tell me now, is it true? Did the Fathers send you? Do they really want Emile to take us to Martinique?'

'Me and Emile. Yes.'

'In secret?'

'Correct.'

She gave me a searching look as she lowered herself into her seat. As for me, I found it hard to contemplate her without dropping my gaze to her belly. I wanted to ask: who is he? What is the name of the man who has put this thing inside you?

'You're sure it's not Emile himself?'

Her question startle me.

'What?'

'This notion to take us to Martinique – is Emile behind it? Is it just his idea?'

'*Absoliman pa.*'

'How can you be sure? Were you there when the Fathers spoke to him?'

'Of course. He spoke to us both together – Cléophas.'

'You swear on that?'

'I was there in the morgue the whole time, I swear.'

She looked perplex.

'And you haven't run away?'

'No. The Fathers are building a new distillery. They need more hands to build it and they need more sugar, more money, more slave. And they cannot afford to buy new. Cléophas says you all belong to them since the old days. They just want you back.'

Nothing I said seem to reassure her. She kept staring at me with the same anxious expression, a deep line between her eyebrows. I wanted to stroke it away. Now that I could see her face more clearly, it struck me that she had been crying. Her eyes seemed larger than usual, swollen and glistening. The way the lamplight hit her cheek-bones and forehead, she seem to glow.

'And how does Emile propose we get away in secret?' she said. 'Some forty slave? Does he think we can fly?'

I felt glad she had ask this for it gave me a chance to play the big Don Diego. Pulling myself to full height, I set my hand on my hip and rested my foot on the spindle of the second chair, taking my ease like a Béké planter.

'Well, there is a way to do it. We go to Petit Havre, not to town. Too busy down there day and night, we'd be caught before we made it to the carenage. No, we go after dark, through the forest, avoid the road.'

'With old people, people in shackles? Some with babies? And me, like this?' She gestured at her own self. 'All in the pitch dark? Is madness.'

I dusted off my fingers to show her how easy it might be done.

'Like eating pastry,' I said. 'I could do it myself.' Though, for true, it's unlikely I could have found the way alone. That afternoon, I had paid scant attention to our route since Emile knew where to go. I just followed him, more or less, and mostly failed to note the landmarks and so forth. Howsomever, I was loath to seem uncertain or childish to Céleste and so concluded: 'We can get to Petit Havre, *pa ni pwoblèm.*'

'Lucien, *ché*, listen. No matter where we go from, this is danger-ous. Taking us all halfway up the island. We might get caught. He could . . . it could get us all killed.'

'We won't be caught,' I told her. 'Like I said, we go through the forest.'

She sighed.

'Well, let's see. I need to talk to your brother.'

With that, her gaze fell to the swell of her belly. This might have been the moment to ask her about it but I found myself struck dumb, any question I had clogged in my throat. Presently, she looked up at me.

'Like what?'

'Like a *zigizi* trapped in a cup. Was he like this when you left? I never saw him so agitated. He seems crazy.'

'He's not crazy, he's—' I stop myself.

'What? What is he?'

'You know what he is.'

She sighed again and the light in her eyes dimmed as though a cloud had passed across the face of the moon.

'But . . . the Fathers will keep him after this, yes? If we go to Martinique – me and him – we would both be at the hospital, in St Pierre, is that so?'

I recalled Cléophas in the morgue, his vague promise that the Fathers might grant Emile his freedom or buy him back and let him set up quarters with Céleste.

'Hard to tell,' I said. 'They might keep him – but they might just send him back to the Dominicans in St Marie.'

'How far is that from St Pierre?'

'A long hike. Impossible to get there and back in a day.'

Not that I wanted to hurt her feelings exactly. But the way she had said 'me and him' without a thought for any other person made my inners ache. A far-away look crept into her eyes. She rubbed her hands across her face.

'Go and eat now, *ché*,' she told me. 'Get some rest.'

Some things never change. Back in the old days, she was forever telling me to do this, do that. I just stood there, biting my cheek.

'We can talk more tomorrow, Lucien. You can tell me about your life in St Pierre. I miss you so much. I thought of you every day. Come here.'

When I made no move, she reached out and took my hand.

'Little britches,' she said. 'My little britches. You're so tall now. You'll soon be a man before you know it.'

Well, she may as well have spat in my eye. I dropped her hand, took a step back.

'I am a man, already,' I told her.

She put her head on one side as she contemplated my face.

'Perhaps you are,' she said. But her last words to me were: 'Take care of yourself, child. And tomorrow don't go getting yourself in the *mèd*.'

Chapter Twenty-Three

No sign of Chevallier or his woman outside in the yard but I could see a dim light burning in their big cabin. In the open kitchen, I found the food Angélique had left, wrapped in banana leaf, some cold fish and plantain. I stood there and dog them down. As my eyes became accustom to the gloom under the kitchen roof, I began to make out the figure of a fellow lying near the embers of the fire. Something familiar about him. For true, he resemble my former playfere Vincent. I tiptoed closer and knelt down for a good look. It was him, no question. He appear to be asleep. Vincent was a few years older than me and apparently full-grown now but I would have known him anywhere. In one hand, he clutched a flask of Kill-Devil; in the other, a monster crab – long *kickeraboo* by the stench.

I was about to leave my old friend to his rest when he open his eyes and stare straight at me. Then he gave a yawn and murmured:

'*Gwan-mè* said you came back.'

'*Me vwala*,' I replied. 'Come to take you to Martinique.'

He yawned again.

'So they tell me.'

'Sent by the Fathers. I'm the only man they trusted.'

Vincent let fly a belch.

'What about your brother? They sent him too.'

'Correct. But mainly they wanted me for the job. Your friend smells bad.'

Vincent look puzzled for an instant then gave a reeling glance at the dead crab in his hand. He must have been drunk as an Emperor.

'Found him on the road,' he said.

'Where did you find the Kill-Devil?'

'Tails,' said he.

'Where is Tails?'

A laugh exploded out of him such that the sweet musk of rum hit me in the face.

'Rat tails. You kill enough rat and show the doctor the tails, he gives you taffey.'

'You get your Christmas taffey soon,' I told him.

'Not soon enough. I wanted it tonight.'

He drop the crab and stash the flask in his pocket. Then he closed his eyes. It occur to me that within the past year his father Joseph had hung himself from a tree. No wonder he sought the sweet oblivion of rumbullion.

'Come on,' I said. '*Dodo.* Let's put you on your mat.'

However, Vincent took exception to being roused. He swung at me with his fists as though he no longer recognise me, ergo I soon gave up and let him rest where he lay.

'What is he like?' I asked. 'This Dr Bryant?'

Vincent gave a long sigh.

'You don't want to know. Him and Bell – they are bad as each other.'

'Your *gwan-pè* said something about them not flogging.'

'Sometimes they make Saturnin do it. But mostly, they find other ways.'

'Like what?'

'Nail your ear to a wall. Bell did that last night to Augustin.'

'I know. But what else? Chevallier refuse to tell us.'

'Bell likes to cut toes, chop them off with an axe. Cuts hands. The week he got here, he cut the hand off Polidor for eating cane.'

'What about the doctor?'

Vincent swore hard.

'His favourite punishment he calls "Martial Medicine". You want to know? Well, here it is.'

He took a deep breath and let it out again, slow. Then he told me. It was a punishment first carried out on a man-nurse known as Martial, hence the name. Soon after Bryant arrived in Grenada, Martial had attempted to run away but he had only got as far as the carenage when they caught him. He was drag back to the hospital and Bryant had him taken down to the mill. First, they tied him up in the bilboes, trussing his head so he couldn't move. Then they forced old Choisie to excrement in his mouth after which they gagged Martial for five hours and wired his mouth shut.

'Once they make you do that, you are broken,' said Vincent. 'Five or six times now, they have done it, to different field hand. That's how they punish my father.'

'What did he do?' I asked. 'Why was he punished?'

'For eating leftovers from the hospital kitchen,' Vincent replied. 'No question, he was never the same after that. Killed himself a few week later.'

I just sat there, not knowing what to say. Who could imagine such a punishment? It was unthinkable cruelty. To lose a toe might be preferable.

'You see?' said Vincent. 'You wish I hadn't told you now.'

He rolled over onto his hands and knees and from there thrust himself upright, almost – but not quite – falling as he lean down to grab the crab. Then he weaved across the yard to one of the middle cabin and hauled himself up the step and inside. When I followed him to the threshold, he was scrabbling around in the dark. After a while, he appeared in the doorway, a small burlap sack in his hand.

'I'm not going,' he said.

Still reeling from what he had just told me, I found it hard to take in.

'Not going where?'

'Not going to no Martinique, be a slave all over again for those monk. French or Englishman. Makes no difference. I'm getting out of here.'

'Where to?'

He glance toward the high forest, somewhere out there in the dark.

'Going to find the Maroon. Lucien, my friend, *boug mwen*, I intend to stay here in this island, hide out and cause some trouble about this place for these Goddams.' He laughed: 'Hee hee!' Then he grab my shoulder and breathed rum into my face. 'But keep quiet. Say nothing to my *gwan-mè* or *gwan-pè*. Not my sister either. Less Thérèse knows the better, then if anyone asks her, she need not tell a lie. So you must keep your mouth shut, *kompwan?*'

'*Wi.*'

He held onto the door frame as he clambered out of the hut and down the steps.

'*Ovwè*, Lucien. Sorry for running off when you just got here.'

'No need to go now. We leave on Christmas Eve. Stay until then.'

He thought for a moment, then said:

'No. If I wait that long I – I might lose heart. Here – take this.' He thrust the stink-crab into my hands. '*Bon chans*, Lucien. Good luck.'

He grab the back of my neck and pull me toward him, pressing his forehead against mine. Then – as though the ground beneath him was a tilting deck on the high seas – he staggered like a sailor out of the yard, away from the quarters, toward the back of Hospital Hill and the mountains beyond.

Chapter Twenty-Four

Hard to say how long I stood there, staring after Vincent into the darkness, trying to take in what he had told me about Bell and Bryant, their gruesome methods of punishment. Some cloud came creeping across the stars, bringing with them the threat of rain. Presently, the smell of fishrot began to turn my stomach and so I threw the crab into the embers of the fire. Deciding to try and get some rest, I turn toward the ramshackle hut and almost leapt out of my shirt at the sight of a silent figure looming toward me out of the night. *La Diablesse!* No, it was my brother. Mary and Joseph! He could out-slink a cat.

'Where's Céleste?' he asked, abruptly.

The light had gone out behind her jalousie. I pointed at the little cabin.

'In there. She wants to see you.'

Emile ground his jaws together, chewing nothing but his own pegs. Then he set off across the yard. Upon reaching the cabin he paused and rubbed his hands all over his face like a madman. I had just begun to wonder whether he might have lost both heart and mind when – at last – he climb the step and tap the wall with his fingertips.

'Céleste . . . *se mwen.*'

After a short pause, I heard movement behind the door, then one of the door leaves opened a crack and my brother slipped inside. The flap closed and then – silence.

By and by, I wandered over to idle in that vicinity. I could hear the murmur of voices inside the cabin but they spoke so low it was impossible to hear their words, hence my eavesdrop short-lived. At least the two of them were talking. Perhaps if he spoke to her, Emile would compose himself and stop acting jumpy as a cricket.

I was about to go and get some rest when all at once the murmurs in the little cabin grew louder and more agitated. Then tout and suite, my brother came storming out and down the step, leaving the doors flapping. I heard Céleste say:

'Wait – listen, *ékout-mwen*—'

But my brother strode across the yard, all set to disappear down the shortcut to town, a steep track through woodland. I hurried over and intercepted him at the edge of the trees.

'Wait. What's the matter? *Côté ou ka allé?* Where you going?'

He spoke in my ear.

'I can't stay here. I'm going to find LeJeune and Thérèse, see if they want to come with us.'

'You should rest. Wait for dawn.'

He kept staring down at the hospital, tugging at his own hair and breathing through his nose like an agitable horse. Despite the sultry night, he was shivering. I had never seen him in such a mistempered frame of mind. With Emile unhinged, the very fabric of the world might unravel. If only I could get him to lie down and rest, he might collect himself.

'Listen,' I told him. 'You're dead on your feet. Wait a few hours and I'll go with you, *pa ni pwoblèm*. We'll go before dawn, whiles Céleste and the rest still asleep. We'll be gone by the time these macaroons sit up and scratch their tail-bone.'

Something in what I said must have struck him – perhaps the prospect that we might be gone before Céleste awoke. I saw him waver and took his arm.

'Come now, let's lie down for a few hour.'

He allowed me to guide him to the ramshackle hut, barely no-
ticing where we went. His eyes remained open but he fail to see in
front of him, too busy staring at all the thoughts of Céleste whirling
about in his mind.

Inside, the cabin was musty and blacker than a blind man holy-
day. Leaving the door open for air, I scrabbled around in the dark
whiles Emile slumped in a corner. No blanket in the place, just an
old white pinafore hanging on a nail and some damp mouse-eaten
burlap on the floor. I draped the apron across Emile but saw at once
a pale flash in the gloom as he tossed it aside. His words came to me
out of the dark.

'Be sure and rouse me at dawn.'

'Of course. Soon as the *'ti gounouys* fall asleep, I wake up.'

A few raindrop began to patter on the roof and, presently, the
heavens opened. I peered outside. The deluge lash the earth all
around the quarters, thundering upon the cane-trash over our heads.
I reached out and pull the door flaps shut so that we were tight-tight
inside. The racket of rain went on and on, battering the roof. It was
like lying inside a giant drum. I heard my brother shifting, restless.

'Emile? What did Saturnin say?'

'Oh – he'll talk to the field hand. Tell us tomorrow what they
want to do.'

'Then what?'

He gave a bitter laugh.

'What does it matter? We're all dog-meat in the end.'

We lay there without a word for a while until, at last, I found the
nerve to ask:

'And what about Céleste? Did you find out – anything . . . ?'

I heard him roll over to face the wall.

'No,' he said. 'Now – *dodo* – go to sleep. *Bònnuit.*'

How was I suppose to look out for him if he never confided in me? He was like a closed-up box within a box with locks. A few days previous, I would have put my life in his hands, no question. Now, I'd scarce trust him to watch a tether goat, never mind lead a motley gang of slaves up-island in a perilsome escape. He might well be unfit for our task – and it was all the fault of Céleste and her belly. At the very least, I resolve to keep a close eye on him next day. Whether he liked it or not, I would go with him when he went to see LeJeune and Thérèse.

I curled up on the bare floor, contriving how I might persuade Emile to let me accompany him, listening to him breathe and wondering if he had lost his mind entirely until, in the end, I dropped off the edge of the world into slumber, lulled senseless by the constant din of rain.

PART FIVE

Grenada

(SECOND DAY)

Chapter Twenty-Five

The following morning I awoke blear-eyed and confused, Emile no longer beside me. Light streamed in through the gaps in the boards. The rain had stopped and the heat of the day was well advance. Someone tap the door and a female voice murmured:

'Lucien? Vincent?'

My heart gave a jump at the thought it might be Céleste. However, when I sat up to push back the flaps, they swung open to reveal a thin girl, somewise older than me. Her head bare; her hair fixed up in plaits. She had a rip in her skirt but her petticoat and apron look clean.

'*Bonjou,*' said she.

'*Bonjou, Manzell.*'

She raised an eyebrow.

'*Se mwen.* Léontine.'

Well, I wouldn't have recognise her. Last time I saw Léontine, she was only peeny-weeny. She handed me a calabash full of cassava porridge.

'From Céleste,' she said.

Since I was hungry as a starve-gutted dog, I set to eat quick-sharp.

Léontine peer past me, into the hut.

'Is Vincent in there?'

'No. Where's Emile?'

'Gone to Megrin to see LeJeune.'

I scramble to my feet, nearly knocking over the porridge.

'What? When did he go?'

'Oh, long time since. You slept through both bells. But have you seen Vincent?'

'No.'

Awake less than a pig whisper and already I was out of sorts. Calling myself all kinds of fool for oversleeping, only to be left behind with women and girls. I tried to squeeze past Léontine, intending to head after Emile, but she block my path.

'Where you going? He will be half across the island by this time. He told us you're to stay here out of sight until he gets back.'

'Did he now?'

'Yes,' she said. 'I must go. The doctor breakfast plates need to be cleared, then I have to wash the floor of his chamber.'

Yet, instead of heading back to the hospital, she hurried across the yard and entered one of the other huts. As I sat down again to finish the porridge, my gaze fell on the satchel inside the doorway. The French doctor, Maillard, resided just down the road. It occur to me that I could run to his house and back in no time at all, deliver the herbs like Cléophas had commanded. Then we would no longer have to cart them everywhere. My brother might want me to hide away all day like a chicken-heart but I was too much the man to sit around doing nothing. No, sir. *Non mèsi.*

When Léontine return she had tied a ribbon around her throat – a faded, crease ribbon that look like it might once have serve to secure a parcel, but a ribbon nonetheless.

'We used to make dirt-pies together,' I said. 'Do you remember?'

'Of course. Everybody remembers you and your brother. Is he really going to take us to Martinique?'

I gave a dry laugh.

'Well now, I'm not exactly sure what he might do, in the immediate.'

'What kind of man is he?'

'Why do you want to know that for?'

'I just wondered. Does he have a woman in Martinique?'

'No. Leastwise, I doubt it.'

Most vexing, for some reason, she kept asking about Emile. I decided to change the subject.

'What about Céleste? Seems to me she's getting a baby. Who is her man?'

Léontine gave a careless shrug of her shoulder.

'*Di mwen*,' I said. 'She must have a man.'

Girl shook her head.

'But if you had to guess – what would you say? Who is the father of this baby?'

'The English doctor,' she replied. 'Bryant.'

I just about leapt out of my linen.

'Why would you say that?'

She shrugged her shoulder again, gave her teeth a little suck.

'I see things. Hear things.'

'You saw her – with Bryant?'

'Not exactly. But everyone thinks it must be him.'

Split me! In my head, I heard the crack of the stick that Emile had snap with his bare hands. If he heard this story, like as not he would find Bryant and do the same to his neck. But before I could ask more, a bell rang down at the hospital.

'I have to go,' said Léontine. 'They're looking for me.' She began to walk away. 'If you see Vincent, tell him he's in big trouble. He fail to show for work this morning.'

'Wait,' I said. 'What you just told me about the doctor. Keep it to yourself.'

'Why?'

'Because if Emile finds out . . . if he starts any kind of mayhem with Bryant, this whole plan is shot, *kompwan*?'

She nodded then hurried off downhill, in the direction of the hospital, leaving me alone. Dazzling sunlight made everything appear bright and hard. A breeze drifted through the quarters at that instant and there seem to me nothing lonelier than the way it whisk the dead leaves around and stirred up the dust.

Chapter Twenty-Six

The Maillard residence stood about halfway along the High Road above town, situated on its own, atop a small inland bluff. Since we had mostly avoided highways the previous day, I resolve to continue in the same vein and pick my way downhill through the trees rather than on the road. Emile had taunted me for crashing about too loud, thus I vowed to try and make less noise. Hugging the satchel to my chest, I crept along on tiptoe, trying to breathe in silence – though as soon as I quitted the quarters, my nerves were all a-jangle and it was an effort to keep myself from panting.

Fortunately, I reach the Maillard place sans incident. The road outside the residence lay quiet and still, shimmering in the heat. Beyond and below the bluff, I could see Fort Royal and the carenage, blue-blue, almost close enough to touch. Plenty of ship down there, at anchor. The scents of swamp water and burnt wood drifted up on the warm breeze. Dogs barking in the distance, someone hammering, the odd shout of laughter. Of course, in my travels since those days I have seen some of the great cities – Quebec and Paris and, of course, London – but back then Fort Royal seem like a great metropolis to me and I would have given my right spleen for a closer look at the town. I had only set foot there once, on the day that Damascene took me to Martinique, but on that occasion, we had hurried through the streets so fast I scarce had time to take it in and what I witnessed of the place I mostly saw from the deck of the sloop as we set sail. It was tempting to go down there and witness for myself the bustle of the quayside and the parade ground.

However, I had already stretch the leash by leaving the quarters and so, with a sigh, I scuttled across the highway and through the garden gate.

Ignoring the foredoor, I crept around the back of the house and stepped up on the veranda to tap the jalousie, just how I use to summon Miss Praxède beforetimes. Everyone spoke of her as the housekeeper or *bonne* for Maillard. Nobody mention that she was – to all intent and purpose – his wife. He had bought her when first he came to the island and they had been together since. Praxède sometimes gave me a sweet glass of *d'leau pain* when I came to fetch the doctor, which happened whensoever the friars needed an extra pair of hands if, for instance, one of them fell sick or perished overnight (they had a terrible habit of dying).

In fact, the person who appeared in response to my tapping was not someone I recognised at all: a *petite cocotte* about sixteen years of age, wearing only a chemise and a flower in her hair. Her skin shone like mahogany. She open the door just a crack and commence to inspect me up and down, the look on her face like I had crawled out from some dirty-dirty hole.

'*Bonswa*, Miss Lady,' said I, with a bow.

She gave her teeth an indifferent suck. Her curls were short and her eyes damp and clouded. By the look of her, she might have been crying all day long.

'What d'you want, banana boy?'

'*Souplé*, may I speak with Monsieur Maillard?'

'Nn-nn. He's down in town, probably at that *salle de billiards*.' She had a lisp and the way she spat out the word '*billiards*' you might think she dislike the game. 'If you go down there you give him a message from me. Tell him that tomorrow he can cook his own damn food.'

I scratch my ear.

'Well now, do you really want me to tell him that?'

'Most certainly,' said she. 'What business is it of yours in any case?'

Rather than trust the bag of herb to this person – who struck me as a fickle type and unreliable – I could just run down express to the billiard hall and hand the jars over to Maillard in person, sound and safe.

'Never mind, Miss Lady. I'll go down there – but—'

'You do that,' said she.

I hesitated. For true, I had a raging thirst and was just in the mood for some *d'leau pain*, spiced up nice and sweet with cinnamon.

'Tell me, Miss Lady – what's your name?'

'Zabette.'

'*Enchanté, Manzell.* But – by any chance – is Miss Praxède at home this morning? Might I speak with her?'

'Not unless you a *zombie*.' When I look perplex, she said: 'That woman been gone to Kingdom-come since the Michaelmas.'

The door had crept open. A faint smell of burning wafted out. On a sudden, I grew dizzy.

'I'm – I'm sorry,' I said. 'Did she get sick?'

'Nn-nn. Shot dead.'

'What? Why?'

She pursed her lips at me and frowned.

'Why you so interested, banana boy?'

'I – I used to know her. I used to call here.'

Her expression soften somewise.

'Well – after he sold her, she ran off and then—'

'Wait – Maillard sold her?'

'Wasn't my fault,' said she. 'Nothing to do with me. I thought he should keep her. She was just getting old is all, near fifty, but

Pierre – Monsieur – he can't afford to feed two of us and he wanted a younger one. Are you going to the billiard hall?'

She press one hand to her side, frowning. The door had inch open further and I saw now that – beneath the chemise – she had a big belly. Another infant on the way. Seem like every female on the island was cooking a baby.

'Well, are you?' said she.

'Am I what?'

'Going to see Monsieur . . . only give him a different message. Just tell him – tell him there's a good dinner waiting for him at home.'

All sorts of distracted notion flicker through my mind. I thought: I never did see a billiard hall before. I thought: but his dinner is burnt. I thought: this girl here is the new Praxède. I thought: poor Praxède – gone *kickeraboo*.

'Who was it?' I asked. 'I mean to say – who bought her?'

Zabette tossed her head.

'One of those new Scotchmen – Mister Mac-Something.'

'And he killed her?'

'No, but she ran away and when they caught her she got herself shot in the back.'

'. . . Why did they not just give her a whipping?'

'Ah, you know, so many rascal been running off lately, Jésis-Maïa help them if they get caught.'

Just then, there was a great crash from somewhere in town, down by the quay, as though a cart had dropped a heavy load. The *blou-coutoum* set a dog to barking somewhere downhill and I must have flinched.

'*Kam-twa*,' said the girl. 'They keep him tied up. Are you sick?'

'What? No.'

'Then why do you want to see the doctor?'

I showed her the satchel.

'To give him this, from *les Frères de la Charité* in Martinique.'

She eyed the bag with interest.

'What's in there? Rum?'

I lifted the flap, to reveal the muslin-wrap jars.

'Just some herb, for medicine.'

'Phhh!' said she, disappointed. 'Well, you know where to find the billiard hall?'

She started to give me directions but as she spoke my thoughts began to drift. I imagined myself wandering through town, getting lost, then being stopped by drunken redcoats. I could picture them, standing in the middle of the street, belligerent, like roosters looking for a fight.

'– so then you turn left off the parade,' Zabette was saying. 'That's if you're facing the water—'

'Listen,' I said. 'If it's all the same to you – can I just leave these herb here, *souplé*? I should really get back to – eh—'

I gestured vaguely toward Hospital Hill. Zabette sucked her teeth again, this time in irritation. She pointed to the floor of the veranda.

'Put them there; I'll see he gets them.'

I set down the satchel.

'*A plus*,' said she and bessy-down but full of disdain. Then she shut the door.

For a short interval, I stood there, prepondering over what she had told me. Poor Praxède, sold on and shot for running away. Shot in the back.

Some creature was scuttling about in the space beneath the boards of the veranda: an agouti, perhaps, or a rat. I heard the sound of scratching and then a series of vile urgent squeaks, one upon the other, as though some small animal was being devoured alive. With a shiver, I step back down into the garden.

Laid out below me, there was Fort Royal: the parade square, and all the bustle of the carenage. Beyond the town, I could see the fort out on the promontory. All at once, I heard a great shout of laughter and a clang of steel from within the barracks, as though the Glasgow Greys might be in the midst of some kind of fighting tournament. With another shiver, I turned on my heel and instead of heading to town I hurried across the road and back into the woods.

Chapter Twenty-Seven

I had scarce gone any distance when I heard the sound of voices; male voices. Looking up, I saw – descending the path through the trees – two men. One I knew at once as the French physician Maillard, though his hair had turned entirely grey since last I saw him and his skin had acquired a yellow tinge. The other was less familiar but I recognise him from the previous day for it was the bacon-face Béké that I had encounter down at the river whiles waiting for Emile. He wore the same garments, same shirt, the broad-brim cloth hat. Neither man carried a gun and so I doubted they were on their way to hunt; rather, they had the air of gentlemen out for a morning promenade. They had notice me already and I could hear them converse in English as they descended the path.

'A half-breed there ahead,' said the stranger.

'Indeed,' Maillard replied.

'Do you know him?'

Maillard squinted down at me.

'It's hard to tell at this distance.' He stopped in his tracks and pointed into the undergrowth. 'Over there, sir, you'll see the other plant I told you about.'

Something deferential in his tone told me that the other man must be his superior – and English, for two Frenchmen, alone, would surely have spoke in their own tongue.

Whiles they paused, peering into the greenery, I had a brief instant to consider my position. Where they stood, I would soon be oblige to walk past them. Of course, I could have slipped away into the trees but that would appear suspect. Instead, hoping that the doctor might fail to recognise me, I dawdled up the track, trying to act unruffled, though my heart beat a taptoo in my breast. Alas, Maillard turn to watch me as I approached and then he swore under his breath:

'*Putain! Lucien? C'est toi?*' He glanced at his companion. *'Je m'excuse. C'est à dire* – I know this boy. Lucien? Is that you?'

As it was, I did my best to sound cheerful:

'Good day to you, sirs.'

The Englishman turn to Maillard.

'Who is this boy?'

'Oh, he used to live here. In fact, he may be of interest to you, Dr Bryant – he's living proof they can speak good English if they wish.'

And so – here was Bryant: the new superintendent of the hospital. He wipe the sweat from his brow, regarding me with interest.

'What a surprise, Lucien,' said Maillard, in his precise English. 'I thought you were in Martinique.'

'Indeed, sir. But the Fathers sent me here on your account, in fact. I have just been at your house to deliver some herb from them. Your girl took them in.'

Dark thoughts about poor Praxède flitted through my mind all the while and I fear they might show in my expression but Maillard seem not to notice. His face look more haggard than I remembered, his eyes dark and flinty.

'Ah! Really? Well, of course, I'm most grateful. I must write a letter of thanks to the Fathers. Perhaps send them some wine.'

'They would like that, sir.'

He turn to Bryant.

'You see, Lucien was born here at the hospital in the time of our predecessors, the Fathers of the Charity. A Scottish nurse-man of theirs took care of the boy, following the death of the mother, a

Mandingo female. This Scotch fellow raised him and fed him and so forth. And, as you can hear, he did learn to speak your language quite well. Most of the friars came to look on him as something of a pet, or so it seemed to me, and one of them took him to Martinique after the nurse died. An intriguing case, I'm sure you'll agree.' He regarded me again. 'I hardly recognise you, Lucien, you're quite grown.'

'Yes, sir. It's six Christmas, more or less, since I left.'

The Englishman – who had been eyeing me suspiciously all through this conversation – now spoke.

'This is the second time I've seen you loitering on hospital property, boy. What are you doing here? Do you have a pass?'

'Sir?'

'A ticket,' Maillard explained.

'Oh yes, sir.'

I took it from the pouch around my neck. Bryant glanced it over before returning it to me. He rubbed his lower lip tween thumb and forefinger whiles continuing to inspect me. Then he spoke to the French doctor.

'Is there any policy on this?'

Maillard narrowed his eyes.

'Policy? Perhaps, my English . . . I'm not sure I follow you.'

'All the Negroes and half-breeds and so forth that were left here by those Charity Fathers now belong to the English Crown. Surely then this boy must also . . .'

'Ah!' said Maillard and wagged his finger. 'I see where your thoughts have taken you, sir, but no. This boy belongs to the French friars in Martinique.'

I cannot express how alarmed I felt at the unexpected turn this conversation had taken. The blood pounded in my ears. It was all I could do not to run off at full fling.

'They took him there several years agone,' Maillard continued. 'Before you – ah – he was gone from here long before the – the change of regime.'

'But surely—' Bryant paused, pointing at me whiles he gathered his thoughts. 'Forgive me, Maillard, but—' He gestured over the hill. 'Those Negroes down on the plantation belong to us.' Then he waved his hand toward where the hospital quarters lay. 'And those up there belong to us.' His finger return to me. 'Why not this one? Surely he is hospital property – or he belongs to the Crown, at least?'

'No, no,' said Maillard. 'He belongs to the French. He's here simply on an errand. I imagine he will soon return to his masters in St Pierre.'

He looked at me, something approaching a warning in his eyes.

Tout and suite I said: 'Quite so, sir. I'm commanded to go back there directly.'

'In that case, why are you loitering here?' the Englishman demanded.

'Sir, I just delivered the herb to Monsieur Maillard. Now I must wait for the boat, sir.'

'When do you sail?'

'Tomorrow, sir.'

'I see.' His lips parted and stretched in an approximation of a smile. 'And where can we find you in the meantime?'

'Sir?'

'Where are your lodgings?'

'Oh – in town, sir. Near the – the carenage.'

'Where, exactly?'

'In rooms, sir, by the – by the billiard hall.'

'Who's the owner?'

I was struggling to think of a name when Maillard clicked his fingers.

'I know it,' said he. 'Run by that Spanish woman. Señora Franco, is that right? The place with the blue door?'

I just nodded, dumbly. Maillard turn to Bryant with a roll of his eyes.

'Terrible place, verminous. But, dear sir, allow me to show you this other plant. I'm expected for luncheon *chez* Mme. Bertrand and I've no wish to keep her waiting.' He drew Bryant off the path. 'It's a remarkable leaf. The hospital Negroes use it in cases of *mal d'estomac*. After you is manners.' He allowed the Englishman to step ahead of him with a last word to me as they picked their way into the undergrowth. 'Lucien, good day to you. I'm sure you have other errands to run on behalf of your masters.'

'Quite so, sir. Good day to you, sirs.'

I went up the track at the most sedate pace I could muster, all the while expecting Bryant to call out, 'Stop! Wait! Halt!' At one point, I glance back and was unnerve to see that – whiles the French doctor had bent down to pluck a leaf – Bryant stood motionless, staring up in my direction, regarding me like a cat might watch a juicy cutlet, a cutlet that is snatched away from neath his whiskers just before he can take a bite.

Chapter Twenty-Eight

Having no desire for any further *vis-à-vis* with inquisitive Englishmen, I hurried straight back to the hospital quarters. So far as I could see, the place still deserted. The cabin where Emile and I had slept was stuffy but I shut myself inside to await his return. I must have dozed off in the heat and fell away into a dream in which I was among many passengers on a sloop. The hull sat low in the water, low enough for those aboard to touch the waves. People kept dipping their hands in the ocean as though to test its temperature. All seemed well for a time until they pull their arms out of the water and then I saw that every one of their hands had been bitten or cut off. The stumps oozed thick red blood and the ship soon became awash with sticky gore.

In a hot panic, I open my eyes to find that Emile had returned. He sat perfectly still, his back against the wall of the hut. Grey mud cake both of his feet and his skin shone slick with sweat but other than that I could see no mark upon him. He had open the door and was staring out into the yard. A heavy stillness lay over the quarters. For a while, I stayed there, motionless, watching him. After my unsettling encounter with the English doctor, it was somehow tranquil to let my gaze rest upon my brother, the slow rise and fall of his chest. But I had to know if he was still half crazy. I sat up, somewise light-headed, perhaps because of all the blood in my dream.

'You look sick,' said Emile.

'I'm not,' I told him. 'Did you find LeJeune?'

'Mm-hmm. I had to wait and wait but in the end I found a way. She wants to come with us, for true. She has a bad master over there. But he promised her a ticket for Christmas Eve so *pa ni pwoblèm.*'

'How did you get to speak to her?'

'Bunch of flowers.'

'Flowers?'

'Correct. I pick flowers from the roadside and took them to the back door of the house, presented myself like a suitor, all bashful and shy, asking to see Miss LeJeune. While the house-boy went to fetch my sweetheart I wandered off far enough that LeJeune would have to come outside, so we could have a private conversation. And that's what happened.'

'What about Thérèse? Did you see her?'

'No. We sent a message into town this morning with one of the *porteuses*, telling Thérèse to come here tonight, if she can, to read the Power of Attorney to us and the field hand.' Here, he paused and glanced around the hut. 'Where's that satchel?'

My guts turned over. I had to admit then that I had gone to the Maillard place. Of course, Emile was displeased, not only that I had left the quarters, but that I had forgotten to bring back the bag which he had promise to return to Cléophas.

'You know what they're like about their goods and gear. Won't lend a thimble without wanting to know when they might get it back. Oh well . . . Did you see Maillard?'

For a twinkling, I did consider lying about my encounter with the two doctors, then thought better and told Emile about meeting them on the path, how suspicious Bryant had been, his questions about who owned me and where I was sleeping.

'Anything else to tell me?' said Emile. 'You bump into any soldiers? What about the Governor? You seen him on your travels? Did General Monckton invite you for tea?'

'It's not funny,' I croaked. 'That doctor will know me if he sees me again.'

'Well, he won't see you. Besides, you have your ticket.' He nudge my leg with his toe. 'What's the matter, *ché*?'

'Nothing. Only – we should get away from here quick-sharp.'

'That's the intention.'

'No, but – do we have to take all these slave? If they're sick or dragging chains, they'll slow us down. And the babies will cry, somebody might hear them. We need to decide who to take and who to leave behind.'

Emile gave me one of his looks.

'We're not leaving anyone,' he said. 'Whoever wants to come with us, we take them.' Then he stretched and sighed. 'Any messages for me,' he asked, apparently indifferent.

No doubt, he was mousing for news of Céleste. She appeared in my mind as she had been the night before. I could almost feel the swell of her belly pressed against me as we embraced, the scent of vanilla. Then I pictured her in the arms of Bryant.

'*Non*,' I replied.

Emile tip back his head and gave an elaborate yawn. He stretch his legs and shut his eyes, but I could see now that he was trembling.

'Well, if anyone wants to speak to me, they can come and find me.'

'Quite so,' said I. 'Best you stay here out of sight, in hiding.'

His eyes snapped open.

'I care not one fly-smut for hiding,' he said. 'You know me. I would stroll down there to that refectory, sit down – plain as day – whiles the Béké nurse-men are at supper—'

'For true, you would.'

'– put my feet up on the table, help myself to their wine. But I won't scuttle about the place like a spider on account of any female – or any man.'

'Correct,' said I. 'Exactly right.'

His words were naught but swagger yet it was a comfort to hear him bluster and brag – though we both knew in our hearts, it was only a sham.

Chapter Twenty-Nine

We emerge from the hut just as shadows began to rise up around the quarters. The sky glowed in shades of yellow and blue. Emile lit a smut-lamp and I set about making a fire, gathering up what dry kindling could be found and picking any salvable cinders out of the ashes. Howsomever, my construction refuse to ignite, no matter how much I blew on the smouldering twigs. Emile crouch down beside me and poked at my careful arrangement of combustibles.

'Want a piece of advice about laying a fire?' he said.

'Not really,' I replied.

'I might be tempted to get a few stick alight first,' he said. 'Then add the coal later, piece by piece.'

'You might be tempted?'

I was about to scoff in his face when he held up his finger and frown to silence me. Then he cup one hand to his ear and open his lips wide. In this manner, he listen for a while. At any other time the sight of him – squatting there, mouth agape – might have struck me as comical but my nerves were in fritters. No telling what he had heard. I held my breath but could detect no sound except the first *'ti gounouys*.

Emile pointed to where the path dip toward the plantation.

'Over there,' he mouthed. 'One man.'

Then, soft as a ghost, he took my hand and drew me behind the nearest cabin: a shadowy and dense-wooded spot. From there, we could see most of the narrow yard. Not a thing happen for a spell, save that a faint breeze caress my skin and the point of flame on the abandon lamp bent and flickered. Just as I began to wonder if Emile was imagining things, a lean figure emerge from the undergrowth on the far side of the quarters: a man, neither young nor old, naked from the waist up, his skin dark as the back of a cedar beetle. He peered warily about him as he advanced into the yard. Not a handsome fellow; I've seen more comely manicou, but his bearing proud. He walked cautiously across the open ground, darting glances to and fro: back into the trees and through the door of each hut he passed. As he drew closer, I saw that he was unshaven, his britches worn and soiled. He held a short whip in his hand. When he reach the kitchen, he came to a halt and gaze down at the flickering smut-lamp.

Only then did Emile step out from behind the hut, moving on velvet paws like a cat, such that the man fail to notice him until he spoke:

'*Bonswa*, Saturnin.'

The driver gave a start then his face cleared when he saw my brother. He drew himself up to his full – short – height and said, in a rasping voice:

'*Bonswa*, Emile.'

'You're early.'

'Belly-ache. I must go to the hospital, see a nurse.'

'Sorry to hear that, my friend,' said Emile. 'We can wait until you—'

His voice tailed away. I saw then that the driver had twisted his lips into a grin.

'There is no belly-ache,' he said. 'I'm never sick. A man has to be strong down there in the field. Only way to survive. I'm sure you understand what I'm talking about.'

He stared at my brother, a glint of sardonic humour in his eye.

No doubt, he thought we led a soft life. I chose that moment to step out from the shadows.

'*Bonswa*,' said I.

At the sound of my voice, the driver turned. His gaze moved over me like a fly walking then he turn back to Emile.

'This your brother?'

'Correct.'

Saturnin sniffed.

'What are you banana boys doing behind there? Shitting in high grass?'

'We heard you coming,' Emile replied. 'But you gave no signal.'

'I saw no need.'

'You could have been anybody.'

'Well, clearly, you boys are expert at hiding.'

Perhaps he meant to imply that we were cowards – or perhaps not. He tap the bull-whip against his leg. There was a pause in which nobody was entirely sure what to say or do. Then Emile found his manners.

'Well, my friend, I'm glad you are in good health. And what of your crops? Have you been able to tend your produce today?'

Saturnin sucked his teeth, dismissive.

'Never mind all that Mandingo palaver. I've no time for chit-chat. I came to tell you, I talk to them this morning, all of them.'

Seeing Emile look apprehensive, I spoke up in his stead.

'What do they want to do?'

Saturnin held out his hands to my brother, as though in appeal.

'You boys are the intelligent ones. What do you think they want?' Never mind the whip, I was beginning to understand why nobody much like this man. He glared at Emile. 'A few thing we want to know first. Some of them need to be assured that if we go with you it will be to toil for *les Frères*. They won't sell us on to some other master?'

'So far as I know,' said Emile. 'They just want their old slave back.'

'So – if we go with you – we would be growing cane? Not indigo – nobody wants to do that stink thing again.'

'No, they gave up on indigo a while back. Better money in sugar. You'll be growing cane and some of you might learn to work a distillery.'

'Making rum?'

'Yes, they want to fashion a new kind, a white rum. Most of you will tend fields but Lefébure wants to build a new distillery and he needs people to work it.'

Saturnin was clearly not averse to the prospect of making Kill-Devil. His eyes began to gleam but he soon grew combative again, perhaps somewise shifty.

'Well, that's all very well but we need to know – they are wondering, all of them – who will be chief field hand over there? If the Fathers have slaves already – then they have a driver.'

'Caesar,' said I. 'He's as fair as can be.'

Saturnin cast nary a glance in my direction; he was only interested in my brother.

'So – who would be chief driver? This Caesar – or me?'

'Well, now.' Emile cleared his throat. 'I did discuss that with Cléophas. He wants Caesar to work the existing fields with his gang as usual. You and your people will be set to clear and plant new fields. But you'll drive your own-own hands; Caesar will drive his.'

'What about once the new fields are planted? What happens after that?'

'Same-same,' Emile replied. 'You drive your gang and tend your own field.'

He said it straight-face but so far as I could remember Cléophas had not mention drivers and who worked what field. Perhaps that was one of the subjects that they had discuss down at the Sugar

Landing whiles I flew about like a damn foo-foo, begging for fishes and rum.

Saturnin rubbed his hand back and forth across his whiskers then asked about provision ground. Emile told him that the Fathers had set aside land for crops.

'You'll have plenty to eat. Cléophas told me to make sure you knew that. And he says any punishment they mete out will be fair.'

At these words, Saturnin gave a dry laugh.

'He would say that. As if it was Paradise here in Grenada with them before. That old Father Damien, remember? He knew how to put stripes on a body. Oh, but – I must apologise. No need to tell you boys about the Pestle.'

He made it seem as though this mention of our father was accidental, yet I wondered whether he had done it express. We might yet come to fisticuffs. Emile looked as though he had a quid of tobacco on the chaw; his jaw worked, hard and tight; his eyes glittering: none of it a good sign.

Saturnin carried on as though oblivious.

'Well – fair punishment and provisions: I'll tell them that. What about dancing?'

Emile looked at him, his features a blank.

'Dancing?'

'These cockroaches – Bryant and Bell – have forbid all the French dances. The Gavotte. The Saraband. Will the Fathers let us dance French again, like before? I like that old French dancing.'

Though clearly exasperated, my brother kept his countenance.

'Oh yes. Martinique is a French island again. Everything French.'

'The Englishmen all gone,' said Saturnin, sounding decisive but all the same looking to Emile for confirmation.

'More or less. They speak French there, like always.'

Saturnin brightened.

'Good. One more thing. The field hand get their Christmas rum tomorrow night, after work. Most of them have tickets to visit sweethearts or family in different parts of the island. Half won't be back until late the following night. Do we have to go tomorrow or could it wait until St Stephen? That way they can have a few day of rest and see their family, say goodbye.'

'*Absoliman pas*,' said Emile. 'Think about it. If they go drinking tomorrow night and visiting around the island, half of them will tell their family they're leaving, everybody saying goodbye and crying, wailing or – just as bad – they'll invite their family to come with us. Every damn slave on the island will hear about it and then it takes just one person to let slip and the troops will be down on top of us before you can spit. Either that or we might end up with too many to fit the boat.'

Saturnin rubbed his whiskers.

'Now you explain it like that . . .'

'Besides, Cléophas won't wait longer than first light on Christmas Day. We have to go tomorrow self. Can you stop them getting into the rum? The last thing we want is whip-cat niggers crashing around the forest.'

'I can try. But there's a couple – the younger men – a couple of hotheads.'

'Anybody drunk will be left behind. So tell me – how many want to go?'

The driver frowned, thinking.

'Hard to say. Some are scared to get caught. They are afraid of being punish. But a few of them still have kinsfolk left behind in Martinique. They're the ones that want to go most, them that have family over there.'

'That's to be expected,' Emile said. 'Did you explain the Power of Attorney?'

'The what?'

'That parchment I showed you. They have to know about it.'

'I'll tell them, word for word.'

'How can you tell them word for word – you can't read.'

Saturnin gave my brother the dead-set with his eye. No doubt, he took a stitch at this reminder of his own shortcoming.

'Thérèse will be here tonight,' said Emile. 'She can tell us if the English Governor sign the paper or not. I'll bring her down to the plantation and she can read it to them. Then they can weigh up the risk, make up their own mind.'

The driver groaned.

'You really have to read it to them? If Bell or any Béké-man finds us there, you with some document, all the way from Martinique—'

'It won't take long. You can post lookouts.'

'– everyone stood talking like a public rencontre, we'll have some explaining to do. Besides, you try getting those slave all in one place together. They wander off, catching rats, making *chouc-chouc* in the bushes. And if you want lookouts, then they won't be there to hear your damn document . . .'

'Well then, put children on lookout,' said Emile, through his teeth. 'I'll bring Léontine to help. Just get as many of them together as you can. Men and women. Do any of them know how to get to Petit Havre on the goat track?'

'Most of them never left the plantation.' Saturnin pulled up his britches, making himself taller by about half an inch. 'But I know the way. Use to visit a girl up at Gouyave if I could get a ticket. Hee hee! Went there plenty of time, over the hills.'

'I remember,' said Emile. 'You stop visiting that girl back when I lived here. Must be ten years ago. *I bon.* The hills are the same; we both know the way. And Lucien too, from walking here.' A pang of guilt twisted my inners but I said nothing. 'Who else?'

'Well – Magdelon was hired out to Beausejour a few years ago,' said Saturnin. 'She might remember how to get there. Petit Havre is just over the next ridge so . . .'

'Good. That's four of us.'

'Same for Céleste,' I said. 'She was hired out to Beausejour too.'

My brother gave a blink that was almost a flinch.

'She might not be coming,' he said. 'Who else? What about Augustin? He used to visit some girl up in Palmiste years ago.'

'Well, that's true,' said Saturnin. 'Except he has a bad case of the blue devils, since Bell made him eat his own ear.'

Emile just looked at him.

'What?'

Saturnin proceeded to tell us that the overseer had cut Augustin down from the cabin wall that afternoon by slicing the ear from his head with a knife. Then straightways Bell had cooked the severed ear on a hot griddle and forced Augustin to consume it.

'Takes a while for a man to get over that, swallowing his own cooked ear,' said Saturnin. 'Not the first time it's happened.'

All at once, I felt giddy, as though I might be sick. Emile caught my eye.

'Lucien,' he said. 'Go and sit down over there.'

I shook my head.

'I'm fine.'

'In any case,' Saturnin continued, 'I doubt Augustin could lead a group. Plus he's still in shackles.'

'Let's see how he is later,' said Emile. 'He's strong in his mind. If he is capable, we must use him. His group will just have to go at his pace.'

The driver pursed his lips as he took this in. Something troubling him but Emile was too agitated to notice. Saturnin took a backward step.

'I should go and see a nurse soon or I'm in trouble if Bell finds out.'

So saying, he began to walk off in the direction of the hospital.

'Make sure they're all there tonight,' said Emile. 'And post look-outs.'

The driver huffed out his cheeks then spat on the ground.

'*Kam-twa*, banana boy,' said he. 'No need to get all fluffed up like a frighty hen.'

And with those words, he set off at a trot, down through the trees toward the hospital. We watched until he was swallowed by the shadows and even then we carried on standing there until we could no longer hear the slap-slap of his feet on the earth. Far out to sea, a few violet cloud had moved in across the horizon.

I glanced at my brother, wondering whether he would stay long enough to see Céleste that night, or if he would run off again with the excuse of speaking to the plantation hands. Another few moments passed in silence. Then he sighed.

'*Vwala*,' he murmured.

'Do you trust that man?' I asked.

Emile sighed again, then replied:

'Would you trust a barracuda?'

PART SIX

Grenada

(SECOND NIGHT)

Chapter Thirty

Under instruction from Emile, we were all to gather in the yard that evening to hear the Power of Attorney. He made sure we had enough lamp around the fire for Thérèse to read by. We knew that Céleste would be somewise late because Bryant had been invited out to supper and had ordered her to admit a new patient to the hospital in his absence. Léontine return to the quarters early since she was not require to wait upon his table. Whiles Emile told Chevallier about our encounter with Saturnin, Léontine kept fidgeting and stroking her lips, all the while staring at my brother until, at last, he asked her:

'*Sa ou fé?*'

She covered her face with her hands. Making a silly sot of herself. Somewise bemused, Emile turn back to the old man.

I gave Léontine a nudge.

'Ho! Listen—' said I, but she was too busy staring at my brother.

I was about to prod her again when we heard a dove hoot in the trees on the Fort Royal side where the path dips toward town. Old Angélique exchange a look with her man then resume stirring the pepperpot.

'That's Thérèse coming,' Chevallier said then hooted in reply.

Presently, a well-fed young woman step into the yard. Last time I saw Thérèse she was a waif in a threadbare shift. Now she wore shoes and respectable clothes, most likely discarded by her mistress: white chemise and dark skirt and a bodice of some kind of sheeny cloth. She had bright ribbons in her hair and dragged along a tatterly old whalebone parasol, so full of holes it would have offer scant protection from rain or sun.

Emile and I jumped up to greet her.

'Look at this handsome pair of fools,' she said. 'Never thought to see you boys again. *Bonswa tout moun. Bonswa Gwan-mè.*'

'*Bonswa*,' Angélique replied. 'Tell me, *ché*, have you seen your brother or heard from him?'

'No,' said Thérèse. 'Why? What's the matter?'

The old woman exchanged a glance with her man.

'Nobody seen him since last night.'

'Probably nothing to vex up about,' said Chevallier. 'The doctor gave him rum. He'll be back when it runs out – but he'll be in trouble.'

Thérèse had acquire some fine affectations down in town. Her skirts too precious for the dirty ground and Angélique had to fetch a clean cloth for her to sit upon. The cast-off parasol must have been her prize treasure, judging from how often her fingers strayed to stroke its old bones. And the soup she declined with the excuse of saving appetite for some sugar-bread promise by the Governor. Of course, Emile had questions for Thérèse – was she in good health? Did the Governor treat her well? And so on – but once Mandingo politesse was served, he turn back to Chevallier. Thereafter, Thérèse set to pinch my cheeks as she did when I was small, always treating me like a newborn.

'Little britches,' said she. 'Look at those big cheeks now.'

She squeeze my face, making all manner of baby talk, despite I reminded her that I was no longer an infant, until – in the end – I told her I had made *caca-merde* in my 'little britches' then – *plaf!* She punch me in the back of the head, all airs and graces gone.

'*Méchan*,' said she. 'Naughty boy.'

Then, like a fine lady just off the boat from La Rochelle, she picked up her skirts and cloth and flounced away. I caught a glimpse of her frilly calzoons as she sat down beside her grandmother and would have kept looking except – in that same instant – Céleste arrived, calling out to reassure us as she approach the yard:

'*Mwen ka vini. Bonswa tout moun.*'

She crossed over to her hut, unfastening her apron as she went. I glanced at Emile, half expecting he might take foot again like a madman but he appeared not to notice that Céleste had even arrived because – all at once – he was deep in conversation with Léontine. Beforehand, he had paid her scant attention but now he seem to hang on her every word as she recounted some skit-brain nonsense about serviettes, perscribing how she was oblige to fold them up fancy fashion for the doctor. Hardly a tale for the ages yet my brother appear to be bewitch by the girl. He kept touching her arm as they spoke, encouraging her to say more.

'Oh really? So you fold it in half, then to a point? Then what?'

His eyes never left her face yet he must have been aware of Céleste for we all heard her call out as she approach the yard. Next time Emile reached out to touch Léontine, he kept his hand on her wrist.

'Well, that sounds complicated, for true. You must have nimble fingers, *ché.*'

And so saying, he stroke them – just as Céleste glanced over and saw him. She knew what he was doing, just as well as I did: playing coquet and courtship, as though he no longer cared for her. My guts ached with shame, for I wished he would stop all this tomfool simmy-dimmy. I tried to catch his eye but he was still pretending to be hypnotise by Léontine. Meanwhile, Céleste folded her apron, slow-slow, and placed it inside her hut. By the time she returned, her face was empty of expression. She lowered herself carefully to the ground behind Angélique and Thérèse, a spot where Emile couldn't see her unless he craned his neck, but he must have had eyes in the side of his head for – as soon as she settled – he reached into his shirt and pulled out the Power of Attorney. Then he held up his hand for silence.

'*Ecoute mwen, tout moun.* Listen, everyone. Thérèse, you know why we are here?'

'*Gwan-mè* just told me. You think you're going to take us all to that *Matinik*.'

'Well – nobody can force you to go with us,' said Emile. 'But if you agree to come, here's how I think we can do it. Léontine – would you mind standing watch? Just keep an eye on the hospital and the shortcut to town.'

Whiles Léontine got up and began to pace the yard, Emile took a stick and drew a rough shape in the dirt, like a fat fish with a tail that curl to a point.

'This is Grenada,' he said and pointed to a spot above the tail. 'Here's the hospital, on the coast by the river.' Then he pointed to a spot further up the island. 'Here is Petit Havre, where we have to get to. Me and Lucien chanced the road once or twice but too many slave out on the highway will cause suspicion. Also, they post soldiers here.' He pointed to a spot just north of the St Jean. 'It's not safe to leave the plantation that way. Our only choice is to avoid the road and head inland.'

He explained that we would have to cross mountain ridges and rivers en route. The only way to climb some stretches would be to haul ourselves up with the help of vines. Anybody old or sick or lame would struggle.

'So we have to help each other. *Kompwan?*'

A few people nodded. The plan was to go in small groups, each a mix of young and old, sick and healthy, led by someone who knew the goat track. That way, the more able could help the others.

'And we must go tomorrow. Christmas Eve. *Nwel toupatou ka*

fête. Everyone will be busy swilling and carousing. We can go as soon as Bryant and Bell leave for the Anglade dance. By this route . . .' He traced a curve in the dirt, from the plantation to Petit Havre. 'What do you think?'

He glanced around at the group. Angélique glared at the map in the dirt whiles rubbing her bad knees. Céleste was staring down at her swollen belly. Thérèse stroked the spokes of her parasol, a worried look in her eye.

'What about Vincent?' she said. 'You can't go without my brother.'

Nobody spoke for a moment. Then Emile sighed.

'Well, nor can we hang on here hoping he will turn up. We have to get everybody to Petit Havre by first light, Christmas Day, otherwise Cléophas will go without us and we'll be stuck here. In the meantime, if the Béké notice the slave are gone . . .'

With a flick of his wrist, Chevallier snapped his fingers.

'They will hunt us down.'

Emile unfolded the Power of Attorney.

'This document is a kind of legal certificate,' he said. 'According to Cléophas it contains permission from the English Governor for us to take you. But though he says it gives authority, he still wants us all to sneak away in secret. Make of that what you will.'

Chevallier scratched his head.

'Makes no sense to me.'

Céleste gave a hiss.

'Either there is permission or there's not,' she said, hotly.

Without even glancing at her, Emile continued:

'My guess is we have no real permission to take you, no permission from the English, that is. But you should look at this deed, then hear what it says.'

With these words, he pass the manuscript to Chevallier who pitched it tout suite at his woman as though it might burn his fingers.

'Careful,' said Emile.

The old man shuddered.

'*Puten documents*. I have a horror of them.'

Meanwhile, Angélique held up the parchment in the fading light, peering at it from several angles, much to the amusement of Chevallier.

'You can read now, woman, can you? What does it say – pray tell? Ho-ho-ho!'

His laugh cut short when she made a fist over his lap, the unspoken threat a punch to his most delicate part.

'*Puten!*' said he, squirming out of her reach whiles she made further show of inspecting the deed and concluded: 'Looks like a genuine Attorney Power to me,' though I would be surprise if she had ever before seen such a thing.

She handed the parchment to Thérèse who scrutinise the page for an instant then cleared her throat and – without stumbling or hesitation – commence to read aloud:

'December 1765. St Pierre, Isle of Martinique. Be it known that this day before Pierre Henri Emerigon, lawyer, and by virtue of his office, a Notary Public for the town and Isle aforesaid, commissioned and sworn, personally came and appeared—'

'Listen to that,' crowed Angélique – who couldn't have look more proud had Thérèse reached into her calzoons and pulled out a live chicken. 'Reads like a born lady.'

'Where was I?' Thérèse peer down at the page. '. . . personally came and appeared Père Edmund Lefébure of the town and Isle aforesaid, and Victor-Thérèse Charpentier, Comte d'Ennery, Governor of the Isle aforesaid both of whom do Declare and Swear that all the Negroes currently residing at the Hospital of Fort Royal town, Isle of Grenada, in and upon the Plantation Tract or parcel of land adjacent to said Charitable Institution are the *bona fide* possessions—'

'What the—' Chevallier cried. 'Who can make head or tail of this nonsense?'

'*Chut*, old man,' said his wife. 'Shut your dirty beak and listen.'

'– *bona fide* possessions of *Les Frères de la Charité* of St Pierre, Isle of Martinique which property the said Lefébure has a right to recoup and reclaim having a Just Title to said Negroes, which are Slaves for Life—'

'Hah!' cried Angélique.

'– either purchased here in these Isles aforesaid by *Les Frères de la Charité* between the years One Thousand Seven Hundred and Thirty-two and One Thousand Seven Hundred and Sixty or born to the said Negroes during that period or thereafter—'

So on and so forth it went, in the most inscrutable jargon, with so many 'aforesaids' and '*bona fides*' such that my recollection is less than perfect. Certainly, my brother and I were described; I remember that part: 'Two Mulatto, male, one Emile, also known as Mandingo, Light Brown colour, impressively tall and well-made, known to be keen-witted, about twenty-eight years of age – and Lucien, his brother, a boy of Light Brown colour, also clever, can speak both French and English to a fair standard. The boy is thought to be about twelve years of age.'

'What do they know,' I muttered, my face hot.

'Hush now,' said Emile. 'Listen.'

The next part explained that we were to be sent to Grenada to reclaim the Negroes of the Fort Royal Hospital and their descendants, including all the field hand and any slave that had been hired out, who were all 'the *bona fide* property of *Les Frères de la Charité*, as both Père Lefébure and the Comte d'Ennery shall and will Truly warrant and forever defend—' et cetera, et cetera.

Then there was a short list of the hospital slave with a brief description of their appearance. A gloom descended as Thérèse spoke each name aloud for to our minds no good ever came of having your particulars recorded in a document. Thereafter, a longer list of field hand: their names with descriptions of each person, beginning with Saturnin and the men, then lastly the women and children. In conclusion, the deed stated that the two Mulatto were commanded and authorise to deliver all the said Negroes to Père Lefébure at *L'Hôpital des Frères de la Charité* in Martinique.

'Thus done and passed in my office in the town of St Pierre, Isle aforesaid, in the presence of Père Cléophas Boudon and Père Roget Boniface, witnesses of lawful age and residing in this Isle who hereunto Sign their names together with the Said parties and me the Notary, in the year of our Lord, One Thousand Seven Hundred and Sixty-five. There being no seal of office I have hereunto affix my private seal.'

Thérèse flicked the broken disc of wax with her finger.

'*I bon*,' she said. 'That's it – except for their signatures.'

'Read them,' said Céleste, darkly.

We waited whiles Thérèse peered at the page. The various handwritings were troublesome to decipher, I knew, having attempted it myself.

'First is . . . Victor-Thérèse Charpentier, Comte d'Ennery, Governor. Then . . . Père Edmund . . . Lefébure. Père . . . Cléophas Boudon. Père . . . Roget Boniface. The last one is Pierre Henri Emerigon, Notary.'

Céleste gave a sniff.

'All French. No Englishmen names?'

'None.'

'*Vwala*,' said Céleste. 'Might as well throw that parchment in the fire for all the good it will do us.'

She rose to her feet with some difficulty, leaning on Angélique and Thérèse for support. Then she began to make a deal of *bloucoutoum* as she gathered up the empty calabash into her skirts.

'Céleste,' said Emile. It was the first time he had spoken to her since he fled the yard the previous night. 'Let me explain.'

She gave a dry laugh, her eyes blazing.

'Explain? Explain how you will get us all into hot water.'

He gazed at her swollen belly.

'Perhaps you should go and lie down,' he said. 'You probably need to rest.'

Céleste pulled in a deep breath as though she might blow fire at him but then she stormed off toward the kitchen with the empty calabash clattering in her jupe.

Emile watched her go then turn to the others.

'This is what you must weigh up. Do you want to come with us, knowing that no Englishman in Grenada has given his authority? Is it worth the risk? You have to balance that against your situation here. I'll say the same to the field hand tonight once we have read them this document.'

He glanced around at their faces. Everyone remain silent for a spell. Léontine – who had been listening whiles she kept lookout – came back to the fire. She tossed a stick into the flames and a shower of sparks flew up and disappeared into the night.

'Well, I want to go with you,' said she. 'No question.'

Chevallier gazed hopefully at Angélique.

'I tell you, it's tempting,' said he. 'I can't take much more of this *bordel* here.'

'What about you, *Gwan-mè*?' Léontine asked.

The old woman shook her head.

'It's too dangerous.'

'But listen, *ché*,' her man said. 'The Fathers would make Augustin a nurse again in their hospital over there. And I can see my own-own sister again.'

Angélique spat in the fire.

'I have to think about it.'

'Me too,' said Thérèse. 'I could never leave Vincent. And I – I have a better life now in town than I ever did here.'

Léontine turned on her, a look of disbelief on her face.

'You are getting too cosy down there, *kouzin*. You could be hired on elsewhere any moment – *plaf!* – if you displease them.'

'For true,' said Chevallier, his eyes still on Angélique. 'Bryant might get a better offer and hire you on again. You could end up in a bad place, girl – very bad.'

Thérèse grip the handle of her parasol. She looked as though she might cry.

'But if I go over there they might put me to cut cane. I'm better off here with the Governor. And what about Vincent? You can't leave him behind.'

There was silence for a spell then Angélique said:

'Child, he might be gone to the mountain.'

'And if he is in the mountain you'll never see him,' Chevallier added. 'Even if he turns up and goes with us to Martinique, you'll still be left here by yourself.'

Thérèse was silent for a moment. Then she said:

'It's not worth the risk. I'm sorry, but I'm staying here in Grenada.'

Angélique nodded, frowning.

'That's your decision, *ché*.'

'Well, I'm going,' said Léontine. 'I want to be with family – *Gwan-pè* and Emile.'

'He's not your family,' I told her.

'That's what we must do,' cried Chevallier. 'We must decide as a family.'

'We will, *ché*, we will,' said Angélique.

They seem to forget that not all of us were related to them. At least Emile and I had each other. The only one among us with no blood ties at all was Céleste – though now, I suppose, she had her baby, albeit just a scrap in her belly.

I glanced up to see what she had made of this last part of the discussion, but no sign of her anywhere and so I sprang to my feet and wandered over to her hut. The door flaps lay open. She was inside, putting on a clean apron. When she saw me at the threshold, she gave me a wan smile.

'There you are,' she said. 'Listen, I need to speak to your brother.'

These words did nothing but fill me with alarm. Her belly made her apron jut out in front. Another picture of her with Bryant came into my mind. I blinked it away.

'What is it? I can tell him.'

'No. Just tell him I want to see him, without everybody listening. Promise?'

I nodded.

'Good boy.'

Her eyes glistened as she smoothed back her head-tie. She embraced me, kissed the top of my head. Then she stepped past me without another word and hurried down the path to the hospital.

By this time, the first bright stars had begun to prick the evening sky. When I turn back to the yard, I could make out Chevallier and Angélique by the fire, filling their pipes. No sign of my brother and the others. I hurried over.

'Where's Emile?' I ask the old couple.

'Down to the plantation,' Chevallier said. 'Thérèse is going to read them the Attorney Power. Léontine went to stand lookout.'

I could scarce believe it. They had forgotten all about me. *Tambou!*

Mortified, I stood there for a moment. My brother would take two *jeunes-filles* with him, leave me behind. Well, devilled if I was going to sit with the old buffleheads. Besides, Céleste wanted to speak to Emile: he would want to know about that.

I slipped into the trees and skelted down the path. A short distance along I saw them up ahead, shadowy figures walking single file, foot and foot behind, Emile bringing up the rear. He must have heard me coming because he glanced over his shoulder, then stopped and waited until I caught up with him.

'Where do you think you're going?' he demanded.

'With you,' I replied, my face blazing, for the girls had turn to stare at me.

'No,' said Emile, with a touch of exasperation. 'Léo and Thé-Thé know every inch of this place, all the calls and shortcut. You've been too long in Martinique.'

Sometimes, the way he talk made me cross as a crab in a bucket. Calling people nurse-names as though he was their sweetheart. *Léo – Thé-thé*. To hear him spout on like that put me off going with them – almost. I threw my arms wide, mortal affronted.

'I know how to conduct myself. I can stand lookout same as them.'

Emile took a long look at me and sighed.

'Talking to you is like talking to a stone wall. I have no time for this. Go back.'

'Please do not insult me,' I cried.

But I no longer had his attention. He turned and set off again. He was gone so fast, the girls had to scuttle to keep up, the three of them soon melting into the darkness, leaving me standing there. I waited for a spell to let them get ahead then crept after them, my brother and his two little *amorets*. I would show him that I was not a baby any more.

Chapter Thirty-One

Since Emile could hear a mouse tiptoe in the grass, I took care to keep my distance and lingered far behind them quite to the River Road and the plantation. I gave them time to cross the St Jean and only then did I venture over the highway myself, careful to check that it was empty of travellers. From there, it was but a spit and stride to the footbridge and the cabins on the far side, now all lit up by flambeaux. Beyond the village, the produce ground: rows of plantain and so forth, grown by the slaves for their consumption. And, in the darkness beyond that, the cane-fields spread out along the valley with the low slopes of Morne St Eloy rising up behind.

I crept across the bridge, bessy-down in case some colonial type might see me against the night sky. Despite this precaution, one lookout knew all about me for I heard a pigeon call somewheres along the riverbank, a warning to those in the quarters. Sure enough, when I reach the entrance to the cabins, Saturnin stood waiting. He look me over like I was a pullet and he was fixing to wring my neck.

'Your brother said it might be you. Likes to tell people what to do, don't he?'

In reply, I gave a shrug, feeling a twinge disloyal.

'He can do what he likes in Martinique,' said the driver. 'For now, I can think of a spot where I can use you on lookout. Guess where Bell is?'

'*Di mwen.*'

'In town, celebrating early Christmas. This ought to be a quiet night. Let's go, little yellowman.'

Without another word, he set off into the yard. I hurried after him, glad to stand lookout. I was just gratulating myself on my manliness when someone leapt on my back with an ear-piercing shriek. I thought the jig was over until I remembered Choisie, one of the old ancients. Poor Choisie lost his mind before I was born and his peculiar pleasure was to throw his stinky carcass onto the back of any unsuspecting mortal. No need to turn my head and look; the smell of him and the way his bony fingers dug into my flesh were all the reminder needed. Old Choisie. A miracle he was still alive. And then I remembered what Vincent had told me about 'Martial Medicine'. It was Choisie who had been made to extrement in the mouth of his father. In as long as it took me to remember this, the driver tangled with the old goat, trying to break his grip on my shoulders. They tussled for a spell until, finally, Choisie sprang loose and scurried off, his strange shuffling gait familiar to me from beforetimes.

Saturnin shook his head in exasperation, then led me on across the yard past a few figures assembled around one of the flambeaux. He pause to speak to a grey-haired pipe-smoker, a man I recognised as Old Raymond. Raymond use to borrow a bible from John Calder, though Calder said the old fellow couldn't read; he just like to leaf through the pages. Léontine crouched nearby, talking to someone curled up on the ground, a scrawny man with a bloodstain bandage around his head and an iron weight chain to his ankle. Took me a short while to recognise him: Augustin. My guts turned over at the sight of the dark patch on the bandage where his ear had once been. Léontine saw me and I would have gone over and spoken to them except Saturnin finish with Raymond and jerked his head at me.

'This way,' he said. 'Let's find your brother.'

Whiles Raymond hobbled off toward the produce ground, I followed the driver to the largest cabin. A couple of field hand loitered on the step, peering inside, but Saturnin push past them and they fell back to let us through. A waft of stale air hit me in the face as we cross the threshold. By the light of a few lantern that hung from the rafters, I glanced around. The cabin was almost full of people: men, women and children; some seated on the ground, half a dozen or so on ramshackle benches and the rest standing. The mood appear to be one of subdued agitation. Some of the slave stared back at me, smile-less. The odour of so many bodies press together was overpowering.

On one of the benches, sat two women, both in spike collar, their names I remembered as Magdelon and Cléronne. Despite the crush of bodies in the cabin, the others left a space around those two; they were in isolation. Nobody wanted to encounter those sharp metal spikes.

Emile and Thérèse stood at the front, struggling to light a smut-lamp with the help of a woman whose name (I seem to recall) was Charlotte.

The strongest young bucks had assembled at the back. Tired of waiting, they had engaged in a game of Crackers, a test of manhood whereby players lay biscuits on a table and thrash them with their genital part. The winner is the man who can break a cracker by thrashing it the fewest times. As we came in, one of them thumped his cracker to shatters and then jump back, laughing and snapping his fingers at the others. Another man – sour-faced at losing – glanced over in my direction. I believe his name was Montout. When he saw me he scowled. 'Damn banana boys,' he said. 'It's an infestation.' And he leapt about, pretending to stamp on cock-roaches. His compeers began to laugh and a few women urge them to hush. This disturbance made my brother glance up and when he caught sight of me he turned on the driver.

'What's he doing here? I told you to send him back to the hos-pital.'

'I'm put him in the field,' Saturnin replied. 'You wanted look-outs. He can go in the near cane-piece, next to Léontine.'

Emile was about to protest when Thérèse accosted Saturnin.

'I need more light to read. Have you no lanterns that work?'

'Lanterns,' scoff the driver. 'Where do you think you are – the Governor residence? What's the matter with that one?'

He nodded at Charlotte, who had just unhooked a lamp from a rafter. She held it aloft for Thérèse, who peered at the Power of Attorney.

'*I bon*,' she said. 'That will have to do.'

'Get rid of the boy,' my brother told Saturnin then he turn to me. 'Go back, or there will be trouble.'

Well, I had been about to tell him that Céleste wanted to see him but, after that, he could whistle if he wanted any message from me. Meanwhile, as though to imply that Emile was no better than a hysteric woman, the driver flapped his hand in the air.

'Boy is fine,' he said. 'I'm put them in the field.'

'You need to hear this document,' Emile told him. 'As much as the rest of them.'

In response, Saturnin spat on the floor and pointed to the wet spot in the dirt.

'I'll be back before that there is dry.'

With a shake of his head, Emile turned away – a dismissal.

'*Annou alé*,' said Saturnin to me. 'Let's get Léontine.'

He strode out of the cabin. I was about to follow when Montout piped up again:

'Little milk-face, you want to play me at Crackers?'

He waved his member at me whiles his friends laughed and snapped their fingers in exultation.

'Let him be,' scolded Charlotte. 'He don't want to show us his peeny *lolo*.'

This cause yet more laughter. Humiliated to be the butt of all derision, I turned and fled, only to bump into Augustin on the step. He grab my hand, wild-eyed.

'Lucien,' he said. '*Mwen kontan wè zot.*'

The clothes he wore were tattered and filthy, his legs streak with mud; at least, I hoped it was mud. His ankles had been rub raw by the shackles. I could smell the putrid blood on his bandaged head.

Another burst of laughter from inside made me shrink from the cabin.

'Never mind them,' said Augustin. When he saw me give a searching glance about the yard, he pointed toward the produce ground. 'They went that way.'

'*Mèsi,*' said I, but he still had a grip on my hand. He gazed into my eyes, a desperate expression on his face.

'I'll see you on the boat to Martinique,' he said.

'*Wi,* I hope so.'

I tried to edge past him but still he clung to me.

'Oh Lucien. I cannot tell you how much I would like that.'

His eyes began to fill with tears. I squeezed his hand and manage to extricate myself, leaving him standing on the step. My pity went out to him but – at the same time – it was disconcerting to witness a grown man cry. Emile had seem to wash his hands of me. And, though I tried to tell myself it was of no consequence to be mocked by the field hands, I found the humiliation unsettling. All in all, I felt as though the very foundations of the world were somehow in jeopardy.

Chapter Thirty-Two

Behind the cabins, I almost collided with Saturnin. He was mighty displease, having retrace his steps to find me.

'What are you doing?' he muttered. 'Hurry up.'

Léontine stood waiting at the edge of the provision ground. The driver led us around the perimeter of this vegetable patch until we had reach the cane-pieces that lay to the east. Here, the cane grew well above head height, the crop almost ready to cut. At one spot, at the edge of the field, Saturnin paused and spoke in a whisper:

'LaFortune? *Koté ou yé?*'

From somewhere in the midst of the grasses came a reply:

'*Isidan chef.*'

The voice of a boy, soft-soft.

'You see anything?' the driver hissed.

'*Non, chef, toupatou trantjil.*'

'Good. Stay there.'

I peered hard into the cane but no sign of this boy LaFortune. In my own mind, I made a solemn resolve to hide myself just as well as LaFortune when I reach my own spot.

We skirted the edge of the field, keeping in the star-shadow of the stalks, and soon stopped at a place with a clear view across the rows of produce. Over at the quarters a few children were running around and, just discernible by the light of the flambeaux, Old Raymond sat smoking his pipe near the smallest hut.

Once again, we had to wait whiles Saturnin stood listening, importantly. In the distance, somewheres inland, I could hear an ox lowing as if in agony. The sound pierce my soul for I did miss my cows, Victorine most of all. She made me laugh, the way she would on occasion rub her snout along the grass or – on cool days – gambol around the pasture for sheer joy, kicking up her heels. For true, I would have given my thumb to be back in St Pierre at that instant, stroking the velvety fur behind her ears.

I must have been lost in my reveries because next thing I knew Saturnin had grab me by the shoulder and shove me into a dense patch of cane at the edge of the field.

'Stay there,' he whispered, his breath in my face. 'If you see any person go over to the quarters or any Béké man anywhere, sing out.'

'Sing?'

He gave me a narrow look.

'You were taught to signal, I suppose?'

In my own mind I said: 'Better than you were, spud, for I have yet to hear you put your lips together and hoot.' But I had prudence enough to maintain politesse.

'Wi.'

'Good. See him over there?' The driver pointed with his whip to the old fellow near the small hut. 'That's Raymond. Now, if you see anybody, you give him a warning. He knows you're here. *Kompwan?*'

'Of course.'

Nothing incivil in that, yet Saturnin subjected me to a long, hard look, just to let me know he did not trust me entirely. Then he wagged his finger at me and whispered:

'I see you looking at my whip. Let me tell you, it can tear skin from flesh, flesh from bone and leave you like a standing skeleton. *Kompwan?*'

Though more incline to ask him if he was dumb as a beetle, I simply nodded.

Beside him, Léontine stood in silence, her eyes downcast. The driver treated me to another menacing glare, whiles – quietly but comprehensively – he blew his nose into his hand. For true, I experience some degree of trepidation regarding what he might do next but, to my relief, he just wiped his slimy fingers on his breeks. Then he trudged off along the edge of the cane-field. I would have like to spiflicate him.

Léontine reached out to touch my arm.

'You'll be fine,' she whispered. 'Someone will come and get you later.'

'When?' I asked her. 'How long do I stay here?'

It came out more pathetic than I intended but, mercifully, Léontine had already scampered off in pursuit of the driver, else she might have deem me wishy-washy.

I watch their progress toward the cane-pieces in the west until I could see them no more. After that, I tried to settle down and listen. This far inland, you could no longer hear the sea but all around me the cane was full of noise. Little sounds that in other circumstances would scarce be worth the fret – a scuttle here, a rustle there – rats, no doubt, or toads; but, all the same, they gave me the twitters. Also, it was hard to find a comfortable stance among the stalks. In the end, I crouch down on my hands and knees. In daylight hours, the cane would provide poor cover there at the edge of the field, but by dark of night it was as good as that cap of invisibility my brother always talked about.

After a while, I saw Saturnin reappear at the quarters, alone, just a squat dark shape against the light of the fires. No doubt, he had shove Léontine into one of the other cane-fields. He exchange a few words with Raymond on his way past but I was too far distant to hear what they said. As Saturnin retrace his steps to the large cabin, Raymond gazed out across the rows of produce as though idly taking in the stars. His face in shadow but, for a short while, he seem to stare directly at me. Then he return to his pipe.

Out there in the cane, on lookout in the darkness, I felt very alone. Hoping to catch a reassuring glimpse of Léontine, I peered across the produce ground and almost stared the eyeballs out of my head looking for her but all was murky in that direction. I just hoped to hellfire that Thérèse would rattle through the Power of Attorney faster than a cryer at a half-day market. Raymond sat within whistling distance, and beyond him I could see one end of the big cabin. My brother was in there, I knew, and that gave me some small comfort despite his bad mood.

With each passing moment, I grew accustom to my situation and soon the scuttles and rustles close at hand became less disturbing. I stretch my ears beyond them until I could have heard an iguana blink over at Morne Rouge – and that was when I became aware of someone – or something – moving through the cane.

The sounds came from the field to the north of the produce ground but they seem to draw closer all the while to where I stood. For an instant, I thought it might be Léontine come to find me, for some reason. But the harder I listen, the more I became convince that this was no slip of a girl. Whoever it might be, they breathe heavily and, once or twice, I heard a clumping tread. Of course, these sounds might have a simple explication. Perhaps a mule had got loose and wandered into the field, perhaps a clumsy goat. Since I did not fancy getting all womanish over nothing and making a numps of myself in front of the plantation slave, I held back on hooting an alarm to Raymond.

For a time, all was silent. I began to think I must have imagine the noises and had just begun to recompose myself when I caught sight of movement in the cane-piece, within a stone-cast of where I stood. The long leaves of the cane shivered and then a dark hunch figure emerge from the field and scuttled along, ever closer to my hiding place.

All at once, despite my scorn of superstitiosity, half-forgot notions of wolf-men and night-hags flooded my mind. Was it *Loup-Garou* come to get me? Or *La Diablesse*?

Raymond sat smoking by his hut, oblivious, but I could no more summon him than I could step out my own skin and fly up in the sky for – if I did make a sound – this thing had crept so nearhand it would pounce on me fast as a viper on a rat.

Closer, closer it came, through the gloaming starlight. I swear, in that moment, I must have been about the worst scared boy in the whole Antilles. As the figure drew near I saw, first, a ghostly face and then a pair of pale hands holding – what? A cocked hat, made of straw. This here was no old-wife tale, but worse: a sneaky Béké with a three-corn hat. Stone me down. I found myself within spit and stride of Addison Bell, the overseer, as he skulked along in the shadows of the cane.

The blood surge through my ears with a sound like a thousand men at march on shingle, so loud I feared that Bell would hear. At one point, when he tripped and almost lost his footing, he mumbled a few words and my inners turned over. Had he brought soldiers with him? But then he muttered again and giggled, it dawned on me that he had address nobody but his own self. He was entirely alone and, by all appearances, as drunk as a tick in tafia. He must have taken it into his head to creep about the plantation upon his return from town, trying to catch some slave doing what he ought not. Evidently, he had no notion that someone might already be hid in the fields. I prayed that he would stumble beyond my hiding place into the night. And, indeed, he did creep right past me but – after only a few more step – he sat himself on the ground, a mere spirt from where I hid. Then he produced a flask from his pocket and took a sip. I was close enough to hear him swallow.

Believe me, I had scarce a breath in my body. All I could do was keep as still and quiet as possible until he decided to leave. Easier said than done. My knees, pressed against the ground for so long, had begun to ache; my throat felt drier than a twice-bake biscuit. Meanwhile, having toss back a few more pulls from his flask, Bell began to stare over at the quarters whiles muttering under his breath. I strain my ears to hear what he said. The way he spoke reminded me of John Calder, though Bell sounded somedeal more loutish.

'Aye, ye damn'd lazy old bas——. Sat there on your a——e. And youse dirty wee black bas——s. Where's that trollop, yer mother? Lying on her tum-tum back, as usual, nae doot, lazy b——ch – ha ha!'

Had he been in less rummy condition, he might have wondered why the yard stood more or less empty, but he could see Raymond smoking a pipe and some pickaninny draggling about the place and that seem to satisfy him. Despite being drunk, it would appear he still had wiles enough to have cross the river well upstream such that he might sneak around to the north and approach the cabins from a direction nobody would expect. Now, he seem content to sit in the dark and spy on the village whiles sipping rum and raining down oaths and imprecations on the slaves. Presumably, this was not the first time he had amuse himself in such a fashion. But how long would he remain there? All I could do was keep still until he grew bored and gave up or – perhaps – fell into a swinish stupor. After a while, he began to hum a tune beneath his breath, a mournful Scots lament, about his own land. At last, with a sigh, he put on his hat and began to stagger to his feet: he was about to leave. I could scarce believe my luck. My knees still ached and – having delay the moment as long as possible – I shifted my weight ever so gently, stretching out my leg in silence.

All at once, I felt a rare, hot and piercing spasm as though some-one had extinguish a segar on my foot and then some horrible crea-ture slithered across my toes. What had bit me I cannot be sure, but the slithering reminded me of when I was a child and a giant centipede – a creature at least a foot long – had stung me, an injury that in aftermath had cause me untold agonies. Although I manage not to yell, I kicked out my foot to shake off the horrid beast then curled up in throes of anguish, causing the dry leaves beneath me to crackle and sigh. All this grand disaster took but an instant to unfold yet, needless to say, none of it occurred in silence.

Bell span around at once.

'What's that?' he whispered. 'Who's there?'

I force myself to take shallow breaths, though sheer fright now made me more incline to gasp. Meanwhile, a burning agony shot up my leg, like a rusty nail dragging poison through my veins. The pain made me light-headed. I thought I might swoon. Bell paced the edge of the field not ten feet from where I lay. Every so often, I caught a shadowy glimpse of his legs between the cane-stalks. Starlight gleamed on something in his hand: the short blade of a cutlass.

'Come out here, ye tum-tum bas——,' said Bell, louder now. 'I'll have ye! I'll slice your belly open and wash my hands in your tripes and trullibubs.'

Slow-slow, I turn my head to peer over at the quarters. I could just see Raymond, a shadow against the firelight. Having heard our commotion, the old slave had put his hands to his mouth and now made three pigeon hoots to alert the hands that something amiss.

Meanwhile, Bell took another step toward the cane.

'Dinna be feart,' he said, more gently. 'I never meant whit I said there the noo. I'll not hurt ye. Dinna worry. Come on oot here. No harm will come tae ye.'

Since all of this he spoke whiles testing the bite of his blade against his thumb, I felt disincline to believe him. In a trice, he lost patience and began to slash at the air with his cutlass, puffing himself up as though preparing to dive into the field. Alas, the insect-bite had drain my strength. I was too weak to crawl any distance and, besides, Bell would have heard me. He took a step into the row longside where I lay, and thrashed about him with the flat of his blade, rattling the cane-stalks, left and right. A few more paces, a slight change of path and he would stumble over me. In desperation, it came to me: my only hope was to scare him away. If I could just frighten him enough, he might scuddle off and shut himself inside his cabin.

And so – I will admit, without properly considering the consequences – I bared my teeth and gave the most convincing and deepest growl from my *répertoire*, low and threatening at first then building to a savage pitch, just like my brother had taught me. It took almost all my remaining vigour. To my surprise, before a second growl had even formed in my throat, Bell staggered back a few paces then turned and fled the field. At the sound of his rapidly receding footsteps, I peered out between the cane-stalks. Alas, instead of running in the direction I had expected – toward his own cabin – he was racing across the produce ground, headed directly for the field hand quarters.

Chapter Thirty-Three

Alerted by Raymond, the field hand had begun to assemble, streaming out of the big cabin. With every passing instant, more people arrived. I could see them as shadows against the fire-light. They all peered out at the figure of their overseer running pell-mell toward them across the rows of produce. Of my brother, I could see no sign. Perhaps he had fled the quarters already, gone back up the hill.

Bell began to shout as he ran:

'There's wild beasts in there, in that cane. Quick now! All of youse! Fetch torches! Fetch torches, ye ba——ds!'

His hat flew off but he raced on without stopping to retrieve it. A low babble floated across the provision ground as the slave began to raise their voices. Then Saturnin pushed his way to the front; his short stature and bullocking demeanour marked him out. Dull-voiced, he began to yell orders:

'Mr Bell now. He says fetch torches. Mr Bell coming. Go quick. Fetch torches.'

A crowd gathered around the driver, all a-clamor, and he spoke to them in low tones, perhaps explaining in illicit kréyòl. When Bell reach the quarters he grab Saturnin, shouting, telling him to make the slave search the cane, pointing at the field where I still lay hid. Some heated discussion and much arm-waving ensued. I'm not sure how well Saturnin spoke English but the overseer seem to have some trouble making himself understood. I got the gist of it from their raised voices: the two men debated the topic of wild beasts and whether they existed in Grenada; the driver seem to think not, whiles the overseer claim to have just heard a savage animal growl in the cane-field. I expect Saturnin had drawn his own conclusions about what had happened and was happy to procrastinate by putting up an argument. Someone found a conch shell and began to blow upon it. Everybody shouting. Then the chickens got themselve loose – whether by accident or design was hard to tell – and all the bird flapping around and screeching and the efforts of the children to catch them only added to the hollow-balloo.

Meanwhile, I had begun to shake uncontrollably. Whatever creature had bit me had gone but the bite itch me something fear-some and I could scarce stop scratching. Fever crept up on me, through my veins. In my mind, I chided myself: if only I had kept still, I would not have been bit. Or, had I held my tongue instead of growling, Bell might have walked past without finding me. My lip trembled as I tried to stop bursting into tears. I considered myself to be no better than a dolt. Now, I had but two choices: try to get back to the hospital as fast as I could pull it – if I could hobble that far – or stay put and hope that Saturnin could dissuade Bell from conducting a search of the cane-pieces. It was the toss of a penny, either way. Whether I limped off into the night or hid, if Bell set sight upon me, I was done for. And if it chance that some field hand stumbled upon me, well, I could only pray he would give me the go-by, rather than turn me in. Most likely the plantation slaves would help me – but how could I be sure?

Alas, when I tried to stand up, my injured foot could take no weight. The only way to escape was to crawl. I began to creep along on hands and knees and then, of a sudden, heard a faint fistle among the dead leaves on the ground behind me. I might have had an apo-plexy right there and then, but when I glanced around it was no overseer or giant centipede but Emile himself coming toward me, his face gleaming in the starlight.

Just then, a shout went up at the quarters as Saturnin split the field hand into gangs and told them to search the cane. Evidently the overseer had prevail. People ran this way and that, calling to each other, lighting torches, dropping torches, grabbing bill-hook, stick and axe. Surrounded by a cohort of slave bearing blades and flambeaux, Bell became a man again. He grabbed a torch from one of the women. Then, with some remark to a nearby gang, he began to stride across the provision ground. The poor hands had to hurry along beside him, hopping between the rows, trying not to step on their precious crops – unlike Bell, who stomped along with scant regard for where his feet might land. He was heading directly for the spot where we lay hid.

Emile spoke in my ear.

'Can you walk?'

My throat had closed over with fear and shame. My lungs were tight. Unable to speak, I picked myself off the ground then felt myself falling forward into a fog but Emile caught me and pulled me onto his back, tucking my legs under his arms to carry me like a child.

'Hold tight,' he whispered.

Keeping his head low, he set off through the field, northward bound, going slow enough not to disturb the cane-stalks, bearing me along, slipping through the tall grasses nice and easy, like a hermit-crab through weed, and I was his shell.

Chapter Thirty-Four

Some kind of fever took hold of me such that I have only patchy recollection of most of that night and the morning that followed. Evidently, Emile carried me back to the hospital quarters and laid me down in the ramshackle cabin. I was dimly aware of him pressing a cool cloth to my forehead. At some later point, Céleste came in. She gave me a kind of medicine that made me drowsy. All night long I fell from one dwam into another. Hard to tell whether I was asleep or awake. Sometimes Céleste appeared, sometimes Emile. Then, later, I woke again and heard them there together, low voices talking at my bedside. I turn my head and thought I saw Emile reach out to Céleste and touch her swollen belly – but it was only a brief impression and then I sank down into darkness again.

When next I open my eyes, the pirate Bart Roberts and *La Diablesse* had taken over the cabin. Old Bart he set a rusk upon a chair, proposing to play me at Crackers. I had never played the game before and, much intimidated, looked around for Emile or Céleste, only to find that they had both disappear. Roberts had already knelt down and now he pulled his virile member from his britches and began to pound the rusk with it, so hard that the diamond cross at his throat did jump, whiles *La Diablesse* looked on lickerously. That cracker must have been as hard as black walnut because the pirate fail to even cause one crumb.

'Your turn, Squeakum,' he said to me and when *La Diablesse* laughed he bowed to her, saying: 'Unless you, Madame, would try first,' which I thought amusing because, of course, she lack the necessary accoutrement. They both turn to me, then, with such fierce looks, I felt oblige to participate. Yet, when I delved into my britches for my own tackle, my hand grasp nothing but air. Perhaps my *lolo* had shrunk inside me or dropped off somewheres; *n'importe quoi*, my manhood was gone.

Of course, I knew this was simply a dream or some kind of hallucination of the senses; nevertheless, I began to panic. *La Diablesse* laugh so hard I could see the furred root of her tongue behind her mossy teeth. Then she flipped up her skirts, revealing her hoof but – worse than that, and to my horror – instead of lady parts she had a *koko* on her bigger than the throwing arm of a harpooneer and with this massive extremity she proceeded to thwack the biscuit, smashing it to fritters. When naught but crumbs and dust remain, she turn to me again and I saw that her prependant had grown a pair of fangs at the end. This grisly apparition rose up in her hands like a giant centipede and then – Mary-and-Joseph! – drew back as if to pounce on me.

Tambou! In my nightmares, I must have been thrashing around on the mat, for next thing I knew Céleste appeared beside me, pressing a damp cloth to my forehead. Not yet fully awake, I blurted out:

'Don't play Crackers with them.'

'What?' she said.

'Don't play Crackers with them!'

'What are you talking about?'

But before I could reply, a leathery hand reached up and drag me back down into the hot dark of sleep.

PART SEVEN

Grenada

(THIRD DAY)

Chapter Thirty-Five

Some time the following morning, I washed up on the shores of slumber, weak as a worm. Bright light bled in between the slats of the hut. My throat was dry. My whole leg throbbed. Even my brain hurt. I groaned. A voice came to me, close at hand. Emile. He sat against the wall, just behind me.

'Here, drink this.'

He supported my head and held to my lips a calabash fill with coconut water. I took a sip. Something had been added to make the liquid sweet and milky. Then I caught a glimpse of my foot and near cried out in anguish. Hard to believe that this grisly appendage was my own. All five toes had puffed up, misformed, like a row of dark and deadly mushroom, my ankle so swollen it could belong to a fat Béké with the gout. Whatever had attack me left behind the imprint of fangs, two puncture marks. I did not care to imagine the size of the creature that made them but they were similar to what I had suffered as a tot when a giant centipede bit my arm.

Emile began to bathe my foot.

'We have to get you better by tonight,' he said. 'Céleste thinks the bite is infected. Did you see what did it?'

'No . . . I'm sorry.'

'What for?'

'For last night.'

'Want to tell me what happened?'

Well, I would rather have pulled out my own tongue with a pliers than admit my mistakes but I force myself to confess that when it seem like Bell might find me I had growl to scare him off, never once expecting him to take leg-bail for the quarters.

'I guessed it was you,' Emile said. 'Soon as I heard them shouting about a wild beast growling in the cane. What was Bell doing? Spying on the cabins?'

'Mm-hmm – and cursing the field hands. He's sick for home. Misses his mammy.'

My brother gave a dry laugh.

'That's a good one,' he muttered. 'Sick for home.'

'Well, I'm sorry. If I hadn't moved when I got bit, he might not have heard me.'

'No need to be sorry. You can't help being bit.'

'But the Power of Attorney . . . they need to hear it.'

He shook his head.

'We were finish. Thérèse skipped reading the names to make it quick. She was done by the time we heard Raymond. The field hand were just debating what to do.'

'But what about Léontine? We should have gone to get her.'

'You think she needs your help? Soon as she heard Bell make a commotion, she hop the twig, came flying through those cabins before he got halfway across the produce ground. That girl can take care of herself. Went off to work this morning with ribbons in her hair. Here, have some more.'

He supported me again whiles I drank from the calabash.

'What did the field hand decide?' I asked. 'Are they coming with us?'

'No decision yet. They're still talking. We'll find out soon enough. Now – do you think you can walk?'

He help me up off the mat but when I tried to step onto the bad foot a lightning bolt shot up my leg and a wave of nauseation ran through me like a poison. My head began to spin and I would have hit the floor had Emile not caught me.

'Easy now,' he said, laying me down again. 'You just woke up. We'll try later.'

He draped a cool cloth across my forehead. An anxious look had crept into his eye but he shook his head and laughed and then – whap! It was gone.

'*Puten mèd!*' said he. 'You got away with it last night, for true. Piece of luck old Bell did not nab you down there. You bear a charm life, britches.'

In my bones, I knew he was wrong. Even little children could stand lookout without getting caught. Though I never saw him, I could picture that boy LaFortune, the one hid in the cane by the produce ground, the one who had spoke to Saturnin. I could just imagine that boy with his compeers, laughing at my ineptitude, my *bêtise*.

A vision from the night before flash through my mind: *La Diablesse*, her massive prependage growing fangs, rearing up, ready to strike. I peered out at my brother from beneath the damp cloth.

'Is Bart Roberts dead?' I asked, trying to sound nonchalant.

Emile paused in the act of washing his hands.

'Bart Roberts, the pirate? He died years ago. What do you want to know that for?'

'Just asking.'

Nonetheless, he looked at me askance.

'Is this something to do with your dream?'

'No,' I said. 'What dream?'

He made a horrified face and waggled his hands in the air:

'Don't play Crackers with them! Don't play Crackers with them!' He began to laugh but stopped when he saw that I had taken offence. 'It was just a nightmare.'

A sudden heat rose up behind my eyes. I glared at Emile, my forehead prickling, my jaw tight.

'You know Céleste wants to talk to you,' I said.

'Yes, we spoke last night.'

'Did she tell you about her child? Who the father is?'

'She did,' he said, abruptly. 'It was some carpenter slave. He and his master did some repairs in the hospital early this year. But they've gone now to Guadeloupe.'

I must confess, I found myself bemused. Could this be true? Or was Céleste only lying to my brother because of what he might do to Bryant?

'That's not what I heard,' I told him. 'Léontine knows who the father is – and it's not any carpenter gone to Guadeloupe.'

My brother narrowed his eyes at me. He took the cloth off my forehead and set to wringing it out.

'Best thing to do, Lucien, is we should mind our own business.'

'But I can tell you who he is, if you want.'

'No need,' he replied.

All the same, I found myself compel to speak the name. I know not why exactly I wanted to provoke him, except that he had mock me for having a nightmare.

'Dr Bryant,' I said. 'Léontine is sure it's him.'

Quick-sharp, Emile leaned forward and spoke, soft and low, close to my face.

'First, you should ignore rumours. Second, mind your own business. Third—'

But instead of continuing, he sighed.

'What?' I asked.

'Nothing.'

'But – what if it is Bryant?'

Emile gave an angry sniff.

'Are you trying to cause trouble? What do you want me to do? Go down there to the hospital, knock him cold as a wedge? Get myself arrested?'

'No,' I said, though I was so angry with him, the idea held some appeal.

'*I bon*,' he replied. 'The important thing is to get Céleste – and all of us – off this island, away from him and safe. I know it's him. Of course I do. She told me about it – what he did. She had no choice.'

'Oh.'

'Yes – "Oh".'

'Then why'd you tell me it was some carpenter gone to Guade-loupe?'

'Because – you silly – I did not want you to know it was Bryant – in case YOU did something stupid.'

'But—'

He put his hand up to silence me.

'Not another word,' he said. 'Not about Céleste, not anything.'

Shame welled up in my eyes in the form of scalding tears. Loath to let Emile know I was upset, I dash them away with my fingers. Above all, I would hate him to think me a weeping baby. He turned away to finish rinsing the cloth, his shoulders hard and set, his neck stiff and unyielding. Even the back of his head seem to disapprove of me. I turn my face to the wall and lay there, eyes shut, until I heard him leave the cabin.

Chapter Thirty-Six

I must have fallen asleep again because I woke to find the morning well advance. Someone was approaching the hut, soft-footed. Imagining Bell or Bryant sneaking up on me, I felt my heart flip over as the door swung open, but it was only Céleste, saying:

'I can't stay long.'

She put her hand to my forehead and knit her brows together. 'Still a fever,' she told me. 'But we must get you walking.'

Since I could put no weight on the injured foot, she help me to the threshold. The heat outside hit my skull like a mallet. I sat down and descended the stairs on my hind quarters. Céleste showed me a pair of crutches propped against the cabin wall.

'No need for those,' I said.

'How will you walk otherwise?' She haul me to my feet and pushed a crutch under each of my armhole. 'Rest on them. Swing forward instead of using that bad foot.'

Giving me orders, as usual. She made me ply back and forth across the flat part of the yard whiles she watched.

'That's it,' she said. 'Keep going.'

'Where's Emile? What's he doing?'

'Never mind him. Just watch your step.'

Hobbling to and fro on flat ground turned out to be simple enough – if tiring – and soon I was hirpling about like a life-long cripple. The problem came to light when Céleste led me away from the cabins, down the shortcut path to town. Ground creepers snagged up the stilts and they stuck in the mud, bringing me to a standstill. Worst of all, when I turned around, we discovered that it was impossible to go uphill. Picturing the many heights that Emile and I had scaled on our journey from Petit Havre to Fort Royal, it dawned on me that any hill on our return would be impassable to me and, with crutches in hand, I would never be able to haul myself up a steep incline by grasping branches and vine as necessary. No mistake, I would require prodigious help to get anywhere on the island.

'Try going sideways,' Céleste suggested, but it was no use.

Just then, I caught sight of my brother picking his way through the trees, silent as a stick insect, watching me all the while. Céleste noticed him a moment later.

'Keep practising,' she said then hurried off through the undergrowth to intercept Emile. They stood together, close-close, and began to talk in low, earnest voices. After a while, they both stared in my direction. My brother seemed low in spirit, his countenance grim as Céleste murmured in his ear. What was she saying? In normal circumstance, I might have wandered near enough to eavesdrop but the crutches made such a ploy impossible. I was stuck on the path, plain and simple, able only to look and wonder, as they murmur to each other. Clearly, they had indeed become reconcile to some extent during the night at my bedside. Emile did look glum but his ill-humour no longer seem to be aimed at Céleste. A lonely ache twisted in my gut, just like beforetimes, when the pair of them would lock together like two half of a shell and me a little fish on the outside, darting hither-thither, trying to nose a way in.

Presently, their *tête-à-tête* ended and – with a last glance in my direction – Céleste hurried off toward the hospital whiles Emile resumed his course through the underbrush toward me. As he stepped onto the path, he cast a glance at my crutches, saying:

'*Bonjou*, hop-leg. I would toss you a coin if I had one to spare.'

'Always mocking, giving joke,' I told him. 'You would crack a jest upon the gallows. Where have you been?'

'The boat-house. Chevallier is set on rowing to Petit Havre because of Angélique, her knees. I just wanted to check the boat is sea-worthy.'

'And is it?'

'So far as I can tell.'

'I see you and *Manzell* are now on speaking terms.'

Ignoring that, he crouch down to study my foot, frowning in a way that made my scalp itch.

'Who else is going in this boat?' I asked.

'Chevallier. Angélique. Léo will go with them to help the old man row . . .'

He stood up. I just looked at him. He gaze back, unflinching. At last, he said:

'You can't go overland on these crutches.'

'Is that what Céleste told you?'

'I can see for myself. Can you walk uphill?' When I fail to reply, he answered his own question: 'No. In which case . . .'

'What about you?' I demanded. 'Are you going in the boat?'

'No, I have to take the field hand. Hardly anybody knows the way to Petit Havre.'

'But I could go with you, in your group . . .'

'Someone would have to carry you half the time. Makes more sense you go by boat. Be safer, quicker.'

I gave a hard laugh.

'So, you two get to go together – all nice and sweet – and I have to sit with those old Arada in a stupid boat.'

'Think about it,' Emile said. 'You saw the terrain. You think you can manage on those poles, up and down ridges, slippery mud, crossing rivers?'

'I'll leave them here, dammit.'

So saying, I threw the crutches to the ground and took a step forward onto my injured foot. At once, a fiery jolt shot up my leg; I hopped back onto the other heel but lost my balance and ended up collapsing on my back at the side of the path. Fortunately, a prodigious patch of fern soften my fall.

Emile just stood there, morose, his arms folded as much to say 'I told you so'.

But then an actual voice called out from up at the quarters – a voice I instantly recognised as belonging to Dr Bryant.

'You there, boy.'

With a start, my brother glanced up. From within my bed of ferns, everything beyond the summit of the path was out of my view. However, I saw Emile swallow hard and then, faster than a firelock, he began to run uphill toward Bryant, calling out:

'Master sir! Sheeps!'

'Ships?' I heard Bryant say, crossly. 'What ships? What are you on about?'

'*Non, non*, sir,' gasped Emile and then I heard him make the sound of a lamb. 'Baa! Muttons. Sheeps. *Mouton de mon mèt. Pédu.*'

'Ah,' said Bryant. 'Sheep!'

'*Pédu! Pédu!*'

'I see . . . You lost your sheep. The sheep that belong to your master, yes?' Bryant continued in hesitant French: '*Non, j'ai* – no see – *pas vu moutons – aujourd'hui. Non.*'

And then Emile tried to explain to him in a mix-mash of kréyòl, French and his five words of English that as he drove his sheep along the River Road they escape from him and ran uphill toward the quarters. He made a jumble of it here and there, but his story came clear enough when done. Meanwhile, I lay on my back, quaking, in case Bryant should notice me. However, it would seem that I was invisible, perhaps due to the abundant ferns and the steep slope of the path where it dip beneath a ridge. The Englishman must have spotted my brother – or at least his upper body – simply because he was on his feet.

'*Pas moutons*,' Bryant was saying. 'No sheep. But do you not speak English, boy?'

'*Kwa?*'

'*Pourquoi – tu – ne – parle – Anglais?*'

'*Ah*,' Emile replied. '*Mon met Fwancé. Ne pal anglé.*'

'I see. Your master – is French, he – speaks no English. *Pas d'Anglais.*'

'*Wi. Mé* – master, sir – *mes moutons.*'

'Yes, yes,' said Bryant. 'Dear God. Well, go and find them then. Wait – wait.' I held my breath until he continued: 'Have you seen a boy? *T'as vu – un garçon? Un negre?* His name Vincent. Vincent? *T'as vu?*'

'*Non*, master sir. *Non. Pa de Vincent. Désolé. Aw revwa*, master sir.'

The yard grew silent and I had to assume that my brother had run off to find his imaginary sheep. Presently, I heard the creak of a doorflap and then another, as the Englishman peered inside the huts, one by one, calling out, sternly:

'Vincent? Vincent?'

I dreaded that he would come poking his nose down the shortcut path; if he did, I was done for, but soon enough the noises from the yard ceased. Though it was almost certain that Bryant had return to the hospital, I was too afraid to move. After what seem like a decade, my brother finally reappeared, strolling down the path from the hospital quarters.

'Is he gone?' I asked.

'*Wi*,' replied Emile. 'Hopefully we will be halfway to Martinique before he comes mousing after Vincent again. But let's avoid the huts for now.'

He heave my sorry bones up onto his shoulder and carried me and my crutches uphill. Steering clear of the yard and the cabins, he took me into the border of a nearby thicket that prospected the hospital buildings and the road to Fort Royal. Emile set me down with my back to a tree and took up a position a short distance away. No pair of sparrowhawk could have kept a closer watch over the hillside but we saw nothing stir except the doctor himself, around midday, riding down to town. From time to time, I heard my brother sigh but not a word pass between us all afternoon. For true, our circumstance required that we keep quiet, yet – no question – it was not for this reason alone that we sat there without speaking.

Chapter Thirty-Seven

M y brother had been hoping for cloudy weather but by sunset the horizon still lay wide open. Clear skies and the threat of a near-full moon toward midnight: conditions could scarce be worse for an illicit escape. Bryant had return from town and the plan was to leave as soon as he and Bell set out for the dance at the Anglade estate. By judicious questioning, Saturnin had learn that Bell was to rencontre with the doctor at the hospital and from there they would ride together to the soirée. Maillard had been deputed to take charge of the sick room that night but since he preferred to remain at home for Christmas Eve he would only put in an appearance if summon by the Béké nurse-men.

Only once the hospital slave began to return to the quarters did we venture out of our hiding place. Quick-quick and quiet, Léontine, Chevallier and Angélique readied themselve for departure in the row-boat, collecting their few possession to take to Martinique. Since I had arrived with only the clothes on my back, I had little to do and so sat on a hut step, resting my leg. All day long, as we sat in the thicket, I had nursed bitter resentment at my relegation to travelling with the old folk whiles Emile and Céleste would go together by land. For true, putting me in the boat made all kind of sense and I understood why my brother had reach that decision. Nevertheless, I felt so excluded I could scarce bring myself to look at him.

'Cover up those light sleeve, *tati*,' he told Angélique. 'Wear something that won't be seen out on the water.'

With trembling hands, the old woman took a brown shawl from her bundle and draped it around her shoulders to conceal her pale chemise. Léontine had put on a dark indigo wrapper, pieced under the arms with check linen, but now she changed her white petticoat for a slate-grey one. Then, hands on hips, she sashayed over to Emile and looked at him sidelong neath her lashes.

'Will this do?' she asked.

He gave her one glance.

'Fine,' said he and walked away, leaving her to stare after him, her mouth open. For a moment, she scuffed her foot around in the dirt. Then she whirled about and slump down beside me on the step. Meanwhile, Chevallier had peel the white shirt from his back. I believe he was entirely sober but the prospect of escaping to Martinique had made him elated and silly. My brother went up to him.

'Have you nothing dark to wear?'

'*Puten!* The Fathers will give me a new shirt, some good cotton.'

'Or not,' said Emile. 'I wouldn't count on them doling out fine linen.'

'They will give me a tumpty-tum shirt, at least. *Pa ni pwoblèm.* Any case, I'm better like this for rowing. I just get all sweated up.'

And he flexed his sinewy arms.

Meanwhile, Léontine fingered my sleeve.

'You should dip this in mud. Darken the cloth. Let me do it.'

She tried to pull the shirt off me but – all of a panic – I hissed at her.

'Ss-ss. Rub mud on your own shift.'

Nevertheless, after my performance the previous night, I had no wish to cause further mishap. Thus, before Emile could order me about, I hopped over to a patch of muck in the shadows. There – as ever, mortified by the many scars on my back – I snatched off my shirt and swirled it in the damp earth until the cloth was the colour of dung. Léontine kept looking over, so quick as I could, I squirm back into the clammy linen, unable to shake the sense that my life had come to its lowest point so far.

My spirit sank further still when Céleste arrive with the news that Bell and Bryant had set off for the Anglade estate.

Léontine jumped up.

'*I bon*,' she said. '*Annou alé*. Let's go.'

Céleste had brought a trait of corncake from the hospital – no doubt, a gift from some patient or one of their relative. She set them down in the kitchen, then walked across the yard to her hut. I watched Emile, his eyes tracking her. Presently, he strolled over and up the steps to lean in her doorway. They began to murmur to each other. I heard her exclaim lightly: 'No, stop!' and then Emile gave a laugh – the first true laugh I had heard from him in a long time.

Angélique kept hobbling over to the edge of the huts, wringing her hands and staring down toward the High Road in the fading light.

'Who you looking for, *Gwan-mè*?' Léontine asked. 'Thérèse isn't coming.'

The old woman gave a sad nod.

'I know it,' she said. 'And Vincent is gone, for true. But what about LeJeune? She should be here by now.'

'That woman can look after herself,' Chevallier told her. 'Always has. She is tough as old turtle. She knows the way to Petit Havre on the goat track. Besides, if she has a ticket she can take the road, pretend she is visiting family.'

Angélique continue to flutter about, agitated, until the old man stroked her cheek.

'Now, *ché*,' said he, kindly. 'Sooner we go, sooner we get there.'

Céleste emerge from her cabin with a small bundle of belongings and my brother wandered across the yard in her wake. She put her hand on my forehead then took some leaves out of her pocket and gave them to me.

'Chew on these if you get hot.'

As she knelt down to examine my foot, Emile began to transfer the corncakes into a burlap bag. I expected him to wish me luck or at least say *ovwé,* but though I waited he made no move to approach me. Instead, he took time to reassure Angélique, saying:

'With your man at the oars, you'll get there in no time at all.'

He handed her one of the bags. Meanwhile, Chevallier stepped in front of me, blocking my view of Emile.

'How far can you row, boy?'

The question took me by surprise. I felt still trembly from head to foot and doubted I would be equal to such exertion. Chevallier studied me, his face most grave until he laughed and punch my arm.

'Only jesting, child. You're sick. Léontine will share the oars. Come now. Let's get out of this place – and fair riddance to it.'

He shouldered his bundle and went to join Angélique in bidding farewell to Céleste. My brother stood to one side, now gazing at me, as though trying to convey something – something important – but whatever it was, I had no notion. He look sad, but most of all he look sorry. Perhaps he felt guilty about sending me in the boat. I certainly hoped so.

Léontine and Chevallier started down the path toward the sea so I turned and limped slowly after them. I could have said goodbye to Emile and Céleste or raise my hand in farewell, but the crutches made such a movement awkward. Despite her bad knees, Angélique overtook me as we descended into the trees, following her man. We had gone some way along the track when it seem to me that I heard Emile call out my name. I glance back but the ground had already dip down such that the lamps in the yard had disappeared and – though I listen hard – I could hear nothing further.

Concluding that it had most likely been my imagination, I set off hobbling again, trying to evite potholes and hating myself and all the world and everyone in it.

Chapter Thirty-Eight

The boat-house stood at the mouth of the river where the hospital estate met the coast. I clocked along, trying to keep up with the others but even old limpard Angélique could move faster than me. We made our way downhill without event, onto the flat span of land at the shore end of the valley. As yet, the moon sat too low in the sky to be seen but starlight glimmered on the surface of the ocean and on the St Jean at its widest point, where it flowed into the sea. By a stroke of good fortune, the ferryman had moored his raft on the north bank of the river and all seemed quiet on our side.

Chevallier made us wait in the trees whiles he check that there was nobody at the boat-house. Across the road lay a narrow span of rough ground then a strip of dirty-looking shore. In the tail of the afternoon, fishermen sat there to mend their nets but by night this stretch of the coast grew quiet. A single horse and rider went by en route to town, followed by a troupe of revellers on foot, then everything fell silent except for the surf pulling restlessly at the sand.

Presently, the old man reappeared and indicated that we should follow him. When we reach the boat-house, he fumbled in his pockets for the key, damning and swearing under his breath. My skin itched all over, in agitation; my ears straining to hear any sound above the waves. Every moment seem to me an age but, at last, the key turn, the doors opened. Léontine helped Chevallier to drag the row-boat down to the sea, leaving me to wait in the night-shade of the boat-house with Angélique.

'Not long now,' she whispered and took my hand in hers. To my surprise, she was quaking from top to toe. I had always been afraid of this old woman with her hocus-pocus but here she was, all a-tremble, yet trying to sound brave for my sake. I saw for the first time that her viperish ways were the result of simple fear. A kind of mournful pity swell my heart and stop my breath.

When Léontine came to fetch us, Angélique hobbled off at once to rejoin her man at the boat. As for me, however, it proved impossible to hobble at any speed because the cursed crutches kept sliding and sinking into the sand. In the end, I had to surrender them to Léontine and hop alongside her, leaning on her shoulder, my shame complete. I could sense the old couple staring at me as we approached and hoped it was dark enough to hide my mortification. Chevallier kept the boat steady in the shallows whiles the old woman hitched up her skirts and clambered into the prow. Then it was my turn. Léontine handed my crutches to her grandmother then grab the stern whiles Chevallier took me by the elbows. He was about to hoist me aboard when we heard a soft hoot from the highway. I turned and saw a figure outlined against the night sky, coming toward us across the sand.

'Who's that?' Léontine murmured.

Of course, I knew at once, would know him anywhere from the set of his shoulders.

'Emile,' I said.

'Oh *puten*,' Chevallier murmured. 'That's it now. Something amiss.'

'*Chut!*' said Angélique. 'It might be nothing.'

The old man released his grip on my arms but I still had to lean on him for support. My brother came right up to the boat. I could tell by the starlight gleam of his eyes that he was gazing at me.

'What's the matter?' Chevallier hissed.

'Change of plan,' replied Emile. 'LaFortune came up from the plantation with a message. The field hand – the fit and healthy ones – are refusing to be slow down by those who cannot keep up. So Saturnin is taking them in one fast group. They've all talked about it and decided.'

'What about the rest?' asked Léontine. 'Those one who aren't able?'

'I'll have to take them,' Emile replied. 'I'll talk to Saturnin, see if I can get him to change their mind. But I doubt it.'

Angélique snorted.

'Why bother coming to tell us? Makes no difference to us here going by sea.'

My brother turn to look at me again.

'Well,' he said. 'I change my mind also. Lucien is coming with me.'

The old woman sucked her teeth at him.

'Boy is lame as a three-legged mule. He's better in the boat with us.'

'We'll manage,' said Emile. 'Give me those crutches.'

She handed them out of the boat and my brother stuck them in the sand. Léontine stared at us, frowning. I saw the old couple exchange an uneasy glance as Emile lifted me up onto his back. He drape me around his shoulders, his elbow behind my knees, my head dangling.

'There,' said he. 'If all else fails, we can go anywhere like this.' He pull the poles out of the sand then bid the others farewell. 'See you at Petit Havre.'

None of them said goodbye. I would have like to watch them set off but the way my brother held me half upside-down, the blood rush to my head and my eyes filled with water, such that I could only see the ground see-sawing beneath us and Emile striding along, his blurry feet sinking deep and deep into the dark sand.

Chapter Thirty-Nine

For sake of expedience, he carried me across the road and only set me down when we got beyond sight of the shore. My spirit soared to be alone with him again, just the two of us, moving through the night-shadows of the landscape. This part of the plantation, the flat old indigo field south of the river, had never yet been planted with cane. With the use of my crutches, I could pick my way across the plain. This was the easy part, down in the valley. I hilched along in silence, managing at times to achieve an almost swinging gait although – under normal circumstance, without injury – I would have been twice as fast. Emile moved along behind me so silent that, once or twice, I had to turn and check that he was still there.

A short distance inland, he overtook me and headed down into a small copse beside the river. Somewise puzzled, I followed him. There, in the trees, just visible, a figure stood waiting. Céleste: her bundle on her shoulder, the bag of corncake in her hands. She and my brother consulted for a while, their heads close together. When they finished, Emile came and spoke in my ear.

'She will go in front, then you.'

Up ahead, Céleste was already just a fleeting dark shape on the river path, heading for the bridge. I hobbled forward, sensing Emile behind me, foot on foot, so close now that I could hear him breathe.

Soon enough, we came to a halt under more trees near the bridge. On the far side, I could see the flickering fires and flambeaux of the plantation quarters. After another hush conversation, my brother continued along the path. Somewhere up ahead, I heard a low exchange of dove hoots as he let the field hand know we were on our way.

Céleste leaned over to speak in my ear.

'We'll get there. Safe and sound.' When I made no reply, she went on: 'Your brother was heart-sick, you know, making you go in that boat. It's better this way. Now we can all be together. Come here.'

She put her arm around my shoulder. I wanted to say something to her about Bryant and what had happen to her but I was unable to find the words. And so I simply allowed myself to lean against her and put my forehead against her cheek. She no longer smelled like vanilla; she smelled like fear. We stood there in silence until Emile returned, then Céleste took my crutches and disappeared with them, into the darkness. My brother bent down to pick me up, this time carrying me pick-a-pack. He bore me along like I weighed no more than a sash. By the time we got to the bridge, Céleste was waiting for us on the other side. Emile carried me across so fast and silent that if you had glimpse his shadow you might have thought he was only a ghost flitting across the river. Howsomever, the thought of being carried into the yard like a cripple fill me with horror. Bad enough for the field hand to see me shuffling along on crutches, but it was better than being borne along as though I were a complete invalid.

'Put me down,' I begged.

'Are you sure?' said Emile, without breaking his stride.

'I can walk, *souplé*, put me down.'

To my relief, he stop where Céleste stood waiting – short of the cabins – and set me on my feet, supporting me until I had a firm grip on my poles. Thereafter, he paused and looked at us, first me then Céleste. I had the sense that he might be about to impart some word of wisdom to us but in the end he just nodded and made a scraping noise at the back of his throat, a clearing of his passages. Then he shook his head – as though dismissing a troublesome thought – and headed on toward the cabins.

Chapter Forty

Wee found Saturnin waiting beside the flambeaux at the entrance to the yard along with two whip-thin boys. He gave my crutches a glance but made no comment. Instead, he muttered something and twitched his whip toward the river. Off the boys went, fast as bat, speeding into the darkness.

'Once they fetch the lookouts we can go,' he told Emile.

My brother drew him aside and they began to speak in murmurs. I hitch past them slow-slow and heard Emile ask:

'What about the rum? Did you stop them drinking?'

'Yes, yes, *pa ni pwoblèm*,' said the driver. 'The cask still sealed.'

'Listen, my friend. Would it not be safer – more fair – if we stuck to our first plan? Go in small group, some able, some not.'

Saturnin gave a snort.

'You want to take the sick and lame go ahead, and welcome. All the fast ones want to come with me.' He grinned. 'We won't set sail without you, never fear.'

With that, he strode off toward the cabins. My brother exchanged a worried look with Céleste then they hurried after him. By the time I reach the yard they were in a huddle with the driver, trying to make him change his mind. A few field hand scurried hither-thither to gather up their meagre duds, but most of them were prepared and waiting to leave. For true, they had already divided themselve into two platoon. Around the main fire stood the able-body slaves, those uncumber by ill health or impediment, mostly men and boys. There were, perhaps, ten women in this group: some girls but also mothers, healthy younger specimen with older children who could travel unaided. The strongest young men – Coco, Montout, Lapin and Philoge – had gathered around a puncheon of rum on the ground. Perhaps they were meant to guard the liquor, and although the seal remained intact, the way they kept slapping the cask and sniffing the staves suggested they would sore have like to taste its content.

By contrast, around a small fire on the far side of the yard, another group had gathered – about a dozen of them. Here we had a different species – at a glance: the old, the weak, the mad, the ramshackle, the encumbered. Old Raymond and crack-brain Choisie; Magdelon and Cléronne in their spike collars; one sick-looking elderly woman sitting on a step with her head in her hands and a few mothers with babes-in-arms and toddling infant who would have to be carried. Longside them stood two miserable-looking young men, presumably fathers to these children. One of the men had a missing hand; his arm ended in a blacken stump. Nearby, Augustin lay curled up on the ground in his fetters, the bloody bandage still wrapped around his skull. We might as well have been a party of cripples bound for Rome.

With a jab of his whip, Saturnin indicated this group to my brother.

'That's your party over there.'

Then he strolled off to join the fast group, *en passant* gazing upon my plyers. He made no comment, simply raised his eyebrows and scratched his chin in a manner design to let me know he was entirely unsurprise that I had got myself in such a pickle.

Just then, I heard a low hoot from the bridge. Someone in the fast group made a reply and then, to my surprise, Léontine came darting into the yard.

'What's the matter?' Emile asked her. 'Something wrong with the boat?'

'We're coming with you,' she replied. '*Gwan-mè* decided we

should not be separated from everybody else.'

Just then, Angélique arrive with Chevallier helping her along.

'Here come the old folks,' said Saturnin. 'Got all frighty out there on their own. Turn tail and run back to camp.'

Chevallier scowled at him.

'We just changed our mind,' said he.

Angélique drew herself up to her full height and pointed at my crutches.

'If that boy can go climb around the island then so can we. I'm quicker than him.'

As though to prove it, she shook her man off her arm and hobbled across the yard, giving the fast group a haughty look as she join the sick old woman on the step.

'*Bonswa, Marigot*,' said Angélique. '*Sa ou fé?*'

Marigot looked up with a start.

'Angélique,' said she. '*Mwen kontan wè zot.* I'm so tired I wish I was dead.'

Meanwhile, Céleste had begun to hand out the corncake. For once, I had no appetite and so stash my piece in my pocket for later. Céleste passed another portion to a young mother who carried a tiny baby strap to her back.

'Here, Rosalie, eat. We may not have time to stop once we get moving.'

'*Mèsi.*'

The young woman broke the cake into pieces. She called out to a little imp who sat in the dirt wearing a baby hat.

'Casimir.'

The child toddled over to her and took the cake. Rosalie held out another to the man beside her, a young fellow. He was so caught up in gazing over at the fast group that he fail to notice until she spoke his name:

'Narcisse.'

With a start, he turned and I saw that he had only a flap of skin and a hole where his ear should have been. Another victim of the overseer. When Rosalie offered him the corncake, he shook his head and his gaze soon wandered back to Saturnin and the others.

Meanwhile, Céleste offered a cake to Choisie. The old crazy only sniffed it once or twice like a cat might surview a morsel.

'Just eat it,' Magdelon told him. 'Eat.'

He inspected the cake minutely. Only after a while did he break off a crumb and push it tween his lips. Chevallier had gone to sit beside Augustin. Céleste gave them both a cake. Chevallier took a bite.

'This is good,' he said, his mouth full. 'I intend to eat like this every day in Martinique. We can ask the Fathers for a loaf like they sell in the market.' He groaned. 'With flour from *La Fwance* – and pastry made with butter that melt on your tongue.'

Angélique paused in lighting her pipe to gaze at him, somewhat caustic.

'He's going to tell us about pastry now,' she said, blowing smoke. 'He ate pastry once.'

A few people in both groups laughed.

'Never mind pastry,' said Cléronne. 'I just can't wait to get rid of this collar.' She plucked at the spikes encircling her throat then gave Magdelon a sideways glance. 'They will take these off, won't they, over there?'

'Oh certainly,' said Magdelon. 'The Fathers will take them off us, for true.'

However, from the expression on both their faces, you could tell neither of them was certain. Behind me, I could hear hush voices. I glanced over my shoulder. The young couple – Rosalie and one-eared Narcisse – had become embroiled in a heated conversation.

Saturnin stepped into the space between the groups and threw his arms wide, saying:

'Once we get to Martinique we shall have our own dance to celebrate. Wait and see.'

Emile – who had been silent up until this moment – gave an exasperated laugh.

'A dance to celebrate . . . have you lost your mind?'

Saturnin scowled.

'We're only – speculating,' said Chevallier. 'What it will be like over there.'

'Speculating!' Emile replied. 'They're not going to set you free in Martinique, you know. Life with the Fathers is not much better than here. Some of you might remember it like that, but you're dreaming. You'll still be slaves. You'll still be getting up every day to work in the field. Those men are still your masters. There's no magical Father is going to ply you with pastry and let you dance all night.'

'But some of *les Frères* are good men,' said a voice from the fast group. 'Better than these English.'

Emile gave another dry laugh.

'You think so? How many of you remember the Fathers that were here before? Hmm? Not all were good men. Père Gabriel, for example, comes to mind. He was one. Père Barnabé. You think he was good? And there were others . . .'

The obvious name, of course – a creature far worse than Gabriel or Barnabé – was Damien Pillon. Since he had died only five years previous, many of the field hand would remember him. I stared at the ground, unable to look them in the eye. My face grew hot. The scars on my back began to tingle.

I expect the field hand were waiting to see if Emile would utter the Pillon name, but when he resume speaking, he simply said:

'I'm sure some of you can think of other Fathers who were not good men.'

Had some person called out 'The Pestle' or even 'Your own papa', I would scarce have been surprised, but every field hand, Saturnin included, remain silent – which, in hindsight, seems an act of kindness on their part. Mostly, they look dejected and uncomfortable. Nonetheless, Emile had not yet done berating them.

'These new Fathers over there in St Pierre, they're just white men from Europe same as any other. Lefébure, from what I hear, is only interested in making rum. What that suggest to me is, he will do whatever necessary to get sugar. He'll work you hard. And Cléophas is no saint. Most of you met him when he was here. You know the kind of man he is. He only wants sugar money. That's why they need you.'

Raymond took a step forward.

'Yes,' he said. 'But, for true, it has to be better than here. Every day now, we are wondering – who will be next? What will they chop off? Will it be a finger, toe, a hand or foot? Who will lose his head? How will they torture us? What terrible thing will they make us do? What will they make us eat? Our own ears – or worse?'

I glanced around at their gloomy faces. Everywhere, eyes were downcast.

Saturnin nodded.

'For true. They treat us worse than they treat their animals.'

'Correct,' someone said.

The driver turned his gaze upon Augustin, Magdelon and Cléronne.

'Want to get rid of these collars and chain?'

'Most certainly,' said Magdelon and Cléronne nodded, whiles Augustin simply looked miserable.

Saturnin turned a jaundiced eye on my brother and when he spoke again he had a mocking tone to his voice.

'Emile, anyone would think you don't want us to go. But you were the one who came here with your document. You're the one who started all this. You're not changing your mind now, are you? Have you lost your nerve? Perhaps you are afraid.'

My brother fell silent for a time. He looked more sad than afraid. Meanwhile, the young woman and her one-eared man seem to have stop bickering. Rosalie sat as though turn to stone whiles Narcisse stood apart from her, arms folded, staring at the ground.

Eventually, Emile spoke again.

'For true, you won't have to speak English. And I believe there will be better provision ground, more food – so they say. They might get the blacksmith to take off the collars and weights. And their punishment might not be as bad as what you have suffered here of late. But – whatever happens – you will still be slave. They will punish you and flog you. And there may be Fathers who will do worse than that in future. I'm not saying Cléophas is one of those, or Lefébure. But who knows what might happen, who their successor might be.'

'*Puten!* We know that,' said Chevallier, his voice husky. 'But it can't be any worse than it is here now.'

My brother sighed and looked around at them all again, the fast and the slow.

'You really want to go? All of you?'

There was general nodding and murmured assent, a few people calling out:

'Yes,' and 'Correct,' and 'Most certainly.'

As these voices faded, I saw Narcisse lift his head as though coming to a decision. Then, slowly-slowly, he walked over to join the fast group. Rosalie stared after him, in shock and disbelief. Céleste noticed him and spoke out.

'Narcisse?'

The young man said nothing; he simply went to greet some of his compeers at the back of the group, trying to melt into the shadows. Rosalie bent her head and hugged her child Casimir close to her chest. The baby on her back began to cry. Céleste hurried over and put an arm around them.

Emile turned to the other young man in our group, the one missing a hand.

'Polidor – you want to join him?'

The young man pursed his lips. His woman glanced up at him, anxious, holding her baby to her breast. He touched her shoulder with his one good hand then lifted the little girl beside them into his arms.

'I'm stay with my family.'

Charlotte smiled up at him.

'Good,' said my brother.

He turn to Léontine, jerked his head at the fast group. 'You could go with them. You know we might be slow.'

'No,' said she. 'I'll stay to help *Gwan-mè* and *Gwan-pè*.'

'Good girl,' replied Emile.

At this mention of Angélique, I notice she was no longer on the step where she had been sitting beside Marigot. As I looked around, she emerge from behind the hut, somewhat shifty in appearance. My heart gave a lurch. What had she been doing?

'Well, let's make sure nothing goes wrong,' Emile said. 'If any of you have to hide anywhere, make sure you take something to drink or hide close to clean water.'

Angélique step forward and stood in the light of the fire.

'Let us see!' she pronounced.

She raised her arm and I saw that in one hand she held a clay jar, corked. Her eyes wide, she threw back her head.

'If there is spirit in this bottle,' she said, 'all will go well tonight.'

She waved her hand around, then – when all eyes were upon her

– pulled out the cork. A wisp of smoke floated up from the neck of the open flask.

'*Vwala*,' she cried. 'We will have a success!'

She grinned around at both groups, showing her teeth. Some people nodded or smiled but this superstitious display of hers only made me feel ill at ease.

Just then, the two skinny boys return with the lookouts, a girl and boy of about the same age, both lithe and fit. They scattered to various hut to collect their paltry gear.

'Is everybody here now?' said Saturnin, counting heads. 'Who is missing?'

'LeJeune,' said Emile. 'She's coming from Megrin.'

'Well, she will have to catch up,' said Saturnin. 'We cannot wait. Are we ready?'

There were a few murmured replies. Céleste handed the remaining corncake to one of the women in the fast group. People began to gather up their small bundles.

'Just leave the flambeaux and fire to burn out,' Saturnin told my brother. 'That way, anyone passing on the road will think we are here. Emile – we will see you at Petit Havre, by the dirty creek, south end of the bay.'

'*I bon*,' said my brother. 'But stay back in the forest until we get there, don't cross the road or go down to the shore. Keep out of sight.'

The driver rolled his eyes as much to say 'fussy-fussy'. Then he hurried toward the growing ground, beckoning his platoon to follow. Quick and fast, they fled after him, Narcisse among the first, his head bowed. There were few goodbyes between the two groups. Some of the fast platoon could scarce look the rest of us in the eye. Others gave a last mournful glance at the unopen cask of rum as they streamed out of the yard, heading for the foothills of Morne St Eloy.

Last to leave were the two lookout, boy and girl. They had scramble to grab a few possession and now they went running to catch up with the others. Part of me longed to go with them. As they skip toward the provision ground, I limped over to the rear of the huts and watched until they disappear from sight in the darkness. Then I hobble back across the yard whiles the others finish their corncake and drank water, under instruction from Emile. Without looking, I could sense their eyes upon me and I knew what they were thinking. They were all wondering whether or not I would slow them down.

PART EIGHT

The Escape

Chapter Forty-One

Emile counted heads: in total, fifteen adult, plus two babes-in-arms and three toddling children. The mothers fed the infant before we set out and whiles they were thus occupied my brother explain the route. Saturnin and the rest could take shortcut but we would skirt the high ground so far as possible. The first obstacle in our path was Morne St Eloy. We would tackle the inland end, where the cane-fields ascended gradually to a wide ravine then down to the next valley. Thereafter, we could make our way, mostly, through the plantation that line the coast.

Magdelon had been retying her bundle but now she looked up in alarm.

'The plantation? What if they have a night-watcher or dogs?'

'We go around the edge of each estate,' said Emile. 'Nowhere near the houses.'

'How long will it take?' Polidor asked.

'We might do it in three hours,' Emile replied. His gaze rested for a flash on my crutches. 'Perhaps four.'

'What about Saturnin and the rest?' Chevallier asked him. 'How long for them?'

'If they go fast, perhaps two hours.'

I glanced around at their faces in the flickering firelight. Nobody looked abundantly ecstatic. Rosalie pulled her boy Casimir closer to her.

'What if they get tired of waiting and set sail without us?'

'No,' said my brother. 'That won't happen.'

'Who is sailing this boat?' demanded Cléronne.

'Two boat,' Emile replied. 'Cléophas on a sloop with a skipper and in a yawl, the man called White who brought us here, an Englishman—'

Magdelon looked appalled.

'English?'

'In the employ of Cléophas,' Emile said. 'His boat might carry ten at most.'

'Cléophas,' said Angélique, full of disdain. 'I would not take his word for a straw.'

'Who could trust him?' said Marigot, the tired old woman. 'Sneaking about the place, shu-shuing in every ear. If he gets those young one aboard he might think that's plenty slave, set sail without us. Then we are left behind whiles the others all gone.'

Raymond gazed around at us, an old-man glimmer in his eye.

'My guess is Cléophas will wait until dawn, like he said. But once the sun comes up, he might not care to be sitting there in shallow water with a boatload of stolen slave. He will want to be away from that bay, out on the high sea.'

'Correct,' said my brother. 'But we will get there long before then.' His gaze strayed across Céleste and then myself and when he continued it seem that he was speaking mainly at us. 'We have to be like the Gommier tree, our roots intertwined. No matter what, we stick together. That's how the Gommier stay strong and survive, standing and growing, even when the hurricane blow. Now, unless anyone has a question, we should get out of here.'

He threw more charcoal onto the fire to keep it burning. Chevallier helped Angélique and Marigot to their feet and the rest began to gather up their gear in haste. At the sight of everyone getting ready to leave, old Choisie became anxious and confused.

'Where are you going?' he asked.

Emile walked over to him.

'Listen, Choisie. We're going for a walk but we must be quiet. You can't go jumping on our backs and shrieking, *kompwan*?'

The old man nodded his head.

'Good,' said Emile. 'Now remember that.'

'Come along now,' said Céleste.

She took Choisie by the hand and led him with Rosalie and little Casimir across the yard. I pegged over to join my brother, who was taking a last look around the quarters. From a distance, with the fires and flambeaux burning, it might look like a normal night in camp, everyone exhausted at the end of a hard week, drinking their Christmas rum. With any luck, nobody would stray off the River Road to vestigate.

'I'll go at the front of the line,' said Emile. 'You stay at the back with Céleste. Send word forward if you need me to carry you. *Kompwan?*'

'Yes.'

We both glanced around the quarters again. The young women were helping each other strap their babies to their backs whiles Polidor attempted to round up the remaining children. My brother threw another log onto the big fire.

'Tell me something,' I said. 'That lieutenant, back in Martinique. He told Bianco you saved his life.' Emile remain silent so I went on: 'What happened?'

I heard him take a breath.

'Well,' he said. 'It was during the invasion, after the English landed. The French took us south, near Fort Louis. We were entrenched in the mountains. But then we were told to attack and – well, it was a mistake. We had to retreat. The English came after us, into the ravine, then up Morne Grenier. In all the chaos, Fournier – the lieutenant – he was shot, injured. I had to throw him on my back, get him off the mountain before those Goddams took our position. Then I carried him all the way to Gros Morne, a safe place there for him to recover. They ordered me to return to my masters. I left him there. Got rid of the uniform and boots, went back to the Dominicans.'

For a while, I stood in silence, thinking about what he had done.

'Why did you never tell me about all that?' I asked. 'You saved his life.'

Emile gave a shrug.

'It was my duty. I had no choice. Same as now.'

Normally, if you asked him something, he would give no satisfactory reply. You might as well try and gather wool from a turkey.

'Emile,' I said.

'*Kwa?*'

'What if they do sail off without us?'

'They won't,' he replied. He reached out and put his hand on my shoulder. 'I'm counting on you now. Keep your eyes and ears open back there.'

Then he strode over to the others who had begun to line up at the edge of the yard and took his position at the front.

Chapter Forty-Two

By this time, the Man in the Moon was awake and almost full, his shocked white face peering down at us from behind the tallest trees, as though he dared not believe his eyes at our audacity. We sneaked along the perimeter of the provision ground and soon turned into the field. Hardly a word spoken as we threaded our way between the rows of cane, heading east along the valley then north toward Morne St Eloy. Saturnin and his platoon long gone. No trace of them remained, not a shu-shu to be heard ahead of us, not the snap of a twig nor the rustle of a leaf.

My brother led the way, one field to the next. Léontine followed him and, in her wake, Magdelon and Cléronne. Some short way behind them, out of range of the collar spikes, came Charlotte with her baby and Polidor who carried their two other infant, one on his back and one in his arms, but he was strong despite his missing hand and the tots both small and light thus he managed a fair pace. The rest of us followed best we could in a rag-tag line. Chevallier walked with the two old women, Angélique every otherwhile fending off his attempts to take her arm. Raymond must have been a tough old cod to survive so long but he was frail now, his gait shuffling; and though Augustin seemed accustom to lugging his weight, that and his great depression of spirit did slow him down. As for me, I made my way between the cane-rows swift as I could kick it, but my foot and leg felt as though they were afire and venom still fevered my blood. For true, I struggle to keep up even with the tardiest of the others, all the while dreading what terrain we might yet encounter.

Most laggard of us all was Choisie. Advanced age and endless toil had bent his spine, his walk a kind of crab-like scuttle with abundant flapping of elbow and scant forward motion. He seem to have remembered what Emile told him for he had yet to jump on any back. But each-every sound startled him and even harmless sights that appeared in his path could cause him distress. A sudden breeze shivering the leaves on a cane-stalk made him jump and the screech of a nightbird caused him to stop dead with his two hands on his ears. In between, he tottered along, every otherwhile muttering: 'Stone me down!' or laughing to himself until someone told him to shut his beak. Time and again, Rosalie and Céleste had to persuade him onward with hushed entreaties.

They also had to contend with Casimir, the oldest child. He prove to be a sulky, wriggling imp who cause more fuss than all the rest together. Halfway through the third cane-piece, near the fork of the river, he threw himself to the ground and refuse to walk further. When Rosalie tried to persuade him, he set up wailing and – disturb by the commotion – the old watch-dog at the mill began to bark. Of course, all this fracas cause great alarm along the line. Mercifully, no dwelling nearby – only a handful of coffee plantation up in the hills – but anyone on the River Road would hear that hound, plus the *bloucoutoum* could wake the sleeping babies who might, in turn, begin to caterwaul. Everyone with a child hurried on, leaving a few of us to comfort the boy. Rosalie hugged him to her breast to muffle his sobs. The remainder of us stood there like stone statue amid the cane, scarce breathing, each of us wondering if any Béké might come poking to discover what had disturb the guard-dog. Then I remembered the corncake in my pocket. I dug it out and showed it to Casimir. He stopped his racket at once, then took the cake from me and began to eat. The old hound gave one final bark that echoed across the valley and then he fell silent.

My brother patted me on the shoulder.

'Well done, Lucien,' he said.

Though Emile offer to carry Casimir, the child insisted on walking with his mother, but at least we were able to proceed.

Thus, by starts and fits, did we creep through the plantation and eventually reach the inland end of Morne St Eloy where the cane-fields began to ascend the lower slopes of the mountain. Here, Emile summon Céleste to the head of the line and came back to stand with me. When the others began to make their way uphill, I did my utmost to follow but the ground was too steep and my crutches kept sliding out from under me. In the end, Emile gave them to Léontine and lifted me onto his back.

Borne along by my brother, I close my eyes. The sound of the others up ahead came to my ears like a whisper half-heard above the din of the peeping frogs: if you listen hard you might wonder if a breeze had rattle the cane. Emile carried me without complaint, though his breathing grew laboured the higher we went. Sometimes, if he staggered or swayed, the cool leaves of cane brushed against my skin.

We found the others waiting for us at the summit of the slope. Emile set me down and rested awhile. From that high point, we could hear the faint sound of music. The Christmas soirée had begun at the Anglade estate and the plaintive notes of violins and other instrument drifted over from behind the hills: the genteel strings such a contrast to the lush vegetation, both wild and cultivated, that flourished all around.

By then, the moon had climbed above the trees and we had a silvery view all the way to Turtle Bay. Inland, a bank of cloud had gathered above the distant mountains. I could hear a stream running through the vale. Down there, the *Chemin des Hauteurs* cut across the valley, marking the northern edge of the hospital estate.

On the far side of the road, an enorm dark shape rose up against the glittering sky, a forested mountain with a high peak. We set off again, descending toward a narrow band of forest near the road. I could just about manage on my crutches. Soon, the ground began to level out and, somewise further on, we reach the first trees. Up ahead, a scrub land of grass and low bush between us and the *Chemin des Hauteurs*, beyond which lay another sugar estate.

After a hush consultation with my brother, Polidor and Chevallier set off to check that the *Chemin* was clear, Polidor heading up to the bend in the road, whiles Chevallier sloped off downhill. Emile lined us up in twos and threes to help each other to the far side. Soon enough, a series of dove hoot came from the highway, our signal that the road was clear. Grasping their collars, Magdelon and Cléronne were first to dash across the scrub land and skitter-scatter over the highway to the strip of open ground on the other side before disappearing into the tall cane. Next to venture forth, Charlotte and Rosalie. Although cumbered with babies and infant, they hurried forth and vanished into the new estate. Then Léontine helped old Marigot and Angélique to safety, followed by Céleste with Casimir and also Augustin who lumbered over, his chain clinking. That left me with my brother and the two old men. Emile presented his back to Choisie.

'Want a ride?'

Choisie needed no persuasion and since he weigh no more than a leaf my brother lifted him with devil the sign of effort. He trotted across the highway in a snap, Choisie riding him much as though competing in a donkey race. Having set off in their wake, I glance back only to see Raymond hesitating on the scrubby ground. I whisper to him:

'Let's go.'

But still he stood there, his limbs struck with some species of paralysis.

'Raymond – what's the matter?'

He kept staring at the road as though transfix.

'I just realised, I never once left the plantation, not since the Fathers brought us from Martinique.'

Choisie and his donkey had already plunged into the cane on the far side. Just then, from beyond the bend came another signal. This time, the trill of a pigeon – a warning. When I listened, hard, I caught the sound of hooves pounding the dirt road in the distance: what sounded like a single rider heading down from one of the coffee plantation in the hills.

'Hurry up,' I whispered.

The old man seemed about to turn and retrace his step to the quarters but I could tell that he would never make it back to the trees before that horse hit the bend and he would be caught on the open ground, lit up by moonlight. Hoping to persuade him onward, I hobbled over and had almost reached him when a figure darted past me. Céleste. She grab Raymond by the arm and began to pull him to the road, the old man scuttling along behind her like a crab caught by his claw. Peggity-peg, I hopped after them as the drumming of hooves grew closer, closer. We started across the road but the horse gallop so fast I realised we would never reach the cane in time to hide. Quick-sharp, I threw myself at Raymond, casting off my crutches as I knocked him to the ground at the side of the highway. In the same moment, Emile came shooting out of the dark. He grab Céleste and dropped with her so that he fell beneath her body, protecting her as he rolled over onto his side, holding her in an embrace.

Raymond groaned.

'Shh!' I said and clamp my hand across his mouth just as a stallion came hurtling around the bend at full tilt, two Béké colonial on his back, a man mounted behind a woman. They rush downhill like a hurricane-wind, shrieking with merriment and calling out to each other in English, the woman shouting 'Faster! Faster!' and her companion yelling: 'No, stop! Stop it! Slow down!' The cataclop of hooves grew so loud as they gallop toward us, I thought we would surely be trampled and when the stallion snorted in passing I swear I felt his breath on my foot. All the while, Emile kept hold of Céleste, wrapped around her, his face buried in the back of her neck, his protecting hands clasped over the swell of her belly, until the stallion hammered past us and was gone, flying down to the coast.

Chapter Forty-Three

After that, Emile became determine to steer clear of any highway. As soon as Chevallier and Polidor rejoined us, off we set again in our slow line, plodding through the rows of cane. Now, of course, we were trespassing. The screech of fiddles up at the Anglade place soon faded until, at last, we could hear them no more. Once we had reach the trees on the low slopes of the next hill, we crept on around the edge of the plantation, mostly inside the skirt of the wood. By then, a bank of cloud had drifted across the moon, throwing deeper shadow. We pressed on toward the coast then turned inland to make our way along the northern side of the mountain, through the forest. The ground here so steep and slippery in places that every otherwhile Emile was oblige to carry me. Once or twice, he had to go back for Choisie who was too weak to claw himself up the steepest slope. Rosalie, Polidor, Charlotte and Céleste helped each other and the children, sometimes carrying them, sometimes handing them upward or down, one to the other.

Thereafter, we made slow progress along what felt like a broad shelf with cliffs on both side: above us, to the right and below, to the left. Sometimes, the shelf became almost as broad and clear as a road; other times, the field hand had to use their cutlass to hack out a path through the wild grasses. Léontine went ahead with my crutches whiles my brother carried me pick-a-pack. The grassy terrain persisted for such a stretch that we fell behind the others, out of earshot.

'Well done back there,' said Emile. 'With Raymond.'

'It was nothing,' I replied. 'Like eating pastry.'

After a moment, his shoulders began to shake and I realised he was silently laughing.

Eventually, the ground began to dip again, descending. The moon reappeared, peeping out from behind a raft of cloud. I could hear the sound of rushing water up ahead. We soon reach the foot of a ravine and found a river in spate after recent rains in the mountains. The others had stop for a rest on the riverbank.

'How much further?' asked old Marigot.

Emile set me beside her among the roots of a tree.

'That depends. If this is the *Rivière de Beausejour* then – not far.'

'Do you not know?' asked Léontine, who no longer seem to favour him so well.

My brother gazed at the starlight sparkling on the surface of the water.

'Can't say I know this stretch.' He turn to Céleste. 'What do you think, *ché*?'

She shook her head.

'It might be the Beausejour. Hard to tell.'

'Well,' said Emile. 'Whatever it is, we must get to the other side.'

'Can we sit here awhile?' said Angélique. 'My knee is killing me to death.'

'Us old ancients need to rest,' Raymond added.

Emile thought for a moment then said:

'Let's find somewhere to cross before we rest.'

And so we headed upstream. Foot on foot we went, one after the other. Along the riverbank, the vines grew thick, climbing and twining. Choisie clambered his way over the tangle of roots and liane like a nimble old beetle but Emile had to carry me again.

At last, we reached a gully where the river broadened out neath a thundering waterfall. In mid-stream there appear to be a number of deep pool and, here and there, the water ran fast over flat rocks. Emile set me down again then turn to the others.

'Let's rest here until we find a way across.'

Whiles Polidor and Léontine went to check whether any spot might be fordable, the women led their children to a stony stretch of river and began to play with them in the shallows. Magdelon settled in among the roots of a prodigious tree and, after a moment, Cléronne sat in front of her and began to rub her feet, quite companiable. Nearby, Chevallier stepped off a low part of the bank into a knee-deep pool.

'Oh, that feels good.' He turn to his woman. 'Come in, *ché*, cool down.'

'Help me, then,' she said and he held her hands as she lowered herself into the water to paddle among the rocks.

Further upstream, Raymond took a calabash from his bundle and filled it from a pool near the falls. Then he carried the vessel over to Augustin and Choisie.

'Here,' he said. 'Cool yourself.'

The three men took turns to splash the water on their necks whilst watching the shadowy figures of Polidor and Léontine pick their way, rock to rock, testing the depth of various pool. Meanwhile, Céleste had wandered up to the lagoon below the falls. She stood on a rocky outcrop and reached into the cascade of water then brought her hands to her face and throat. Emile set off toward her then seem to change his mind and return to where I sat.

'Come on,' said he. 'Let's cool you down.'

He carried me to the outcrop of rocks and set me on a fallen tree at the side of the lagoon. Céleste cupped her palms together neath the torrent then came over to us, careful not to spill a drop, as though to let us drink. However, soon as she got close enough, she threw the water at my brother in jest. Most of it caught him in the face, so unexpected that he spluttered and I could not help but grin. Céleste laughed so hard, she almost lost her footing and fell into the lagoon. My brother began to bespatter her and she kicked a deluge back at him. Then they both turned on me. I had to lean down and scoop handfuls of water at them best I could in order to retaliate.

All at once, Emile paused in the act of splashing me. Something caught his attention on the riverbank: Polidor, dashing low toward us. Downriver, various shadowy figures scrambled out of the water, ushered infants into the trees. I could just make out Augustin and Raymond cowering with Choisie beneath some overhanging branches on the bank.

'Someone coming,' Polidor hissed as he dived into the bushes.

Céleste slipped in beside him whiles Emile drag me down behind the fallen tree. Somewhere nearby, one of the babies began to whimper but the cries were muffle so quick I could only guess that his mother had stuff something in his mouth to hush him. For a while, the roar of the rapids fill the air. Me and my brother hunker down in silence, listening, watching, scarce a breath between us. Then, sure enough, I heard the crack of a twig or bamboo, just audible above the falls and then, coming closer, the whush-whush brustle of someone struggling to make their way through dense foliage.

In my mind, I was seize by the notion that Bell had discover the abandon quarters and was bringing a parcel of troops to catch us. Could it be that he had only pretended to go to the Anglade dance? Had he followed us all the way here? For a sudden, the breath left my body. But then Emile put his hand on my shoulder, reminding me that he was there, and I felt somewise reassured.

At last, a shadowy figure emerge from the underbrush. Not the overseer, unless he had took to wearing petticoat. A woman – a house-slave by the looks of her – picking her way up the riverbank with a degree of stealth, evidently – like us – searching for a place to cross. She had just passed a patch of rushes at the edge of the water when someone, somewhere, hiss like a goose. The woman gave a gasp and turn to peer at the river.

'Who's there?' she cried, in fright.

Another sharp hiss then a small figure rose up from the rushes: Angélique. A moment later, Chevallier stood up beside her.

'Is that you, LeJeune?' said Angélique.

The woman clutched at her breast.

'Jésis-Maïa! You trying to kill me, *tati*?'

'Pffft!' said Emile, beside me. 'It's only LeJeune.'

He help me to my feet whiles Céleste fetch my poles. The others had already gathered around LeJeune, speaking in low voices. Beneath the starlight, she looked much older than last time I had seen her, worn out and scrawny.

'Why you coming this way?' Chevallier asked. 'You could go easy on the road.'

'Not tonight,' said Lejeune. 'My master in a temper. Hmm. Mm-hmm. Tore up my Christmas ticket. Had to wait for him to get drunk so I could sneak off. That's why I'm late.' She glanced around at the rest of us. 'Is this all of you? Where is everybody?'

'The faster ones went on ahead,' Céleste explained.

'Faster ones?'

'Young field hand,' said Angélique. 'Boys and men, young women. They're up ahead somewhere. Anybody quick on his feet, they went first in another group.'

LeJeune glanced around at us again, this time seeming to notice our cumbrances and afflictions: the collars and shackles, the crutches, lost wits, babies and so forth. I could see her mind working fast-fast.

'Well,' she said. 'I'm quick on my feet, I suppose. Hmm – I am, for true. Perhaps – perhaps I should try to catch them. Mm-hmm – that's what I'll do. Who wants to come with me?'

She looked around at us again but – when nobody made reply – she continued:

'Oh well, I'll just go on and catch them, I suppose, if that be the case. Hmm. Best get moving, find a way across this river. See you at the boat. *A talé . . . a talé.*'

So saying, she picked up her skirts and – with a brief wave – set off again at such a pace she soon passed out of sight. We stared after her, in silence. Behind me, the waterfall crashed on, boiling, relentless, as loud as a million angry bumble-bee. An air of gloom had descended once again over the entire party.

'Look at her flap and run,' said Céleste. 'Chicken-hearted.'

'For true,' I said. 'She probably needs to lay an egg.'

Weak attempt at humour though it were, at least it made my brother and a few others chuckle and the mood lightened somewise.

Emile pointed to a narrow pool near the far side.

'Over there might be our best bet.'

It occur to me that the fallen tree I had been sitting on might bridge the gap between the riverbank and a pile of flat rocks in midstream and so I suggested we might try to move it.

Emile, Léontine, Charlotte, Polidor, Chevallier and Rosalie joined forces and by a process of pushing, rolling, lifting and toppling the trunk – under direction from Céleste – they manage to manoeuvre it into place. Sure enough, it was a near perfect fit.

Emile, panting, slap me on the back.

'Well done, bug,' he said. 'Good man.'

Well, that was the first time he had ever call me a man. My heart swelled up like a globefish.

Chapter Forty-Four

Those who were able walked across, carrying the children. The rest of us – including Angélique, Choisie, Raymond, Augustin and me – were oblige to shuffle over on our hind quarters, Augustin pushing his weight ahead of him.

On the far side of the river, we carried on downhill. After descending toward the coast somewhile, we reached a dirty-dirty creek and followed the sluggish water a short distance to a break in the trees ahead. The creek flowed across a road and into woods on the other side. Most of the cloud had drifted off by then and the moon shone down on the highway, gleaming in a milky puddle like the pearl of an oyster. Took me a short while to recognise that this was the coast road, where Emile and I had scuttled across on the day we came to the island. We had reach Petit Havre, at last.

This spot by the creek was where we had arrange to rencontre the fast group. My brother hesitated among the trees, a stone throw short of the road. When I poled up beside him, he put his arm around me and murmured in my ear.

'We made it.'

Such foolhardy temptation of Providence made me wince but Emile too lost in his thoughts to notice. We scan the darkness around us, looking for field hand, and Raymond gave a few tentative hoot but though we waited, nobody presented himself.

The others gathered around and Emile spoke to us in a low voice.

'Keep your ears open. Saturnin and the rest may have been delayed.'

Angélique snorted.

'They probably sailed off already. Be halfway to Martinique by now.'

'They might have gone down to look at the boats,' said Emile. 'Let's cross the road here. We can see the bay from the cliff on the other side. Watch your step.'

Magdelon and Cléronne kept lookout whiles the rest of us slipped across the highway to the belt of woodland along the cliff-edge. Emile came over last of all. We crept forward through the undergrowth and – beyond a gap in the trees – the bay spread out below us, shining in the starlight. The two drogher that had been there early in the week had gone. Emile pointed to a sloop at anchor between the two fist of headland.

'That must be Cléophas,' he said.

The Daisy had been moored up closer to shore, the skiff empty but ready in the water at her stern. I could see no movement on any of the vessel. The fast group might have been hiding in the trees that fringe the sand, but it was too dark to tell.

'I'll go down, see if they're there,' said Emile. 'Let's go back across the road; it's safer.' He turn to Choisie. 'We must be quiet, *tonton*. Can you keep hush a while longer?'

Choisie mocked his tone, sour-face.

'Mim mim mim mim mim mim mim?'

My brother mutter to me.

'Try to keep them quiet.'

We cross the road once more and retreated somewise into the forest. Emile sent the two women in collars to stand watch. Then he threw his arm around my neck.

'*Tjenbé rèd*,' he told me. '*Pa moli*.'

Still clasping me, he reached out to Céleste and drew her into the embrace. After a moment, I wriggled out of their grasp and step back, leaving them to stand there, as one, for a few heartbeat, their cheeks press together. Then Emile released her and bounded over the road toward the bay, until he was just a fleeting shadow among the trees on the other side. Céleste watched him go, her fingers on her own face where his skin had touched hers. After a moment, she turned away, smoothing both hands across her head-wrap.

Meanwhile, some of the women had settle down among the gnarled roots of a black sage. Raymond and Augustin perched on a fallen tree trunk nearby and I went to join them. Céleste led Choisie over and sat him down beside me. The smelly old soul rested his head on my shoulder. Eyes shut, I listen to the sounds of the forest. *'Ti gounouys.* Toads. Some kind of nightbird. Choisie breathing through his mouth. The creak of bamboo. The soft coo of a distant pigeon. Choisie sat up and poke me in the ribs. Another coo from a pigeon, more urgent. I open my eyes. Was that a real pigeon? Or a warning from the lookouts?

'*Mèd*,' said Raymond, and stood up.

A third coo – this time answered by another – and then a figure emerge from the darkness: Saturnin. Raymond and Augustin mutter to each other in relief. I haul myself up onto my poles. Never thought I would feel glad to behold that driver, but now the sight of him help to calm my scudding pulse. He peered around at us, then spoke to me.

'Where's your brother?'

'He went to find you. Where's the rest of them?'

The driver jerked a thumb toward the far side of the bay.

'There's another creek over there, sweeter water. They were thirsty.' He grinned at me. 'I'll bet you thought we had gone without you.'

'Well, no,' I said. 'We saw the boats. Is Cléophas onshore?'

'Nobody seen him yet.'

'What about White, the Englishman?'

'Not him either. The beach is deserted. What I want to know is, how are we suppose to get out to that boat. Hardly one of us can swim.'

'There's a skiff,' I told him. 'They'll send it ashore to fetch us.'

'You seem to know everything,' he said. 'Almost as much as your brother. Well, he probably found the rest of them by now. We may as well go down there.'

I hesitated.

'Emile told us to wait here.'

'Suit yourself,' said Saturnin. 'Sooner we get on this boat, the better. Get this damn sea-sailing over and done with.'

He turn to leave, but before he could take another step, Céleste put her hand on his arm to stop him.

'Wait,' she whispered. 'What's that noise?'

Still as pillars, we stood and listened. A low rumble drifted across the land, just audible above the night sounds of the forest. A distant thunder. At first, I thought it came from the east. Next, I was sure it came from the south. I peered up through the canopy of branches. Hardly a cloud in the sky, just a thousand stars scattered across the heavens, twinkling, like God had spilled a bag of diamond dust and tiny stones. Saturnin cocked his head to one side and frowned.

'*Cho!* Will they make us set sail in a storm?'

'Hush,' said Céleste. 'That's no storm. Listen.'

We fell silent, every one of us straining our ears. The low grumble continued, a little louder, a little closer. Now, from somewheres among the trees came an urgent pigeon-coo – a definite warning – followed straightways by the thud of naked heels on dirt and the rushing sound of a person running redshank through the forest. Then Magdelon came crashing out of the darkness, holding onto her collar.

'Horses,' she panted, in a loud whisper. 'About half a dozen.'

'*Mèd*,' said Saturnin. 'Probably a parcel of Goddam swillers, raising hellfire for Christmas. Get back from that road – take Choisie and the children. Go on. Hide. Just stay back until they pass.'

I glanced around. Chevallier and Angélique had already disappeared. Shadowy figures receded into the darkness. Rosalie push Casimir into the undergrowth whiles Magdelon led Choisie away from the highway. Meanwhile, Saturnin crept to the edge of the forest and crouch down behind some bushes, at a place where he had a view of the road. He waved his arm at me, urging me out of sight but my gaze was drawn to the break in the trees where I had last seen my brother. It occur to me that – even on crutches – I might have time to head down to the bay and find him, make sure he was safe. I turn to Céleste and found her staring at the same spot, no doubt a similar notion passing through her mind. For an instant, it looked as though she might dart across the road but then she grab my elbow.

'Come on,' she said. 'He knows what to do, better than anyone.'

She helped me into a thicket of sapling where slender branches and liane had wove together to form a cave of leaves. The thicket stood next the highway but we had no time to seek cover elsewhere, and the night would conceal us provided we kept quiet. Somewheres behind us, I could hear that puling Casimir, but the horses so loud they would likely drown him out. I peer back through the foliage to check on the others. Augustin was still staggering to and fro in search of a hiding place, his iron weight in both hands. Raymond had step behind a nearby campèche but now he scuttled out again.

'Ss – ss – go there,' he hiss. Then he dived into a sparse patch of ferns, leaving Augustin to haul his weight and chain behind the tree.

All this while, the riding party kept approaching at reckless pace. Now, they had rounded the corner and I could hear the chink-chink of several bridle. The sounds echoed around the bay, making it hard to tell how many were coming. Magdelon was right, I reckoned: six riders, possibly more, perhaps on their way to Gouyave in pursuit of further rum and revel. At least if they were drunken they might be less alert. Closer, closer, they came, until the din of metal horse-shoe on dirt fill the night, the clank of snaffle-bits, the poor animals grunting and panting. The riders hurtle past, oblivious to the hand-ful of figures sweating and quaking here and there at the edge of the forest. On they flew down the highway, leaving the scent of stables and hot leather drifting in their wake.

Yet, before I could heave any sigh of relief, the sound of the hooves changed as the horses slow down. They faltered, slowed again, then came to a halt further on, where the dirty creek cross the highway. Without all that thunderous Tantivy, the night resumed its usual level of clamour, above which I could just make out the sound of the men striking up a muttered conversation among themselve but the forest-chatter drowned out their words and it was hard to tell if they were English or French. I waited a short while then gingerly peered out between the branches of our leafy cave.

At first, I could see only a cluster of moving shadows. I counted five, then six horses, their heads bent to the creek. The riders had dismounted and stood in the night-shade beneath the trees. Snatch-es of the conversation drifted to my ears and I thought I recognise something familiar in the cadence of their voices. Seem to me that at least two of them might be Scottish, like my old protector, John Calder. As I watched, one of their number wandered across the road and proceeded to drain his pump. The moon had bathe that side of the highway in silver light such that I could see the man clearly, his cocked hat like a giant bat perch low on his head. Something about that three-corn made me uneasy: the pale trim just visible in the moonlight. Then one of his companion joined him. This second man wore a high cap or mitre, military style. My inners gave a lurch. He had to be an officer or dragoon, and the man in the three-corn, it dawned on me, was a musketeer. I saw now their uniform, the red jackets black neath the starlight, pale cuffs and collars gleaming. They both carried havresacks and cartridge boxes on their backs. This must be some of those Glasgow Greys we had heard about, a mounted party of troops from the fort, most likely on their way to relieve their fellows at one of the redoubts on the coast.

Céleste slipped her hand into mine and gently squeeze my fingers. I understood what she meant: the men would ride on as soon as they had watered their horses; all we had to do was wait, quiet-quiet. Sure enough, moments later, some bustle of activity among the little group indicated that they were about to set off again.

However, instead of remounting, they took their horses by the rein and – on foot, one by one – began to lead them into the woods on the bay side, picking their way between the trees, heading down to the shore. Céleste breathed in sharply. Her grip on my hand grew tighter. We watch the last stallion flick his tail as he high-step in among the trees until the darkness swallowed his vast rump. In the same instant, with a whish in the undergrowth, Saturnin pushed his way into our thicket, at a crouch.

'See that?' he said. 'You think they know something?'

Céleste and I gazed at each other for just a flash, each of us thinking of Emile, the need to warn him. Then, as one, we made a move but Saturnin seize Céleste by the arm and me by the collar.

'Are you mad?' he said. 'I'll go down and warn them. You take these others into the hills.'

'And then what?' Céleste asked, hotly.

'Hide somewheres and wait. We'll find you.'

I glared at him, struggling to extricate myself, and would have wriggled out of my shirt had not Céleste grab both my arms and held me tight.

'Do what he says. I'll fetch your brother and the others.' She turn to the driver. 'You take this boy and hide him, make sure he's safe.'

Before either of us could protest, she slipped away between the saplings. A fistle of foliage and she was gone.

Cursing under his breath, Saturnin drag me out of the thicket. Augustin had emerge from behind his tree, his weight in his hands like an offering.

'Don't just stand there,' said the driver. 'Move!' To me, he said: 'Hold onto those poles.'

Despite his small frame, Saturnin hauled me onto his back and began to carry me uphill, away from the road. Augustin fell into step behind us. We had gone but a few paces when – down by the shore – a scream pierce the night, followed shortly thereafter by the startling crack-whish of a musket, a report so loud that it echoed across the foothills. Saturnin stop dead in his tracks.

'*Puten!*' he muttered.

Another burst of gunfire, this followed swiftly by more shots, then other firelocks banging and balls whistling among the trees, the din ringing out to reverberate around the cove, provoking further disembody screams and the sound of a general chaos: people running pell-mell through the woods by the shore, calling out to each other in a panic above the crack of musketry and harsh Béké voices, yelling:

'Stop there! Stand still! You there! Halt!'

And then, above all that and the din of the night, another rumble came to my ears from the direction of Fort Royal, where the highway rounded the bend and began to descend to the bay: a different sound this time: boots – many boots – hard leather hitting the pack dirt of the road. Well-shod men, perhaps a score of them, running in cadence, heading in our direction. Same instant, I heard a bark, answered by another, and then several dogs began to howl and yelp all at once.

Whoever was coming, they had brought with them a pack of hounds.

Chapter Forty-Five

The next few moments are confused in my memory. I know that Saturnin stood in silence until the clamour of the dogs began to wane as they headed down toward the sea. Then, he fled uphill among the trees, quiet as he could, me slung over his shoulder, topsy-turvy. I heard more yelling from the bay, more shots. Various shadowy figures fled longside us, running this way and that like crazy-ant. Upside down, it was hard to recognise anyone. I saw only feet and skirts skitter-scatter, hear Saturnin shu-shu at them:

'Up there! That way!' and 'Quick-quick!'

I recall the rushing darkness. Augustin lumbered along behind, bearing his weight before him, his fetters jingle-jangling. Several of the others skirred along with us to begin with but it seemed as though some of them soon sheered off or surged ahead. Twigs and branches scratch my face, the air knocked out of my chest as the driver tried to run bearing my weight and then a great thwack as my head hit something hard – most likely one of those slim tree trunks that lay half-fallen here and there amid the undergrowth. Blue and white points of light span before my vision as on we went, up into the foothills. Augustin kept up with us a fair while but soon the clank of his chain faded into the night. I could still hear yelling and the dogs barking down at the shore but the sounds grew dim the further we got from the coast until, finally, they died out.

After that, it was just the driver and me on his shoulders. He pounded on through the trees, staggering uphill, mostly. Then, we slithered down a muddy bank and with a splash we were in a creek.

Water flew up and drench my face and shirt as Saturnin tried to wade upstream but he stumble twice and I near lost my crutches. With a curse, he stagger to the other side of the river and I had to cling to his back as he crawled up the bank. On we went again, toward the heights, pausing once or twice whiles he looked about him until, finally, just below the crest of a ridge in the foothills, he set me down beside a stand of bamboo. Then he bent over to recover, his breath tearing at his lungs. I sat there, on the damp ground, shaking. In my mind, I kept hearing the bang of firelocks ringing out around the bay and the cries of anguish. I felt winded still, from the shock of it all, wondering what might have happen to Emile and the rest.

Presently, a faint sound interrupted my thoughts, a clink-clink drifting toward us from further down the slope. Saturnin shot upright. We both listen hard for a while until it became plain that what we could hear was the muffle jangle of fetters. The driver gave a low hoot and presently Augustin came staggering up to join us, panting like a half-dead mule. He flung his iron weight to the muddy ground and it landed with a thud. Then he stood there, his chest heaving. Meanwhile, Saturnin stared up into the dusky foliage above us.

'This tree here,' he said, to Augustin. 'Help me lift the boy.'

Together, they hoist me into the lower branches. I was able to pull myself aloft to where the leaves were thickest and made myself as snug as I could astride a stout branch. Then something tap my good ankle. I reach down. Saturnin had clambered up to hand me my plyers. I grab them, one by one, and stow them beside me.

'*Mèsi*,' I whisper to him.

'Stay there until you're sure the soldiers are long gone.'

'And then what?'

'Try to get back to Martinique.'

'What? How?'

'That I cannot help you with, little man.'

'But what about Emile? Céleste?'

'They can look after themselve, *pa ni pwoblèm*.'

The distant bang of a musket shattered the night.

'*A talé*,' the driver muttered as he slithered down the trunk, out of sight. I heard some further murmurs down below and then Augustin called out, soft-soft, asking if there was room for him in the tree. Above me, the foliage gleamed in the starlight, a cradle of branches a ways further up where someone might find a perch. I whisper down:

'*Wi.*'

Ensuite, I heard the two men scuffle around amid the tree roots, along with a few thuds and the tingle-tangle of fetters and when I peer down through the leaves I could make out their shadowy figures: the driver trying to help Augustin clamber up the trunk – but his weight and shackles were too much hindrance and so, after a while, they gave up.

Saturnin shu-shu up to me again:

'I have to go.'

A crunch of dead leaves, then silence, until a low voice called out:

'Lucien?'

It was Augustin.

'I'm here. Where are you?'

'In the bamboo. You sit tight up there.' Just then, the hounds set up barking again; this time closer than before. I heard Augustin murmur: 'I should be quiet now.'

After that, he said nothing further. I clung to the tree trunk, all my senses alert, my foot dangling and throbbing. The night air filled up with the frantic high-pitch sound of frogs and bat and, once in a while, from downhill, the howl of a dog. Up above me, high in the sky, the Man in the Moon now wore a torn and tattered wig: two fluffy shreds of grey cloud, one each side of his head. He gaze down upon me, a mad old judge, ready to pass sentence.

Chapter Forty-Six

So much time passed, I felt as though I was about ninety years of age and had spent 200 of them up that tree. At one moment, a bat flew past my face so close that the warm breath of his wing brush my cheek and I near fell from my perch. Then, in the distance, I heard someone advancing uphill. My pulse hammered along in my veins. I clench my thighs to the branch and peer through the foliage, hoping to see Emile or Céleste. The scrambling footsteps grew closer, closer, until I perceived a shady figure, toiling up the slope: Lapin – one of the fittest field hand – a young man several years older than myself. He pass by the clump of slim bamboo stems inside which Augustin had conceal himself and then disappeared into the night. Presently, Lapin was followed by three more field hand. I could guess who they were in outline, the other Crackermen: Montout, Coco and Philoge. They were gone in an instant, vanished up the slope. After a while, another fugitive came scrabbling upward, this time a woman. She pulled along a girl, about ten years of age, too old to be on her mother back. The woman murmur to the child as they went along:

'Here we go, you keep hush now . . .'

From behind the screen of bamboo, Augustin hiss to her, called her name:

'Ss – ss. Claudette. *Isi-a!*'

She paused at the foot of my tree, and I heard her say:

'*Augustin? Se twa?*'

'*Wi. Isi-a! Vini la. Cache-twa.*'

Clearly, the woman thought about it for a twink, then I heard her say:

'*Non, mèsi. Bon chans, Augustin. Bon chans a twa. A plis!*'

She set off once again, muttering more words of comfort to her daughter:

'Mm-hmm, now, there we go again. We'll find our own-own place to hide. You hold onto me now, baby one. You just hold on tight, that's right.'

And off they went, creeping uphill, until her whispering melted into the dark.

After that, silence again, if you discount the tree-frog. Listening to their voices, I lost track of time. Of course, I had heard those creatures every night of my life. We were all so accustom to *'ti gounouys* that sometimes we scarce heard them at all. Yet, that night, their incessant silly squeaking almost pierce my brain. At first, they seem to call to each other but, as time went by, I wondered if they might not be trying to warn me and then I grew giddy and began to think that they were trying to alert the soldiers to my hiding place. My ears ringing. Convince that I might fall, I clung harder to the tree. With no distraction save my fears about what might have happen to Emile and Céleste, it was as though those little peepers were intent on driving me out of my mind.

On a sudden, I distinguish another sound: a soft yelp, close enough that I could hear it above the clamour of the night-creatures. My scalp began to tingle. Nobody came, nobody came – until, at last, I saw movement in the shadows: just a pale flash sneaking uphill, a low, sleek shape flitting between the stands of bamboo: a white dog, there he was, nose to the ground. A shiver cross my shoulders. He came bounding right up to my tree and snuffled a while at the roots. Then, tail wagging, he smelled his way over to the bamboo thicket where Augustin hid. Two sniffs at the base of the canes and then the hound set up a savage bark. At once, I heard the tramp of men in boots and two figures came running: more Glasgow Greys. I could see the outline of their hats, one high mitre cap and one three-corn: a stocky, clean-shaven officer and a mackerel-back soldier of the rank and file. The pale facings of their red coats and their white breeches and stocking gleamed in the moonlight; the havresacks and cartridge-boxes showed as dark shapes at their backs. Muskets raised, they closed in behind the dog and began to yell into the thicket:

'Ger yersel' oot here now.'

'Come oot, or we'll shoot ye.'

The officer pointed his musket at the bamboo whiles the tall soldier ventured forth and began to thrust his bayonet between the canes. One thrust. Two. I winced, as though I myself had been stab. Three!

Augustin called out:

'*Mwen ka vini! Le chyen, le chyen!*'

'What's he saying?' the officer shouted.

'He's feart of the dog, Sergeant,' said the musketeer. 'Wait now.'

Grabbing the hound, he dragged it off a short distance and slipped a leash around its neck. The stocky sergeant bellowed again into the canes.

'Right now, you. Out you come.'

Slow-slow, Augustin emerge, bearing his fetters before him. The dog kept barking and bucking but the redcoat held him fast. Poor Augustin, his bandaged head was hanging – but then – whap! – he looked up and flung his lead weight at the sergeant. The man dive to the side just in time; the weight missed him and fell to the ground. Augustin tried to grab it and run, but the soldier recovered quick-sharp. He swung back his musket and hit Augustin on the head with the butt, a blow that felled him. By this time, the dog had gone stark mad. The sergeant stood over his captive, bayonet fix and pointed, as if to stick him through, and spat down at him:

'I'd like to get my hands in your guts for a wee while.'

He might indeed have done Augustin harm but, just then, up-sprung a commotion of shouts and tramping boots. More white breeches and stockings. Alerted, no doubt, by the clamour, half a dozen more Greys came at a run, accompanied by a black and tan hound as big as a horse. A bewhiskered man in a high mitre hat called out:

'Hold there, Sergeant Grant. Stand back.'

This new bearded fellow must have been the superior for the sergeant put up his bayonet and retreated a few step.

'Yes, sir, Captain Ross, sir.'

Poor Augustin curled into a ball as the white dog snapped at his ankles.

'*Le chyen! Le chyen!*'

Ross turn to the mackerel-back musketeer.

'Munro,' said he. 'Whisht that thing and get it away from there or I'll shoot it.'

The soldier drag the white dog back. As for me, I kept one eye on that black and tan hound. For a brief spell, he rolled around on the dirt, then sprang up and trotted off into the darkness, sniffing the ground, following the scent of the field hands.

'Right,' said the captain. 'Munro – you and McPherson take this prisoner down to Lieutenant Hewett. Then I want you both to go up the other side of the bay with the dog, see what you can find. Tell Hewett to take the slaves he's got back to the plantation but leave some men on watch at the beach.'

'Sir.'

Two of the redcoats pulled poor Augustin to his feet and made him pick up his weight. Munro let the hound off the leash and then he and his compeer began to prod the prisoner ahead of them down the slope. Fetters clanking, Augustin hung his head as he stumbled along, the dog a pale streak, running circles around him.

Someone called for the black and tan beast and when it came galloping out of the undergrowth, tail wagging, the remaining soldiers headed uphill. Soon, the glow of their white breeks faded into the night. To be sure they had gone, I listened until I could no longer hear the soft tramp of their boots. The dog lingered a while to sniff the bamboo until the men called him again from some distance. He set off but, in passing, did pause to mouse around the roots of my tree. He sniffed and wheezed, sniffed and growled. Then he tilted back his meaty head and looked up into the branches. For a few moment, his eyes glittered like black glass and then he began to bark. My heart drop to my dangling feet. In the darkness, amid the foliage, I doubted he could see me. Yet, he knew I was there and, if he kept up that racket, the men would come hurrying back to vestigate and I would be discovered for true.

At a loss, I grab one of my crutches and hurled it down at the dog, hard as ever I could. By some miracle, the crossbar struck him bang on the snout with an audible crack. He yelped and scrabbled away off up the hill, complaining to himself. I fought to calm my own breath and listened until all sound of him had ceased. Thereafter, I waited – and waited – but the great hound did not return and neither did those musketeer.

PART NINE

Fugitive

Chapter Forty-Seven

Saturnin had advise me not to move until the redcoats had gone. But how was a person suppose to know when that might be? I stayed put for what seem like the course of ages. It began to occur to me that if I sat there until sunrise, I would most likely have to wait for darkness to fall again the following night before I climb down. The thought of remaining in that tree, hour upon hour, all through the next day made me squirm. Of course, it would be safer to stick where I was but if I moved under cover of night, I could seek out some hiding hole closer to the coast and – in so doing – I might find my brother or, at least, discover what had happen to him and Céleste and the others. Surely Emile would have manage to evade the clutches of the Greys?

My mind in a ferment, I sat there in my leafy cage, trying to guess how long it would be before the rosy light of dawn bled up into the sky: two hours, I reckoned, perhaps three. Finally, I could bear it no more. Concluding that my best option was to creep closer to the bay before sunrise, I listen for a long time to ensure that no man was near. Then I let my remaining crutch drop from the tree. It hit the earth below with a dull clatter that made me wince. I waited to see what might happen. After a while, hearing nothing untoward, I slither down the trunk and fell to the earth in a heap. Sprawled among the roots of the tree, I peered this way and that. At every turn, I saw phantom figures in the shadows but some time went past and no soldier came rushing forth to apprehend me. So far as I could tell, I was now alone in that part of the forest.

I scrabbled across the ground to retrieve my fallen plyers. Then, I heave myself upright and stood in silence, listening, listening, just as Emile would have done. Little by little, it began to dawn on me that quitting that tree may have been a mistake. My brother would have perched up there for days if necessary. Cursing my own impatience and lack of wit, I attempted to climb back up the trunk but, without the help of Saturnin, even the lowest branches were beyond my reach.

Hampered by crutches, the safest option – to head for the heights – would be out of the question. My only course: to descend to the bay. Although my leg burned like the fires of hell, the swelling in my foot appear to have subsided somewise. Thus, I began to pick my way downhill, ears alert to any sound beyond the customary din of the night. If some redcoat saw me now, I was doomed, for I could no more take foot than ride a travelling carpet.

'Emile is not here,' I told myself. 'Emile is not here. But I'm going to find him. Yes, I am. I surely am. I'll find Emile and Céleste and then together we can try to get back to Martinique. *Tjenbé rèd, pa moli.*'

Hard work, limping along in the dark on those plyers, tottering netherward toward the bay, my eyes and cheek stinging wet. I must have been sweating like a bloated old Béké-off-the-boat.

Chapter Forty-Eight

It took forever and a day to hobble back down the foothills, inch by inch. The closer I got to the bay, the more I strain my ears to hear any sound – especially the hoot or coo of a bird that might suggest I was not the only one still at liberty. Yet, though I hirpled all the way back to the coast road, I encountered not a single human creature, neither soldier nor slave.

I paused at the edge of the woods, near where the sweet creek cross the highway, the sky above me still lit by stars. Presently, I heard the sound of wheels on dirt and soon a donkey-cart came rattling along from the direction of Gouyave. The tumbrel sped past, a Béké driver hunched over the reins; behind him, in the cart-bed, a heap of something, most likely fruits. Perhaps he was bound for some kind of festive market in Fort Royal. Once he had gone on up the road, I waited until a bank of cloud drifted across the face of the moon and only then did I venture forth, hopping over the road and into the trees on the other side, fast as my crutches would carry me. Back in the shadows, I stood stock-still but could hear no sound of movement and so I set off again, slow-slow, peggity-peg, toward the sound of the sea.

The air smelled faintly of smoke. At first, I thought it must be the lingering scent of gunpowder but presently, through the trees, I saw a flickering orange light: the flames of a bonfire on the beach. Full of dread, I crept closer, one peg at a time, until I reach the edge of the woods, and was able to peer out from behind the wide trunk of an old almond tree that grew on a slant toward the water.

About halfway along the narrow strip of sand, a handful of Greys sat around the fire. I could see other shadowy figures in tri-corns pacing the shore. Two men – one of them an officer – stood conferring beside a few tethered horses. No trace of the hospital slaves. As I watched, the clouds moved off to reveal the moon once more and the water of the bay shone like quicksilver. Not one vessel at anchor out there which led me to wonder where the boats had gone. Most important, where was Emile? And what of Céleste? Had they been captured, marched back to the hospital estate like Augustin? For aught I knew, they might have escape to sea with Cléophas, or fled to the mountain. Or could they still be there somewheres, at Petit Havre, hidden among the trees?

One of the horses whinnied and I glance back at the two men. They had approach the fire and whiles the officer spoke to one of the rank and file, the other bent forward to light a segar. As the flames lit up his face, I recognised him: Bryant. The officer addressed him again, pointing into the trees, across the headland and back up into the hills, perhaps explaining how we had been ambush.

Just then, one of the watchmen on the foreshore turned and began to stalk along the sand toward my end of the bay. Deciding to take leg-bail, I hitch back into the seclusion of the woods and return to the highway, alert all the while for a dove or pigeon call, but I heard only the tree-frog screaming at each other.

I hopped across the empty road and slithered into a ditch near the sweet creek. For a time, I lay there out of sight, considering my position. I could hardly stay there forever, hobbling about Petit Havre till Kingdom-come, hoping to stumble upon my brother or Céleste. Saturnin had advise me to return to Martinique but how that might be accomplish on my own I had not one iota. Besides, there would be no leaving without Emile. If I could find the Maroon then I might throw myself on their mercy but, in my heart, I could not shake the fear that they might betray me. Having chawed over every option six times and more, I resolve to return to Fort Royal. At least there I might learn what had happen to my brother and the rest.

The sky grew light, turning first pink and yellow then palest blue. I tested my injured foot and found, to my relief, that I could put some weight upon it, just enough to limp along unaided. Ergo, I thrust my crutches into a pile of dead leaves and crouch there in the ditch to wait. Soon enough, more wagons and wains would come rolling en route to town. If one of those carters stop to water his mules, and if I were quick, it might be possible to scramble up and hide among his produce and in that manner sneak a ride all the way to Fort Royal.

Chapter Forty-Nine

By then, the sound of whistling-frogs had begun to fade until only one little fellow persisted in peeping and, in the end, even he grew tired of his own silly voice and stubbled it. I kept my head low and listen for vehicles approaching from the north. Soon enough, a wagon did appear but the driver carried on without stopping at the creek. Next came the first few *porteuses* striding past, the traits on their head piled high with bright green christophine. They lifted their skirts and splash straight through the shallow water. Then another cart appeared but that one also sped on toward Fort Royal *sans pause*.

I had begun to despair of any driver stopping when I heard the squeak and rumble of wooden wheels and a mildewed mule cart came along, ding-dong, and slow to a halt just a spit from my ditch. Gingerly, I peered out. The mules – a pungent pair – had already dip their heads to the creek. The vehicle bore only a partial load on one side of the cart-bed; a tar cloth covered the produce. It struck me that I could very well conceal myself neath such a canvas. The carter climb down from his perch and went over to the bay side of the road to drain his pump. He could have been forty-five or fifty years of age and was – perhaps, by his appearance – a free Negro, but no day of rest for him it would seem. He wore a waistcoat and breeks woven from cane trash, an excentric costume that I thought might be design to make him stand out in the marketplace.

Whiles his back turn, I rolled up out of the ditch and limp low-low to the cart. Quiet as a creeping nun, I ducked under the canvas and lay on my side, my eyes squeeze shut. Just in time for, moments later, the axles creaked as old Trash-breeks swung himself into his seat. Presumably, he was taking some few pig carcass or somesuch to the Christmas market for it smelled like meat under the tarpaulin, meat on the point of turning. I open my eyes, but all the carcass lay behind me in the dark and I dared not turn over in case Trash-breeks might, at that moment, glance back and wonder why his dead pigs moving. He shook the reins and the tumbrel set off again, splashing through the shallow river and on along the highway.

I tried to waft in some fresh air by raising the cloth a crack. Meanwhile, the cart-bed tilted as we climbed up out of the bay and around the headland. The carter kept to the coast road, slowing down now and then to ford a stream or climb an incline. Every time I lifted the cloth to snatch a breath of air, I caught a glimpse of the landscape: a blue-green flash of sea; a blur of trees; black rocks receding.

My thoughts raced ahead. We would probably cross the St Jean on the ferry at the river mouth. I could leave the wagon before we reach there but then would have to find a way over the water myself, in the open. There might be soldiers everywhere; my bad foot would slow me down and mark me out; everyone would be on the lookout for runaways. All in all, I concluded that it would be for the best to stay in the tumbrel until the last possible instant, even if that meant going on the ferry: a log raft that the Béké pull back and forth across the water by winches. Provided I could remain out of sight neath my tar cloth during the crossing, I could escape on the far side, somewheres on the approach to the waterfront, beyond which point the chance of slipping off unnotice by some passer-by slim. Once we left the ferry, I would have only a short interval to throw myself off the cart-bed and limp into hiding without being seen. Then I remembered that the trees grew thick down by the store-houses at the mouth of the river. I could hide there until sunset, then make my way to a more secluded spot on Hospital Hill.

The closer we got to town, the more anxious I became. Morning sunlight beat down on the tarpaulin. The stink of meat made my stomach turn and my skin ran with sweat. Although the day had just begun, I knew that the streets around the market and parade square would already be busy as a nest of ant. Onward, onward, the cart jerked and jolted, and in what seem like no time at all, we left behind the headlands of St Eloy and came to a halt on the northern bank of the river St Jean.

The ferry must have been moored up on our side for as the carter jump down he bid someone 'Merry Christmas' in English, then there was a chink-chink as coins exchange hands. Trash-breeks coaxed his mules onto the rudimentary craft, such that I heard the knock of their hoofs on the logs. Under the weight of the cart, the raft tilted and sank a few inch and, at this sensation, the mules brayed and honked and tried to back off but the carter murmur to them until they settled.

We were about to cast off when I heard the sound of horses approaching at a canter. I peered out neath the cloth at the road behind and nearly died of apoplexy when I saw two men dismount: Dr Bryant and the redcoat officer. I drop the cloth at once and shrank back against the pig-meat. Something fleshy and bony flopped over me, a leg of pork. Revolted though I was, I dared not shift further lest the men notice the tar cloth move. As they coax their horses onto the raft, I lay there, quaking, afraid the redcoat might order the carter to throw back the tar cloth and show his produce, in case it concealed runaways. Howsomever, after returning a 'Merry Christmas' to the ferryman, the officer fell silent. Presumably, any runaways were expected to head for the wilderness of the interior, rather than back to town.

I heard a splash, then another, as the hawsers hit the water. The Béké raftman called out to his fellow on the far bank; the winch clattered into action and we began the slow drift across the river. Although the mouth of the St Jean could hardly be judge wide, the apparatus was stiff to turn, thus the crossing often took a while. I listened out for any chit-chat that might pass between the men about the escape but Trash-Breeks uttered not a word and, apart from a few bland remarks about the weather, the others made the crossing in silence.

Even as the raft settled against the southern bank of the river, the carter had resume his perch behind the reins. At the click of his tongue, the mules scrabble back onto solid ground and we rattled and groaned up the slope, away from the ferry landing. With any luck, Bryant and the redcoat would canter on ahead. However, as they led their horses off the ferry, I heard the south bank raftman call out, asking about the 'trouble' over at the plantation. I dared to lift the tar cloth just enough to see Bryant and the officer pause to talk to him. Their attention thus diverted, I took the chance to dis-gage from the pork-leg but in grasping the trotter I almost screamed out loud – for what I had grab was not the pettitoe of a pig but the fingers of a human hand. Though I dropped it in a flash and squirmed away, I had time enough to feel knuckles, nails, a thumb. The hand so stiff, I knew at once that the rank smell beneath the cloth was the stench of human death. Such revulsion rose up in my tripes, it was all I could do not to vomit. My throat constricted and a whimper escape me. I tried to breath shallow and lie still as a log, though I felt like bursting out of my own body. The cart kept rolling and, presently, one of the men at the ferry landing gave a chuckle. It would seem they had notice nothing.

Having recovered somewise, I force myself to turn my head and raise the cloth just enough to admit a shaft of light. First thing

I saw, the face of a stranger, a girl, naked entirely. Her eyes and mouth open but the life had left her body. Her cheek and shoulder branded. Perhaps she had been a field hand in the north of the island. Behind her, in a tangle of limbs, several other cadaver, more naked strangers, men and women, brands on their faces and backs, all dead of some cause or causes unknown. Having satisfied myself that none were from the hospital estate, I drop the cloth and lay still – or at least as still as I could, for my whole body shook with fear and revulsion. Were it not for Bryant and the officer, I would have leapt from the cart and hid in the trees but I heard them bid the raftman 'Good day' and then the clop of hooves as they set their horses to follow the tumbrel at an easy pace.

I had just resign myself to being trapped when the wagon change direction and instead of proceeding along the highway to town, we turned up the River Road. I lay there wondering anew what our destination might be, praying it was not the plantation, which must surely be crawling with musketeers. Yet, before I had even recover from my surprise, we turned again and began to climb the poor-made track that cut up and across the back of the hill. In sum, we were headed directly for the hospital itself. All at once, it dawned on me that the carter must be taking these bodies to the morgue where – no doubt, just as our surgeon friars like to do – Bryant would dissect them. As soon as we reach the hospital, the corpses would be unloaded and I would be discovered.

My blood raced as the mules drag the cart on and on, up the track. That part of the hill had been cleared but not yet cultivated and the fields were bare as bleach bones. The nearest trees lay some distance off, back at the coast or up on the high ridge. Bryant and the redcoat continue to ride in our wake. There was no question that if I threw myself out and hobbled away, they would see me and give chase.

At every instant, I tried to goad myself to jump. The incline grew steeper, then steeper still and the cart slowed until we reach such a crawling pace that Bryant and the officer overtook us at last and I heard the clatter of hooves as they reach the battery and rode through the tunnel. The cart lumbered on in their wake and soon entered the same passageway with a great din of grumbling wheels that rattled and rebellowed off the stone walls and floor at deafening pitch. Here, for true, was my one desperate chance to escape. Grip by what felt to me like a reckless madness, a great folly, I slither to the edge of the cart-bed. From there, I drop to the hard floor of the tunnel with a jolt that jarred my entire anatomy. Clench like a fist, my body aching, I lay there, ready for rough hands to seize me or some harsh voice to raise the alarm.

Nothing of the sort. The squeak and rumble of the cartwheels continued, echoing off the walls and ceiling. I waited – waited – until, presently, I dare to look and saw Trash-breeks and his horrif-ic load lumber on, oblivious, out into the daylight of the hospital courtyard.

No time to waste, I hobble back out of the tunnel, fast as my foot would allow, and crept along the battery then up into the trees.

There below lay the hospital cabins, apparently deserted. Giv-en what had happened, a wise man would avoid those huts in daylight and so I limped uphill and found a secluded spot from where I could survey the terrain. The High Road behind town ran below me and there, on the bluff, sat the residence of Maillard, the French doctor. Only a few days previous, I had been at his door, delivering herbs, though that visit now seem to belong to a different life, a life not my own. Sitting there nursing my foot, I recalled the squeaks and scuttles that had come from neath the veranda and – at once – my mind and eyes fixed on that structure, for it seem to me there must be a space below the floorboards where a person might hide. Such a spot would remain tolerable cool in the daytime and the house stood close enough to both town and plantation that, if need be, I could sneak back and forth after dark.

The road was clear save one *porteuse* striding along. When she disappeared into the hospital courtyard, I looked around again. Not a soul in sight. My heart in my throat, I stagger to my feet and half hop, half limp downhill to the edge of the trees opposite the Maillard place. Beyond the gate, the garden lay empty. The jalousies at the front of the house had been prop open but I could see no movement inside. I stole across the road and down the garden path. The veranda – a raise wooden porch – ran along three sides of the building. Behind some ringworm bushes and wild hollyhock, I found a spot where a few boards in the upright end-piece of the structure had rotted and broken. The resulting hole looked about wide enough to squeeze through. I crouch down and peered inside. There was indeed a fair-size void beneath the floorboards and, in places, the earth had been washed out by rains, leaving some deeper hollows.

Normally, the thought of what vermin might lurk under there would fill me with horror, but I had to get out of sight until dark and – given the events of the morning – I felt more than equal to sharing berth with a few rodent. However, rather than come facety-face with some rat and his cousin, I push myself into the gap, feet first. Took but a twinkling to wriggle inside and slide along the damp dirt into the shadows. A few tiny lizard went scuttling as I scrambled in but so far as I could see they were the only creatures in the vicinity. Nevertheless – just in case I had to make a quick exit – I stretched out near the gap in the end-piece, to wait. The floor was low; there was scarce room enough to sit up. The air smelled of wet earth and mould and to that I added the high rank smell of my clothes and body. It was hotter under there than I had anticipated, and more humid. Exhausted, and with nothing to do but wait until nightfall, I lay there for what seem like hours.

Chapter Fifty

By and by, beams of sunshine began to stream in through the spaces between the boards. In the slatted light, I was able to examine my foot. It still looked angry but least it had benefited from some few hours of rest. I put my eye to a crack in the veranda but could see little except a clump of wild hollyhock. Thus, quiet as I could, I drag myself along the damp earth to a spot behind the steps and peered out through another gap. The garden steamed in the forenoon sun. Beyond and below the tree-clad bluff, the town sat baking in a haze of heat. A million-million insect sizzled like they were frying in a pan. Just across the yard, a water-barrel stood by a small out-house, only a spit and stride away from me but I had no spit; my mouth was dry as dead crab shell. I could have kick myself for forgetting about water. Though I felt dizzy from thirst I dare not leave my hiding place.

That morning felt like the longest of my life. I flinched at each unexpected sound; any movement I glimpse from the side of my eye – the twitch of a leaf, the dash of a lizard – made my inners jump. Every passing moment seem to last an hour, every hour, an eternity. Out there in the world, Christmas Day had dawned. From what I could hear, Maillard and his girl Zabette were enjoying a quiet time together, mostly conducted in the bedroom. Every otherwhile, I hear them exchange a few word but their bed-talk was only a murmur.

Too anxious to sleep, I just lay there under the porch, fretting. Foremost in my mind, of course, was Emile, his whereabouts. It seemed unthinkable to me that he would have allowed himself to be captured. I wondered about Céleste and the others, how many of them had manage to escape. The only way to find out was to leave my hiding place and take a sneaking look at the village over in the plantation. Failing that, I could take the more perilsome course of going into town and attempting to see Thérèse. Since she work for the Governor, she would surely have heard something and might be able to tell me who had escape. However, either alternative would be foolhardy in daylight and so I had to wait – and wait, and wait – until nightfall.

Eventually, the doctor and Zabette drag themselve out of bed. I heard the creak of the bedstead, his heavy footstep, the odd bang of a pot or scrape of a chair leg on the floor. At one point, Zabette emerge from the house. She wore just a shift ruffled up over her protruding belly. I spied through the gaps in the boards as she went back and forth, first fetching water then picking beans, singing to herself a lullaby, most likely to serenade her unborn child.

Watching her, I fell to wonder whether I should enlist her help. She might know – or be able to find out – what had happen to Emile. In plus, I was desperate to slake my thirst and perhaps she would, with some persuasion, bring me food and drink. On the other hand, it was hard to know if she could be trusted. She had struck me as the kind of person who would act according to her own selfish need. For all I could tell, she might betray me or let slip something that would drop me in the suds. As I lay there, perpondering, I ask myself what Emile would do in the same circumstance. Of course, would never forget to take water into hiding. But would he do all in his power to discover what had become of me? No question, he would.

After much back and forth of this sort, I decided to alert the girl to my presence and was about to whistle, soft-soft, when a heavy heel thudded overhead. The sudden fear of discovery surge through my veins like needles. I gazed up through the cracks in the boards. There stood Maillard, dressed only in a shirt, his bawbles dangling like two fig against his bare legs. He ask the girl when his food would be ready.

'*Tousuit*,' she replied.

The doctor lingered there smoking and the heavy scent of his segar soon drifted down below the boards. After a while, he began to sniff the air and glance about the veranda, a look of disgust on his face. I worried that the stink of my clothing might have reach his nostrils but, thankfully, he simply went back inside. When the girl had finish picking beans, she too entered the house and, in time, cooking smells and the clatter of cutlery on china denoted that they had begun to eat. After the meal, they retire for another *siesta* and the house fell silent.

Presently, night crept out of the shadows to surround the house. As soon as all fell dark for true I crawl to the hole in the veranda and listened. Only when I felt certain that Zabette and the doctor were asleep did I wriggle out into the garden, behind the screen of holly-hock. No light showed at the windows, thus I crept to the barrel and took a long drink. The water tasted green and warm. I grabbed a hand of banana from one of the trees then limp down the path and across the High Road into the forest.

There, in the darkness neath the branches, I pause long enough to slonk down some fruit. Few cloud that night, the stars silver-bright points of light in the vault of the violet sky. Having hidden the banana peels, I crept uphill to where I could survey the hospital. A few light showed in the *réfectoire* but all seem quiet in the sick rooms. The hospital slave cabins on the side of the hill still gave every appearance of being abandon: no smut-lamps or fires, no movement, not a soul to be seen. I waited for a short time but nothing changed:

the huts were deserted. Unsure what conclusion to draw from this, I set off for my next place of destination: the plantation village. My plan was to creep close enough to talk to someone or, at least, have a look and see what could be seen.

Taking a traverse route up the slope of Hospital Hill, I pick my way through the undergrowth, hobbling along, step by stealthy step. In this painful manner, I soon reach the summit. Not a whisker of any soldier up there but I made sure to avoid the redoubt nonetheless and cross the spine of the hill, well beyond the battery. Thereafter, still on the slant, I continue down the other side to the campèche thicket where Emile and I had paused on the day we arrived on the island. From that spot, I could survey the valley laid out below me in the light of the moon.

First thing I notice was the bridge that span the river: someone had fix flambeaux on posts all along the rails. Two Glasgow Grey musketeer stood watch, one at either end. New torches big as bonfires also burned around the village. To the south, I could see at least four Greys on patrol and no doubt there were more men posted beyond the torchlight, somewheres out there in the dark. If I tried to cross the bridge they would challenge me. Even if I walked up to the ford and came sneaking back down through the cane on the far side of the river I would get nowhere near the quarters with all those flambeaux and men on guard.

I could see a few children running around the yard. Then another movement caught my eyes: a woman shuffling along beneath one of the flambeaux. Her short steps and hesitant movement made me think she must be in shackles. My pulse began to race. Could that be Céleste, in fetters? Howsomever, she moved out of view before I could be sure. After that, I saw nobody else. No sign of Emile or anyone who resembled him.

For a brief spell, I just stood dumbly on the spot, hoping that the musketeers might disperse, but in my gut I knew they would be there all night. I began to consider the long wait until dawn when I could at least spy on the field hand as they set out to work – until I remembered that the next day was St Stephen. Now, on account of the escape, it was out of the question that any hand from the estate would be given a ticket to go a-visiting for Christmas. Nonetheless, you might lay hard money that Addison Bell would demand his day of rest. I could only suppute that everyone would be confine to quarters, kept under guard all through St Stephen and overnight until the next morning.

That was too long to wait. I had to find out about Emile, wherever he might be. If I could be sure he were still on the loose then I would head inland and try to find him, though I little relish the prospect of those louring mountains and the Maroon. But for aught I knew, he was down there with the other captives in the field hand quarters. Only way to find out was to speak to Thérèse. She might even know the names of any runaways who had escaped. Thus, I crept back over the hill and began to make my way down toward Fort Royal.

I tell you, my heart was like ice.

Chapter Fifty-One

I retrace my step back to the High Road, where the Maillard place still lay in darkness. Further down, I passed another isolated house and three yapping-snapping pot-lickers tore out and followed me. They would have liked a piece of my ankle no doubt and might have taken it had I not menace them with a stick. Eventually, they tired of barking and scamper back up the hill leaving me to continue my descent. By some miracle, those penny-dogs were the only creatures I met on the way down and I manage to reach Rue de l'Hôpital without encountering a single human soul. There must have been a soirée at one of the big houses nearby for I could hear the polite screech of violin. Most people would be at home with their family. Nonetheless, I kept alert as a four-eye fish. If Grenada were like Martinique at Christmas time then there would be one bacchanal in the place as night progressed, especially once all the house-slave and the like were release from their duties, with people of all sorts masquerading through the streets in outlandish fancy dress and paint. As I pass the parsonage, an old bacon-face clergyman came out of the garden. My inners took a leap but he waddled off downhill without a glance at me. Almost at once, a well-dress couple emerge from the churchyard – not long off the Béké-boat, by the look of their ghost-white faces – but they were too bound up in each other to pay me much heed. As they turn down toward the carenage, I stepped into the grounds of the church to allow them to walk ahead.

In plus, there was a part of me wanted to see the grave of Damien Pillon. I wandered along the path. Moon and starlight made the tombstones glow like pewter but the light was too dim to read any inscription. The Pestle would have to wait. I return to the entrance. An urn of trumpet-like flowers had been laid on one of the graves just inside the gate. All at once, I recall that Emile had found a way to talk with LeJeune by pretending to be a suitor bearing a posy. Not much of a disguisement, for true, but the ruse had work for him and might for me. Fortunately, no need to rob the dead of their floral tributes since all sorts of plant and tree grew around the graves. In haste, I snatched a few spray of blossom and foliage then crept out of the churchyard and carried on down to the corner of Rue Gouvernement.

To my relief, all seem quiet along there. The street was lined with gardens behind which stood a number of official building and the residences of Viscounts and Honourables. Most of the mansion appear to be empty, the windows dark. Perhaps the inhabitants had gone to some party elsewhere in town and no doubt many of the house-slave would be visiting up the island with their Christmas ticket. From what I could remember hearing as a child, each successive Governor occupied the same great mansion on the street and a big flag always flew from the porch. Sure enough, about halfway along, I found a place with a huge King Jack hoist above the veranda. The house stood well back from the road beneath large trees. A carriage drive curved up through well-tended gardens with lawns and shrub. I peered through the fence for a closer look. At the back, to one side, I could make out a stables and, on the other, what look like an out-kitchen. Although the mansion lay in darkness, the kitchen door stood open and light spilled out from behind the jalousie.

With my posy clutched in front of me as a talisman, I walked up the drive, trembling like a newborn goat. At every step, I expected a dog to come charging around the corner of the building or some butler to appear and turn me off the property. However, I made the out-kitchen sans incident. I only wished Emile had been there to see what I had done. No doubt, he would be proud of me.

Peeking through the open doorway, I obtained a partial view of the lamplit interior. And there sat Thérèse, plucking a pigeon. I almost cried out at the sight of her familiar face but then an old house-slave appeared at the threshold, wiping her hands on her apron. She looked at me down her nose.

'What do you want, boy?'

'Miss Thérèse – I'm here to see her.'

At the sound of my voice, Thérèse glanced up with a start and leapt to her feet.

'Jésis-Maïa!' She slung the half-pluck bird on the table then hurried over, feathers flying *tout partout*. 'If you please, Josephine, let me speak to this boy alone.'

The old woman glared at me, suspicious.

'Who is he?'

'Just a boy,' said Thérèse.

'I can see that,' said Josephine, still glaring. 'How old are you, child?'

'Sixteen,' I replied.

She gave a snort of disbelief.

'Give me a little while,' said Thérèse. 'I just need to talk to him.'

The house-slave threw her a warning look.

'Governor will be back soon.'

'Please,' Thérèse pleaded. 'Just go over to the dining room, set the table.'

Sucking her teeth, the old woman set off toward the main house. Thérèse drag me inside the kitchen and shut the door.

'Did anyone see you come up here?'

'No,' I said, handing her the flowers. 'Don't fret. I was going to be your suitor.'

'Yes – well . . .' She sighed. 'You might be too young for me. What do you want? Be quick. We can't hide you.'

'I know. I just want to know what you've heard.'

'Not much.' She sighed. 'Just that they sent soldiers to Petit Havre and most everybody got caught.'

She told me that the redcoats had been keeping an eye on any boat in Petit Havre and *The Daisy* had caught their notice. When the bigger sloop dropped anchor in the bay, they sent word to town. As soon as the escape from the plantation was discovered, someone had put two and two together and troops were despatched at once. A number of slave were still on the loose but Chevallier, Angélique Le Vieux and Léontine had all been captured.

'How do you know?' I asked.

'The Governor told me because they are family. Everyone is being kept down on the plantation, field hand and hospital slave alike.'

'How many got away?'

'I don't know.'

'Did he mention Emile? And Céleste? Were they caught?'

'He only told me about my family. Nobody else. I'm sorry.'

On an instant, my thoughts became a blur. Thérèse reached into her apron and gave me a handkerchief. I wiped my eyes.

'Not crying,' I told her. 'It's just smoky in here. That oven – the lamps.'

'Mm-hmm. Look, Emile and Céleste might still be free. All I know is, there's to be an inquiry. They've been questioning the slaves. The Governor wants it all done by the turn of the year.'

I thought for a moment.

'What time are you expecting him?'

'Soon. But you can't see him. He would have you arrested.'

'I know – but you could speak to him. Tell him the truth.'

Her eyes flash with sudden fear.

'Tell him Emile was only carrying out orders,' I continued. 'The Fathers, they hired him. He had no choice.'

'But – I'm not suppose to know. I had to pretend I knew nothing about the escape, else I'd be over there on that plantation with the rest.'

We stared at each other. Something snuffed out inside me like a spent wick.

'If I were you, I'd leave town, right now,' said Thérèse. 'Go up to Sauteurs or somewhere. Stay out of sight. Try to get back to Martinique.'

'Not until I find Emile.'

She gave me a grim look.

'If you had any sense, you'd go. Where have you been hiding?'

'Up at the Maillard place, under the veranda.'

She looked alarmed.

'Does he know you're there?'

'No.'

'What about Zabette?'

'The girl? No. I'm keeping quiet.'

She sighed again.

'Are you hungry?'

'Mm-hmm.'

She cut open a few avocato, spooned out the stones then gave me the fruit.

'Thank you.'

Lips pursed, she watch me as I ate.

'Look,' she said, at last. 'If you want to help your brother, you should get Cléophas to come back here and speak for him. Get word to him in Martinique.'

'How am I suppose to do that?'

'Someone going on a boat could take a message. The Governor

might listen to Cléophas. He's a monk. A white man.'

She open the door and stood at the threshold, pretending to shake feathers out of her apron but in fact checking to ensure that all was quiet. Then she came back in.

'Go now. Take the footpath down this side. Not the drive.'

She pause for an instant, a sad smile on her face. I could tell she was torn at having to send me away.

'Never mind,' I told her. 'I'd be a fool to hide here.'

'For true – but where will you go?'

'Back to the veranda, until I know what to do. I'll let you know if I move.'

'No,' she said. 'Don't come back here.'

'Well, if you hear anything about Emile, will you let me know? Send a message?'

'I'll try. What about Zabette?'

'What about her?'

'You ought to ask her for help. She might know someone with a boat. Or she could get someone to tell some person going to Martinique to take a message to Cléophas.'

'That's a slim plan. Ask this one to tell that one . . .'

'Well,' she said. 'It's about the only plan you've got. That girl owes me a favour. You tell her I said she should help you, any way she can. Tell her if she doesn't, she will have me to answer to.' Thérèse thrust more avocato at me and I shove them in my pockets. 'Now, be careful, Lucien. *Bon chanse.*'

Then she gave me a little shove toward the threshold. I step past her into the night and slipped away down the shadowy side path, holding my breath until I was on the street. From there I went haring up Rue de l'Hôpital and back to the Maillard place as fast as my bad foot would allow. Zabette and the doctor must have been asleep for the house lay in darkness. I was up the path and under the porch so quick I forgot to take water with me again. Down in town, those Béké violin were still screeching and now – from a plantation across the bay, near the old town lake – came the rhythmic sound of *tambour*, clapping and singing; some slaves permitted to *fé la fèt* for a few hour because of Christmas. They were playing one of those Congo dances and the boisterous drums on top of the shrieking violins in town made a strange music, discordant and unsettling.

Chapter Fifty-Two

Next morning I started awake, sore in every bone, my head befuddle, my mouth dry. Heavy rain splattered off the foliage all around the house. My head ached from thirst. If Maillard and Zabette had been still a-bed I might have risked a dash to the water-barrel but I could tell – from the nutty scent of coffee that drifted down through the floorboards – that they were up and about, right above my head, in fact, on the veranda. Unable even to eat my avocato for fear of being heard, I lay there listening to the doctor turn the pages of his blasted newspapers that came all the way from *La Fwance.* Since St Stephen is a day for visiting, I hoped that – sooner or later – they would quit the house, allowing me to visit the barrel. Soon, a rattle and bang of pots and pans told me that Zabette had gone inside to cook. I turn my head and stared out between the cracks in the boards, beyond which I could see the falling rain. If only I could crawl outside and part my lips, let the water from the heavens trickle down my throat – but I dare not move.

In time, Zabette emerged and they began to eat at the veranda table, their conversation desultory with no mention of the runaways. As they finish their meal, the rain grew lighter, then stopped altogether. The sun began to shine. Maillard smoked a segar. Presently, I heard the scrape of chair legs and his boot-heels striking the floorboards as he strode inside. I did not detect the girl, her light step flitting across the porch; only saw her through the cracks as she went down into the garden and passed out of sight. She reappeared with a hoe a moment later, wandering among the damp rows of beans, tilling the earth here and there. Soon, Maillard came back out and stood at the top of the steps. I heard him inform Zabette that he was going up to the hospital. When she asked if he wished her to make him a supper, he replied, shortly:

'*Oui.*'

Then he went inside the house again and, after a short interval, the building shook as the front door bang shut.

The girl continue to poke her hoe among the beans, glancing every otherwhile toward the road, a scornful expression on her face. Presently, she stop work and stepped a few pace across the garden. Shading her eyes with her hand, she stared into the distance, and I surmise she was watching the doctor walk up the road. Eventually, she must have been satisfied that he had truly gone. She threw down her hoe and went inside the house. Not long after, I heard the creak of the bedstead. It would seem she had decided to snatch her *siesta*.

I waited for as long as it might take her to fall asleep. Then, desperate to slake my thirst, I crept to the end-piece and squirmed out into the hollyhock, waiting again until sure that the coast was clear. At last, I hurried to the barrel and dip my hands in, again and again, gulping down the warm, green-tasting water – until a voice behind me said:

'You must be thirsty.'

I span around to see Zabette on the veranda.

'Wondered where you were hiding,' she continued. 'I saw you from the window last night, sneaking up the path.'

Uncertain whether to flee or stay, I just stood there, my heartbeat fast as a hummingbird wing. She took a step forward and peered at me.

'Jésis-Maïa! It's the boy with the herbs. Where were you? Under the porch?'

I gave a tentative nod.

'No need to be afraid,' she said. 'Nobody knows you're here except me.'

'I'm not afraid.'

'Well, you look like you saw *La Diablesse*. Are you one of those runaway from the hospital?'

'. . . Not exactly.'

'You told me you came from Martinique . . . is that the truth?'

'I – I best not say.'

'Hm-hmm,' she said. 'Well, I would bet you know something about what happened over there at the plantation. You better go right now. If he finds you here . . .'

'Please,' I said. 'Let me stay a while. Just tonight. I'll be quiet. And – you know Miss Thérèse, down at the Governor House?'

Zabette frowned.

'What about her?'

'Well, she said you should help me. She said – you ought to.'

'Did she now?'

'Yes. In fact, she said she was sure you would help me because she wants you to.'

The girl put her hands on her hips and stared at me as though she might blast my head off. But in the end, she cursed under her breath and then swept off into the house. Perhaps she was not so stupid after all, if she had watch me sneak along the path the previous night and been smart enough to keep quiet about it so far. Or could this be a ruse? Had she run off to fetch some Béké neighbour?

I was on the point of fleeing when she returned, carrying two bowl. She came down the steps and headed behind the hollyhock.

'Come in here,' she said. 'No one can see past these.'

For true, the bushes were thick enough in places to conceal us. I followed her and sat against the wall of the house. She squatted down and set the two bowl in front of me. One was full to the brim with a murky-looking *mabi*. The other contain some scraps of *akras* and beans, perhaps the remnant of their meal. I slonk back the drink *cul sek* then set about the food. Zabette studied me crossly as I ate. Eventually, she said:

'You cannot stay here, little man. You must go when it gets dark. What's wrong with your foot?'

'Nothing. I got bit. It's almost better.'

The girl raised her eyebrows then sniff the air.

'And what's that smell? You stink.'

'Dung,' I lied. 'I was in a dung-cart.'

She waved her hand in front of her face.

'Whoo boy! You reek so much they might smell you from the road. You know they're on the lookout for runaways?'

'Yes. What else have you heard?'

'Not much. They are keeping them all on the plantation for now, even the hospital slave. They flogged the driver. Demoted him. Now they are talking about branding them all on the face. Bryant wants to stop them straying, build a fence around the village. Pierre – Monsieur Maillard – he has gone up to the hospital to find out if there's any more news. It was him that discovered the slave were gone in the first place.'

'Is that so?'

'*Wi*. He got summon to the hospital to tend a sick soldier. Went looking for a nurse at the quarters. Well, that's when he saw the place all deserted and told the men in the sick room. Somebody went to the plantation, found all the field hand gone – *et vwala*.'

'Then what?'

She tossed her head.

'Well, there were soldiers at the hospital, visiting their sick compeer. Some rode to the fort to raise the alarm and the rest went to the Anglade place to fetch Dr Bryant and that overseer. Pierre says the troops got to Petit Havre just as the slave were about to board the boats. They rounded up all but five.'

'Who got away? Did he mention someone called Emile?'

'Is that you?'

'No. Céleste or Emile? Did he mention those name?'

'Nn-nn.'

'Well – how many of the four are men? How many women?'

'Two women, I think; one man; two children.' She stood up. 'I'll bring water so you can get clean. And I'll wash your clothes. But you must leave as soon as it's dark. You hear me? You can't stay here.'

While she was gone, I tried to figure out how to persuade her to send a message to Martinique. I had doubts about how much more to expect from her. But – somehow – I had to get word to Cléophas.

By the time Zabette returned, I had finished eating. She brought with her a bucket of water, some rag and a large white cloth.

'Take off those stink things and get yourself clean,' she said, crossly.

Thankfully, she turn to keep watch on the road whiles I scrambled out of my clothes and began to scrub at my skin with wet rags. Just in case, I kept my back to the wall, to hide my scars.

'How long before Maillard gets back?' I asked her.

'Hard to say. He could turn up any time so . . .'

'Miss Zabette – can I ask you another favour?'

She scowled at me over her shoulder.

'What?'

'I have to get word to one of the Fathers. I need him to speak to the Governor here. Could you send a message?'

'Where is this Father?'

'In Martinique, St Pierre.'

'What?' she cried, then lowered her voice again. 'That's another island! How am I suppose to get a message over there?'

'Miss Thérèse said you might know some free man or a boatman. A fisherman or someone. Plenty boats go back and forth every day between here and there.'

'Nn-nn. I know no boatman. I hardly leave this house. Who does she think I am?'

'But – do you have a cousin or a friend who knows someone?'

'A friend, he says . . . a cousin! As if I know anybody.'

On she went, complaining. I drop the rags into the bucket, feeling the hope drain out of me. Zabette threw me the white cloth.

'Put that on while I wash your things. Be quick.'

The cloth turned out to be a garment: a shift; plain white with no frills or flounces, but a girlish shift nonetheless.

'*Non mèsi*. I can't wear that.'

'Well, that's all there is,' said she. 'If I give you his clothes he might notice they're gone. Put it on. Hurry up. You want to lie around naked under there with your little *lolo* flopping around for some rat to chew?'

The thought made me wince. She turned on her heel again, saying:

'I'll get you something to drink.'

With no little reluctation of spirit, I pull the shift over my head. It just about fit me though it was tight in the shoulders. At least it covered my back. At the thought of my scars, a picture of Saturnin pass through my mind. Saturnin, who had help me to escape when he could have fled, now demoted and flogged. The fact that I had disliked him at first and given him cheek made me want to bash my head with my two fist.

When the girl returned, she handed me some banana and a calabash of water and I stowed them under the porch. Then she clasped her hands on her jutting belly.

– 313 –

'Listen,' she said. 'I might not be able to send a message but I can find out more about what happened. When Pierre comes back I'll get him talking, see what else he knows about the runaways, if he knows their names and so forth.'

'And then you can tell me.'

'Well, if he sits out on the porch you can hear for yourself.' She picked up my clothes. 'I'll put these to dry at the end of the garden where he won't see. Now, be sure to wait until dark before you leave. Take care he does not catch you. Get in there quick.'

She watch me worm my way under the veranda. The shift constrain my movements, kept snagging in the broken boards. Zabette waited until I was out of sight and then she went back into the house. I had no energy to crawl very far inside the space. In the end, I just curled up near the end-piece. Outside, in the garden, I could hear the birds and insect all chattering to each other nineteen to the dozen. I was nothing to them. They were not even aware of my existence.

Chapter Fifty-Three

I must have slept for a while. When I woke again, the stink of segar smoke was strong enough to churn my stomach. I heard a faint tapping sound above me on the veranda and then Maillard gave a chuckle.

'My move,' he said.

More tap-tap sounds then he laughed again. He was playing chess, I realised. I had seen many a friar, head bent over a battered old checker board. At first, I assume that a French visitor had come to call but then Zabette spoke.

'How can you . . . ?'

'Here, with this one . . .' Tap-tap. 'And now . . . I do this and – checkmate. I win.'

The girl let fly a curse and I heard a clatter as though she had overturn some of the chessmen, then a soft clack-clack as someone began to replace the pieces.

'So,' Zabette said. 'Where did they find them?'

'Hmm? Oh – in a cave.'

'At Petit Havre?'

'No, along the coast at Black Bay.'

She had been as good as her word, got him outside and induced him to talk. I wondered how much of the conversation I had missed while asleep. I could have kick myself.

'No, that one goes there,' said Maillard, his attention on the chessboard. 'And that one there. That's it.'

She prompted him again.

'All five of them were in this cave?'

'Yes. The entrance is apparently well concealed and they might have remained hidden except the little boy began to cry just as some redcoats were returning, having searched up the coast. Rather foolishly, of course, they decided to send just one soldier to escort the child and the two women back to the plantation.'

His self-important voice jarred on me like a file on teeth.

Zabette asked: 'So – what happened, exactly?'

'I'm told she started to cry out and groan as they came within sight of the river and then she hunched over on the ground, screaming that her baby was coming. Well, the other woman knelt down to tend to her and apparently Céleste persuaded the guard to run and fetch water in his flask. But by the time he returned, she had vanished. It would seem she had only pretended to go into labour. She has a few months of her term left, of course, the soldier could not know that . . .'

'What about the other woman? Did she not try to escape?'

'No, when the redcoat got back he found Rosalie with her son Casimir, sitting at the side of the road. She must have thought the risk of running again too much. Probably knew the boy and the baby on her back would slow her down. Of course, the soldier had to take them to the quarters before he could raise the alarm, meaning that Céleste was long gone by the time they started to search for her.'

'So – how many are still to be caught?'

'Just Céleste. She's the only one still on the loose. Oh – and the brother, of course, Lucien. He'll turn up soon enough, no doubt, poor little chap. Bryant is very keen to get him. And you can be sure Emile will be watched day and night. They would be disappointed to lose him.'

At once, I was alert in every fibre of my being. Maillard remained silent for a moment then continued:

'In any case, apparently, it's worthless.'

'. . . What is?'

'The Power of Attorney. Emile told the slaves he had permission to take them to Martinique. That's why they all went with him. At least, that's what they are saying. They thought the document gave him authority from Governor Melville to take them. They claim that Emile misled them, that it's not their fault. They were duped by him. At least, that's the story. Apparently, they all say the same under questioning.'

'Hmm,' said Zabette. 'If that be the case then why do they need go sneaking off in the dark without a word to anyone? Sounding suspicious to me.'

'*Exactement*,' the doctor replied. 'Only a fool would swallow that nonsense. No, they're simply trying to save their own skin by blaming Emile.'

'And will it? Save their skin?'

'Who knows?'

They fell silent and after a while I heard the tap-tap sounds of their game recommence. I lay beneath them, astonished. It felt like a punch to the guts. My brother, betrayed by our compeers, even those from the hospital. They were nothing but talebearers, and false tales, in plus. To protect themselve, they would lie about what Emile had told them. I scarce had time to choke down those bitter pills before the conversation continued.

'So, this Emile,' Zabette said. 'Why did they not put him on the plantation with the rest? Why is he in the common jail?'

'Because he is the ringleader, they must treat him as a criminal. They need him under lock and key. He's an intelligent creature, always has been. I'm not surprised he was among the last to be caught. And – there we are, too bad for you – *échec et mat. Voilà.*'

'What? You won – already?'

'You weren't paying attention. Now, enough of this. Make some food. I want to go back up there later, find out what's happened.'

I heard the girl stand up and the whisper of her feet as she went inside. Maillard lingered, moving pieces around on the chessboard. I willed him to follow her, for my entire body ached with all that I had heard. Betrayal and misery, misery and betrayal. Tears pricked my eyes and every sign told me that I would be sick: my mouth had filled with water; I broke into a sweat. Quiet as I could, I rolled onto my side and lay there, trembling, fighting back wave after wave of nausea until, at last, the doctor stood up and went into the house.

Chapter Fifty-Four

By some miracle, I kept the vomit down. I could hear the murmur of voices as Maillard and Zabette ate their meal. Meanwhile, my thoughts were in turmoil now that I knew Emile had been captured. Even if I got as far as the courtyard of the jail, it was the toss of a penny whether I would be able to find a way inside unchallenged. Provided his cell had a window, I might be able to call to him from outside. But I had no idea where they were keeping him. No doubt, they would arrest me on the spot if I strode up to the prison entrance and ask to speak to him. Perhaps I might sneak inside by pretending to make some kind of delivery. But the guards would likely know the regular tradesmen. Even walking past the prison, down Young Street, might be dangerous, not least because the building stood near the guardhouse and the fort. For true, there were plenty boys like me in Grenada. I would hardly stand out in a crowd. Nevertheless, I'd have to be careful, otherwise both of us would be in jail.

I fretted and thought, thought and fretted until, eventually, a plan began to form in my mind. Perhaps, under different circumstance, I would never have conceive such a thing. But as I lay there sweating into the shift that Zabette had provided, an idea struck me and once the notion entered my brain I could not rid myself of it. The more I mulled it over, the more I became convince it might work. As the afternoon waned, I grew increasing high-strung and began to wish that the doctor would hurry up and leave for the hospital. Yet I was oblige to wait, not daring to make a sound, just in case.

At long last, I heard Maillard stride about the place, making preparation to leave, then the foredoor slammed. Presently, Zabette came outside and – through the gaps in the boards – I saw her wander down the garden, out of sight. After a short while, she return with my breeks and shirt, her gaze trained on the road, no doubt keeping watch on her master as he went up to the hospital. She vanish behind the hollyhock then appeared at the hole in the end-piece and handed in my clothes.

'Here,' she said, in an undertone. 'They're dry.'

'That's most kind, Miss Zabette. Thank you. But I have a favour to ask, if I may.'

And then I explain to her the idea that my brain had been cooking. She listen to what I said then told me I was crazy: it would never work. However, in the end – after some desperate persuasion on my part and many objection on hers – she agreed to help.

Chapter Fifty-Five

Somewhile later, I found myself dressed entirely in garments that belong to Zabette: her shift, a petticoat and a dark but faded cotton gown. My plan was to head into town after nightfall and survey the prison to see if there might be some way to speak to Emile or help him escape. Zabette gave me a floppy old straw bonnet that conceal my face and though I still had a limp I could mostly hide it with short girlish steps. I practised walking up and down behind the hollyhock, while Zabette kept an eye on the road.

'What do you think?' I asked.

She threw me a withering look.

'You might pass for a *porteuse* from the mountain.'

This gave me an idea and I ask Zabette to provide a trait of produce from the kitchen garden. She dared not pick much in case her master notice that someone had pilfer his legumes but she stuffed a basket with my clothes and cover them with a thin layer of beans. It was difficile to balance anything on the bonnet and so she showed me how to carry the basket on one hip. The *porteuses* went barefoot which was just as well since the only shoes Zabette possess were too small for me. As a final touch she put a flower in my hat and so my disguise was complete.

'Just as well you got no beard yet,' said Zabette. 'But if I were you, I would stay away from lamplight. What exactly will you do down there at the jail?'

'Find Emile. Speak to him if I can. Perhaps sneak inside. Get him out.'

'You won't get inside. All this *bordel* about the escape, you can bet they have extra guards on duty. Probably they got your brother chained up in a cell with no window.'

'I'll talk my way past the guard and find him.'

She shook her head.

'Whatever you do, never speak. You might pass for a girl in the dark but talk out loud you'll be in the suds. And pull that bonnet down, hide your hair.'

Before I went, I made sure to eat some fruits and take a long drink from the water-barrel. By the time I was ready, thick cloud had crept across to cover the stars and the sky was black as the bottom of a well.

'Remember to bring back my things,' said Zabette. 'Put them under the porch. But only at night. You must never come back here in the daytime. You hear me?'

'Yes. Well – goodbye then.'

I set off across the garden and was about to step through the gate when she came trotting up behind me and grab my arm.

'*Tjenbé rèd*, little one,' she whispered in my ear. '*Tjenbé rèd. Pa moli.*'

Then she race back down the path.

Full of trepidation, I set off for Fort Royal. There was so much to remember, such as taking small step, lowering my gaze like a girl and only glancing up on occasion to check my progress. The tree-frog peeped their heads off as usual and the air was perfume with a mix of burnt charcoal and night-scented flowers. I found it strange that the world could be so ordinary when such devilish events were taking place: my brother locked up like a criminal and me mincing it along the highway in a bonnet and frock.

Few light showed in town. Everything seem quiet and lonely until I reached Rue Gouvernement. The Governor must have been holding a soirée, for his mansion all lit up. Perhaps Thérèse was somewhere in those rooms, serving guest. As I drew near, a group of raucous gentlemen left the house and began to stroll down the carriage drive. To avoid them, I hurried on to the corner. Just ahead a stretch stood the guardhouse and the entrance to the fort so I dived quick and fast around onto Young Street. To my dismay, I practically bumped into a boy about my own age, some kind of a simple-hearted French soul, his whey-face just visible in the dark. He began to toddle longside me, brandishing his arms, talking earnest gibberage and generally making a racket. My plan had been to take a look at the jail, glide past no fuss or bother, but this noodle would draw the attention of any clod within a mile.

I chanced an urgent whisper:

'*Allez!*'

Probably, most people taunted such a boy or gave him a shove to be rid of him but it was not in me to harm him. Perhaps that was why he stuck to me like a wart, or maybe he took me for a kin spirit: an ugly misfortunate with a strange, mincing gait. Alas, we were getting close to the jail. Hoping he would go away if I heard him out, I stopped at the corner to let him finish his pistle, whatever it might have been (for I altogether fail to follow the story). When at last he fell silent, I patted his shoulder then tried to steer him up Rue Pradine, away from the prison. This only caused him to embark upon a whole other tale and so, my head fit to burst with frustration, I began to walk up Pradine myself, hoping to lose him before the carenage. Halfway down – Praise Be to Great Jehosaphat – he hirpled up a set of stairs to the first floor of what look like an eating-house and there gave me a wave before vanishing inside.

Quick and fast, I retrace my step to the corner. From that angle, the prison lay out of sight, set back from the road behind a court-yard. A row of warehouses lined the left side of the street, deserted at that late hour, their doors shut tight. Though it were a relief to be alone again, my guts churned with anxiety. Howsomever, nothing else for it, I took a deep breath and began to make my way down Young Street, the basket prop on my hip. I pass what look like a new hotel on the right and then, all too soon, there was the courtyard and the jail, all the windows dark and barred. I could not have told you which were the cell. Several big iron cresset suspended from the roof threw flickering light across the façade. In passing, I stole a few glances at the yard. Two redcoat soldier stood guard either side of the door. I could sense them watching me as I continue down the street. Then, one of the guard commence to make a clucking sound with his tongue as though to summon me like a dog. Clearly, my disguise had fooled him: he took me for a woman. The urge to run almost overcame me. I faltered and stumbled. Both men laughed and it was a relief to reach the next building – a private dwelling with no lights at the windows – and step beyond their view. Just past the house, I came to a wide lane. It was black as a cellar up there and so I turned off the street, hoping to gather my thoughts and decide upon some course of action. My mind had gone blank with fright and I was desperate to hide, if only for a moment, to recover.

I could have thrown myself to the ground in despair. I saw now that even to make contact with Emile might be impossible. The thought of approaching those guard chill my blood. Even if my female garb fool them for a while, as soon as I spoke, the jig would be over. At the back of my mind, I had conceive some half-bake, hare-brain scheme to hoodwink my way into the jail. But it took courage to carry out such a plan, courage I lacked entirely. In short, I was a coward. I could have spat upon myself. All at once, my stomach heaved. I had to lean against the side of the house to spew into a drain. Afterward, I stood there, my forehead pressed against the wall, wishing I could disappear into the masonry.

The sense of my own inutility soon became too much to bear. I had to move, to shift my thoughts. At a loss, I decided to take a look behind the houses. Perhaps the lane led to the back of the jail; perhaps another entrance. Of course, any prison door would be locked or guarded, any window barred, but I was clutching at shadows. At the very least, perhaps I might call out and hear my brother reply.

In fact, the lane ended in a yard beneath the vast mound of rock crowned by Fort Royal. From many streets in town that familiar sight is hidden by buildings but now as I turn the corner the fort came into view against the night sky and my eyes were drawn to the torchlight that blazed at intervals along its bastions. Then another glimmer at ground level cause me to lower my gaze. There, in the yard, burned a bonfire and assembled around the flames, a group of men: Glasgow Greys, about a dozen of them. The firelight flickered on their dark figures and threw shadows across the back wall of the prison. I stop short and my mouth fell open. The shock made my hand fly to my face, exactly like a girl. This may have worked in my favour and made me seem more womanish because in that moment one of the redcoat notice me and called out:

'Good evening, Miss Yellow.'

His friends laughed as he jumped up and commence to stroll toward me.

'Come here, pretty,' he said. 'I want to show you something.'

As he spoke, he reached inside the front of his white breeches. Without waiting to see what he might produce, I began to back off down the lane. A fresh burst of laughter came from the men in the yard. The soldier called out:

'No, wait. Come here, girl.'

I turned and fled, clutching my basket to my chest. Fortunately, he was too much of a swaggerer to run after a woman in sight of his compeers, though he followed me at a brisk pace nonetheless.

On I staggered, shedding beans in my wake. At the end of the lane, I paused. A right turn led nowhere but the sea. If I headed left, I would have to pass the front of the prison again and, for aught I knew, those two guard might like naught better than to join the soldier in his chase. Across the street lay a short alley that seem to end at a steep hill behind the warehouses: a poor option but the best available. I could hear the redcoat plodding along the lane relentless and so I dodged around the corner and across the road. There, I press myself into the night-shade of the building and – after edging along the wall – darted up the vennel. Provided the shadows of the warehouse had hid me, the soldier might assume that I had fled up toward the town square.

The alley was not much more than a channel for foul water. Now limping again, I pick my way alongside the open drain to the end. Sure enough, at the back of the building lay a short yard beyond which an area of uncleared ground rose steeply into the night. Alas, my ducking and dodging had not fool the redcoat for I could hear him now, the creak of his boots as he strode down the alley. With little choice, I began to scramble up the overgrown slope. Not quick enough, for the soldier rushed out of the dark and, grabbing me from behind, he drag me back down into the yard. Then, pulling me to him, he reached around and up inside my skirts and clamped his hand on me. What he found there must have been quite a surprise for he yelled out in revulsion and jerked away so violently that he fell to the ground on his latter end. Seizing my chance, I scrabbled up the slope without looking back. How I kept a grip on the basket I have no idea, but I was reluctant to abandon it and my clothes. At the top, I found myself once more on Rue Pradine. Dragging my foot, I hirpled along fast as I could, past the road that led to the guardhouse then, at full tilt, out of town and up the High Road.

The Maillard place lay in darkness. I knew Zabette would be a good deal disappointed if she saw my face again. Yet, I had nowhere else to go. In the bushes at the roadside, I threw off the skirts and dressed in my own clothes. After waiting awhile to be sure nobody had followed me, I crept down the garden path and – whisht as a worm in cheese – inch my way through the end-piece of the veranda. The bonnet and so forth I left next to the hole. Inside, I crawl to the furthest corner, hoping to remain unseen if Zabette poked her head in to retrieve her garments.

There, I cowered, picturing my poor brother, chained up in some dank and gloomy cell. I hardly dared imagine how they might punish him. Had our roles been reversed, of course, Emile would have found some ingenious way to help me escape, no question. Whereas I had failed even before I began. Curled up in a miserable ball of shame, I had to press my face into my arms to muffle my sobs, all the while wondering what we had done to deserve such a life.

PART TEN

A Return

Chapter Fifty-Six

————————

Next time I open my eyes it was dark as a tomb neath the porch. The sappy racket of tree-frogs fill the night. Half asleep, I could scarce see a thing thus almost leapt out my own skin when the warm air moved and someone spoke my name, soft like a breath.

'Lucien.'

With a start, I scrabble backward. My head graze the underside of the veranda.

'Zabette? Is that you?'

The voice hiss back:

'*Non, se mwa.*'

My heart just about thudded through my ribs.

'Emile?'

A shadow grab my wrist and push something hard and furry into my hand. Bony claws scrape my palm.

'*Se mwa* – Descartes.'

The boy from Martinique. Was I dreaming?

The boy tug my elbow.

'Come,' he whispered. '*Annou alé.*'

My arm hurt where he had grab me. Clearly, this was no dream. Could he have paddled all the way to Grenada in his canoe? My mind swam in a fog of confusion.

I heard him set off on hands and knees toward the end-piece, leaving me reeling, trying to make sense of how he might have track me down to this unlikely place. Weak as a newborn turtle, I floundered after him and clambered out of the veranda to find him waiting for me at the side of the house. The clouds had disappeared, leaving a clear sky. Bats swooped about like specks of soot in the chimney of the night. Behind one of the jalousie overhead, a lamp glowed. Someone inside was awake, perhaps Maillard, up late, reading his newspapers. The jaundice lamplight spill down upon the boy.

It was him all right – Descartes.

He pointed to the window then put one finger to his lips. Tentatively, I extended my hand into the stripes of light and saw in my palm an old rabbit foot mounted in silver; the one that Cléophas kept in his pocket for luck.

Cléophas.

Before this thought had even spiral through my sluggish brain, the boy grab my elbow again and pull me away from the house, only letting go once we had cross the highway. Then he set off into the forest. I stumbled after him, blindly, my heart beating out of rhythm like a bird fluttering behind the cage of my ribs. A short distance uphill, the boy came to a halt just far enough into the trees that we could talk in low voices without being heard by anyone on the road below. I open my mouth to speak but before I could question him Descartes was already talking:

'Where is it?'

'What?'

'That rabbit foot. He said show it so you know it's him.'

I handed back the lucky charm and Descartes shoved it into his britches.

'Let's go,' he said. 'Someone wants to talk to you.'

'Is he here?'

'Not here – but not far.'

'He's on this island?'

'Yes. Hurry up.'

With that, he skipped off through the undergrowth. I had to hurry after him, no time to think. We clambered uphill toward the fortifications. Soon enough, the trees cleared and we came to a wall, part of the redoubt, where someone sat, silvered in the moonlight. A man. He jump down lively as we approached. A Béké – but not Cléophas. I readied myself to flee until I recognised him: Bianco – or Mr Theobald White, whatever his name might be.

'You look surprised,' said he, in English.

'But – how did you find me?'

'That house-girl told us. Whatshername, works for the Governor – Thérèse. When we heard she was not among the runaways we went to see her, find out what she knows. And here we are.'

Took a moment for this to sink in. Descartes retreated a short distance to lean against the wall. Presumably, since we spoke in English, our words were *baragouin* to him.

'But I thought – were you not at Petit Havre, sir, with the Father, when the soldiers came?'

'I was. Well, Cléophas was out in the sloop, *The Alcyon*. We were in *The Daisy*.' He nodded at Descartes. 'I was about to send him ashore in the skiff to start bringing you all aboard when the fireworks started. Lucky for us, there was enough breeze to take off sharpish.'

'So – you never went back to Martinique . . . ?'

'No. We just sailed around the island, found a quiet bay to drop anchor. Cléophas has been lying low in case he is recognised, but me and the little fellow here have been into Fort Royal a few times.'

'Sir – where is the Father?'

'Just outside town – in a ravine.'

He gestured vaguely to somewhere beyond the carenage and I saw that he had been holding his cutlass at his side all this time. The blade gleamed in the moonlight. I drag my gaze back to his face.

'Please, sir, can you take me to him?'

The Englishman gave a sniff.

'That's not the plan,' said he. 'You will, of course, be returning with us to Martinique, I'm sure you're glad to hear. But first, the Father wants you to do something for him. I'm to take you to the plantation.'

For many reasons, I did not fancy the sound of this, one bit.

'Please, sir – I must speak to Father Cléophas first. It's important.'

White cast a disgruntle glance over at Descartes then tip back his head and gazed up at the stars. He might have been asking the gods to bear witness to his trials on this earth or perhaps he was simply calculating the hour. At any rate, in the end, he gave a sigh then lowered his gaze once again to me.

'Very well,' he said. 'But we must be quick about it.'

He clicked his fingers and the boy jump to his feet. I wondered who was now tending to my beasts back in St Pierre but there was no time to ask Descartes, for the Englishman was already waving his cutlass at us.

'*Alley-alley, veet*,' said White. '*Venee. Eessee.* This way.'

And he turned his back on us and strode off into the trees, swinging his blade.

Chapter Fifty-Seven

We quit the redoubt and headed away from town along the forested hillside above the carenage bay. Presently, we reached a stream and followed it down to where it crossed a highway. The Englishman led us over to the other side. There, he turn to Descartes and pointed into the undergrowth.

'Wait here out of sight,' said he. '*Attand eesee*. Keep lookee-lookee. *Regardee*.'

Then he beckon me to follow him further into the woodland. We kept alongside the stream, descending toward the bay. The path was overgrown and treacherous. White chopped and hacked at the undergrowth – sometimes unnecessarily, in my opinion – but he did like to swing his arm. For a while, we laboured along through the vegetation and eventually reached a place where two coco-palm had fallen across the stream. Their collapse had left an expanse of the heavens visible overhead and silver-blue starlight luminated the bare patch on the riverbank where we stood.

'Wait here,' said the Englishman, then disappeared into the forest. Presently, I heard a machete swish-swish and then a solitary figure emerge from the undergrowth. I recognise his robes at once: it was Cléophas. At the familiar sight of him, I cried out:

'Father—'

'Husht,' he whispered. 'Keep your voice down. Now, come here, child, where it's lighter. Let me look at you.'

I stumbled on a tangle of roots as I approached him. He sheathed his blade then put his hand on my shoulder and gaze down into my eyes.

'You've done well, boy,' he said. 'Even your brother has been caught. But not you! Lucky that you went to see Thérèse – otherwise we might never have found you. But you're limping. You took a fall.'

'Oh – that's nothing. I was bitten.'

'Confounded pot-lickers. A nuisance all over this island.'

'No – not a dog, Father – if you please. Giant centipede, most likely. Father – they put Emile in jail.'

'So I heard. We will talk about that. But first, I want you to tell me something.'

Though desperate to help my brother, I knew the most sensible course was to hear him out and thereby retain his favour. Ergo, I just said:

'Father. As you wish.'

'Good boy. Now, I'm assuming – now that St Stephen is over – work on the hospital plantation will resume in the morning. But tell me, has the cane harvest begun?'

'No, Father. On some estates – but not the hospital. They've been felling trees, stockpiling wood for the mill. So far as I know their harvest will begin on the second day of January.'

'I suppose you know which part of the estate they are clearing.'

'Yes, sir, the back of Hospital Hill.'

'So if they're sent out today it will be to fell trees there on the hillside.'

'Well – I can't be sure, Father, but that seems likely.'

'Very good. White tells me there are redcoats all around the huts at night. But what about in the daytime? One assumes the overseer keeps an eye on them, same as in Martinique.'

'Hard to say, Father.'

'One assumes they would normally be watched over by the overseer and the driver, same as in Martinique.'

'Yes, Father. But now, they might keep soldiers on them when they are in the field, because of the escape.'

He frowned.

'Well, if they are under guard, it makes everything more difficult. I myself cannot afford to be seen at the plantation, of course. People remember a priest. The overseer would definitely remember me from last time – or Bryant would, if I was unfortunate enough to bump into him, which is quite possible. Whereas nobody pays any heed to a little black imp. You're seven-a-penny.' He seem to drift off in his thoughts awhile before continuing: '*Et bon.* Now tell me – have you had any contact with Céleste? I believe she escaped again.'

'Yes, Father. But I haven't seen her.'

'Well, we shall just have to try and find her somehow, get her to the boats. Now – you should be on your way. Mr White will explain everything as you go.'

'But Father – what about Emile?'

Cléophas gave a sigh.

'It's such a pity he got himself caught. I had thought he would make a success of this venture.'

At first, I could scarce trust myself to reply. I had to swallow before speaking.

'Father, if you please . . . what do you think might happen to him?'

'To Emile? Well, it's hard to say. Depends on a number of things. But, if you ask my opinion, I find it hard to believe that he'll escape a flogging. And – I doubt they will let him return to Martinique. They'll probably keep him here, put him to work on a plantation. Of course – just our luck – we will then owe the Dominicans the price of him – but we really have no choice . . .'

'Father – how many?'

'How many what, child?'

'How many lashes?'

'That I know not.' He scratch the back of his neck. 'I believe they gave the driver fifty so – perhaps – a hundred? Flogging stings at the time, of course, but most men get over it. Someone like your brother should be back to good health tout suite.'

A hundred lashes. Into my mind flashed a picture of my brother flinching under the whip, his back glistening with blood and gore. I push the image aside.

'Father, I was thinking—'

'Yes, my son?'

'If only there was someone who could speak to the Governor and explain everything. If the English knew that Emile was simply acting on instruction – carrying out orders – then they might not whip him.'

'Well, perhaps . . . but I doubt it.'

'Do you know anyone that could speak for him, Father?'

'Sadly, no. At least, not anyone who would be of much assistance in such a matter. Mr White is – I should say – how can one put it? I'm not sure his – his credentials or reputation would – be adequate to recommend him.'

'But there must be someone else, Father, if you please, someone right here, who could speak to the Governor . . .'

Cléophas put his hand on my shoulder.

'I know what you're thinking, boy.'

I stared at the ground, kept silent.

'But, of course, there's one small flaw in your plan. You know very well that if I presented myself to the Governor . . . what would you have me say to him? Excuse me, dear sir, that naughty Negro you have locked up in the jail – well, it was me who instructed him to take the slaves from the plantation. But please don't flog him and be a good fellow and give him back to me.'

'. . . I know not, Father, what you might say exactly—'

'But you must realise that the English would, at the very least, put me under watch, if not detain me. And then where would we be?'

'Father—'

'Lucien, I have already put myself at considerable risk by not immediately scurrying back to Martinique. If I announce that I am here, or present myself to the authorities—'

'But Father, could you not explain to them that the slaves belong to *les Frères*? That we had the right to take them?'

'Alas, it's – rather more complicated than that.'

'But if you spoke to the Governor at the inquiry—'

'It's not a public inquiry, boy. Get that out of your head. The Governor will simply have been listening to various reports – from Bryant, the overseer, the slaves and so on. They will be telling him what he needs to know. And that is that.'

'But Father, if you could just speak to him—'

Without warning, he struck me several blows about the head, so fast that I had no chance to dodge out of the way.

'Not another word,' he said. 'Your brother will just have to take his lashes and there's an end to it. Enough now. Mr White will accompany you to the plantation.'

My ears were ringing; my cheek stung. Cléophas rubbed his hand, as though he had hurt himself in striking me. My gaze burn so hot as I stared at him in the darkness it is a miracle he did not reduce to a cinder right where he stood. I considered launching myself at him, intending to go through him like a thunderbolt. He was bigger than me but I reckoned to get a fair few kicks to his head and scallions before White came running and together they overpowered me. Indeed, I might have done it too – with no more remorse than winking – except I knew it would be little help to Emile. Besides, just then, I heard a dim crack like bamboo splitting underfoot and the Englishman emerge from the trees.

'Wait here,' said Cléophas, to me.

He hurried over to White and they began a whispered consultation. Eventually, the Father return to where I stood.

'Sunrise will soon be upon us,' he said. 'Mr White will explain everything as you go.'

My jaw hurt. My hands hurt. Every muscle in my body was clench tight-tight. A sob swelled and ached in my throat.

'But Father – what about Emile?'

Cléophas made a weary sound but when he spoke again his voice was gentle.

'Dear boy. I've told you, there's nothing we can do. Look on the bright side. You yourself are safe. And your brother is a strong man. He will recover. Now promise you won't do anything foolish.' When I made no reply, he repeated himself. 'Promise.'

'I promise.'

'You won't do anything foolish.'

'No, Father.'

They were just words. They meant nothing. My mind was numb. I had no idea what I might do.

'*Et bon*,' said Cléophas.

The Englishman set off and I hesitated until the friar put his hand in the middle of my back and began to push me along. Realising I had no choice, I followed White. Cléophas fell into step behind me and we clambered uphill in single file, me between the two of them, a prisoner. I just kept putting one foot in front of the other, my mind blank, at first, then it began to jump all over the place like a scalded frog. All at once, it came to me: I would have to speak to the Governor myself. Only I could save Emile from what seemed like an inevitable flogging.

When we reach the road, Descartes crept out of the trees to meet us. He handed over the rabbit-foot charm and Cléophas stashed it within his robes, asking the boy:

'Do you still have your ticket?'

Descartes touch the pouch around his neck.

'*Wi, mon pè.*'

'And you know what to do?'

'*Wi, mon pè.*'

'Very good. If you can't find her by – say – midnight, just go back to the boat. We'll see you there.'

Quick-sharp, the boy scurried off down the road, heading for town. Within moments, he had melted into the night.

'Where is he going?' I ask Cléophas.

'To find Céleste and take her to the boats – if he can. We suspect she may go to seek help from Thérèse – so he will begin there.'

Meanwhile, White was slashing with his cutlass at a low-hanging branch. The Father addressed him in English.

'If they are under guard – well – use your judgement. And stay away from town.'

'Fret ye not,' muttered the Englishman and began to wipe his blade on his britches. Cléophas turn to me.

'Once you've finished at the plantation, Lucien, Mr White will escort you to where the boats are waiting at Petit Bacaye. Do you know where that is?'

'No.'

He pointed along the road, away from town. 'Follow this high-way to the far side of the island. You cross a river, then another, this one smaller. Keep going until you come to a third river. That one is smaller still and muddy. It leads down to Petit Bacaye. There's a small bay with a tiny island just offshore to the right. That's how you know you're in the correct place – the little island. If you set out from the plantation of a morning, you should be there by noon.'

He made me repeat these directions then gave me a quick blessing.

'Good boy,' he said. 'Now off you go. We have to leave your brother for now but – all being well – you and Céleste and hopefully some others will be in Martinique by the day after tomorrow and you can reacquaint yourself with your precious beasts. You will be pleased to know we hired a boy especially to look after them.'

In my mind, I could see the cows – their black, shining eyes and velvety nostrils – but for once, in picturing them, I felt only emptiness.

White had already set out across the road. I had no choice but to follow him. On the far side, I glance back to find the Father lingering at the edge of the woods, watching us, but when I turned again a moment later, I could see nothing, not even the trace of where he had stood. Everything had been swallowed up by the dark beneath the trees.

Chapter Fifty-Eight

Now, the Englishman made me walk ahead of him, perhaps to ensure I did not straggle or – more likely – sneak off behind his back. From time to time, he slash needlessly at the underbrush with his cutlass. I could only wonder what Cléophas wanted us to do at the plantation. Indeed, the very prospect of going there fill me with sick anxiety. The sooner I could give White the slip, the better. In my mind, I had yet to figure out how I might insinuate myself into the presence of the Governor. However, for now, White strode foot and foot behind me and there was little I could do except climb fast enough to avoid being hacked across the back of my legs.

We took a traverse route up the slope and emerged onto the spine of Hospital Hill behind the battery then continue down the other side to the campèche thicket. There, White paused in order to survey the field hand quarters. The flambeaux had burned out but the Glasgow Greys still on guard: in the dim starlight, I could just make out a few shady figures in uniform at either end of the bridge. As yet, I could see no sign of activity in the village. White did stare down at the huts for a good spell then, with a flap of his hand, indicated that I should precede him along the ridge toward the hospital fortifications.

Although that patch of hillside had been cleared in some bygone era, the forest had soon resumed its relentless creep and – inch by inch – invaded the trenchments. White must have been there before because he went directly to the end of the battery where a thick curtain of vines and leaves hung down. He pull back the creepers and guided me into the narrow space between them and the wall. Then he stepped in after me. Conceal by this screen of vegetation, we were invisible to anyone who might pass by, even close at hand. Thin starlight filtered in through the foliage. I could just make out the Englishman, a shadowy figure beside me in the dark.

He sat down against the battery and I heard him uncork a flask. Soon, the burnt-sugar smell of rum began to fill the damp air in that confine space. White smacked his lips together. He had scarce uttered a word since we left Cléophas.

'If you please, sir,' I whispered. 'What are we doing here? What's the plan?'

He took another sip of rum.

'We wait,' he said.

'What for, sir?'

'First bell.'

'Then what?'

'You'll see.'

I lean back against the wall. No matter what happened, I had a feeling that I would soon be in the suds. Either they had cooked up some scheme to steal the slaves in broad daylight (heaven forbid!) or they wanted me to sneak into the quarters, for some reason, once everyone was out in the field. Neither prospect held any appeal. If only I could get beyond range of that cutlass. It might mean hitting him on the head – but with what? A rock? A branch? A bare fist? And though my foot had healed somewise, I wondered how far and how fast I could run.

Once again, I glanced over at White. The flask had fallen to the ground. His head had drop forward onto his chest. He appear to have drowsed off. With one finger, I gave the flask a push and could tell by the light weight that he had finish the rum. I was trying to suppute whether it might be possible to slip away through the vines without waking him when my speculations were interrupted by the faint sound of laughter in the distance. Cautiously, I parted the screen of leaves and liane and saw – in the first rosy peep of daylight – a group of soldiers, about ten of them, walking away from the huts and the bridge, toward town. Evidently, the overnight watch on the quarters had stood down. A few of the men jostled each other and, once more, their laughter floated up to the battery. Then the first bell began to ring up at the hospital, so loud they could probably hear it in Brazil.

White snorted. His eyes snapped open.

'Redcoats are going back to town, sir,' I told him.

He shot forward to peer through the foliage. For the immediate, I put aside the notion of escape and looked out again just as the Greys entered the patch of woodland at the coast and disappeared from view.

'Did any come to replace them?' asked White.

'Not so far as I can see.'

Just then, the bell down at the plantation struck up its own racket in answer to the one at the hospital. As if by magic, tiny figures began to emerge from the cabins. At that distance it was hard to distinguish one person from another. I even fail to spot Addison Bell at first, but then I peered again and there he was, leaning against one of the huts: straw tri-corn and pinkish skin, his sleeves roll back, arms folded.

Within a short while the whole gang had assembled and then they set out for the bridge. Two or three had coils of rope on their shoulders and most of them carried tools of some sort: saws, axes, mattocks, shovels and big long iron-crows. The sun glinted on the blades as the line of slave cross the river. Only when they reach the other side, did I begin to recognise individuals among them. In first place came Augustin, his head still bandaged but now free of his shackles;

in his hand, a short whip – the one that Saturnin used to carry. So, Bell must be trying him out as driver, probably to punish him, for no man could be more ill-suited to the task. After him came the big men: Coco, Lapin, Montout, Philoge, all in shackles. Then Polidor and Narcisse and the boys and girls of the fast group, followed by Charlotte and the other women, two or three of them in shackles. Ensuite came Magdelon and Cléronne, discernible as ever by their collars and the gap – fore and aft – where the others gave them a berth. Next, Raymond, apparently – despite his age – still fit for field work. In his wake, Saturnin, limping along in fetters. Then Léontine: the way she stalked along showed how wretched she felt with her new low status as field hand. Behind her, old Chevallier, looking somewhat bewildered. No sign of Angélique Le Vieux. Perhaps she had been left behind at the quarters to cook food or supervise peeny children with old Marigot. Trailing Chevallier came Rosalie, also shuffling along in chains, her baby on her back.

Last of all, Addison Bell. He walked with a measured pace, his gaze fix on the slaves ahead of him.

'No soldier guard,' said White. 'Good. Now, where are they headed?'

'Most likely that open patch there, sir, the felling on the side of the hill.'

'Well. Let's see if you're right.'

We watched the line walk away down the road and then turn up the slope where the hillside lay bare.

'Blow me sideways,' said White. 'Full marks to the nigger.'

Whiles the others streamed up the slope like a line of ant, the overseer spoke to Old Raymond, who set off in the direction of the mill. Presumably, he had been trusted to fetch the cart. Bell watched him go, having no doubt instructed him to return quick-sharp. Meanwhile, up on the felling, the field hand set to work without delay. They knew what to do; had done this many times before, no need to be told. The strongest and fittest were in charge of toppling trees and rooting out any stumps that remained in the ground whiles the rest began to trim branches and stack logs. Magdelon and Cléronne seem to be giving instructions to the hospital slave. By this time, Bell had left the road and was walking uphill among them, watching them work. A great sense of urgency hung over the hillside, as though the slave wish to prove to the overseer how industrious they could be.

'Now,' said White. 'We'll wander on over there and I'm going to hail that overseer and engage him in conversation. You saw me play the dummie – well, now you will see me pass myself off as a new settler from England. I'll ask that Scotch shabaroon about the weather or somesuch – or I might pretend we're lost, I have yet to decide.'

'But – if you please, sir – if I go down there, they'll recognise me.'

He glared at me out of his side eye. He was drunker than I had thought.

'You like to be difficult, do you, boy?'

'No, sir.'

'. . . Where was I?'

'Talking to the overseer.'

'Yes. Good – you're paying attention. I'm testing you, boy, testing. So – while I'm talking to him I want you to tug my sleeve as though you need to speak to me.'

'Who am I suppose to be?'

'You're my boy, of course. Now, I'll ignore you but you just keep tugging until I shoo you away. Then – here's the fun! I want you to drift off far enough that Bell cannot hear you – and you must wander over and pretend to pass the time of day in some nigger-talk with a few of your fellows in the field as they work – but really you'll be giving them the message. Komprendee?'

'Yes, sir.'

'Good. Sound as a bell. Sound-oh.'

He took up his flask then tip back his head and shook the last few drop of rum into his open mouth.

'But sir—'

'What the devil, boy? Pestering me.'

'The message – I need to know the message.'

'I'm just coming to that. The message is that they can still escape, as planned. They just have to get to the far side of the island at Petit Bacaye. Tell your fellows they must get there by dawn tomorrow because after that, the boats will be gone. We can't afford to wait any longer. Now, you tell them how to get there – you remember the directions the Father told you . . . ?'

'Yes.'

'. . . and make them promise to pass on the message to their compeers once we're gone. You got that?'

'Yes, sir. But—'

'I haven't finished. Now, I'll be keeping an eye on you so just give me the sly nod once you're done. I'll finish my conversation with old Jocky-numps, tell him we must be on our way and I'll call you back to me. I might give you a cuff around the ear at some point, as a convincer – but you're not to hold it against me – and then we'll stroll off and be on our way.'

'Like eating pastry,' I said.

'What?'

'Nothing, sir – but the problem is, as I was saying, they will recognise me.'

'Well, the Negroes might – but has the overseer ever set eyes on you?'

'. . . No, sir. He almost saw me once – but it was night and I was hidden.'

'So – what are you worried about?'

'I'm just – the slaves might peach on me, sir. They already peached on my brother. They could tell Bell who I am – to gain his favour. Then what?'

'They won't do that,' said White. 'They won't peach on you to your face.'

'But how can you be sure?'

'For my part, I cannot,' said he, sounding cheerful. 'But Cléophas is convinced they won't. He says he knows how their minds work. They trust you, he says, and you're a likeable chap – despite your temper – and smart. That's why he sent you and not that little dark bugger – who is not, as it transpires, the quickest crab in the creel. Cléophas reckons you're a better prospect.'

I thought of something else then.

'Bryant knows me,' I said. 'The doctor. If he turns up I'm dog-meat.'

'Well, you'll just have to hope he stays away. In that case, it would get too hot for me. Much too hot. I might have to turn Judas – and nobody wants to do that. Even to a half-breed. But you would understand that I had no choice.'

When I fail to reply, he nudge me with the haft of his cutlass.

'Would you not, boy?'

'Yes, sir.'

We sat there, for a short while, in silence. Then I said:

'What if more redcoat come along now to guard them this morning? Do we still try to pass on this message with a gang of soldier watching?'

White put his finger in his ear and jiggled it, saying:

'Such a circumstance would be – less than ideal.'

Well, that summation certainly fell far below the fact – but I must have ruffled him for he pocketed his flask and stood up.

'Let's go,' he said.

Cautious as two cat, we crept from behind the vines. The battery above us lay empty, not a soul in sight. I looked out over the plantation. The sun had yet to chase all the shadows from the fields. No wind that morning. Across the whole entire valley, the cane stood motionless, the vibrant jade of all the leaves soften by the pearly haze of daybreak.

White gestured that I should walk ahead of him, downhill toward the River Road.

'*Alley-alley, veet,*' he said.

And – since he prodded me with the flat of his cutlass blade – I had no choice but to comply.

Chapter Fifty-Nine

Once we reach the River Road, the Englishman made me walk beside him. He strolled along, whistling, the cutlass at my back. Hospital Hill rose up to our right. The first part had been cleared entirely but further inland, where they were working, tree stumps and cut branches litter the ground. As we drew closer to the felling, White sheathed his blade but kept one hand on the haft whiles, with the other, he grab my collar such that he had me under his control. My heart felt like it was beating in my throat. Up on the slope, the gang continue to labour, heads down, attentive to their work. Although the hour was early, there would be nothing unusual in the sight of a Béké on the road with a brown boy by his side.

By this time, the overseer had reach the top of the felling. He stood on a tree stump, tapping his whip against his leg, staring down toward the mill, keeping an eye out for Old Raymond. A few of the men had tackled a stubborn stump near the roadside. Narcisse dug around the base whiles Lapin and Philoge sawed at the roots in the hole and Saturnin examine the proceedings and gave advice. As he shuffle gingerly around the others, I saw that the back of his shirt was stained brown and red with blood, old and new, from the flogging they had given him.

Magdelon stood chopping wood halfway up the slope with a few other women. Nearby, Rosalie trim branches, her baby strap to her back, despite her fetters. Beside her, Charlotte and Cléronne helped Léontine and Chevallier to gather and stack the logs.

As we drew near to the field hand, the Englishman release my collar, staring uphill at Bell, no doubt wondering how to hail him in a way that would appear natural, given how far he had strayed from the road.

'Come down from there, confound you . . .' White muttered and began to curse hard beneath his breath. Just then, the ox-cart came into view, rolling along the highway from the mill. Bell leapt from his stump and began striding down to meet it. En route, he shot a glance in our direction and briefly took our measure before losing interest in us.

'Here we go,' muttered White. 'You do exactly what I told you.'

The cart came to a halt beside the felling. Raymond peered at us as he climb down from the seat and when he recognise me his mouth fell open. I stared back at him, pleading with my eyes, begging him to say nothing. He gave me a nod, scarce perceptible, and began to fiddle with the breeching strap on the harness whiles darting glances in our direction, clearly bewildered to see me turn up in broad daylight in the company of a strange Béké.

White was already hailing the overseer.

'Good day to you, sir. How do you do?'

As Bell return the greeting, his gaze passed over me again. The very fact that I appear to be the slave of another fellow was enough to render me almost invisible. White came to a halt in the road, not far from the cart.

'Tell me, sir, is this the way to Fort Royal? I fear I may have taken a bad turn.'

''Deed you have, sir,' Bell replied. He pointed to the sea. 'Back that way, turn left at the coast. Follow the road straight into town.'

'Ah, thank you,' said White. 'I knew we had gone wrong somewhere.'

The overseer had already turned his attention to the cart and –

finding fault with the amount of debris in the back – began to berate Raymond. With Bell thus distracted, White glared at me, a reminder that I should tug his sleeve rather than stand there, stiff as a hollow tree. Then he called out again to the overseer, who had just ordered Raymond to clean up the back of the wagon.

'That's a fine Scotch accent you have there, sir. Where do you hail from?'

'Mugdock,' said Bell.

'Mugdock?'

'A village outside Glasgow.'

Meanwhile – at the sound of a strange voice on the road – some of the field hand had paused in their work to gaze down at where we stood. Magdelon and Cléronne, Léontine, then Charlotte – Saturnin, Polidor, Augustin: I saw the recognition in each of their faces as, one by one, they turned and spotted me.

'Indeed? I'm a Devonshire man, myself. Tell me, sir, I'm – eh – looking to buy some land here. Thinking of settling in Grenada, you see. Would you recommend it?'

The overseer made a sour face and straightways came strolling over to where we stood. By chance, White had struck on a subject close to his heart.

'I'd think long and hard before settling here,' said Bell. 'It's a damnable place.'

'Really?' the Englishman replied. 'How so, sir? What do you find objectionable?'

'Well – where to begin? The flies, the musquitos, the heat, the diseases and pestilence, the storms, the food, the people – the French in particular – I have no time for them. I could give you a list as long as your leg.'

The field hand made a great show of activity whiles no doubt they strain to hear every word the two men exchanged.

'Dear me – that does sound bad,' said White. 'All the same, I like the look of the place. Tell me, what lies up yonder, further along this road? Any old Frenchy plantations for sale, by any chance? I'd want to buy in this part of the island – near town, you see – I'd rather not end up in the back end of nowhere.'

Bell glance behind him to check on the slave. The Englishman took the opportunity to glare at me again and so – as soon as Bell turn back toward us – I did as White required and tugged his sleeve. Imagine my surprise when – with a sudden fury – he raised his elbow and thump my head, a clanging blow. Whiles I was still reeling from that, he aimed his foot at my latter end and gave me a kick that jarred my bones.

'Leave me be while I talk to this gentleman,' he cried, then addressed the overseer again: 'Devil the boy, never gives me peace.' Then to me, he said: 'Go over there and do something useful. Help that nigger.'

Cursing him in my mind, I limped over to the wagon. Raymond had found an old sack and was flapping it around to clear out the dust and twig. We exchanged a nod and I began to scrape the debris off the cart-bed with my bare hands. Turning away from the two Béké, the old man interrogated me with his expression but before I could mutter a word I saw Rosalie approaching with Léontine, their arms full of split logs, their eyes full of questions. Rosalie took small, shuffling steps and – as she reach the rear of the cart – she pretended to trip over her fetters. Her pile of wood tumble to the ground beside me. Quick-sharp, I bent down to help collect the fallen logs, thus we were partially hidden behind the wagon. Léontine began to throw wood into the cart-bed, making such a racket that we could whisper, unheard by White and Bell.

'What in the hell are you doing here?' Léontine asked.

'Emile's in jail,' I muttered, in reply.

'Bell told us. Have they hurt him?'

'Not so far as I know. What about you?'

'Not me,' said Léontine. 'Not yet. But they flogged Saturnin and they have threaten us with more whipping.'

I bent down to help Rosalie, asking her:

'Which way did Céleste go?'

She jerked her head toward the far side of the valley.

'Into the cane, over there, like she might be heading for the mountain.'

Up on the slope, the field hand laboured on, every otherwhile darting glances at us, trying to figure out what was happening. We continue to dump the logs in the cart with as much noise as possible.

'Cléophas is still here with the boats,' I told them. 'Petit Bacaye. If you get there by dawn, you can still escape. Follow the road out of town, then—'

'Save your breath,' hissed Rosalie. 'I know the place. But none of us will go. Everyone terrified. Wondering how they might punish us.'

'And we're under guard again tonight,' Raymond added.

I stood up to hand him more wood and check on the two Béké. They were still deep in conversation, Bell saying:

'Of course, it's up to you, but I'd invest your money in England, not this godforsaken hell-hole.'

White attempted to catch my eye, but I bent down again behind the cart to help Léontine with the last of the logs.

'Where is your grandmother?' I asked.

'Looking after children.'

'Will you try to get to the boats?'

She shook her head.

'I doubt it. What about you?'

'I'm going to see the Governor, try to stop them flogging Emile.'

'Are you crazy?'

'*Dousman*,' hissed Raymond.

Bell had begun to stroll toward the cart with the Englishman on his heels. I had never seen White anxious before but he look close to it now. I stood up with the last piece of wood – just in time, because Bell slap the side of the cart and shouted at us.

'Get a move on, you women. Go and get more wood. And use these. What do you think they're for?'

He snatch two baskets from the cart and threw them on the ground. Léontine and Rosalie grab them and made themselve scarce, not daring even a backward glance. White stared at me, attempting to divine if I had been able to pass on the message. When I gave him a furtive nod, relief spread across his countenance.

'Well,' he said. 'We must be on our way – thank you, sir, for your advice and recommendations. I shall be sure to visit the billiard hall.' He turn to me. 'Hurry up, boy. *Alley-alley*. We haven't got all day. Farewell, sir, farewell.'

He put a guiding hand on my shoulder and led me away. Once or twice, I glance back, wondering if any of the slave would peach on me now that we were leaving. Bell strolled over to watch the men who had begun to lever up the tree stump with iron-crows. The women had resume chopping wood but every so often they would raise their heads and stare after us. So far as I could see, none of them seemed as though they had any intention of having a quiet word with Bell.

White tightened his grip on my shoulder.

'Stop looking back,' he muttered.

Only when we were beyond earshot of the felling did he begin to question me.

'How did you fare? Did you tell them?'

'Yes, sir.'

'You gave them directions to get there?'

'One of them knows the place. She can tell them.'

'And they understood we can only wait until dawn?'

'Yes, sir.'

Somehow, I had to get away from him, but it would have to wait until there was nobody else in sight. Already, on the road ahead, I could see a number of *porteuses* and a man on a donkey. Cléophas had told White to avoid the town but, evidently, he intended to ignore that instruction and pass through Fort Royal on the way to Petit Bacaye. My best bet was to wait until we were well beyond the carenage, where the road ran through a thick swathe of forest. There, I could make a run for it, dive into the trees and then – once I'd lost old Bianco for sure – I could turn back to town and find the Governor.

The Englishman kept interrupting my thoughts with questions about the slaves.

'What did they say when you spoke to them?'

'Not much, sir, it was difficult.'

'Will they try to escape? How will they get away?'

'Sir, they're scared out of their wits. And they'll be under soldier guard again tonight. So . . . I cannot say, sir.'

White frowned and then grew silent. Presently, he took out his cutlass and started to massacre any roadside grasses that offended him in passing, an apparent foul mood which lasted until we reach town and his gaze fell upon a rum stall at the quayside. Only then did his face brighten.

'*Alley-alley*,' he said to me. '*Veet*. Let's get me a breakfast.'

Chapter Sixty

Various merchant had set up stalls along the wharf for some kind of seasonal market, a continuation of Christmas. The esplanade throng with people. White headed straight for the rum stall and ask the merchant for a taste. The stall-keeper gave him a glass but the first tafia that White essayed was not to his liking and so he demanded another bottle. Then he and the merchant fell into conversation about the virtues of the different kinds of Kill-Devil on the stall.

Meanwhile, I notice people drifting up a side street to the parade square. Something about to happen up there, I guessed, perhaps some kind of marching display by the Glasgow Greys with their shrill Scotch pipes. As I watch the townfolk milling around, it occur to me that the Rue Gouvernement lay just beyond the square. I glance back at White. He had leaned across the counter, deep in conversation with the rum seller. Just as a kind of experiment, I took a backward step away from the stall, then another. And another. The merchant had just poured White a third glass. I kept on stepping backward, allowing myself to merge with the crowd. Then, in a flash, I turned and slipped away, expecting White to call out or chase me, but I heard nothing, only the din of people around me, chattering and shouting and laughing. I moved with them, up the side street, scarce able to believe my luck. All being well, I could cut across the square then dive along to Rue Gouvernement and try to gain an audience with Melville.

At the far end of the side street, the way into the square was block by slow-moving people, chiefly a drove of English sailors in

Monmouth caps and wide trousers who were dawdling at the corner. I had to stand on my hind legs and peer beyond them. So far as I could see, a great swarm of townfolk had gathered in the parade ground. Some among them had sought shade beneath the few acacia tree that grew around the edge of the square. I could see various fine-timbered redcoat strolling around among the bacon-fed merchants and planters, the shopkeepers in aprons. A few rosy-cheek ladies twirled parasols; others had children clinging to their skirts. Here and there, longside the French and English, a number of free men and women; their well-tailored garments distinguish them from the slaves of all ages, most of whom stood attendance on a master or mistress, whiles the remainder bore traits of produce on head or hip. The heat of the sun would have nailed a man to the dirt. Everyone was talking at once and the clamour of conversations echoed off the buildings on all sides.

The crowds look thickest in one far corner of the square, where the road began to rise toward Hospital Street and the hills beyond. Above the heads of the populace, I could make out a group of Béké soldiers and officials, taking their ease on horseback. With a start, I recognise Bryant among them, in conversation with an eminent bewigged personage whose expensive garb marked him out as Governor Melville. The lavish gold braid of his officer-jacket glittered in the sun. He sat astride his stallion, listening to Bryant without looking at him.

All this, I glimpsed over the shoulders of the weather-beaten Jacktars in front of me as we proceeded slowly into the square. When, at last, the sailors stepped aside, I push forward; my view expanded and something else in the far corner caught my eye: a wooden structure; two sturdy post about eight feet tall and join together at the top by a long beam; the whole apparatus painted black. A cart sat between the posts, a low tumbrel, harness to a pye-ball mare. On her back sat a thin, sallow-face fellow. Two more men stood in the rear of the cart: ordinary Béké in shirt-sleeves, one with dark, curly hair. The other, who wore a straw hat, was examining a noose that had been strung from the cross-piece of the gallows.

'They are hanging one of their own,' I thought to myself. 'Poor Curly there. I wonder what he did to deserve his fate?'

Then Curly moved aside, and I saw that the tumbrel contained a third person. All at once, my heart knew what my mind would not accept. His hands were tied behind his back; he had a dirty bandage on his thumb. I knew him at once; his form and outline imprinted on my brain. Apart from the bandage, he was dress the same as last time I had seen him, though now his clothes were filthy and torn. Emile. Curly was speaking to him, his words lost in the din of the crowd. As I watched, the man in the hat took a step behind my brother and slip the noose around his neck. Emile just stood there, apparently in a daze, and allowed him to adjust the knot. Curly was still talking in his ear, pointing to the joist above them as though in explanation. Emile tilted back his head but it was hard to tell whether he was gazing at the cross-beam or the sky – or, indeed, whether he could even comprehend what the man was saying.

My knees turn to air then gave way beneath me. I sank to the ground. Before me lay the beaten earth of the square. Tiny stones and grit imbedded in the dirt. The imprint where a barrel had been rolled. A piece of something bumpy-green that look like a shred of avocato peel. Oh, to be a stone, a barrel, a shred of peel, a piece of grit, for none of them had feeling. These Goddams would murder Emile in front of me. Of course, I should save him – but how, among this crowd, these soldiers? In which case, if I were a man, I ought to hand myself in and face the consequence longside my brother. Where was my courage? Where? If only I could turn back time. We could steal *The Daisy* from White and sail away. Or take foot to the mountain instead of the hospital. Oh, to feel nothing.

Meanwhile the multitude surge forward on all sides. Someone walked into my back and cursed, then another man stumbled over me. Various angry people told me to stand up but I just sat there, stunned, too afflicted to move until several pairs of hands haul me to my feet. Somewhere a baby was screaming. All the heat of the afternoon seem to be concentrated where we stood. Sick in my stomach, my head light, I raise my eyes. There was the gallows again, swimming in my vision. The man in the hat was now speaking to my brother whiles gesturing at the crowd. Emile stared out across the sea of faces. His gaze swept past the place where I stood but I was too small and too far away. The pye-ball mare took a few restless step and the tumbrel rocked back and forth as the rider reined her in. My brother staggered; the rope at his throat grew tight then slackened off as he regained his footing. I found myself calling out in panic:

'Emile!'

My voice hoarse and ragged, mostly swallowed up by the noise in the square but a few people glanced over to see who had shouted. Before I could cry out again, someone grab my shoulder, hard. It was White, with his pesky rummy face. He thrust my head into his sour armpit and spoke in my ear.

'Shut your trap. You want to get yourself arrested?'

When I tried to shout again, he clamped his hand over my mouth. Kicking and twisting, I tried to break free. As we struggled, I glimpsed the people and parade ground in flashes. A well-rigged man took the hand of the boy next to him as they both stared at the gallows. Two penny-dog rolled around in the dirt. A few redcoat contemplated our scuffle with interest. For true, White was strong, stronger than me. Though I resisted, I soon grew weak in his grasp and he began to drag me away. More heads turned. One of the soldiers looked as though he might stride over to investigate us but then another voice rang out, this time from the tumbrel.

'Be quiet. Let the prisoner speak.'

At once, keen to see what was happening at the gallows, the soldiers turned away – as did everyone else. A general cry went up for silence. On the cart, my brother drew back his shoulders. His lips moved but his voice was too low. In order to hear him, those beneath the acacias were oblige to quit the shade. They hurried forward and launched in among the ruck. The mass of people surge toward the tumbrel, straining to catch what Emile said but his words were lost in the roar of voices – both French and English – demanding quiet.

'*Silence!* Listen! *Écoute!*'

Meanwhile, White man-handle me out of sight behind one of the trees. He slam me against the bark, spoke through his teeth into my face.

'Be quiet. Want to get yourself caught?'

'Let me go.'

'To do what? You'll end up like your brother there. Stupid boy. What are you running for? Your only hope is to come back with us to Martinique.'

'Please . . .'

But he held me there, against the tree trunk. All at once, the crowd grew quiet.

My brother was speaking, his familiar voice tired but determined. Just a few broken sentences carried to where we stood, a mix of kréyòl and French.

'. . . *je suis esclave* . . . nothing but a slave . . . I had no choice . . . I was given orders . . . *mwen te gen okenn chwa* . . . *on m'don lòd* . . .'

A woman at the front shrieked out:

'Speak English, you dog!'

In retort, a few of the French in the crowd yell back at her. Then people began to jeer and curse in both languages and the cacophony escalated. Emile faltered, his voice overwhelmed. White pinned an arm across my chest. He peered out from behind the tree and soon gave a bitter laugh.

'What is it?' I asked.

'Fisticuffs,' he said. 'They're fighting.'

'Who is fighting? Emile?'

'No – silly fools in the crowd, French against English.'

He clamped one hand across my mouth and began to drag me toward the empty side street. I stumbled along in his grasp but, by the time we had reach the corner, the crowd-brawl had broken up and a hush descended on the parade ground once more. White glance back to see what had happened.

I could not help myself. Could not help it.

I turn my head and look toward the gallows.

Chapter Sixty-One

What I saw can never be unseen, never forgotten. All my life, over and over again, that same scene repeating in my mind. At one shift, time seem to slow down yet quicken. The two Béké leap off the back of the cart just as the pale-face rider kick the flanks of the mare. Off she sets, at a trot. The tumbrel rolls forward causing my brother to sway and lose his footing. His toes scrape along the cart-bed for a few moment and then the vehicle lurches away, leaving him to drop but a few inches. There he hangs, suspended, swaying gently like a human pendulum, his hands still tied behind his back. Presently, his toes begin to point downward. His body quivers and then, in tiny increments, his knees draw up until he appears to be sitting in mid-air. I want to close my eyes, to turn away – but find I cannot for if I do I will never see my brother again. This sad and grisly image is the last I will have of him. A strange and crazy dance it is; his movements so graceful they seem deliberate – but I must assume that they were involuntary.

White craned his neck to get a better view. He grip my collar. All at once, I knew I must get away from him. I ducked and step backward, wriggling out of my shirt, leaving it empty in his hand. Sametime, I shoved him so hard that he hit the ground. Then I ran off down the empty street.

The sun beat down on my skin, bright and dazzling, burning hot, but inside myself I felt dark-dark, black as night, and every particle of me shivered as though frozen to the marrow.

I stumbled onward, blindly. Saying my brother name.

Emile.
Emile.
Emile.

Chapter Sixty-Two

I heard White shout but when I turn the corner and look back he was still trying to get to his feet. I kept running along the wharf – also now deserted. Everyone had gone to the square. Halfway along the esplanade, I glance back again and saw White turn the corner, giving chase. I ran faster, past the last houses, toward the red cliffs on the edge of town. Here, the trees began. Old Bianco had fallen behind, out of sight. At the first chance, I dived into the undergrowth and began to climb. I crawled up the sheer overgrown rock face using the thick screen of bushes, hanging on with both hands to liane. About halfway up, I could go no further so I stopped, one set of toes in a crack in the rock, the other foot on a thin branch. Somehow, I knew in my bones that the Englishman would search for me alone. If he call for help, made a fuss, people would ask questions – and the last thing he wanted was questions. I concentrated on regaining my breath, counting to fifty and more before I heard him down on the road, stumbling and grumbling, apparently reluctant to venture too far from town.

A line of ant crawled across my arm but I moved not a sinew. I waited and waited. After a while, I peered out through the foliage and saw White retreating back down the road toward Fort Royal, no doubt intent on consoling himself with a tot of rum. Only when my hands and feet grew numb did I clamber down from my perch and head away from town, slipping into the woods by the coast as soon as I was able.

When I finally came to my senses, I found myself on the narrow

shore north of Fort Royal, near the mouth of the river. I cannot remember how I arrived at the waterside or how long I had been standing there. The memory of what happened at the gallows was already
seared into my brain, burned into my breast.

Gradually I became aware of a horrible sound, a sound that grat-
ed on my ears, waking me from my nightmarish stupefaction: a
guttural scream, like a cry of terror, repeated, over and over. It made
my skin crawl. For a moment, I wondered whether I myself might
even be the source of this racket, my grief turned into violent lam-
entation, for it almost sounded like someone giving voice to the agonies of torture, whether spiritual or otherwise. But then I turn my
head and saw a group of fishermen on the shore. They had gathered
around, bent low, each with his machete, hacking a huge turtle to
death. The screams of the helpless beast, the din of its death throes,
added to the horror in my heart. I had to escape from that terrible
place, escape the torment I felt inside.

The sea looked clean and soothing and so I walked into the green
shallows, let them lap at my ankles. The water felt only a mite cool-
er than my skin. I stepped in further to where it tickle my knees.
Every so often, a wavelet gave me a gentle push but I push back,
kept wading until the breakers crept up past my waist then further
still, though the water rocked and shoved against me. Once it was
around my chest, I lifted my feet and let my body topple and roll. I
close my eyes and open my mouth, allowing myself to slip beneath
the salty waves. A cold current did suck me in, gently at first, and
then it began to drag me down and away.

PART ELEVEN

Tjenbé Rèd; Pa Moli

Chapter Sixty-Three

My life ought to have ended there and then. By rights, I should have handed myself in to stand beside my brother on the gallows, but I had a lack of courage, the kind of courage that Emile possessed. All my days, I have lived sorrowfully with that knowledge. That is why – when I imagine him now – I like to think of him as an old man, taking his ease in the conservatory of this stately built house where I am employed. His hair is grey. He walks with a stoop. I pretend that somehow I saved him and that we work here together, tending the gardens and hot-house. I have long conversations with my brother and consult him on the best way to grow vines and vegetable. Alas, all that is simply my imagination. I let him down and – in my grief and shame – surrendered myself to the ocean like a coward.

However, my life did not end there. Apparently, the fishermen saw me wade into the water and when I sank beneath the waves and fail to reappear, two of them swam out to look for me. Since they hunted daily for shellfish they were familiar with the currents along that stretch and well use to diving. They soon found my limp body not far from where they saw me disappear and brought me back to dry land. At first they took me for dead but one of their number turn me over and squeeze the ocean out of my lungs until I could breathe again. Though I had not drowned, the salt-water in my chest scorch so bad I thought it would be the end of me. They laid me in the shade of the boat-house to vomit and recover. After a while, three of them return to work, dividing up the turtle meat to take to their masters, whiles the oldest man kept watch over me.

In due course, when I could sit up, he started to ask questions. Who was my master? What was I doing there? Did I know how to swim? I avoided answering mostly by coughing, pretending to be incapable of speech. However, it seem to me that he had guessed who I was because he began to talk about the escape and the missing boy, the boy from Martinique, brother of the ring-leader.

'If I was that boy, I would be careful,' he said. 'If I was him, I would leave this island first chance I get, go back to Martinique. For true, I couldn't help such a boy myself. But I would tell him, get away from here. They will hang you, boy – that would be what I would say to him.'

As soon as I regain some strength, I gasped a few word of thanks to him and stumbled away into the strip of forest between the beach and the coast road. Somewheres in the midst of those woods, I curled up neath an almond tree, too chicken-hearted to return to town, too stupid to know what to do except lie there weeping and wait for the fishermen to leave for the day. Once they were gone, I had resolved in my mind to go back into the water and drown myself, for true.

After a while, I began to wonder how long they might leave Emile on the gallows. By carrying out the execution in the most public place where the whole town would see, they had ensured that the news would spread across the plantations from Salines to Sauteurs. No doubt, the Béké would cart him to the hospital estate in a few days and display his corpse to scare the runaways into continued submission. Then, most likely, they would dig a shallow hole somewhere on the low slopes of Morne St Eloy and drop him in. I could only think about all this for moments at a time, before the pain made my heart ache so badly that I had to thrust it from my mind.

Toward the end of the afternoon, I heard the fishermen pack up and leave, cursing each other and giving joke. I waited a while and then crept back to the edge of the wood. The sun had put fire to the sky in the west. I quitted the trees and walked to the edge of the pink and orange sea. In less than an hour, it would be dark. I took one step, then another – but as soon as my toes touch the water I realise that I no longer had the courage to wade in.

I was not even brave enough to put an end to myself.

Chapter Sixty-Four

S ome time after nightfall, I found myself stumbling along the
back of Hospital Hill. Below me, in the valley, I could see
lantern blazing all around the field cabin and the shadowy figures
of redcoats at either end of the bridge and around the perimeter
of the quarters. I trudged on, and kept trudging, my leg sore
again after running from White. At the inland end of the hill,
the mill lay in darkness. Once the harvest began, in a week or
so, the place would be lit up all night long. As I slipped on past
the buildings, the monster hound began to make a racket, a deep
bow-wow, but I knew he was tied up and I no longer feared him.
Somewise further on, I join the highway where it pass the riverbank. Back on the day we had arrived in Grenada, my brother
had drag me down the other side to hide from those Capuchin
monks on mules. We had lain among the rushes and Emile had
held me tight-tight. Now, that day seemed like a lifetime agone.
In passing now, I turned my head the other way, too broken to
even look for the place.

Soon, the road curved east through a valley, around the back of a
hill. As I carried on inland, through the night, my leg ached worse
and worse. Every time Emile came into my head, I began to panic
and had to fight for breath. My heart throb so much with guilt and
shame, I had to keep pushing all images of him from my mind. My
overwhelming urge was to lie down at the side of the road and fall
into the sleep of death. Years hence, some fellow might stumble
upon the huddle of my bleach bones and wonder who I had been

in life. To keep going, I had to chant to myself, under my breath, in time with the rhythm of my walking, step and step:

'*Tjenbé rèd. Pa moli.*

'*Tjenbé rèd. Pa moli.*

'*Tjenbé rèd. Pa moli.*'

Sometimes, only the thought of Céleste kept me putting one foot in front of the other. Céleste in the morning, with drops of water glittering in her hair; Céleste in the afternoon, the dark curve of her arm as she reached out to wipe the forehead of some patient; Céleste in the evening, giving joke, a spark of merriment in her eye. I tried to imagine where she was right at that moment. Since it was night, she might have sought shelter. Where would she hide? Her belly so big, I doubt she could climb a tree but perhaps she might find one with low enough branches. Or perhaps she was already in the high mountain, in a cave. Somewhere near fresh water. She would have found herself some fruit to eat, to keep her strength up. She might even have gone to the big lake, to look for those Maroon. They might take pity on her and give her shelter. Whatever the case, she was so practical and sensible, no matter what her situation, she would make the best of it. If anyone could survive in the forest, it was Céleste.

Twice that night, the rumble of hooves behind me broke into my reveries and I had to leave the road quick-sharp, slip into the shadows. First time, a fat planter laggered along on his mule; the second, a group of men rode past with purpose, though whether they were hunting for me or Céleste, or simply on their way to one of the eastern towns, I could not say. At last, the road began to curve north-east and soon after, between two distant hill, I caught a glimpse of the sea, the sheen on its surface made steel-bright by the stars. Here was the far side of the island. I had to wade through a fast-flowing river and thereafter, the highway swerved inland for a while, then I came to another creek. I remembered what Cléophas had said about three rivers, the third one, muddy. Sure enough, a stretch further on, where the road took a sharp turn inland, I came to a little dirty creek, and a gap in the trees on the coast side, not much more than a goat track. Here, I turned off the highway. The track ran level at first then veered left down a steep slope, deep into scraggy woodland. I stumble down the bumpy path and soon arrived in an area of shrubs and palm growing in a wide bay between low hills. Beyond the trees, I could hear the soft rhythm of the waves. I walked toward the sea and out onto a narrow strip of sand.

A yawl had moored up out in the cove. From what I could tell, it was *The Daisy*. No movement on board but perhaps they were asleep. To the right of the boat lay a wooded islet, a small black mound against the stars. Looking at it, I supputed I might be able to peer down from its summit into the yawl, provided the sea was shallow enough to wade out. With this in mind, I pick my way along the black rocks to the narrowest strait between shore and island. There is scarce any tide in the Caribees but the water was at its highest level and in the dark I had trouble judging its depth. Deciding to wait a few hours until the ocean receded and the light improved, I found a dry spot among the roots of a great tree and settle down to wait.

I must have nodded off because when I awoke some hours later the tide had gone out somewise and the sky had turned from milky silver to pale lemon. Now, I could see the reef and rocks surrounding the islet, black below the green shallows. I stepped into the water and began to feel my way out, one slippery step at a time, over slimy submerge rocks and jagged coral that bit into my feet. I reach the little island and scramble up through the dirt and bushes from one rocky outcrop to another, all the way to the summit. There, below me, sat *The Daisy*, about twenty feet away, moored in a deeper channel of water, the skiff tied to her stern. In the dim light, I peer down into her hull and saw the peeny figure of Descartes curled up in the stern. Cléophas lay amidships, wrap like a slug in a blanket. No Bianco. Most likely, he was keeping watch on the bigger boat, *The Alcyon*, further out to sea or along the coast.

Something about seeing Father Cléophas there gave me pause. In my mind eye, I could picture my cows, Victorine and the rest. I imagined what it would be like to be back in Martinique, alone, no Emile in the world. And then I pictured Céleste, struggling through the wilderness of the high forest, supporting the mound of her stomach with her hands, making her way to the mountains of the interior.

Without warning, Descartes rolled over and sat up. He took a sleepy glance at the shore and, having reassured himself that no troops had camped there, waiting to pounce, he scratched himself and gazed out at the faint light dawning on the horizon. Presently, when he looked up and saw me standing atop the islet, staring down at him, his mouth fell open. Quick-sharp – to stop him calling out – I put my finger to my lips and motion for him to be quiet. He blinked a few times and then slowly nodded.

I mouthed to him: 'Céleste?' and gestured to indicate a big belly, then pointed to the ground beneath my feet as much to say 'Has she been here?'

Boy shook his head: 'No.' He raised his hands with a shrug of his shoulders, telling me: 'Who knows?' Then he gestured at the mountains, with another shrug.

For a time, I stood there on the little summit, undecided, feeling the grit and stones beneath my feet. Descartes gaze back at me, wondering what I might do. After a moment, I raise my hand in farewell. The boy gave me a nod and raised his.

I turned and clambered down the islet in silence and then, piece and piece, made my way back to the shallows. The water felt warmer now. Either I had grown use to the teeth of the coral or I chanced upon a less arduous route to dry land. Once ashore, I scrambled along the greasy black rocks. All the while, Descartes sat upright in the stern of *The Daisy*, watching me. When I reach the narrow strip of sand, he raised his hand again in farewell and I raise mine. I walked along the sea-strand and hid myself in among a mangrove swamp from where I could still see *The Daisy*. Some time later, the Father roused himself from sleep and spoke to the boy. The murmur of their low voices floated to me across the water. They kept an eye on the shore as the sun rose higher in the sky. Only when it seem certain that no slave would arrive to join them, did Cléophas raise the canvas then he lifted anchor and they set sail toward the open sea.

I watched until they were only a dot on the horizon. Then I retrace my steps through the scrubland in the bay and on up the track. Once I regained the empty highway, I walked along it for a short while then turned inland, into the trees. Far in the distance, early cloud rose up behind the mountains, like billowing smoke. I set a course across country toward the highest peaks. The sky had begun to turn lavender. Soon, it would be another hot morning.

A Note from the Editor of this Narrative

Although the narrative ends there, I feel honour-bound to relate what little else is known of its author. The original of this manuscript, along with associated letters and papers, came into my possession last year when my neighbour, Miss Amelia Conder, gave them to me shortly before her death. Miss Conder first discovered the documents some twenty years ago, while attempting to catalogue the contents of the library in her parental home, following the death of her mother. The papers were found inside an unmarked box. Initially, Miss Conder failed to see much significance in these pages and simply stored them away. At the time, she was grieving and also overwhelmed by the sheer scale of the documentation left behind by her deceased parents; a fact that is entirely understandable when one learns that her father was Josiah Conder, the author, editor and noted abolitionist, who had died in 1855, leaving behind a vast personal archive.

Close examination of the letters in the box suggests that the widow of Thomas Pringle – another noted writer and abolitionist – had sent the documents to Miss Conder's father. As you may know, Pringle brought to public attention the story of a former slave, Mary Prince, and presumably had intended to do the same with this narrative. Apparently, illness prevented him from working on the manuscript and, after he died, his widow gave it to Conder in the hope that he might undertake the translation. Miss Conder only found time to sort through her father's archive last year when – perhaps with some awareness of her own mortality – she began to put her affairs in order. It was then that she rediscovered the manuscript. Having glanced through its pages, she later confided that she had thought immediately of me, her neighbour.

Miss Conder and I had more than a passing acquaintance ever since, a decade previously, I had succeeded in coaxing Snowflake, her parakeet, off the roof of my porch and back into his cage. Subsequently, we became friends; inasmuch as a schoolmaster in early middle age and a lady well advanced in years can be so described. I teach languages at our nearby Dulwich College and Miss Conder was aware that, in my spare time, I had been attempting to write a novel on the subject of Fédon's Rebellion in Grenada: a nugget of history that has always fascinated me because my great-great-grandfather was killed in that conflict. Miss Conder passed the papers on to me since it was her impression that the memoir delineated events of that era in the Windward Islands. At first, upon realising that the documents have no bearing whatsoever on Fédon, I was discouraged. However, as I read on, my disappointment was replaced by excitement.

In a covering letter to Josiah Conder, the widow Pringle explained that the manuscript had been brought to her husband in the October of 1812 by a polite half-caste gentleman of middle age who introduced himself as Mr Dove. When questioned, the visitor confided that his late mother (formerly a slave) had been employed for several decades as housekeeper at a great house in Suffolk. Dove himself still worked at the same establishment as chief steward. He explained that following the death of the elderly head gardener, the manuscript had been discovered amongst the old man's belongings. This gardener, a mulatto, had also been a slave and was an old friend of the visitor's mother.

Alas, the widow Pringle does not record the ensuing conversation in full, but from what she does write, it would appear that the wealthy master of the great house in Suffolk – Captain Dove – had once presided over a merchant ship that plied a trade between Bristol and the rest of the world. On one of these voyages, en route from Tobago to Jamaica, his crew had spied a skiff drifting along without purpose, somewhere north-west of Trinidad. The occupants – a Negro woman and a young mulatto man – were slumped, motionless, at the oars. The crew took them for dead but when the skiff was brought alongside, signs of life were detected. Not only that but – in the stern, beneath an awning constructed from the woman's petticoat – a small half-caste boy was discovered. The three castaways were lifted aboard and questioned by Captain Dove once they had recovered. Only the young man could speak English. He called himself Lucien; the Negro woman's name was Céleste. Lucien was reluctant to communicate at first but when the captain explained that he traded exclusively in goods – his present cargo, an assortment of glass window-panes and wrought-iron balconies – and that, furthermore, he was a firm abolitionist, the young man became more forthcoming. Apparently, after living in hiding for several years in the mountains of Grenada, the fugitives had set out some ten days previously in an attempt to reach Trinidad where they believed they might live freely, due to what they had heard was a more moderate Spanish regime in that island.

Initially, the captain was uncertain what to do with these runaways but, over the ensuing voyage to Jamaica, after spending much time in their company, he grew rather fond of them and, when his boat docked in Kingston to off-load a consignment of balconies, he kept the fugitives hidden in his cabin. Thereafter, they returned with him to England, to his home in Suffolk, where he gave them paid employment. Céleste became nurse to his young daughters, while the captain hired the young mulatto to work alongside him on his ship, which he did for over a decade. Ultimately, Lucien left the sea to work on the captain's Suffolk estate, first as a ground keeper and ultimately as head gardener. Mrs Pringle was a keen horticulturalist, which might explain another detail that she mentions: apparently, Lucien (who never married) achieved great success in growing flamboyant Grenadilla plants and avocados in a glasshouse, much to the delight of the captain who enjoyed nothing better than to show off these exotic vines and fruits to visitors.

It would seem that Céleste brought up her son, the little half-caste boy, alongside the children of the great house. The boy progressed from the position of footman to butler and thence to steward. Over the years, Pringle's visitor confided, the captain had come to treat him like the son he never had, even giving him his surname – Dove. Here, apparently, Pringle asked his visitor – this Mr Dove – for his Christian name, and was told that Céleste, his mother, had named him Emile.

A NOTE ON THE TRANSLATION

The original account is written throughout in the same neat copperplate hand, yet in a mixture of languages, with some parts rendered entirely in French and others in English, while the whole is broken up with numerous passages in what I have learned is a kind of early French Creole or kréyòl. My sense is that the author was fluent in all three tongues to the extent that – carried away by the telling of his tale – he sometimes forgot which language he was writing in. As far as the Creole was concerned, I was initially at a loss. However, I have been fortunate enough to strike up an enjoyable correspondence with Mr Lafcadio Hearn, now a resident of Tokyo, who lived for two years in Martinique and has written most engagingly about the French West Indies. With his assistance, I completed my translation. I have retained a smattering of the Creole patois to give a flavour of it to those readers who may be unfamiliar with its cadences; it is a tongue rather like French in some respects, and rather unlike it in others. For the most part, I have honoured the author's rhythms and grammatical quirks and have undertaken only modest changes to the original, where a degree of modernisation seemed appropriate.

Of course, the genre of slave narratives, so popular fifty years ago, arose partly as a response to the notion that Negroes could not write. Indubitably, there are those who will claim that such a fully-formed literary work as this manuscript could not have been authored by a self-educated former slave. I simply point those readers towards other accomplished slave accounts, such as *The Interesting Narrative of the Life of Olaudah Equiano, The Narrative of the Life of Frederick Douglass* or Linda Brent's *Incidents in the Life of a Slave Girl.* One element that marks this account as unique is that it does not attempt to record the author's entire history from birth into slavery, and on into freedom, but focuses instead on a short period: just a few weeks in December 1765. Presumably, at one time, the author intended to seek publication, but the reasons why he never did so remain unclear.

Edward A. Nichols
86 London Road, Forest Hill, London.

Afterword

BY JANE HARRIS

Here are some historical facts upon which *Sugar Money*, the novel, is based.

Please be aware – this Afterword is full of spoilers.

In 1738, the French Colonial Government in Grenada built a hospital overlooking the main town of Fort Royal (now known as St George's). By 1742, the hospital had been handed over to the care of a band of mendicant monks or friars: the Brothers of Charity of the Order of St John of God – *les Frères de la Charité* – who had been running a hospital in the neighbouring island of Martinique for almost a hundred years. The friars looked after the sick but, in order to fund their charitable works, they also ran plantations alongside their hospitals – plantations which relied on the labour of enslaved people. The poverty-stricken friars took out loans in order to purchase these slaves, some of whom they trained as nurses to work alongside them in the hospital. The rest of the slaves were set to toil on the plantations, growing indigo and sugar cane.

By the mid-1750s, it became clear that the superior of the Grenada hospital – one Father Damien Pillon – was more interested in making money from his sugar factory than in caring for the sick. He survived several challenges to his rule until his own death in 1760. Soon thereafter, the French authorities resumed control of the hospital and the few remaining, inexperienced friars were sent back to Martinique, leaving behind all their possessions – including the enslaved people. Subsequently, the British invaded Grenada in 1763 and took over the hospital.

In August 1765, one of the mendicant friars – Father Cléophas – travelled from Martinique to Grenada and attempted to persuade the enslaved people who worked at the hospital to return with him to Martinique. However, the British authorities soon got wind of his intentions. They sent him packing and he was obliged to go back to Martinique empty-handed. Determined to succeed, Cléophas hired a 'mulatto' slave from the Dominican friars in Martinique and sent him to Grenada with instructions to round up the enslaved people and take them to the bay at Petit Havre (now known as Halifax Harbour) from where a waiting boat would carry them to Martinique. Conditions must have been grim under British rule because – despite the terrible risks involved – the slaves agreed to go with him.

However, the plot was discovered and troops were dispatched in pursuit of the escapees. The soldiers recaptured the majority of the runaways and arrested the mulatto, but although eleven slaves did manage to escape to Martinique, the British insisted that they be returned immediately to Grenada. The recaptured slaves unanimously pleaded that the mulatto had persuaded them to escape by assuring them that he had the English Governor's consent to take them. In the end, the mulatto was condemned and hanged, the only person executed. He protested to his last breath that he had only done the duty of a slave by obeying his masters. An inquiry into the incident showed that Father Cléophas had himself 'debauched' a couple of the runaways. However, no friar was ever apprehended, charged or punished for 'theft' of the hospital slaves.

The decision to execute the poor hired man was unpopular in Grenada and contributed to the discontent, both of the free French who remained on the island under British rule, and of the Grenadian enslaved. Indeed, the evident growing hostility among the slave population led to the proposal, in 1766, of a bill entitled 'For the Better Government of the Slaves etc.' This bill was intended to legislate for Grenadian planters to be more humane in their treatment of enslaved people. Alas, the bill failed to pass and, just one year later, in 1767, the slaves did indeed revolt. Troops from the garrison quashed the rebellion and several slaves were killed. Thereafter, estate owners who had used violence against their mutinous slaves lived in fear of being massacred. The execution of the revolt's ringleaders only increased hostility to the British among Grenadian slaves and the free French. In the aftermath, the British did tone down their harsh regime somewhat but their unpopularity continued, as evidenced by the Fédon rebellion of 1795: a failed uprising against British rule in Grenada, predominantly led by free mixed-race French-speakers, the purpose of which was to abolish slavery and return power to the French.

Condemnation of the slave trade increased over the ensuing years until the British abolished the practice in 1834 and the French eradicated slavery in all its possessions in 1848.

Acknowledgements

This novel was inspired by events that are described in *Grenada, A History of Its People* by Dr Beverley A. Steele, and also in *Conception Island* by Raymond Devas. My touchstone book, to which I returned again and again, was *Two Years in the French West Indies*, by Lafcadio Hearn (and, in Chapter Six of *Sugar Money*, I quote from Hearn's description of the market sellers of Martinique). I found John Angus Martin's *Island Caribs and French Settlers in Grenada* extremely useful, as was *Voyages aux Isles de l'Amerique*, by Père Labat.

Of the many accounts of plantation life and slave narratives that I read, probably those I found most inspiring were *Sugar and Slavery, Family and Race: The Letters and Diary of Pierre Dessalles, Planter in Martinique, 1808 to 1856*, edited by Elborg Forster and Robert Forster; *Mastery, Tyranny and Desire: Thomas Thistlewood and his Slaves* by Trevor Burnard; *The Interesting Narrative of the Life of Olaudah Equiano*, edited by Angelo Costanzo; and *Creole Testimonies, Slave Narratives from the British West Indies, 1709–1838*, by Nicole A. Alijoe.

Once again, Francis Grose's *Classical Dictionary of the Vulgar Tongue* was invaluable, as was the *Dictionary of Caribbean English Usage*, compiled by Richard Allsopp.

Finally, I'm indebted to the works of Robert Louis Stevenson, whose novels have inspired me since childhood.

THANKS

My research for this book was greatly assisted by Dr John Angus Martin, historian and former Director/Curator of Grenada Museum, who gave me access to a vast archive of photographs, drawings and maps and showed me the site of the original hospital in Grenada. Historian Dr Stephen Mullen kindly read the manuscript of *Sugar Money* and gave me detailed feedback on its historical accuracy; and Dr Curtis Jacobs and historian Lucy Inglis pointed me in the right direction in the early stages of my research.

I'm grateful to the staff of the Archives Nationales d'Outre Mer in Provence, France, and to those at the National Archives at Kew, London, for allowing me access to historical letters, documents, maps and plans. I'm indebted to the British Council and to the former head of Glasgow Libraries, Karen Cunningham, who together funded and organised my research trip to the West Indies as part of their Trading Tales project. Thanks are also due to the following for their help with geographical, military and sailing research: Sarah Hopkins, Travis Gottshutzke, Peter Mackenzie, Alex Stevens, and Jamie and Amber of Conservation Kayak, Grenada.

Much gratitude to Grenadian legend, hiking guide and naturalist Telfer Bedeau, who took me on a hike across the island from St George's (Fort Royal) to Halifax (Petit Havre), following the route of the journey made by my characters.

Huge thanks to the following who gave feedback on all or part of the manuscript: Richard Beard, Andrew Binnie, Rena Brennan, Adam Campbell, Geoff Cooper, Polis Loizou, Jacob Ross, Elia Rulli, Tom Shankland, Gillian Stern, and Alex Stevens.

Many thanks to my editor, Angus Cargill, for his patience and enthusiasm, to Stephen Page for his encouragement, to Donna Payne for her great design and to all at Faber & Faber, including Maria Garbutt-Lucero, Katie Hall, Eleanor Rees and Kate Ward. I'd also like to thank my agent, Jonny Geller, for being super, and also Catherine Cho, Kate Cooper, Alice Lutyens, and all at Curtis Brown.